WEST HEADS HOME

A NOVEL

BY
Peter Farnham

D1057649

ISBN: 9798854313513

Cover design by: Peter Farnham

Library of Congress Control Number: 2018675309

Printed in the United States of America

PART I: THE WORLD

CHAPTER 1
i

San Francisco
3 OCT 69

"Hey Sarge, *fuckin' California!* Look out the window."

Arthur's eyes popped open, and with a small gasp he sat up. *Puppa I'm sorry—*

His seatmate, a Spec/4 from the First Air Cav, said, "You okay? Sorry to startle you."

"No problem," Arthur said. The troubling dream still resonated but was already fading. "Weird dream is all."

The pilot began speaking over the cabin PA system. "Guys, we'll be landing this mother in just a couple minutes. If you look out the left side of the aircraft you'll see the Golden Gate Bridge and San Francisco, California, in the good old U S of A. The *WORLD, GUYS!"*

The cabin broke into applause.

Arthur looked out the window at the approaching California coast, the Golden Gate Bridge like a tiny ladder across the entrance to the bay. The flight from Tan Son Nhut by way of Tokyo had been a long one. *But that was America down there.* He yawned, still tired, but smiled.

He looked at his reflection in the window. He ran his hand over the red-blonde hair, long enough to part but still GI short. He would let the wispy mustache grow out; he had gotten fond of it. His face looked thinner than he had remembered. It occurred to him he hadn't seen himself in a mirror in months. *C-rations and life in the jungle didn't do much for weight gain,* he thought. Never big, he now doubted he weighed 120 pounds.

The prettiest of the half-dozen stewardesses, a leggy brunette, got on the horn at the front of the passenger cabin. Laughing good-naturedly at the whistles and cheers and exuberant offers of marriage, she said, "Gentlemen, on behalf of the entire flight crew, we want to be the first to welcome you home."

Cheering erupted, Arthur joining in with the best of them. He looked out the window again. It was real; he wasn't dreaming. He had made it. Great day in the morning, he had. He was back in *The World*.

ii

After landing and a short bus ride to Oakland Army Terminal, Arthur, still wearing his jungle fatigues, was in line to get fitted for a new uniform, even though he was being discharged. While this surprised him, he had learned in his eighteen months in the military not to ask questions. *Just get it over with so I can get out of here.*

He got to the head of the line. "Name?" the clerk said.

"West, Arthur L., Sergeant."

The clerk squinted at his list. "From Belfast, Maine? First Infantry Division?"

"That's me."

"Wait here, Sergeant." The specialist got up and walked to a door and knocked. He went inside.

The man behind Arthur in line groaned. "Man, what'd you do?"

"Don't even know," Arthur said.

A lieutenant came out of the office with the specialist. The lieutenant said, "Sergeant West?"

"Yes sir."

"Come with me." Arthur got out of line and followed the lieutenant.

Another guy in line behind him yelled, "You in deep shit now, Sarge!"

"Goin' back to Nam!" another guy called.

A third guy sang the *Dragnet* theme—"DUMP-de-DUMPDUMP!"—and this provoked a fresh round of guffaws. Arthur grinned at the needling.

6

They entered the lieutenant's office. "Have a seat, Sergeant," the lieutenant said, picking up the phone.

Arthur did so as the lieutenant dialed.

"Good morning, sir, this is Lieutenant Backus. Sir, I have Sergeant West in my office...Yes sir, he just arrived. Very well. I'll send him right over." The lieutenant hung up.

"Sir, excuse me, but what's going on?"

The lieutenant shook his head. "Chaplain Abeles will explain everything to you."

iii

"Arthur," Abeles said, "I'm sorry to be the bearer of such unwelcome news, but the Red Cross has notified us that your Aunt Esther has, regrettably, passed away."

Arthur put down the soda Abeles had given him. "Passed away?" he said quietly.

"Yes, I'm afraid so. Not quite a week ago." Abeles waited a moment, clearly expecting Arthur to react in some way. When he did not, Abeles continued, "I'm told she passed very peacefully, however. The funeral was two days ago. Arthur, God's will is often difficult for us to-"

"She died a *week* ago?"

Abeles nodded. "Six days ago, actually. Arthur, the army made every effort to get the news to you before now. Unfortunately, you've been in transit, and they were constantly just missing you, starting from when you left Dau Tieng. We almost caught up with you in Tokyo, but your plane left minutes before the base chaplain arrived. Arthur, the army handles large numbers of people very well, but handles individuals very poorly. I'm sorry. Is there anything I can do?"

Arthur shook his head. "I knew she wasn't well," he said. "But..." He drummed his fingers. *It was still a shock.* "How did you find out?"

Abeles consulted a piece of paper before him. "A friend of your aunt's, a Mrs. Sylvia Hall?"

Arthur nodded.

"Mrs. Hall contacted the Red Cross, and they contacted us."

"I see. I'll call Mrs. Hall and thank her."

"That would be very nice, Arthur. Do you have any other family?"

"No."

After a moment, Abeles said, "Arthur, I've found prayer helpful in these situations. Would you like a few minutes by yourself?"

"No, sir, not necessary." He shivered, unaccountably cold. *Aunt Esther, dead?* It didn't seem possible. Arthur stood. "May I go now?"

"Of course, Arthur. God bless you." Arthur returned to the fitting line.

iv

Two hours later Arthur was standing in the cab line. His new dress tunic had all the appropriate badges—Big Red One patch, buck sergeant stripes, and two overseas bars. He had also stopped by the PX and bought the six ribbons he was entitled to wear, as well as a combat infantryman's badge. After he had pinned on these insignia and finished dressing, he had looked at himself in the mirror, in uniform for the last time.

Not bad, he had decided.

The cab line, although long, moved pretty quickly, and when it was Arthur's turn he opened the rear door and tossed his duffel bag in the back. The bag was far lighter than he was used to, only containing his old uniform and jungle boots, and some toiletry articles. In his wallet was about three hundred dollars, his last month's pay.

A girl sat beside the driver. *His girlfriend?* Arthur wondered. She smiled as he clambered into the cab after the duffel. She was pale and slender, with short brown hair and a faint dusting of freckles. She wore a shift, sandals, and a pair of granny glasses. A daisy was inserted behind her ear. "Where to?" the driver said.

"San Francisco Airport."

"Are you going home?" the girl asked.

"Ayuh."

She smiled. "You must be from New England."

"Maine."

After a moment, she said, "Are you just back from Vietnam?"

He nodded.

"Bad vibes," she said, shivering.

"Kill anybody?" the cabby asked.

Arthur considered this a moment. "It's possible. But I don't think so."

"Women and children?" the girl said.

"What?"

"Did you kill any women or children?"

Arthur looked at her, searching for the smug arrogance of the self-righteous. Amazingly, it appeared to be a straight question, asked in the tone of someone inquiring whether he preferred Fords or Chevrolets. He decided to answer her straight. "No. No women or kids."

"How do you know?" she asked. "You said it was possible you killed somebody. How do you know it wasn't women or kids you might have killed?"

He started to explain, but then said, "Just do, is all. I never did such a thing, and no one else I knew did, either."

"Well you have to admit it's happened, right?" the girl said. "I mean, you read stories in the papers—"

Arthur nodded. "Didn't say it never happens. But it's actually rare. Very rare. Not like what you may have…read in the papers."

"All right. I know it must be difficult for you. But I think it's a terrible, destroying a defenseless country," the girl said. "It ought to stop."

Arthur said nothing, uncomfortable with the conversation. *Did everyone think we were murdering people?*

He looked out the window until the girl turned back to the front. A moment later, Arthur caught her looking at him in the rear-view mirror. She returned his glance, smiling secretly.

Fifteen minutes later, the cab pulled into the drop-off lane outside the airport terminal. "Okay, General, here you go," the cabby said. "That'll be fifteen bucks."

Arthur paid him. "I'm a sergeant, but thanks for the ride."

"General, sergeant, whatever," the cabby said.

"Good bye," the girl said. As the cab pulled away, the girl looked at him over her shoulder. He waved to her, and she wiggled a couple of fingers back.

v

Arthur listened to a phone ring in a living room across the continent. In the middle of the fifth ring, it was picked up. "Hello?"

The operator said, "I have a collect call from Arthur West. Will you—"

"Oh heavens, yes, of course we'll take it!"

"Go ahead, please."

"Arthur? Arthur, is that really you? Where are you?"

"It's me, Mrs. Hall. I'm—I'm in San Francisco."

"Oh, thank God you're home. Arthur, did the Red Cross reach you?"

"They did." *It was good to hear a familiar voice again.* "They told me the news here after I'd landed."

"Arthur, I'm so sorry. Esther was a treasure. You were so lucky. If it helps any, she went quietly. The cleaning lady found her sitting in front of the fireplace. She'd been crocheting. The work was still in her hands.

Such beautiful crocheting." Mrs. Hall began to weep a little.

"I'm—I'm glad she didn't suffer," he said. He wiped his nose on his sleeve. *I can't believe I'm standing here bawling.*

"Arthur, she told me she left everything to you. The house, the car, even some money. Don't know how much, but enough so you won't have to worry about getting a job right away. When are you getting in, and do you have anyone meeting you?"

"I'm due in at Portland around six tomorrow morning. I'm on Braniff."

"We'll be there, Arthur."

"Long way to drive," he said.

"Arthur, it's no problem," she laughed. "We'll be there."

"Well…thank you," he said. He gave Mrs. Hall his flight information.

"Arthur, there's a lot to catch up on, and I'll fill you in when you get back. I know Henry Junior will want to see you."

"Say hi to Hag for me, and thanks for taking the call."

"We'll see you tomorrow, Arthur." She hung up.

Arthur shouldered his duffel bag and began searching for his gate.

"Hello, you," a voice behind him said.

Arthur turned, and his eyes opened wide. It was the girl from the cab. "What are you doing here?" he said, smiling.

"I asked Roger to come back and drop me off." She smiled and came up to him, standing very close. She smelled like flowers and sun-dried cotton. She said, "My name is Amanda."

"Amanda."

"Yes." After a moment, she smiled again. "So, should I just salute, and keep calling you 'Sergeant'?"

He grinned back. "No, no, of course not. Sorry. Name's Arthur West."

"Is that what they call you? Arthur?"

"Arthur? Nope. My friends call me Preach."

"Ahhh, Preach. Well, it's very nice to meet you." She stepped closer still. She said softly, "Tell me, Preach. Would you like to come home with me?"

Arthur looked at her, open-mouthed. "Come home with you?" *What the heck was going on?*

She arched an eyebrow over a hint of a smile. "Do you always repeat everything anyone says?"

"No. But…"

"But what?"

"What about your cabby friend?"

She dismissed him with a toss of her head. "Roger's just someone I know. I ride with him sometimes. I meet interesting people that way. Like you."

"Like me?"

"Yes. A soldier back from the wars, but you still looked very lost," she said. "Like a lost kitten."

"Lost kitten?"

"You're doing it again," Amanda said.

Arthur laughed. "I guess I am. Sorry. Again."

Amanda said, "And you don't have to keep apologizing. Come on, do you want to stand around in this airport all day?"

"Amanda, I've got a plane ticket—"

"Turn it back in."

"People are expecting me tomorrow morning at—"

"Call and tell them you're okay."

He stood and looked at her, amazed at this remarkable turn of events. He had to admit he was tempted, but he wanted to get back to Maine. Then, as he thought further, it occurred to him…*why?*

He had already missed the funeral. The house and car would keep. He had no one waiting for him, and Amanda was here. She was also cute and seemed to like him.

Possibilities for the next few days occurred to him.

It would be fun. And he was sure due for some of that.

He chuckled, and decided. "Amanda, what the heck. Let's go."

Fifteen minutes later—ticket returned, the Halls called—Arthur and Amanda were in a cab headed north on Highway 5.

.   .   .

CHAPTER 2
i

**The Haight, San Francisco
3 OCT 69**

Amanda directed the cabby to the corner of Page and Clayton. The area was a curious mixture of lovingly restored Victorian town houses, and others of the same era that were decidedly less cared for. "The Haight's changing," she said as the cab pulled over. "Rents are starting to go up, and a lot of places you could afford a year ago have been bought by rich people now."

"Still looks like a cool neighborhood," Arthur said. He paid the cab fare and pulled his duffel bag from the trunk. He looked at the townhouse in front of them. "Do you live here by yourself?"

"Oh no," she laughed. "Four of us live here. We split the rent and utilities. Come on." She started up the steps. Arthur followed.

From the entryway, stairs led to the second floor, and the hall to the right stretched to the rear of the house. A curtain of beads hung in the entrance to the front room. The house smelled of smoke and incense. Amanda said, "Come with me. I'll show you where to put your things."

Amanda led him to a second-floor bedroom in the rear of the house. The bed was a double mattress on the floor, covered with a down comforter. Stereo components sat on brick and board shelves against the far wall, and a low, circular table sat in the middle of the room, two beanbag chairs around it. The walls were covered with watercolors. An easel sat in the brightest spot in the room, an end table covered with jars of paint and brushes sitting beside it.

Lucy in the Sky with Diamonds wafted down from the third floor. "So, uh, where do you want me to put my stuff?"

"Anywhere."

Arthur placed his duffel in the corner, out of the way. "Mind if I sit down?"

"Please do." Arthur sat in one of the beanbag chairs, then unbuttoned his tunic and loosened his tie. Amanda chuckled as she sat in the other chair.

Arthur smiled. "What's so funny?"

"I've been wondering if you ever unbuttoned anything, or took off your tie or…relaxed."

He smiled. "I've been out of the army for two hours, Amanda. In the army, particularly if you're a sergeant, you don't go around in public with your tunic unbuttoned or your tie unknotted. Habits are hard to break."

"Hey, it's all right." She reached under the table and pulled out a baggie of marijuana and a small pipe. "Would you like to smoke some grass?"

He smiled. "Sure, I'd like that." Amanda crushed up a pinch of grass into the bowl, lit it, and they shared a few tokes.

Then Arthur heard the front door open, and people talking as they ascended the stairs. "Hello? Anybody to home?" a female voice called.

"Come on up," Amanda called.

"Fee-fi-fo-fum…I smell people having fun! *Fun police, fun police!*" a male voice boomed, followed by giggles. Two massive people walked into Amanda's room.

"Hello," Amanda said. "Pilgrim and Roxie, this is Preach. He just got out of the army today."

"All *right,*" Pilgrim said. He was bearded, wearing bib overalls and a beat-up pair of Keds. "You oughta come to the protest tomorrow. Golden Gate Park, man. A band's playin', lotsa freaks, lotsa good vibes—supposed to be a really nice day, too."

"Cool," Arthur said.

"Hiya Preach." Roxie beamed, giving him a toothy smile. She was pale, a round, moonlike face beaming beneath the kerchief hiding her hair. "Got any of that dope left?" she asked Amanda.

"Sure," Amanda said. She passed her the pipe and grass.

Footsteps creaked across the floor above them, and a moment later came downstairs. A guy entered the room. "Hey man," Pilgrim said.

"Hey, Pilgrim," the guy said. He was about Arthur's size, with flaming red hair in a wildly teased Afro. He wore black horn-rimmed glasses, a long-sleeved, American flag t-shirt, and bell bottom jeans. He was barefoot. "Roxie," he added, nodding to her. He glanced at Arthur and Amanda, but said nothing.

"Doyle, this is Preach," Amanda said. "He just got out of the army today."

"Hey," Arthur said. Doyle nodded.

"Were you in Vietnam?" Doyle asked, eyeing Arthur's service ribbons.

Arthur nodded. "Just got back."

"Preach is coming to the protest tomorrow," Roxie said. She shook her head. "The war makes me so mad. All that killing, women and children." She glanced at Arthur. "I mean—"

Arthur shook his head. "I know everyone thinks—"

"Holy crap, it's time for *Star Trek!*" Pilgrim said, glancing at the table clock beside Amanda's bed.

"Great!" Doyle said. Pilgrim, Roxie and Doyle headed downstairs.

They don't even want to listen, Arthur realized.

After a moment, Amanda said, "Do you want to join them?"

Arthur nodded. "Sure, why not? I haven't watched TV in a year."

They followed the others downstairs to the living room.

The *Star Trek* episode was about a group of space hippies under the spell of an insane holy man, who was leading them to a paradise on a supposedly mythical planet called Eden. It struck Arthur as the most embarrassingly silly hour of television he had ever watched. He was almost unable to endure one scene without laughing, when Spock began jamming on his Vulcan harp with the band the space hippies had formed.

"Wow," Roxie said. "This is so cosmic. Like..." she grasped for the appropriate word. "Like...*wow!*"

"This show is always such a metaphor," Doyle said, shaking his head. "How could they have cancelled it?"

Amanda said nothing, instead watching Arthur, who met her amused glance from time to time as the show progressed, getting sillier with each scene. He was grateful when Pilgrim brought a bag of potato chips from the kitchen, of which he ate more than his fill; he hadn't eaten since breakfast on the plane that morning.

Finally, at the conclusion of the episode (the leader proved to be a false prophet and although Eden was beautiful to look at, every plant on it was poisonous) Amanda said, "So what did you think, Preach?"

Arthur looked at her, trying to keep a straight face. "Interesting," he said.

"Especially the part when Spock started rockin' out with his harp," she said carelessly.

Arthur couldn't help it. He chuckled. "Especially that part. Those wigged-out Vulcans." Amanda giggled.

Doyle glanced at Arthur, studying him a second, but said nothing. Pilgrim and Roxie, oblivious, began rolling a joint.

Amanda said, "Come on, Preach. Let's go back upstairs and get you unpacked." She stood, and Arthur rose to follow her.

"Amanda, I..." Doyle started, then stopped.

Amanda turned. "Yes, Doyle?"

After a moment, he said, "Nothing." He looked away.

"Hey Doyle, look at my new *Green Lantern*," Pilgrim said, waving it at him. "You can read it when I'm done if you want."

"Cool," Doyle said. As Arthur followed Amanda out of the room, he felt Doyle's eyes on them.

ii

Amanda shut the door and turned and looked at Arthur, and her hand went to her mouth and she started laughing. He started too, and after a moment was laughing so hard he had to flop down in one of the beanbags.

"Shhh," Amanda said. "They'll hear you."

"I'm—I'm sorry," he said, gasping.

"Every time I looked at you down there I had to look away," Amanda managed to whisper. "That is the dumbest episode of *Star Trek* ever made."

"You got that right," Arthur said. "But your friends sure seemed to like it."

"Oh, you know it. Pilgrim and Roxie never miss an episode. They don't answer the door when it's on."

"Like—*wow*!" Arthur said, and that got them laughing again.

"Yes, wow." Amanda finally stopped laughing. "My. I haven't laughed so much in months. Thank you. It's good to laugh like that." She crossed to him, leaned down, and kissed him chastely on the lips. He closed his eyes and returned the kiss, blood pounding in his temples. *It had been so long,* he thought. *With a round-eyed girl, at any rate.* They parted and, looking into her eyes, he gently stroked her arm. *She felt so smooth.*

He kissed her again, gently parting her lips with his tongue. After a moment, she pulled slightly away from him and looked at him thoughtfully. "Do you want to ball me?" she asked.

He was flattened by the question, but struggled to sound casual. "Of course, but—but only if you want to. I don't—"

"It's okay, you," she whispered. "I want to ball as much as you do." She stood and pulled off her shift and was naked before him.

All right then. He was out of his uniform in seconds.

iii

When Arthur awoke it was dark outside. A single candle burned on the dresser. He did not feel rested. Amanda lay beside him on her side, looking at him. "How long have I been asleep?" he asked. From the speakers across the room came soft music, somehow evoking waves breaking on Lincolnville Beach on a moonlit night.

"Four hours," Amanda said. "You fell asleep right after. Do you know you moan in your sleep? You were trying to talk, too. Something about your father?"

Puppa. He remembered nothing of the dream. "Sorry. I was tired. It's been a long day. I didn't sleep well on the plane. What's on the stereo?"

18

"*Then Play On.* Fleetwood Mac."

"It's nice."

"Preach?"

"Ayuh?"

"Tell me about Vietnam."

"Tell you what?" he said. *He had not expected this.*

"Well—what was it like? Is it a pretty country?"

He considered this a few moments, then nodded. "From the air, yes, it's beautiful. Green everywhere. You've never seen so many shades of green. Trees, bushes, paddies, water, all different, from almost yellow to a green so dark it's almost black. You fly over it in slicks and"—

"Slicks?"

"Helicopters. The ones you ride in, not the gunships. You fly over it and look down and see all this green thousands of feet below you. And the sun's reflecting off the rice paddies and...I don't know, it's really beautiful from the air. Hard to describe."

He looked at the ceiling, continued quietly. "And then you get down in it, and start walking. Man." He shook his head. "Pretty soon you're wondering how something that looks so beautiful from the air can be so terrible to walk through on the ground. Mud and water everywhere and undergrowth so thick that sometimes you can only move through it by falling up against it and knocking it down, then standing up and doing it again and again until finally you get through it. And the bamboo's actually got spikes. They might even be poisonous, for all I know." He held his hands up for her to inspect. The backs of his hands were covered with small scars. "Cuts from bamboo. They got infected. Some guys wore gloves to protect their hands. Wish I had." He stopped and looked at her. *I'm babbling.* "Sorry, don't mean to rattle on."

"It's all right."

He got up and crossed to the window and looked up at the stars. The moon, a glowing crescent, shone above the city. "The moon's huge over there, like a pie plate or something when it's full. Don't know why. Maybe being close to the equator. It's like you're on another planet. I've never seen it so big before. In Maine in the winter sometimes it looks big, but not like in Nam."

She came up behind him and lightly stroked his shoulder with her nails. "Preach, what's combat like? Did you fight every day?"

He turned and looked at her, her eyes gleaming. *What the fuck?* He shrugged. "Not even. Most days you're just walking through the jungle, dirty, hot and tired. That's what war is, mostly." He decided not to mention the fear, the blood, and the screams.

And rats.

"You've got some ribbons. What are they?"

He scoffed, flabbergasted. "Come on, Amanda, I—"

"No, I really want to know."

After a moment, he said, "An air medal. Some others."

"What's an air medal?"

"You get it for taking a lot of helicopter rides."

"What others did you get?"

"Vietnam campaign ribbon. Vietnam service ribbon. National defense medal." He pointed them out on his tunic. "Everybody gets those."

She looked at his tunic, and said, "That's four medals, but you've got six. What are the other two? What's that purple one?"

Arthur was silent a moment. "Purple Heart," he said.

"I've heard of that one. Doesn't that mean you got shot?"

He scoffed. "Got a scratch one night. I didn't even have to get dusted off. Here, let me show you," he said.

He crossed to his duffel bag and pulled out his shaving kit. From the kit, he withdrew a film can, and shook out a small piece of metal that looked like a pencil lead, about a half-inch long. "That's what the docs pulled out of my arm. They gave it to me…after." He put it back in the film can. "Hardly enough for a Band-Aid. I know a lot of guys that deserve their purple hearts. I don't."

"What's the other one?"

He didn't answer.

"Preach?"

"Silver Star," he finally said.

"Oh my," she said. "Don't you have to do something brave to get that one?"

Arthur said nothing.

"So tell me. What happened?"

Arthur shook his head. "No."

"Come on, I want to hear about it. Let's get back in bed, it's cold." Arthur nodded, and slid under the comforter. She joined him, and rolled over to face him again.

"Please?" she said. "Tell me?" She stroked his abdomen with her nails, stirring him.

He looked at her. "Do you really want me to tell you?"

"Oh yes," she whispered. "Oh yes, Preach, I do."

He nodded. "Well, I guess I…" He knew he was avoiding the issue. *How to begin?*

"Every day, a chain of random events happens," he said. "Like, in the morning when patrol starts, you take point in the left file, and another guy takes it in the right. No reason. It just shakes out that way, you know? Then, an hour later, you walk around the left side of a stand of bamboo and your buddy in the other file walks around the right. Then *pop pop!* And he gets lit up and you don't, but it would've been you if you'd been in the right file instead of the left. You understand?"

"Perfectly," Amanda said.

"Sometimes, something that doesn't seem important at the time turns out to be real important when you look back on it," Arthur said. "Life-changing important, you know?"

"So what happened?"

And then he told her. He spoke, uninterrupted, for twenty minutes.

iv

"So," he finished, "they pinned the Silver Star on me a couple of months later. A few cents worth of metal and a piece of ribbon. Don't even mean nothin." He sighed. "I'm sorry. Laying here, telling you war stories."

"Preach?" Amanda said after a moment, eyes bright and luminous.

"Ayuh?"

"You..." she stopped. "Never mind."

"What?" he said. "Come on. You were going to ask me something."

"No, I wasn't."

"Come on now. You were. What?" He looked at her. *"What?"*

"Are you sure?" she said. He nodded.

"What I was going to ask you was—" Her eyes glowed in the darkness. "You liked combat, didn't you?"

He stared at the ceiling again, silent a very long moment, stunned at the question. *Holy moley.*

Finally he spoke. "I never thought about it. But...You're right. I did. I was good at it, you see? God help me. Combat was...a rush, Amanda, a rush like you wouldn't—"

"Shut up," she whispered, and feverishly rolled over onto him.

.   .   .

MEMORY

Northern Mekong Delta, RVN
1 APR 69
0943 Hours

Arthur looked out of the slick and watched the Vietnamese countryside pass by thousands of feet below him, the wind from the open doors cooling him after the long double-time through the jungle to the LZ they had just left a few minutes before. He liked flying in the slicks; it was one of the few enjoyable things about the infantry.

But the pleasant ride did nothing to quell the sense of foreboding he had about the next few days. Everything felt wrong.

First was the haste with which the company had moved this morning. Captain Buchan had had the company saddle up within a half hour of daylight, barely giving them time to make coffee and eat. They had then near double-timed through the jungle to the LZ where they were picked up and were now being flown...somewhere.

Second, they had just gone into the field near Lai Khe yesterday on what was supposed to be a week-long operation. That this mission had been canceled not even one day into it indicated a serious emergency somewhere.

Third was the nature of the terrain passing by, thousands of feet below him. His unit up to now had operated almost exclusively in remote, heavily forested areas far from villages. Below him, stretching far into the hazy distance, were rice paddies, shimmering in the mid-morning heat, dotted with villages, the checkerboard paddies held together by thin red strands of dirt road. Arthur checked his compass. They were heading almost due south. With all those paddies below, plus roads and lots of vills...this could only be the Mekong Delta.

"We gonna be riffin' in that?" Lurch yelled over the roar of the Huey's propellers. At six-eight, Lurch was the tallest man in Lima platoon.

"Looks like it!" Arthur yelled back. Lurch muttered to himself.

The slicks began to descend toward a half dozen columns of purple smoke rising from a lengthy stretch of rice paddies between two wooded creeks. Arthur yelled, "Saddle up!" When the slicks were below the trees, he flipped off the safety on his M-16. When, inches above the paddy, the slick hung motionless, Arthur leapt out—and promptly sank to his knees in paddy water.

The rest of the squad bailed out behind him and slogged, cursing, past the front of the aircraft, toward a dike thirty meters in front of them. The flight of slicks took off, banking to the right as they rose above the tree line and disappeared.

Within five minutes the rest of the company had arrived, and they moved into the woodline next to the paddy and halted. LT headed to the company command post for an officer's conference. Once he came back, he called a squad leaders meeting.

"Last night," he said, "a ruffpuff outpost about three klicks from here got hit bad. Beaucoup casualties. This morning, they found a dead gook outside the wire, wearing an NVA uniform. That got everyone's attention at brigade; aren't supposed to be any hardhats in the area. Well, it sure as hell looks like there are now. We were the closest available unit, so we're supposed to find and destroy this NVA outfit. Gotta still be in the area."

LT continued, "There are also beaucoup civilians in the area. So this is not—I say again, not—a free fire zone. We're not to fire unless fired upon, or unless we actually see targets carrying weapons. Of course, anything moving around after dark's fair game. Also, there may be mines and booby traps in the area. Questions?" There were none. "Okay. Saddle up."

They were moving moments later.

As the morning wore on, they began to see civilians. A dirt road a hundred meters away was dotted with a variety of traffic. A boy in short pants, no more than five or six, herded six huge but docile water buffalo with a stick. A clutch of Buddhist monks in orange robes strolled by. Two young women wearing ao dai pedaled past on rickety bicycles, waving and smiling.

"Fuckin'-ay, pretty little babysans," Nose said, waving back and leering.

"Fall out, take a break," LT called back.

"About fuckin' time," Bear said.

Arthur was grateful for the break; he, like all of the others, was wet, hot, and thoroughly miserable.

"Hey Preach, we supposed to eat standin' up?" Pappy called. Grizzled and hard at 39, Pappy was the oldest man in the company by a good ten years.

"No. Sit on that berm over there." Arthur indicated the dirt road they had been paralleling. As the men sat, he said, "Team A, eat. Team B, keep an eye out."

Pappy pulled off his mud-caked boots, revealing his bony, water-wrinkled feet, toenails thick and yellow. Like most grunts, he didn't wear socks.

Turnip, a skinny black kid from Chicago, rolled his eyes, and winked at Arthur. "Put your damn boots back on, Pappy. I can't be lookin' at them ugly ass feet."

"Look at this, then," Pappy said, displaying his middle finger.

"My man," Turnip laughed.

"My ass," Pappy said, with a hint of a smile.

Arthur grinned; the friendship between Pappy and Turnip was a constant source of amusement to the others.

"Man, I can't wait to get out of this shithole," Bear said, opening a can of meatballs and beans. "First place I'm going after I get home is fuckin' Amsterdam."

"Where's that at?" Nose asked.

"In Holland, dumbass," Bear said. "You know, windmills and wooden shoes and shit? A buddy of mine was there last year. He said it is out—fucking—standing. Dig it." Bear leaned forward and whispered, "Whores are legal. You walk by a whorehouse in the Red Light District and they're all sittin' in the windows, showin' what they got."

"Yeah, right, Bear," Pappy scoffed.

"I ain't even bullshittin'," Bear said. "Anyways, that's where I'm headed. Soon as I get outa this fuckin' place."

Then Nose said, "Hey, where's all the civilians at?"

The road was suddenly empty.

"They take siestas here?" Pappy said.

"That's in Mexico, ya dumb fuck," Garcia said, "not in—" then an explosion shattered the quiet.

The men instantly slid off the berm into the paddy.

Before the echoes of the blast had stopped, high thin screams began from the front of the column. "Mother fucker I'm hurt! Oh, fuck me, I'm hurrrt mother MOTHER JESUS!"

"Medic!" someone yelled. "Get a medic up here!"

Red from the waist down, Blue Berry, a rifleman in Mike Platoon, lay shrieking in the middle of the road, a large piece of him, also red, a few feet away beside a smoking hole in the road. His hands fluttered helplessly.

"Stay off the berm!" LT yelled. "Stay in the paddy!"

The company medics reached the man, and one of them plunged a syrette of morphine into his pale arm. Blue Berry's cries echoed across the paddies as the medics

*worked on him. In the paddy, Captain Buchan's RTO spoke
urgently into his radio, calling for a dustoff.*

*Gradually, as morphine and shock set in, Blue
Berry's cries faded to groans, and then the dustoff
appeared, hovering above the paddy water as a half dozen
of Blue Berry's buddies wrapped the now silent casualty in
a poncho liner. They carried him as gently as possible to
the slick, another man carrying the leg.*

"Fuck," Bear said, looking away.

*Once Blue Berry and his leg were aboard, the slick
lifted off, banked, and sped away.*

*After a moment, Garcia said, "Goddamn gooks
knew. That's why they disappeared."*

Arthur nodded. "I think so."

"Okay let's get movin', people," LT called.

No one was hungry any longer.

CHAPTER 3

i

The Haight, San Francisco
October 4, 1969

Arthur awoke with a start; although still dark
outside, he could hear traffic, and after a moment noticed
the first hint of dawn beginning to appear through the open
window. He glanced at his watch.

Almost five-thirty.

He looked at Amanda next to him, the draped sheet
at once hiding and revealing the swell of her hip curving
down to her slender waist. He heard faint whistling as she
breathed, and he smiled. *It was kind of cute, her snoring.*

He got up as quietly as possible and pulled on his
boxer shorts and a t-shirt. Amanda stirred. "Whassat?" she
mumbled.

27

Arthur whispered, "Shhh, going downstairs, can't sleep."

"'Kay," she said and rolled over. He left the room, quietly pulled the door closed, and went to the kitchen.

To Arthur's surprise, it was clean—dishes in the drying rack, no food out, countertops and the floor spotless. A bag of garbage was neatly tied shut, next to the back door. On impulse, he took the bag outside and put it in one of the garbage cans in the alley. The day was cool, but promised to be gorgeous.

When he came back in, he began to look for coffee, and after a minute found a jar of instant. He put on water to boil. He was just putting a spoonful of the crystals into a mug when Doyle walked in, still wearing the American flag shirt and jeans he had been wearing the day before. "Hey," Doyle said.

Arthur nodded. "Couldn't sleep. Making coffee. Hope you don't mind."

"Be my guest, man," Doyle said, yawning. "You got any extra hot water?"

"Ayuh." Arthur got another cup from the shelf. "Like it strong?"

"Yeah."

When the water was hot Arthur poured. "Got any milk?"

"Nope," Doyle said. "We ran out yesterday. Sorry about the instant. I've usually got some fresh ground around, but Pilgrim and Roxie are behind on their food money."

Arthur looked around. "You take care of the kitchen?"

"Oh yeah. That used to be Pilgrim's and Roxie's job. You can imagine what the place looked like then." He chuckled. "I buy cookbooks and shit. I want to be a chef."

Arthur smiled. "I'll buy some real coffee today. My present to the house. Milk, too."

"Groovy man, thanks a lot." More silence as they sipped their coffee. "So, in Nam, did you kill anybody?"

That question again, Arthur thought. *Why did everyone ask him that?* He shrugged. "Don't think so, no."

Doyle waited a moment for Arthur to explain, but when he didn't, he shrugged. "Far out." He sipped again. "So, you like Amanda?"

Arthur nodded. "Sure. You've known her awhile, I guess."

Doyle sipped his coffee reflectively. "Coupla weeks. I met her in Golden Gate Park and she brought me home. Just like she did you. I've been livin' here since."

"Really?" Arthur said, keeping his tone casual although he felt anything but. *Doyle and Amanda had...?*

"Yeah," Doyle said. "Fucked my brains out that first night and for a few days after, but then zippo after that."

Arthur put down his coffee mug, stunned. "You were her...boyfriend?"

Doyle chuckled and shook his head. "Amanda doesn't have boyfriends," Doyle said. "Just, you know, sex partners, like. I lasted almost a week, which was actually pretty good. Some guys don't last two days. Hell, she's fucked half the dudes in the Haight and workin' on the rest, seems like."

"Well," Arthur said. Uncertainly, he continued, "It's... different with us." He realized how lame that sounded.

Doyle smiled. "You wouldn't believe some of the guys she's brought back here. Needle freaks, a couple of 'em. Meth, smack. And Roxie told me about some really creepy guy from Utah a few months ago. Some Indian name, I forget. Very heavy, he even freaked Amanda out." Doyle finished his coffee and stood. "Welp, gonna go back upstairs and try to crash again. Thanks for the coffee. There's some pot in the living room. Help yourself."

"Thanks," Arthur said, speechless and seething. *Holy moley, what next?*

As he finished his second cup of coffee, Roxie lumbered in. "Good morning," she said, smelling of marijuana. "So you gonna wear your uniform to the demonstration today?"

"Don't think so," Arthur said. "I'll see if Doyle'll loan me some clothes. Where's it going to be?"

"It's going to end in the park, but it'll start down on the Embarcadero. There'll be speakers and all, and a coupla bands. Ought to be a trip, ya know?"

"Sounds like fun."

"Oh yeah, demonstrations are far out. You meet people, party and all. This one's gonna be huge. Like a hundred thousand people."

"Think it'll do any good?" Arthur asked. "I mean like help end the war and all?"

"Nah. War'll just go on, I guess. But in the meantime, we'll sure party!" Roxie said.

"Amanda gonna go?"

"Definitely. At big events like this, she likes to sketch. People, the scene, you know. She sketches real good. Guess you saw all her paintings." Roxie stood. "Gonna go smoke some more dope, get my morning buzz on. Catch you later." Roxie headed for the living room.

As Arthur sipped his coffee, he thought about whether he should go to the demonstration. They had been few and far between in Maine. The university up Orono was not exactly a hotbed of antiwar sentiment. He had also not been opposed to the war before getting drafted, assuming that the government knew what it was doing.

He chuckled to himself. *How fucking stupid was that?*

But he decided that if everyone else in the house—especially Amanda—was going, he would, too.

Golden Gate Park, San Francisco
October 4, 1969

Late that morning, Arthur sat beneath a tree in the park near Stanyan, when he saw Amanda across the street, holding her sketch pad. He waved. "Hey, Amanda!" She saw him and smiled. She had still been asleep when he had walked the few blocks to the park an hour or so before with Doyle, Pilgrim, and Roxie. "Pull up a piece of turf," he said.

She joined him, leaned over and kissed him on the cheek.

"Hey you," she said. "I finally got up. I wanted to sketch the march." The lead elements were just starting to arrive. She opened the pad. "Could I see a sketch or two?" Arthur asked.

"Sure," she said. She flipped through the pad.

They were portraits, mostly, character studies done with quick, economical lines: children playing; a hippie strumming a guitar; a mounted policeman, the sketch somehow capturing the horse's movement. Arthur thought her sketches were better than her watercolors. "These are good," he said.

Amanda laughed. "Thanks," she said. "I just knock them out. A few I work on more. Where are Roxie and the guys?"

"They said they were going to try to find a good place to sit up front." Amanda looked around, glowing in the late morning sunlight. *She is gorgeous,* Arthur thought. He was glad he had decided to stay there a few days. He smiled and leaned toward her. "So…" he whispered, "you wanna go back to the house and…you know?"

"I want to sketch right now," she said, smiling. "Maybe later."

Arthur sat back, disappointed. "Oh. Well, okay." *So much for that.*

She smiled. "There's no need to pout."

"I'm not pouting," he said.

She giggled. "You're pouting."

"I am *not. Jeez.*"

Amanda looked at him, not giggling anymore. "Okay, so you're not. No big deal. I still want to sketch."

"Sorry." *Relax,* he told himself. "You're right. I was pouting." Amanda didn't respond. *Okay then,* he thought. "So what's going to happen when all the marchers get here?" he asked. More and more people were streaming into the park now.

"There's going to be a rally with speeches and all. At the athletic field." Amanda gestured toward the far end of the park. Then she exclaimed, "My God, look at *those* people."

Arthur looked up. There were five of them. All wore white togas, and headdresses made up of rainbows of feathers. All visible flesh was painted stark white and their faces were further covered with wavy black lines, like contour lines on a map.

"I have got to sketch them," Amanda said. She flipped to a new page in the sketch pad and started roughing in the new subjects, eyes darting between them and pad as she drew.

As they approached, one of them made eye contact with Arthur. The man started to look away, but then snapped his eyes back. After a moment he smiled slightly, almost to himself, and then moved on.

"Did you see that?" Arthur said.

"See what?" Amanda said, sketching.

"One of those guys. He kinda smiled at me."

"Sure he did." She smiled doubtfully.

"No, really," Arthur said. *No way he had imagined it.*

Then, the man caught Arthur's eye again, grinned openly and nodded, but moved on before Arthur could decide what to do.

Amanda noticed, this time. She smiled. "Gee, Preach, you're right. You might have a friend there."

Arthur grinned. "I have no idea who he is."

Amanda smiled again. "I bet if you gave him your phone number he'd call you. Lots of gays in San Francisco, you know."

Arthur laughed. "No, that's not it. It's like he knows me or something." He stood, puzzling over the mystery but not sure what to do. He decided he had probably just imagined it. "Let's go find the others."

iii

Doyle, Roxie and Pilgrim had found places about fifty yards from the speaker's stand. The field was filling up fast. "Uh-oh," Doyle said, "here come the radicals."

A group of several hundred people, almost all male, were yelling and chanting angrily, red banners and NLF flags waving. Arthur was okay with protesting the war, but he was not very happy to see this—open support of the people who had been trying to kill him just a few days before. But he refrained from commenting.

They were almost all bearded, and clad in veritable uniforms of corduroys, turtleneck sweaters, and tweed sports jackets. They marched to the front of the now-seated crowd, and took position directly below the speaker's stand.

Moments later, a speaker took to the podium. *"GOOOOD AFTERNOON, EVERYBODY!"*

The crowd roared back a greeting.

"It's a gorgeous day here in Golden Gate Park, but it sure ain't a gorgeous day for our country!"

Noisy cheering, boos and catcalls erupted. A man behind Arthur yelled, "Shame on Nixon!"

33

"People in Vietnam are dying by the thousands every day from a war our government is fighting!"

"Nixon sucks!" the man behind them yelled.

"And the Citizens Coalition to Stop the War in Vietnam is here today to call on our leaders to stop the insanity!"

"LOBOTOMIZE NIXON!"

"So to start off, let's welcome Congressman Don Prescott!" There was a smattering of applause. Prescott was tall, square-jawed, hair fashionably long. As he began with the ritualistic denouncing of the war, a group of men behind him began setting up a drum kit, amplifiers and microphones.

"Looks like there's gonna be a band soon," Roxie said. "Wonder who? I hope they're good."

After railing against the war for several minutes, the congressman finally got to his real message. "Now people, we all want the war to end," he orated. "But it can't happen without money!"

The radicals in front of the podium began to boo.

"No one wants to talk about it—"

More booing.

"—but it's true!"

The booing changed to screams, and the radicals began gesticulating.

"I see those middle fingers," the congressman said.

"Give Nixon the finger!"

"But I ask you to put your index finger up beside it—and stick a dollar bill or a five or a ten or a twenty between them"—

"Tell Nixon to stick it!"

"—and give it to the marshals coming around to collect it!"

On cue, a swarm of people with buckets and white armbands fanned out from the base of the speakers stand and began circulating among the crowd.

The roars of disapproval from the radicals became louder, the obscene gestures even more blatant. The rest of the crowd began to grow restless.

The congressman, sensing the changing mood, abruptly left the podium, and the master of ceremonies took over, smoothly shifting gears to the next item on his list. "Thanks, Congressman. Keep up the good fight! And now, please give a warm welcome to Gold, playing at the Fillmore this weekend! Gold, everybody!"

Amanda turned the page of her sketchbook and began sketching the band.

As the band started playing, the radicals near the speaker's stand started booing, but the music drowned them out. *"All right!"* Roxie said. She stood up and began to dance, and a moment later Pilgrim joined her. Amanda began sketching them.

Arthur noticed the five guys in white robes again, circulating through the crowd a short distance away. For a moment he considered approaching them. *But what would I say?* He decided against it.

After a short set, the band retired to the back of the stage. The master of ceremonies returned to the microphone. "Gold, everybody. And now, our next speaker is—*Hector Figueroa, from La Raza!"* The radicals began to roar their approval.

Figueroa came to the microphone. "Thank you, thank you," he said to the crowd. Then, the bass player unplugged his instrument, causing a small burst of feedback to squeal from the speakers flanking the podium. "But before I get started…" Figueroa's face contorted in fury and he bellowed, *"LET'S GET RID OF THIS HONKEY BAND!"*

The radicals roared, ecstatic.

The bass player, exasperated, tossed his hands in the air and walked off the stage, the band following.

"VIVA LA RAZA!" Figueroa bellowed.

The radicals roared back.

"What the hell's he saying?" Roxie said.

"Long live the race," Doyle said. "La Raza. You know, like their culture or some shit."

"WE'RE HERE TO STOP THIS FUCKING HONKEY WAR!"

Roars from the front of the crowd, but not much else from the rest.

Figueroa turned his fury on the crowd. *"THIS IS NOT A PARTY! THIS IS NOT WOODSTOCK! YOU PEOPLE BETTER GET SERIOUS!"*

This provoked a smattering of boos from the rest of the crowd, although the radicals bellowed their approval.

"YOU PEOPLE, YES, ALL YOU HONKEYS! YOU ARE THE PROBLEM! YOU ARE NOT INTERESTED IN JUSTICE! YOU JUST WANT TO SMOKE DOPE AND LISTEN TO ROCK MUSIC!"

Pilgrim chortled. "Sounds pretty good to me!"

"Change to stop the war?" a marshal said, holding out a plastic bucket. Arthur put a couple of dollar bills in the bucket. "Gee, thanks, man," the marshal said.

"Well," Doyle said, "that does it. You shamed me into doing something, man. Gotta help stop the war, you know?" He got up. "Gonna get a bucket and help collect money," Doyle said. He took off after the marshal.

Figuroa continued, *"I'M ASKING ALL BLACK AND LATINO AND NATIVE AMERICAN PEOPLE TO JOIN ME IN SOLIDARITY AND WALK OUT OF THIS INSULTING AND BULLSHIT HAPPENING RIGHT NOW!"* Figueroa roared. The radicals at the front of the audience erupted in approval, their flags waving like leaves in a windstorm.

The boos became louder, more constant. Nearby, a young couple stood and folded their blanket, others joined them, and soon a steady stream of people were leaving the rally.

Amanda continued to sketch. "Well, this is going downhill fast," Arthur said. "How to break up a rally—insult the audience."

"Mmmm," she said, concentrating on her sketch.

"Think I'm going to head on back to the house," Arthur said. He stood. "See you later?" he asked hopefully.

Amanda nodded. "I'll be along in a while. I'm going to do a few more sketches."

"Okay," he said, disappointed but trying not to show it. He started working his way back through the crowd.

A hundred yards from the athletic field a path wound through a grove of trees. As he approached the grove, the guy in the white robe emerged from it and stopped in front of him. *Something about him,* Arthur thought.

The man looked at Arthur and smiled. "Preach, as I live and breathe."

And then Arthur made the connection. He grinned broadly. "Dick Osgood. Wow."

Dick started laughing. "It took you long enough, asshole. How the fuck you doin'?"

. . .

CHAPTER 4
i

The Haight, San Francisco
October 4, 1969

"So," Arthur said, passing Dick the pipe. After a moment he grinned broadly. "You've changed a little, man."

Dick was in mid-hit and started laughing, which got him coughing convulsively so that he spewed smoke, tears

37

and snot. This got Arthur laughing too, and it took them almost a minute to recover.

"Jee-zus, don't do that, Preach," Dick gasped when he had caught his breath enough to speak.

"And I love the feathers."

This set them off again. Finally, wiping the tears from his eyes, Dick took a sip of water and sat back. He sighed. "Damn, it's good to see you, man," he said. He took off his headdress and set it beside him on the sofa.

"Ayuh," Arthur said. "Three years?"

Dick nodded, smiled. "So what have you been doing, man?"

Arthur considered this a moment. "Finished high school. Ran the FoodMart in Searsport awhile. Got drafted. Went to Nam. Got back yesterday. That's about it." *Three years in twenty-five words or less,* he thought.

"Yesterday?" Dick said.

Arthur nodded.

"Holy shit. What was Nam like?"

Arthur shrugged. "Made it home." He was silent a moment. "How 'bout you?"

Dick looked away. "Been out here awhile," he said. He shifted in his seat, rubbed his cheek reflectively.

"So what's with the makeup?" Arthur said.

"Just greasepaint," Dick said. "Me and my friends, we decided to get freaky today."

"Who's we?"

"Guys I share a house with, over in the Castro. Gay guys, but what the hell, different strokes and all that, you know? They don't hassle me or anything."

Arthur cocked an eyebrow at him.

Dick grinned. "Always liked the chicks, man, you know that," Dick said. "But I've evolved, ya know? More tolerant than I was back home." He shook his head. "Home. A fuckin' trailer in the woods. Workin' in a slaughterhouse." He leaned forward and leered, "It sure ain't like here. A lot of chicks see me in this getup and think I'm a holy man or something."

"Yeah, right," Arthur scoffed. "How's Jeanette, holy man?"

Dick's head jerked up. "Jeanette?"

Arthur smiled. "Come on, Dick. You think everyone back home is stupid or something? The two of you disappearing the same day?"

Dick said nothing for a few moments, then nodded reluctantly. "So you figured that out, huh?"

"Wasn't hard." Arthur waited.

Dick sighed. "Jeanette and me worked our way across the country, doing odd jobs. She'd waitress, I'd wash dishes. Then she got big time into drugs when we got here. Crystal and all. Heavy shit. She finally took up with some biker and split. Ain't seen her in close to two years." He asked, "So, how's...Wilma? And the boy? Sometimes, I...miss 'em, you know?"

Arthur shrugged. "Holding up okay, last I heard. Her folks were helping out. Yours too, I think."

Dick nodded but said nothing.

After a moment, Arthur said, "Got some bad news about my family, though." He told Dick about Aunt Esther.

"Jeez, that's too bad," Dick said. "She was a boss lady. I always liked her. When's the funeral?"

"Already happened." Arthur explained. "So, I thought I'd hang out here for a while." He smiled. "I met this girl, see."

Dick grinned. "Sharon ain't on your radar screen anymore?"

Arthur smiled back. "Nope." The front door opened.

Roxie shrieked when she entered the living room. "God, look, Pilgrim! It's one of *those guys!*"

Dick nodded quietly.

"I am not believin' this," Pilgrim said.

Amanda entered, and smiled at Arthur. "I told you," she said, a hint of triumph in her voice.

Arthur chuckled. "An old friend. Not a new friend. We're catching up on our lost youth, right, Dick?"

Dick nodded. "Hello," he said.

"I'd like to sketch you," Amanda said. "Dick."

Dick smiled. "I am honored."

Amanda sat across from him and opened her sketch pad.

"So where's Doyle?" Arthur asked.

"Out collectin' money to stop the war," Pilgrim chortled. He rubbed his hands together. "Well, let's get high and see what's on the tube, huh?"

The excitement Dick's presence had generated soon disappeared as they became immersed in an old Humphrey Bogart movie.

"There," Amanda said, a few minutes later. She leaned back from her sketchpad. "Finished."

"May I see?" Dick said.

"Of course." She turned the sketchpad toward him.

"You sketch well," Dick said. "It's a gift, you know."

"Yes." Amanda nodded quietly. "I know."

The front door opened again, and Doyle entered, eyes gleaming. "Look at this!" he said. He held a donations bucket from the rally. "Must be twenty-five bucks in here!"

"Cool," Roxie said, taking another hit.

Doyle nodded at Dick. "Who's he?"

"Friend of mine," Arthur said. "Dick. From Maine."

Doyle snickered. "Far out, Dick-from-Maine. I'm Doyle."

Dick nodded.

Doyle sat down on the sofa and dumped the bucket of change and bills onto the coffee table. He began to count. "Man, look at all this bread!" he said. "Enough to replenish the pantry for sure."

"Wait, you're keepin' the money?" Arthur said.

"Damn straight," Doyle said.

"Though it was to stop the war," Arthur said.

"Jeez, everyone collecting it was keepin' it," Doyle said. "I bet half the money that got collected won't get turned in."

Arthur kept silent.

"What? *What?*" Doyle said.

"Hey, do what you want, man," Arthur said.

"Gee thanks," Doyle sneered, "like I need your permission. You got a real attitude problem, man."

This was too much for Arthur. He leaned forward in his chair. "You're the thief, Doyle, not me."

"Preach, please!" Amanda said quietly.

"Whoa," Roxie said. "Preach, come on. There are other ways."

"Jeez, will you guys lighten up?" Pilgrim asked. "Tryin' to watch a movie here. Come on, Preach. Calm down and take a hit."

"No. I'm gonna go for a walk," Arthur said. "Dick, you want to come?"

Dick shook his head. "No," he said, glancing at Amanda. "I've been walking all day. I'll hang out here."

"Amanda?"

"No," she said. "I think you need to be alone right now, Preach."

Arthur considered this a moment. He decided he had probably overstepped. "Okay," he said. "I'll be back in a half hour." He started out of the room, then stopped beside Doyle. "Sorry man," he said.

"Sure," Doyle said. "It's cool." But Arthur could tell it wasn't. He left the house and started toward the park. He looked at his watch. Five-thirty. The shadows were lengthening, the warmth of the day fading.

At Stanyan he turned right and walked past a hotel to Fulton. A few blocks down he found a corner grocery and bought a quart of milk and a pound of fresh-roasted coffee beans, which he had the counter man grind for perk. He went back outside, the evening growing pleasantly cooler. Above, the evening star glowed in the purple sky. To the west was the gloaming's brilliant fire.

Arthur smiled, the sunset making him somehow feel better. He returned to Stanyan, whistling. He stopped when he realized the tune—*Rose of Culloden*. His mother used to...

A vague sense of disquiet filled him. He headed back toward the house. He had been gone an hour.

ii

He let himself in. The TV was still on, but the room was dark otherwise, the gray from the TV screen casting a silvery glow throughout the room. "Welcome back," a voice said from the living room.

"Hey, Doyle," Arthur said. "Where'd everybody go?"

"Who cares?" Doyle said. "What'd you buy?"

"That coffee I mentioned this morning. Want some?"

"Sure." They went back to the kitchen and Doyle got out the percolator. Arthur sat at the kitchen table and watched Doyle make the coffee, carefully measuring out the grounds. "Thanks for the coffee. And the milk. Sorry I gave you shit earlier."

"Don't worry about it," Arthur said. Then he heard something. "What's that?"

"What's what?" Doyle said.

"That. Listen." He cocked his head toward the front of the house. "Hear it? Some kind of thumping."

"Oh yeah," Doyle said. "I think that's Amanda, gettin' to know your buddy, Dick." Doyle chortled. "Dick's dick."

"*What?*"

"Hey, I told you she wasn't into long-term—"

But Arthur was already out of the kitchen, heading for the stairs.

He charged up the stairs and ran down to Amanda's room. He grabbed the doorknob and tried to turn it, but it was locked. He could hear them inside. He pounded on the door.

"Amanda!" Arthur called.

"Go away!" she yelled back.

"Open this door!"

"GO—A—WAY!"

The pounding continued. Arthur stared at the door, stunned, for several moments, then scratched his head, at an utter loss for words. He turned away and headed back to the stairs.

He sat on the sofa in the living room, the TV still on. Heart pounding, he fixed himself a pipeful of marijuana. After a time the pounding upstairs stopped, and the house fell silent.

A few minutes later, Doyle came from the kitchen carrying a couple of mugs of steaming coffee. "Here you go, man," he said.

"Thanks."

They sipped in silence a few minutes. The door upstairs opened. Arthur heard her coming downstairs. She appeared in the door of the living room off the entry hall. She was holding Arthur's duffel bag. "Here's your bag." She laid it on the landing. "Everything's in it. Your uniform, shoes, whatever."

"Amanda, can I ask a question?"

"No." She turned and went back upstairs.

Arthur jumped to his feet. "So, that's it?" he called after her. "That's *it?*"

"Yes."

"Well..." he started, "Well—that's just great, Amanda. That's just *great!*" He started ranting, unable to help himself. "And tell that jerk up there that he isn't my friend anymore! The two of you have a nice life! Have a real—" He heard the door to her room shut with an irrevocable finality. He took several deep breaths, trying to still the hammering in his chest.

He slammed his fist into the wall beside the door, then clutched his fist, muttering under his breath. He went back into the living room and sat down.

"Ain't women a gas?" Doyle said. "Can't live with 'em, can't—"

"Shut up, Doyle," Arthur said, wearily.

"Hey, it's cool," Doyle said. "It's cool." He looked at Arthur obliquely. "So this guy Dick is a buddy of yours, huh? Some bud—"

Arthur leapt to his feet and in two quick strides was on Doyle, straddling him in the recliner. He grabbed his shirt and shook him, his face inches from Doyle's nose. "One more word, Doyle! One more word and I'll punch your lights out, you hear?"

"I hear, man. I hear." And then, unfortunately, Doyle started to laugh.

Arthur nailed him square in the nose with a right cross. He heard the crunch as the cartilage popped. Blood spurted down the front of Doyle's shirt as he yelled in pain.

"Shut up, man!" Arthur yelled and hauled off to punch him again, when someone grabbed him from behind and pulled him onto the floor.

"Stop it Preach, what the fuck are you doing?" It was Pilgrim. He flipped Arthur over and straddled him, holding his arms down.

"Let me up, Pilgrim!"

"Get a grip, man," Pilgrim said, refusing to let go. "Get a grip and I'll let you up!"

Let—*me*—UP!" Arthur struggled as hard as he could for a few more seconds, but Pilgrim outweighed him by a good hundred pounds and was stronger to boot. Arthur finally relaxed, exhaled sharply, and lay still. "Okay man, you win," he said.

"Good," Pilgrim said. He did not move.

"You can get off me now, I'm cool," Arthur said.

Pilgrim peered into his eyes a long second. "Okay, then." Pilgrim gradually relaxed his grip, then slowly got off Arthur and stood, carefully placing himself between Arthur and Doyle.

"Ged the fuck ouda here," Doyle said, clutching his nose. "You ard welcome here adymore."

Arthur sighed as he stood. "Doyle, I—"

"Jus' ged the fuck oud." Doyle stood.

"You better go, man," Pilgrim said.

As Arthur calmed, he became embarrassed. "Okay, I'm going." He looked at Doyle, and shook his head ruefully. "Doyle, you probably don't much care, but I—I shouldn't have punched you, man."

"Gread," Doyle said. "By dose thanks you."

Arthur said nothing to that. After a moment, he said, "I'm wearing your clothes. I'll change and then I'm gone, okay?"

"Fuck 'em," Doyle said. "Keep 'em." Doyle disappeared toward the kitchen.

"Time to go, Preachee," Pilgrim said.

"Okay, man. I'm gone." He walked out the door. Pilgrim closed it behind him, locking it.

Arthur changed into his uniform again before leaving the porch, folding Doyle's clothes neatly on the doormat. He then walked down the steps to the street. He felt guilty—he did not know why—and vaguely ashamed. *I shouldn't have lost control like that,* he thought.

He heard a tapping behind him. He turned. Amanda was in the window to her bedroom, looking down on him. She was naked. She wiggled her fingers at him, her expression gentle, regretful, almost sad. Then she turned away.

Man alive, he thought. Arthur turned away and headed toward Stanyan and Golden Gate Park.

. . .

CHAPTER 5
i
Golden Gate Park, San Francisco
October 4, 1969

A few minutes later Arthur reached Stanyan and the park beckoned across the street, the dark trees ominous. A small hotel was behind him. He decided to check in there, and then return to the airport in the morning and fly home. *So much for a nice weekend in San Francisco.*

"Strawberry!"

He looked up at the voice—that of a woman, frantic, frightened, standing just across the street, calling into the woods in the park. She was about his age, long blonde hair, granny-glasses, wearing a sundress and sandals. She cupped her hands again.

"Strawwwwwberreee!" she called. She was shaking.

Arthur crossed to her. "Can I help you?"

The woman whirled around. Her voice shook. "Yes sir, please. My baby's in here somewhere." She gestured deeper into the park. She smelled of marijuana and alcohol. "My husband's looking for her but—" Her composure left her and she began to sob. "Oh please help me, please! You can't imagine what this place is like after dark, especially for a little girl."

"Of course," he said. It hadn't occurred to him that the park might be dangerous. "Have you called the police yet?"

She gasped, eyes widening. "No! No cops! They'll take my baby. They'll say I'm unfit, you understand?"

46

Arthur nodded. "Okay, no cops. You wait right here. I'll go in and look around."

"Oh thank you," the woman said. "She's four years old, blonde hair. Carrying a pink bunny. Her Bun-rab, she calls it. We got separated at the rally. I just turned around for a second, and—" The woman began to sob again. "Oh God."

"Okay, try to take it easy. I'm sure she's fine." Arthur disappeared into the woods, beginning to regret getting involved. But he was committed now.

He stopped in a small clearing to orient himself.

The rally had been at the athletic field, approximately halfway into the park, a good fifteen minute walk. He knew it would be difficult to find the girl. He tried not to think of what might happen to her if he didn't. But the very act of trying not to think about it caused the thoughts to form, like thunderclouds on a hot summer afternoon.

Arthur entered the park, feet crunching on the cinder-covered paths. The moon was up now, its silver light dappling the ground through the thick canopy overhead. He hurried on, tempted to simply disappear and leave the woman and child to their fates. But around a sharp turn, he heard rustling bushes, and smelled alcohol and sweat lingering in the air, someone having disappeared just before he came into view. He knew then he had better continue looking.

A few minutes later, he reached the field where the rally had been. It was empty except for the trash and debris covering it. The speaker's stand had been taken down. Then as he reached the other end of the field, he heard quiet weeping. "Who's that?" he called.

Soft sniffles were his only answer. He approached cautiously.

There, sitting at the base of a tree, was a little girl about four years old, clutching a pink bunny rabbit. Arthur knelt in front of her. "Hi."

"Hello," the girl sniffled.

"I'm Preach," he said.

"I'm Strawberry," the little girl replied.

"Is this Bun-rab?" he asked, pointing to the rabbit.

"Yes. Mister Preach, will you help us find my mommy and daddy?"

"Sure I will, honey. Sure I will. Come on. I know right where your mommy is." He stood, took her hand, and they began to walk east. Arthur turned toward the northern boundary of the park. He decided to walk along the perimeter, figuring it was safer along the street.

He soothed her as they walked along, Strawberry clearly happy to be with a grownup now. Then he heard a voice calling off to his right, inside the park. "Strawberry! *Strawww-BERRREEE!*"

"Daddy!" Strawberry exclaimed. "Mr. Preach, that's my daddy!" She let go of his hand and began running toward the voice. Arthur followed. *At last,* he thought.

"Daddy! Daaaa-deee!"

"Strawberry! Strawberry, it's Daddy! Where are you, honey?" Arthur heard pounding footsteps on the path.

Then the father emerged from the darkness a few yards to their right. "Honey, here I am, oh thank God you're—"

He stopped when he saw Arthur.

But Strawberry ran into his arms and he swept her up. "Oh sweetie, I'm so glad I found you, so glad so glad…"

Strawberry gestured to Arthur. "Daddy, this is Mr. Preach, he was taking me to Mommy and—"

"Great," the father said, looking uneasily at Arthur. "Listen, I don't want any trouble." He looked at his daughter, then eyed Arthur warily. "Did this man hurt you, honey?"

"No, Daddy."

Arthur, appalled, stared at the father. "Now listen, pal, you don't think I—"

"I don't know what to think," the father said. "But I know you better get going now. The cops might want to talk to you if you don't."

Arthur stared in stunned disbelief. "Sure," he said slowly, the anger starting to grow. "I understand. And there's no need to thank me for finding your daughter or anything. Guess you and your wife were too stoned on pot and cheap wine to keep track of her yourselves."

"That's not true!" the man yelled. Then he fell silent, and after a moment quietly said, "Listen, just be thankful I'm not calling the cops." He backed away. "Come on, Strawberry, let's go find Mommy."

"Your wife's on Stanyan," Arthur said, calming. "She asked me to look for your daughter. Ask her when you see her." The man looked at him, and after a moment, he nodded. Arthur figured that was all the thanks he was going to get.

"Good bye, Mr. Preach," Strawberry said.

"Good bye, Strawberry," Arthur said.

"Hush now!" her father said sternly.

Arthur watched them disappear down the street along the park's northern boundary, and then he sat down on a nearby bench. He was shaking, angry, and needed to regroup.

After a minute or two, calmer, he headed toward that hotel he had seen on Stanyan. He figured he was less than fifteen minutes from a hot shower and a meal. He picked up his duffel bag and began to walk back toward the east through the park.

In a particularly heavily wooded section, a sob came from behind a bush to his right. "*Ayudame*," a voice said. "Hello? Is that someone? Help me, *por favor*. I'm hurt."

"What's wrong?" Arthur said, not leaving the trail.

"I'm hurt. *Dos pendejos*, they beat me up."

A man staggered out into the path, hand pressed over one eye. He was short, and very fat. He whimpered softly, "I can't see out of this eye, man. I think they popped it or something."

"Here, let's take a look." Arthur bent forward, wishing there was more light.

He heard a small sound behind him, but it was too late. Two people grabbed him from behind simultaneously with the man in front leaping at him. *"HEY—"*

One of the guys behind punched him hard in the kidneys. Arthur gasped but kicked at the man in front of him. He missed and the man kicked him in the crotch, mostly missing but not entirely. Arthur yelled in pain and then the men threw him to the ground, raining blows and kicks on him. He lost consciousness within moments, mercifully before the pain from the kick to the side of his head had even registered.

ii

His first sensation was one of enormous thirst, his throat harsh and grating as he tried to breathe. He coughed and shivered in the gray, cold light of the foggy dawn. *Gotta get water.*

His second sensation was pain, his head and torso a battlefield as he tried to sit, gasping with the effort.

His third sensation was incredulity.

Ambushed. I got ambushed.

He looked around warily. His left eye refused to open fully, but he could see out of it, sort of. His duffel lay nearby, its contents scattered in the grass near him. A sudden thought caused him to reach around to pat his hip, and he gasped as his shoulder protested the sudden movement.

His wallet was gone, of course. Then he saw it on the ground nearby. He picked it up. All his cash was gone, but his military ID and Maine driver's license were still there, thankfully. He also found fourteen dollars and coins in his right front pocket that his attackers had overlooked. It was change from the twenty he had used to buy the coffee and milk the afternoon before.

Just great. Now I'm almost broke, too.

He put the bills back in his wallet, and began to check himself out. He gingerly moved every part of his body, starting with his feet. After a minute or two, he satisfied himself that nothing was broken. But he could feel a cut on his scalp above his left ear, to go along with the damaged left eye.

Next, he tried to stand, and after a couple of attempts, did so, although a bit shakily. He walked around in circles for a minute or two, regaining his balance.

I've got to get cleaned up.

He found a water fountain nearby, and after gulping mouthful after mouthful of the cold, delicious water, he took out a handkerchief, wet it, and wiped the blood off his face and scalp as best he could, then washed his hands. The handkerchief, now pink, he discarded. He went back to his duffel and collected his stuff. He had a moment of heart-stopping alarm until he found the film can with the shrapnel scrap, still in his shaving kit. Relieved, he put the can in his pocket. *Better to carry it there,* he decided. He picked up his duffel and quickly exited the park. He crossed the street and looked at himself in a storefront window.

The cut on the side of his head was smaller than expected, and it was not bleeding anymore. He had also developed a pretty impressive shiner.

But he was alive. He supposed he was lucky.

His efforts at tidying his uniform had been only partially successful. The knee of his trousers was torn and a button was missing from his tunic. Blood speckled his khaki shirt. *Gotta get out of this uniform.*

Then he remembered Doyle's clothes, and walked as fast as he could back to the house on Page. When he got there, he breathed a sigh of relief. Doyle's clothes were still on the front steps. Knowing everyone inside would still be asleep, he stole onto the porch.

Xin loi, Doyle. He quickly changed.

A minute or two later, wearing Doyle's shirt and jeans, plus his own tunic and jungle boots, Arthur stuffed his uniform pants and the bloody shirt and tie into a trash can at the corner. He almost put the new dress black shoes he had been issued into the trash can as well, but then decided that would be a waste, so he put them next to the can, figuring someone who needed them would take them. He took off his badges and ribbons and started to toss them as well, but then, not knowing quite why, he put them in the pocket of his tunic. He turned from the house, and walked north to Geary.

With a last look behind him, Arthur West turned east, toward the rising sun.

And Maine.

. . .

PART II: MAINE
CHAPTER 6
i

Waldo County, Maine
June, 1949

There are two Maines.

The first is the Maine of stately mansions along picturesque stretches of the coast, the mansions built by clipper ship and whaling captains from the profits of voyages made a century or more before to Siam, the Japans, and old Cathay.

It is a Maine of galleries, cozy restaurants, summer cottages and sailboats, in a hundred little coastal towns named Port Clyde and Tenants Harbor and Rockport and Camden.

It is a Maine of concerts during summer evenings on village greens, almost every green with a monument honoring the men from there who died for union and freedom in the War of the Rebellion.

It is a Maine of lobsters, clam chowder, blueberry pie, and baked Jacob's Cattle beans.

It is a Maine of stern islands a hundred yards offshore, the pines growing thick to their rockbound, seaweed-covered shorelines, surrounded by seagulls and lobster buoys and fog.

It is the Maine the tourists love; it is also the only Maine most of them see.

But there is another Maine, one of lumber mills and chicken farms, in factory towns like Millinocket, Farmington and Brewer. It is a Maine of working people, of time clocks and dinner buckets—a hard Maine, a Maine of bleak, always tenuous prosperity.

It is a Maine of clapboard houses needing a coat of paint, standing alone in windswept fields, the black pines around the fields ominous in the gray rain of a late spring afternoon.

It is this Maine into which Arthur Leon West was born in June 1949, in the Waldo County General Hospital in Belfast, twelve miles from the sagging, rented saltbox on a hill near Swanville his parents, Horace and Maude, called home.

ii

May, 1953

Arthur was an only child, which was fortunate because Horace Greeley West was not a wealthy man. He took his responsibilities as a husband and father seriously, however, and worked hard at providing for his wife and son. He did not drink, thus avoiding the alcohol-fueled rages that sometimes overcame some of his coworkers at the Belfast chicken plant, where Horace worked four nights a week in the live hang room.

The live hang room was a squawking chicken's first stop on the processing line that turned it into broiler and fryer parts. Horace's job was to take the chickens out of the tiny wire cages in which they arrived, packed sometimes fifteen to a cage. He then hung them upside down in shackle-like brackets, the penultimate step before their throats were slit. It was tiring, sometimes painful work. He wore a leather apron, gloves and goggles, but rarely did he leave a shift without pecks and scratches from the fear-crazed birds.

It was a job few people sought, but Horace was glad to have it. A dollar an hour in 1953 was worth something. And, by doing a little blueberry raking in season, a little logging some days, and a little small engine repair others, he managed to keep his family fed, housed, and clothed.

Of course, a vegetable garden, apple tree, and laying hens helped, as did the deer he shot and the perch, bass and horned pout he took out of Waldo County's lakes and ponds. Horace took quiet pride in his marksmanship and fishing skills, honed sharp by necessity.

Although Horace had been known to poach a deer occasionally, and slightly under-report his always meager income each April, he would never accept charity. The ban extended to family as well. Arthur's Aunt Esther, Maude's older sister, left comfortably well off by her late husband, had offered financial assistance more than once, but had always been turned down.

But if Horace was a proud and stubborn man, he was also clean and sober. He did not use foul language. In fact, he rarely said much of anything at all. Arthur had asked his mother about this once.

"Your father is a good man, Artie," his mother had told him. "If he doesn't speak much, don't take that as a sign that he doesn't love us. Some men are like that."

"Okay, Momma," Arthur said. He went to bed that night proud of his father. He wanted to be just like him when he grew up.

iii

March, 1954

Since Horace was almost always gone Sunday mornings when Arthur got up, every Sunday a neighbor, Sylvia Hall, would pull into the West's dooryard in the family station wagon. The Halls owned a prosperous dairy farm occupying both sides of the Swan Lake Road three miles north of Belfast.

Mrs. Hall was a large, powerfully built woman, her face red from years of exposure to the sun and wind, but her pale blue eyes were kindly and she always spoke with a gentle smile. Her two sons, Harrison and Henry Junior, sat in the back seat.

Arthur and his mother would ride with them to church in Searsport. Arthur usually sat in the rear-facing back seat. After the first few trips, Henry Junior, about Arthur's age, began to sit back there with him. As they talked over the weeks, Arthur's first friendship was formed. In truth, talking with Henry Junior each Sunday was the only thing about church he liked.

"We got a television," Henry Junior announced grandly one Sunday morning on the way to Searsport. "Daddy picked it up last week in Bangor."

Arthur was impressed. He had heard of television before, but had never seen one except in a store window in Belfast. "Wow, Hag," he said. "Is it really like movies?" For inexplicable reasons, virtually everyone who knew Henry, except his mother, had started calling him 'Hag'.

"Sort of," Hag said, "like old movies, in black and white. And there are commercials all the time. Those are things they show to try to sell you stuff. Sometimes they're funny. 'Brusha-brusha-brusha, with the new Ipana! Brusha-brusha-brusha, it's better for your teee-eeeth!'" Hag laughed. "Ipana toothpaste. Daddy said he'd buy us some."

"Wow. What are the shows like?"

"Wicked good," Hag said. "*The Howdy Doody Show* is funny. He's a puppet, Howdy Doody. His friend is a man named Buffalo Bob. *The Lone Ranger* is a good show, too. *'Hiyo Silver, away!'* It's on in the afternoons. Come over some time and watch."

"That'd be fun," Arthur said. He had never been to Hag's to visit.

"Mommy, can Artie come over tomorrow and play?" Hag called over his shoulder to the front of the car.

"I suppose, Henry," Mrs. Hall said, "if it's all right with Artie's parents."

"Can I, Momma?" Arthur called.

"We'll see, Artie," his mother said.

iv

"Momma," Arthur said after the Halls had driven away that afternoon, "Hag got a television set last week. Do you think Puppa could buy us one?"

"I don't think so, Artie," his mother said, fumbling in her purse for the house key.

"But why, Momma? Hag says it's really neat."

"Your father likes his radio, Artie. Besides, a television set costs a lot of money."

"Oh." It had not occurred to Arthur that money might be an issue. "Does Mr. Hall have more money than Puppa?"

Arthur's mother smiled. "I don't know, Artie. But your father has money enough to take care of us. Besides," she added, "it's not polite to talk about how much money people have. Do you understand, Artie?"

"Ayuh, Momma," Arthur said. After a moment, he said, "So can I go over to Hag's tomorrow? You heard Mrs. Hall say it was all right."

His mother smiled and unlocked the door to the house. "We can ask your father about it when he gets back."

v

"Puppa?" Arthur said that evening after supper. His mother had pan-fried some of the dozen white perch his father had brought home that afternoon. She had also served boiled potatoes and peas mixed together in hot milk, the butter Arthur added to his potatoes coloring the white of the milk with rich yellow droplets. Black flecks of pepper added to the dish, one of his favorites.

His father looked over the top of the *Republican Journal* as his mother cleared the table. "Ayuh, Artie?"

"Hag asked me to come over to play tomorrow afternoon. Can I?"

His father considered this. "Long way to go by yourself."

"Only a few miles," Arthur said. "I can ride my bike over. Besides," he said, carelessly, "Hag got a new television set. Hag says we could watch while I'm there."

His father considered this a moment. "Don't know as I like you riding your bike over there by yourself just yet, Artie. But, I could probably drive you. Is it okay with Hag's folks?"

Arthur nodded. "Hag asked me in the car on the way home from church today and his mother said I could come."

Arthur's father nodded, and went back to his paper.

"Thank you, Puppa," Arthur said. Another thought occurred to him. "Puppa?"

His father put down his paper again. "Ayuh, Artie?"

"Why don't you go to church with Momma and me?"

After a moment, his father said, "Did you enjoy your supper tonight, Artie?"

Arthur nodded. The perch, fresh caught through the ice on Half Moon Pond, were firm, delicately flavored, and delicious. He had eaten two, and part of a third.

His father said, "Keeping you and your mother fed, that's the Lord's work too, I guess." He picked up the paper again. "Think you could help your mother with the dishes?"

Arthur smiled. "All right, Puppa."

vi

October, 1956

One of Arthur's strongest memories of his mother was a ballad. One afternoon he was playing with toy soldiers on the kitchen floor while his mother prepared dinner. She was whistling softly as she peeled potatoes, a plaintive, haunting melody that made Arthur feel…older, somehow. "Momma, what's that song you're whistling?" he asked.

She smiled down at him. "It's an old song from Scotland called *Rose of Culloden*, Artie. Your great

58

grandmother used to sing it to me when I was little. I don't remember the words now, only the tune."

"What's Culloden, Momma?"

"It's a place in Scotland, Artie. A battle was fought there a long time ago. The English under Prince William beat the Scottish clans. It was the last battle fought in the British Isles."

"Is the song about the battle, Momma?"

She put down her peeler, thought a moment. "Sort of. It's about a young girl named Rose and her lover, Robert. They were betrothed—that means they were going to marry," she added quickly, anticipating his question. "When Robert doesn't return from the battle, Rose runs to the battlefield to look for him. She finds his body and brings him back home to bury him. The song ends with her an old woman, who never marries another. Instead, she goes mad from the grief and spends each night walking bloody Culloden Moor with a lantern, calling out the name of her betrothed in the hope that one night he'll answer and they'll be together again."

Arthur was silent a moment. "That's a sad story, Momma. Are we Scottish?"

"Partly. Your great-grandmother was a McLachlan. She came here from Canada almost a hundred years ago. Her proudest boast was that the Mclachlans fought at Culloden. In the front rank." His mother laughed. "Your great-grandmother didn't care for the English, Artie. She used to call Prince William 'Stinking Billy'."

Arthur laughed. "That's funny."

"It is," his mother chuckled. "So Artie, you come from a proud family, whose only mistake was fighting for a lost cause. Lots of people fight for lost causes. And some die for them, sadly enough."

Arthur nodded. He went back to his toy soldiers. A moment later, the soft strains of *Rose of Culloden* again filled the kitchen.

vii

Arthur became ill a few days later, on a cold, rainy afternoon. Arthur walked in the front door after school, coughing. His mother looked up. "Hello, Artie. How was school today?"

"Fine, Momma. We started a book called *Dick and Jane*. And I read, Momma. I read!" Arthur coughed again, several times. "I'm the first one in the class who can read!"

His mother put down her spoon. "That's wonderful, Artie. Let me feel your forehead." She did so, and frowned. "You feel kind of warm to me." Then she noticed his feet and pant legs. "My goodness, Artie, you are soaked! Let's get you out of those clothes. How did you get your pants so wet?"

Arthur laughed, coughing again as he undressed in the kitchen. "Waiting for the bus after school. Hag and me were seeing who could make the biggest splashes." Hag and Arthur had become inseparable over the previous summer.

"I don't know why you boys have to play in puddles on a day like this." She passed him a towel. "Here, dry your legs off."

"It was fun, Momma." Then Arthur began to cough again, loudly and persistently this time. "I'm sorry if I did wrong."

His mother smiled. "Oh that's all right, Artie. Boys will be boys. Let's get you to bed." And so his mother put him to bed, assuring him it was just a cold and most boys got them this time of year and he would be better in the morning.

But Arthur's temperature was 101 when his father returned from his shift at the chicken plant, and so he stayed home from school the next day. But by evening, in spite of his mother's attentions, Arthur was flushed and red, his skin hot to the touch, and he could not stop coughing. His temperature had passed 102.

"He needs a doctor, Horace," he heard his mother say that afternoon before his father left for the plant.

"Ayuh," Horace said. "I'll call from work."

Dr. LaPointe arrived after dark. After examining him, he put his stethoscope back in his bag, threw away the tongue depressor and washed his hands. "Mrs. West, Arthur has pneumonia. I'm going to have him admitted to the hospital in Belfast."

"Yes, Doctor. How…how much will the stay in the hospital…how long—"

"I don't know, Mrs. West. But Arthur needs to be hospitalized, the sooner the better. They'll be able to give him better care than we can give him here."

Arthur's mother was silent a moment. "Of course, Doctor. Can it wait until Horace gets home in the morning with the car?"

"You have no way to get to the hospital before morning?"

"No, Doctor."

"Very well. I'll take you myself." He stood. "Arthur needs to get dressed. You also might want to pack a small bag for him."

"Of course. Thank you for your kindness." She reached for her change purse. "What do we owe you?"

"Don't worry about that right now, Mrs. West." The doctor turned to Arthur. "Young man, I've got good news for you. You're going to get to stay in the hospital for a few days. Would you like that?"

Arthur was not sure whether he would or not, but he nodded anyway. "Yes, sir."

They left a few minutes later.

viii

The next couple of days were very mysterious to Arthur. It seemed as if he could remember them and not remember them at the same time.

Arthur remembered arriving at the hospital. It was so brightly lit, especially after the dark ride from his house to Belfast. His mother held him the entire way. He could not stop shivering, even though he felt hot.

After that, things got more confusing. He could remember people in white coming in, and being bathed with cool water and getting shots. He had no trouble remembering *them.* He also could remember seeing his mother and father pretty regularly. His mother seemed always to be there, in fact, and he was pretty sure he had heard them talking more than once. This was unusual in itself because his father spoke so little. What was even stranger was that they seemed to be having a fight.

"Won't hear of it Maddy. I'll work another night or two at the plant and get more logging work days—"

"Horace, the hospital is expensive and Esther can pay for it. And I can help. I can take in laundry and mend and—"

"No Maddy, you aren't going to start working and that's an end to it."

His mother must have agreed because Arthur did not remember any more conversations like that one.

Two evenings later the fever broke. Arthur awoke and sat up. He looked around the room. Then he saw his mother asleep in a chair by the door. "Momma?"

She opened her eyes with a start, looked around a moment, and then saw Arthur sitting up, eyes clear and bright, and her hand went to her mouth. "Thank you, Jesus," she whispered.

"Momma? Are you all right? Are you crying?"

"No Artie, I'm not crying. I'm fine." She dabbed at her eyes with a handkerchief, then crossed to the bed and hugged her son. "How are you?" She felt his forehead, then stroked his hair as she pulled him more tightly against her.

"Fine, Momma, I'm fine," Artie said, trying to extricate himself from her grasp. "Can we go home now? I'm starving."

"I'll go get the doctor, Artie." She hurried from the room.

ix

Arthur was discharged from the hospital the next day. The stay cost the family five hundred dollars, money they did not have. But Horace was a man who paid his debts, and so if repaying the hospital meant more work, Horace would do what had to be done. He was not the complaining kind.

So Horace added more hours at the chicken plant and got a second job as a contract woodcutter for a Bucksport sawmill. During those increasingly rare hours when he was home, he was usually tinkering with some piece of machinery or another for one of his neighbors. Thus, in spite of his near constant exhaustion in the weeks following Arthur's illness, the debt for Arthur's stay in the hospital began slowly to shrink.

x

November, 1956

Horace died just before Thanksgiving. He was hauling logs out of a stand of timber on a hillside near Brooks when he apparently miscalculated the pitch of the slope and the John Deere tipped over, pinning him beneath it. Spilled gasoline then caught fire somehow, probably from contact with the hot engine manifold. Or at least that was the sheriff's conclusion, based on the smoking remains of Horace, the overturned tractor, and a charred acre of forest left at the scene after the fire was brought under control.

Horace was buried three days later in the Searsport cemetery. Arthur wore his best clothes, a blue serge suit and Buster Browns, to the funeral, even though the suit was hidden beneath his winter coat, and the shoes by his galoshes. Wearing your best clothes to a funeral showed respect.

Arthur and his mother kept their emotions under tight control during the service and the reception afterward. They had cried long and deeply at home, of course, in private.

Horace had no life insurance.

. . .

CHAPTER 7
i

Belfast, Maine
July, 1958

Arthur awoke early on a sunny Saturday and went into the kitchen, where he poured himself a bowl of cereal. School had been out for three weeks now. He found it hard to believe that he would be starting fourth grade in September. *He was nine—that seemed so old!*

He planned his day as he ate. First off, he would bike over to Hag's, then go by Clement's, and then they would bike to the quarry and go swimming. But then he heard his mother stirring. He sighed. He had hoped to be off before she got up.

His mother shuffled into the kitchen, gray hair uncombed, clutching her bathrobe around her, threadbare slippers audible on the linoleum floor. It was unusual for her to be up this early. It was not eight yet. Of course, she had gone to bed last night before it was fully dark, so maybe she just wasn't tired now. Still, she had been sleeping more and more lately, he realized. Before they had moved to Belfast from the farm last year, he'd never been up in the morning before her. He had never had to fix his own breakfast either. Now it happened all the time. She was even missing church now. "Hello, Momma," he said.

"Hello, Artie," she said. She put the kettle on, and sat down at the table by the window.

Arthur told her of his plans.

"All right, Artie," she said tonelessly. "Be careful at the quarry. And be home before curfew, all right?"

"I will, Momma. Hag's got a watch; he'll tell me. Can I get a watch of my own sometime, Momma?"

His mother smiled wanly. "Maybe for Christmas."

Of course, his mother had said *'Maybe for your birthday'* two months ago, the first time he had asked. But he only said, "Yes, Momma. Well, I've got to go now." He kissed her good bye—she smelled old, musty, slightly sour—and clattered down the wood stairs to the alley below, where he had parked his old Schwinn the evening before. He grabbed his swimsuit from the line out back and dropped it in his basket. He was soon pedaling furiously down Congress Street.

ii

Clement's dog, Nero, a black-and-white spotted creature of decidedly mixed ancestry, began barking incessantly when he spied Arthur and Hag pulling into the dooryard. Nero yanked at his chain, tied to the bumper of an ancient Ford mounted on cinder blocks in the debris-filled yard surrounding the trailer.

"Hush, Nero," Arthur said, but was ignored. Nero always barked when someone new showed up. "Clement!" he called.

No answer.

"Clehhh-mmmunnnt!" he and Hag yelled.

They were just getting ready to yell again when the front door of the peeling doublewide opened, and Clement's father appeared, barefoot, wearing khaki work pants and a sleeveless undershirt. Mr. Paul was smoking a cigarette. "What do you two want? Don't you know it's early yet?" Behind him was Clement's little sister, May.

"Is Clement up yet, Mr. Paul?"

Mr. Paul turned into the darkness of the trailer. "Clehhh-meeeeee!"

From within the trailer came a frustrated scream. *"Je-zoos, Marvin! You try to raise de dead or wat?"*

Arthur wished Clement would hurry up.

Finally, Clement appeared, slipping around May and under his father's arm. Clement was small, even for a fourth-grader. When he was with Hag and Arthur, people who did not know him frequently mistook him for a little brother tagging along with older kids. "I'll be back later," Clement said to his father.

"And take that damned dog with you," Mr. Paul said. He flicked his cigarette butt into the yard, then went back inside and shut the trailer door.

iii

After they arrived at the quarry, the boys parked their bikes and then put on their swimsuits, splashed into the water, and swam the forty yards to the far end of the quarry. Nero swam with them a short way, then returned to shore, shook himself dry and lay down in the sun. The boys climbed onto a small outcropping just below the surface and sat in the sun-warmed, shallow water, enjoying the day.

"Well, there it is," Hag said, gesturing to the towering cliff halfway down the length of the quarry. It loomed over the quarry, mocking them.

The quarry had long since been abandoned, and over the decades had slowly filled with water from rain, snow melt and seepage. The water was a hundred or more feet deep as close as six inches to the limestone walls, which completely encircled the water except in one spot, a small rocky beach known by all the local kids as Pebble Beach.

When the quarry had been in operation, the beach was the top of the road the quarrymen had used to get to the bottom. The limestone walls ranged in height above the water's surface from just a few feet to more than twenty.

All the local boys knew the twenty-footer simply as "The Cliff." Jumping off it was a rite of passage as soon as boys had learned to swim well enough to be trusted in the water out of parental view. Most boys found the courage to make the jump before they were ten years old. Hag and Arthur had accomplished the feat a week before, but not, it must be admitted, without a minute or two of hesitation. Clement, however, had been unable to make himself jump.

"So who's gonna go first?" Hag said.

"I'll go," Arthur said.

Okay," Hag said. "I'll go next. Then you can go, Clement, okay?"

"Okay," Clement said quietly.

"Come on, let's swim back," Arthur said, and dove into the water. A minute or so later they were back on Pebble Beach; they then walked around the quarry until they were standing at the top of The Cliff. Hag tossed a couple of empty beer cans into the woods. Nero continued to snooze on the beach in the sun.

Arthur looked down into the water below.

It's so far... What a long drop... You can do it... You did it before... Got to show Clement it's easy...

"Well go on," Hag said.

"I'm going, Hag, I'm going," Arthur said. He gingerly walked to the edge, curled his toes over the sharply cut limestone. He looked down one more time—a mistake, he realized—then bent his knees, took a deep breath, shut his eyes, and yelled, *"GERONI"*—

He hurled himself into the void.

"—MOOOOOOH!" After what seemed an eternity he struck the water feet first and shot below the surface. He

began kicking, then opened his eyes and saw green, watery light ten or so feet above him. As he kicked back toward it he became aware of the black depths below him.

He had a quick, deliciously fearful vision of some rapacious beast rising from the depths and grabbing his leg with taloned fingers, pulling him struggling down into the cold darkness, feasting as it ripped chunks of his flesh from his legs. But then he broke the surface and yelled in the sunlight, *"Weeeooo, I was flyin'!"*

"Good jump, Artie!" Hag called. Clement was silent. "Now you, Hag!" Arthur yelled, treading water. He kicked back ten or so more feet to give Hag a clear field.

"On three!" Hag yelled. He assumed a ready position similar to Arthur's, then began to rock rhythmically forward and backward. "One. Two. Three!" And he jumped, yelling, *"WHO GOOOOOOSED THE MOOOOOOSE!"* on the way down. Hag struck the water and sank, then broke the surface a moment later. "Damn, that's fun!" he yelled. "Ain't it fun, Artie?"

"You betcha!" Arthur yelled back, making sure Clement could hear. On Pebble Beach, Nero began to bark.

Clement peered over the edge of the Cliff at the two boys treading water beneath him.

"Now you, Clement!" Hag called.

"Okay. Okay, I'm comin'," Clement called weakly. He walked to the edge. He stood with his toes just beyond the edge of the rock and looked down.

Arthur called, "You can do it, Clement."

Clement nodded. Then his knees began to shake. He gulped in air. "Okay. Okay, on three," he said. "One...two...*three!"*

He did not jump. He was frozen, immobile. "I—I can't!"

"That's all right, Clement, take your time!" Arthur yelled up. "Hag, I'm going to go up top. Maybe it'll help if someone's with him." Arthur swam to Pebble Beach and walked around to the top of The Cliff.

Clement remained standing at the edge, looking down but unable to make himself move. "Shit, I can't do it, Artie," he said, miserably.

"Sure you can, Clement," Arthur said.

Then behind them came a low laugh, startling them. They turned. "Go on, Clemmie, go ahead and jump. What's the matter, you *scared?*"

It was Oscar Loudermilk.

Oscar was five years older than Arthur and his friends, but had to repeat seventh grade and so was still in elementary school. Oscar, naturally big for his age, lorded it over the younger, smaller children on the playground, always careful to exercise his tyranny out of sight of the teachers. He had been a friend of Hag's older brother, Harrison, but they had drifted apart. It was not just that they were not classmates anymore. In truth, Harrison had long since tired of Oscar's foul mouth and petty cruelty.

"Hello, Oscar," Arthur said.

Loudermilk ignored Arthur, then turned to Clement. "C'mon, Clemmie," he whined sarcastically, "Hurry up and ju-ump! You're holding up the li-ine!"

"You go ahead," Clement said. He started to retreat from the edge.

Loudermilk blocked his retreat. "You're chicken is what you are!" Oscar yelled triumphantly. "Ain't that right?"

"No!" Clement said. "Just don't want to, is all."

Oscar flapped his arms like chicken wings. *"Clawwwk-pawk-pawwwk!"*

"Leave him alone, Oscar," Arthur said.

"Shut up, Artie Fartie," Oscar said. He turned back to Clement. "Well come on, Clemmie. Jump, if you're not chicken!"

"No, Oscar," Clement said, turning pale. "I'm not going to jump, I'm—I'm—"

A slow smile formed as an idea jelled. Oscar began to advance on Clement. "Either you jump…or I'm going to help you jump."

Clement began to back up. "No, Oscar, that's not"—

"Oscar, leave him alone!" Arthur yelled again.

"Who's gonna make me?" Oscar said, turning and glaring at Arthur. "You?"

"I'm gonna tell, Oscar!" Hag yelled from the water.

"Oooooooohhh, scare me one time," Oscar said, advancing on Clement again as Arthur watched helplessly.

Finally, Clement could back up no more; at this point Oscar lunged for him. "Let go of me!" Clement yelled as Oscar latched onto his arm, pulling him toward his pale, meaty body.

Oscar began to laugh as Clement thrashed. Arthur watched, ashamed, wondering what to do. Oscar easily fended off Clement's terrified punches and kicks, then braced himself, grabbed Clement's hands with one hand and put the other arm around Clement's waist, lifting him off the ground. Clement started to sob.

Oscar laughed, and began to swing Clement out over the edge of the Cliff. "One!"

"NOOOOOO!"

"Two!"

Clement's screams became guttural, primal. "Don't do it, Oscar!" Arthur yelled.

"And…three!" Oscar yelled, heaving the screaming Clement out over the water.

Clement, arms and legs furiously wind milling, plummeted to the water below. He struck the water on his side, causing a huge splash.

Arthur watched, appalled, as Clement came to the surface, sputtering and sobbing. Hag swam over to him. *"You bastard!"* Hag yelled up at Oscar.

But Oscar leaned over the edge of the Cliff, pointing and laughing. "You just been baptized, you little queer!"

Then, with startling clarity, it dawned on Arthur what to do. He lowered his head and charged.

Arthur plowed into Oscar and shoved with all his strength as he made contact. Oscar, overbalanced, squawked in surprise as he lurched forward from the impact, windmilled for a heart-stopping second as he fought to regain balance, then tumbled off the edge and plummeted toward the water twenty feet below. He belly-flopped, causing a splash that sent waves across the entire surface of the quarry.

Oscar surfaced a moment later, howling in pain. *"Shit-a-Goddamn, I'll kill you, you prick!"* It was clear that only Oscar's dignity had been damaged.

"Now you've been baptized, Oscar!" Arthur yelled in triumph. *"This Preacher's just baptized you! How do you like it?"*

Hag, who by rights should have been on Pebble Beach, dressed and halfway home by now, began to laugh in spite of his best efforts not to. "Yeah, Oscar, and just how do you shit a goddamn? Just like a regular turd?" Even Clement, still shivering, had to laugh at that.

"What're you laughing at? *Stop laughing!*" Oscar raged. And he began to swim clumsily toward them.

But Hag and Clement were far better swimmers than Oscar, and reached Pebble Beach in plenty of time to escape. Arthur ran down from the Cliff and joined them.

Then Clement got angry. *"You fucking cocksucker!"* he yelled. He picked up a rock the size of a small apple and threw it at Oscar's head. Missing only compounded his rage, and he began barraging Oscar with rocks as fast as he could pick them up.

His aim was ineffective, but his invective was right on target. *"Asshole! Coulda killed me! Fuck you and your grandpa and your grandpa's cousin, you piece of dog shit!"*

Oscar bellowed, *"Stop it! Can't you take a joke? Quit it or you'll wish you had!"* But, he stopped swimming toward the beach. After a particularly close miss with a large rock that would have done serious damage had it connected, Oscar even retreated—not much, but enough to be able to dodge Clement's missiles with little trouble— and treaded water balefully as he watched them with hate-filled eyes.

Nero stopped barking when he saw this look. His tail became deadly still and then, amazingly, he began to growl, his hackles standing almost straight up. Arthur had never seen Nero do this before.

Oscar noticed, too. In an effort to regain his dignity, he yelled, *"Gonna kill your dog, Clemmie!"* he taunted. *"Gonna shoot him! See if I don't!"*

"Not if I shoot you first, fat ass!" Clement screamed, *"and don't! Call! Me! CLEMMIE!"* He punctuated each word by chunking another rock.

But it was clear now that Oscar was far enough away to be safe. So after a few more tosses, Clement, exhausted, dropped his last rock. He looked at Hag and Arthur. "Let's…Let's go now." He struggled to keep from crying, and succeeded, mostly.

The boys took turns dressing, the others keeping Oscar at bay with the occasional rock whenever he tried to move closer to shore. Arthur found Oscar's bike and let enough air out of the tires so they were flat, and slipped the chain off the chain ring and cassette to slow his pursuit. Finally, they all jumped on their bikes and pedaled furiously away, Oscar's howls of anger and promised retribution echoing from the quarry walls as they departed.

iv

As Clement hooked Nero back onto his chain, he said, "Thanks, Artie, for helping me today. Maybe we oughta start calling you Preacherman now, huh?"

"Look at it this way," Hag said, smiling. "At least you've been off the Cliff now."

Clement laughed. "See you later, Hag," he said as he went inside. "You too—Preacher."

As Arthur pedaled home, he knew that whatever the other consequences that came from this day, the three of them had made a lifelong enemy in Oscar Loudermilk.

.   .   .

CHAPTER 8
i

Waldo County, Maine
August, 1958

One morning late that summer, a week or so before Labor Day, Arthur and Hag pulled into Clement's dooryard for another, last foray to the quarry. The Paul yard was still.

What was different?

Then Arthur realized—no barking. Nero's chain lay limp in the dooryard.

Arthur dismounted his bike and knocked on the door of the trailer. A few moments later, it opened. Mrs. Paul stood massively before them, hair in curlers, smoking a cigarette. "Watchu want?" she asked.

"Clement around, Mrs. Paul?" Arthur asked. "We were going swimmin'."

"Clemmie out back with his papa," Mrs. Paul said. "They bury poor Nero."

"They're doing *what?*" Hag said.

"Clemmie tell you," Mrs. Paul said, starting to tear up. She shut the door. The boys looked at each other, and raced around the corner of the trailer.

Clement and his father were digging a hole at the edge of the woods. May looked on. Arthur and Hag approached quietly, and then stood off to the side while Mr. Paul silently swung a mattock, loosening big clots of earth in the bottom of the hole. After a half dozen swings, Mr. Paul would stop, and Clement would then shovel out the loosened earth. Nearby, one of Nero's paws protruded from beneath the burlap sack that had been placed over him.

"Jeez, Clement, what happened?" Hag said.

"We went into Belfast last night," Clement said. "Found Nero shot dead when we got home."

"Just lyin' there at the end of his leash," Mr. Paul said. "Shot through the body."

The only sound was the mattock and shovel, and the sniffling of Clement's little sister. After a moment, Arthur said, "Any idea who..." although he knew.

"Nope," Mr. Paul said. "But if I ever find out, there's going to be one goddamned dead dog-killer in Waldo County."

"You could tell something from the bullet, I bet," Hag said. "On *Dragnet* they send bullets to the crime lab all the time, and the lab guys can always tell what gun it was fired from."

"Bullet came from a hunting rifle, a thirty-ought six," Mr. Paul said, digging. He chuckled bitterly. "Probably no more than a thousand of 'em in the county, sheriff says. Hell, I've got one. He's got one. Hag, your father's probably got one, too. No way we can find out who done it for sure, even if the sheriff was willing to try...which he ain't, for a dog. Asked already."

The hole was finished twenty minutes later. Arthur and Hag helped Mr. Paul and Clement lower Nero into the grave, then helped push the earth in over the dog. When the hole was filled, Mr. Paul tamped the earth down with the shovel and started to walk back to the trailer.

"Ain't we going to say words, Daddy?" May asked.

Mr. Paul stopped, thought for a moment, came back to the grave, and stood silently next to his daughter. He put his hand on her shoulder, and looked down. She rested her head against her father's hip.

No one said anything for a moment. Then May, voice tiny but firm, said, "Nero is a good dog, God. Please watch over him and make sure the angels scratch him behind the ears sometimes. He really likes that. Amen." This of course set off the boys, who began to tear up, hard as they tried not to.

Mr. Paul snorted abruptly. He shouldered the mattock and shovel, and turned away. "Damned dog," he said brusquely. He went from the grave, walking with hurried steps to the trailer. A moment later May followed.

The boys looked at each other. "Oscar," Arthur said.

"Ayuh," Clement said. "Gotta be."

"Why don't we tell the sheriff?" Hag said.

"No way to prove it, Hag," Arthur said. "He'd just deny it."

"So what are we going to do?" Hag said.

Clement said grimly, "Nothing. For now."

As Arthur went home, he considered the degree of malevolence that would be needed to shoot a dog in cold blood. It was then he realized that some people were…broken. Something in Oscar was either missing—or should be. Arthur was not sure which was more frightening.

November, 1958

By the time school started in the fall, it was clear
that Oscar had gotten away with Nero's murder. Of course,
he could not resist confirming to Clement his
responsibility. He did this not through confession, but
rather through what was, for him, masterful subtlety. On
the playground one afternoon he grinned at Clement, then
pantomimed pointing and firing a rifle at him while slowly
and deliberately nodding.

"Doesn't Oscar have a dog?" Hag asked one day
after school.

"We are not going to kill a dog, Hag," Arthur said.
"That'd make us as bad as he is. What are you, crazy?"

"Hag, a dog can't help who its owner is," Clement
agreed.

"Well, okay, that's true," Hag said. "But let's tell on
him for beating up kids at school. He does it all the time,
doesn't he? We can tell without letting anyone know it was
us."

"He'd think it was one of the kids he beat up telling
on him, and just beat him up again," Arthur said.

"Then let's tell Clement's dad Oscar shot Nero,"
Hag said. He turned to Clement. "Didn't your dad say he'd
kill whoever it was killed Nero if he found out?"

"My dad's all talk," Clement said. "He wouldn't kill
Oscar. Too chicken."

Arthur and Hag looked at him.

"Well, he is," Clement said.

June, 1959

It was late afternoon on the first Saturday of June.
School was going to be out for the summer on Wednesday,
and it had finally gotten hot. Arthur, Hag, and Clement
rounded the last turn on the gravel road that led to the
quarry, looking forward to the first swim of the season. The

water would be warm on the surface after baking in the sun all morning. The trees surrounding the quarry had only just begun to cast their afternoon shadows on the dark green water.

When the quarry came into sight, they stopped and stared, straddling their bikes. A new, red Ford Fairlane was parked just above Pebble Beach. No one was in sight.

"Hell's bells," Hag said.

"Anyone recognize the car?" Clement said. No one did.

"Where are they, you think?" Arthur said.

"Who knows?" Hag said. "Let's leave. We can come back tomorrow."

"No," Arthur said. "We've got as much right to be here as they do. We'll just keep away from them, is all. Leave our bikes up here."

They wheeled their bikes into the woods, laying them down behind a thicket of vines and scrub pine. Just before they started changing into their swimsuits, Arthur held up a hand. "Hold it a second."

"What's—"

"Listen."

Bursts of laughter were barely audible off to their right, further back in the woods, well away from the quarry. "You think it's the teenagers?" Hag asked.

"Probably," Arthur said. An idea occurred to him. He grinned. "You want to try sneaking up on them? See what they're doing?"

Clement grinned back. "I'm game if you are."

"Are you guys crazy?" Hag said. "What if they see us?"

"We'll be careful," Arthur said. "Come on, let's go take a look."

"Not me," Hag said. "I'm stayin' right here. You go if you want to."

"Okay," Arthur said. "You watch the bikes. Come on, Clement, let's go."

"Guys, I don't think—" Hag started, but Arthur and Clement were already moving quietly through the woods.

As they got closer they could begin to pick out distinct words, fragments of sentences.

"This is wicked good"...

"Never had it before"...

"Another one"...

A few more feet and a small clearing became visible. Arthur and Clement crouched slowly behind some low scrub, so they could see without being seen.

Oscar and four of his brown-noses sat in a circle facing each other, swigging from cans of Narragansett they were passing around. As each took a swallow, he tried to belch, every successful belch eliciting laughter from the others. Oscar's belches were the loudest of all. As each can was finished, one of the boys tossed it into the woods behind him. A can flew toward Arthur and Clement, but dropped well short of them. No one turned around.

After a few minutes, the boys had polished off all the beer they had brought. Arthur had counted eight cans tossed into the woods. Then Oscar said, "Okay, so who wants to do it?"

The boys looked at each other. "You sure about this, Oscar?"

"Ayuh. Brother and me do it all the time."

"Well…" one of them said, looking at the others for encouragement. They all looked at each other and at Oscar, and nodded tentatively. The boy continued, "But we've all got to swear never to tell anyone."

Oscar laughed derisively. "God damn right we'll swear," he said. "I swear I'll kill any one of you who tells. How about that for swearing?"

"Okay, Oscar," the first one said. "I swear I won't tell."

In short order they had all sworn not to tell anyone about…whatever it was they were about to do. By now, a John Deere tractor could not have pulled Arthur and Clement away.

Oscar and his companions stood, alarming Clement and Arthur, who almost got up to run. But then, astonishingly, they dropped their trousers and underpants around their ankles and sat back down Indian style, still in a rough circle. "Closer," Oscar said. They all wriggled in closer, forming a tighter circle. "Closer!" More wriggling, shifting. At last Oscar was satisfied. "Okay, now grab the guy's pecker next to you." Oscar started to grab, but no one else followed suit. He stopped. "Well, come on—*grab!*"

"Let's—let's all do it together," one of the other boys said. "On three, okay, Oscar?"

"Buncha morphodites," Oscar grumbled. "Okay, on three, then." They all nodded. "One—two—*three.*" The movement was executed as Oscar directed.

A couple of Oscar's companions flinched, then giggled. "Now what?" one of them said.

"Start jerkin'," Oscar said, and began stroking the member of the toady next to him. Within seconds, everyone's hands were vigorously pumping, and their conversation stopped.

Arthur watched, stunned. *What were they doing?* He glanced at Clement, who turned at that moment and caught Arthur's eye. Slowly, a twinkle of laughter began to dawn in Clement's eyes, and then he was shaking, turning red with the effort to keep from laughing out loud. This of course caused Arthur to want to laugh too, and soon he was also shaking.

One of the boys grunted loudly. "I'm—I'm first! Shit, I'm first, goddammit!"

"Well don't stop, I'm almost comin' too!" the kid to his right grunted.

Arthur had no idea what they were talking about, but he had seen enough. He also knew that every second they lingered from this point on put them in serious danger of a beating, if not worse. He motioned for them to withdraw, and Clement nodded, still shaking, tears streaking his cheeks. Ever so slowly—they knew they would pay dearly if they were caught now—they began backing up on their hands and knees, moving only a foot or so at a time, carefully avoiding sticks and other debris.

When the clearing was no longer visible, they stood and moved more quickly, arriving back at the bikes a minute or so later. Clement could contain himself no longer, doubling over as the laughter overwhelmed him. Arthur shushed him, but joined in as quietly as he could, as much from relief at not getting caught as at the humor of the situation.

Hag looked at them blankly. "What's so funny, guys?" They did not answer, too busy giggling. "Come on, *tell me!*"

"Shhh," Arthur hissed, wiping away a tear. "Let's get out of here. We'll tell you in a minute."

As quietly as possible, they walked their bikes through the woods to the road. As they mounted up, Clement looked down at the Fairlane. "Got to be Loudermilk's," he said. "He's the only one of that bunch old enough to drive."

"Loudermilk?" Hag said. "Loudermilk's back there?"

"Boy, is he ever," Clement said, and he and Arthur began to laugh again. "Wait, I'll be right back." He dropped his bike and dashed down to the car, squatting beside one of the tires. After a moment the car began to settle. When the tire was completely flat, Clement dashed back. "Now we can go," he said.

They pedaled furiously away.

Hag did not believe it when they told him.

"Swear to God it's true, Hag," Clement said. "And they didn't want anyone to know about it, either. Oscar said he'd kill anyone who told."

"But...why?" Hag asked. "Why would they do *that?*"

"Don't know," Arthur said. "But I'd sure like to find out."

"I'll ask Harrison," Hag said. "He'll know. He's sixteen."

"Okay," Arthur said, "but don't tell him what we saw. Let's keep that a secret for now."

Clement looked at Arthur, nodded thoughtfully. "Okay. At least for now."

iv

Arthur and Clement were even more astonished when they heard Hag's explanation on Monday on the playground during lunch recess.

"Jackin' off?" Arthur said.

"Ayuh. Babies come from it," he said. "I don't quite understand that part, but...anyway, Harrison told me them doing it to each other like what you guys saw is a 'circle jerk'. He said it's something queers do."

Clement and Arthur looked repulsed. Arthur had no idea what a *queer* was, except it was something no boy he knew wanted to be. "You didn't tell him what we saw?" Clement asked.

"No," Hag said. "He asked but I didn't tell."

Arthur was silent a moment. Then he said, "You know, we can fix Oscar good with this, guys."

"How?" Hag said.

But Clement needed no explanation. "Yeah. We can." They began to talk.

v

The next day, Arthur, Clement and Hag crossed the playground and sat down on the bench that Oscar and his toadies usually used. They opened their lunches and began to eat, chatting idly. School would be out for the summer tomorrow morning.

A few minutes later, the eighth graders were dismissed for lunch, and Oscar and his entourage emerged from the building, walking toward their usual bench. They stopped and stared at the three younger boys. "Get up, Artie Fartie," one of them said. "That's our bench."

"Don't see your name on it," Clement said, continuing to eat.

"Don't get smart, little man," the toady said.

"What's your favorite beer, Artie?" Clement said. "Mine's Narragansett."

"Mine too," Arthur said.

"And…and mine," Hag said.

Oscar's companions looked at each other. One of them, wide-eyed, said, "Oscar, I've got to go now." He left hurriedly.

Oscar glared at Clement, sneered, "Ayuh, like you drink beer. *Clemmie.*"

"We do so drink beer," Clement said. "We drink it out by the quarry. And don't call me Clemmie again, you fat piece of shit."

This was too much for Oscar. "Why you—" He leaned down to grab Clement.

Clement jumped to his feet and fearlessly back-pedaled a step or two. "Hit me, Oscar, and I'm going to start yelling right now about what you and your friends here were doing out at the quarry Saturday afternoon. Then we're going to tell our teacher. Then she'll call your folks." Oscar's companions glanced nervously at each other.

Oscar tried to brazen it out. "You—you didn't see anything, you little pimp. You're just makin' it up."

"What's a morphodite, Loudermilk?" Clement said. "Is that like a queer?"

At this, Oscar's toadies shifted uncomfortably. Two more drifted discreetly away.

"And how'd you get your flat tire fixed, Oscar?" Arthur asked.

Oscar's mouth was silently working. The last toady muttered something to Oscar and left as well. Oscar, suddenly alone, glared at Clement, but there was something else in his eyes now, something they had never seen there before.

"Oscar," Arthur said, "Don't touch any of us, ever again. Or any of the kids you pick on. If you do, we'll tell everybody we know about what we saw. Our friends, our folks, the sheriff, everyone." He smiled. "And all our friends'll tell their friends. Every kid in town will hear about it. Hag will tell Harrison, too. You'll be at Crosby in the fall. Think about the jokes."

Oscar was silent a moment, then he muttered, "I'll get you for this." He glared at Clement. "Especially you."

Clement smiled. "Not if I get you first, asshole." He sat back down. He returned to his lunch. Oscar stalked off.

"Jee-zus," Hag said, sighing with relief as he watched Oscar cross the playground. "I was scared shitless. You think it'll work?"

Clement shrugged. "We'll see. But yeah, I think so."

.   .   .

CHAPTER 9
i
Belfast, Waldo County, Maine
September, 1959

Arthur's mother continued to deteriorate. She rarely left the apartment now, sleeping most of the time, only getting up for a few hours from late morning to dusk. When awake, she usually sat in the kitchen, drinking tea. She mostly ate white bread with butter, sugar so thickly sprinkled on the butter that Arthur could hear it crunch as she chewed.

She rarely got dressed beyond her bathrobe and slippers. Her bathing was also becoming less frequent, enough so that Arthur was finding it increasingly unpleasant to be in her presence.

As his mother worsened, he tried different tactics in his interactions with her, hoping to change her back to the mother he had loved.

Arthur tried being cheerful. "Momma," Arthur would say, smiling brightly as she slurped her lukewarm cup of tea, "Here's a joke Hag told me today. Why did the moron throw his alarm clock out the window?" He paused. "Because he wanted to see time fly!" He laughed. "Get it, Momma?"

His mother would look at him with red-rimmed eyes and nod. "I get it, Artie."

"Great, Momma. Say, why don't you get dressed and we can go for a walk, maybe to Johnson's for a sandwich. It's really nice outside."

"No, Artie, I'm too tired." She would then retire to her room, more often than not.

Next Arthur tried talking to her as though he were the parent and she the child. "Momma, you've got to get dressed today."

"All right, Artie." She continued to stare out the kitchen window, chewing her sugared bread.

"Here. I laid out some clothes."

She dropped the bread and stood abruptly. "Let me rest now and then I'll get dressed." And she would retire to her bedroom and close the door.

He tried appealing to her sense of motherhood. "Momma, remember those potatoes and peas in milk you used to make? We haven't had those in a long time. They were sure good."

Her eyes had perked up at this, and she had smiled. "Artie, you're right," she had said, enthusiasm in her voice for the first time in months. "They would be good, wouldn't they? Why don't you go to the A&P, and I'll fix them right off when you come home."

"Great, Momma. I'll be right back!" He kissed her, took two dollars from the cookie jar and ran to the A&P. He eagerly purchased potatoes, a brown paper bag full of unshelled peas, and a quart of milk, then ran back to the apartment.

He burst in the door, panting from his run. "Here's the potatoes and peas, Momma. I'll shell the peas and you can peel the…" He looked around a moment, then heard snores emanating from his mother's bedroom. His shoulders slumped and, despondent, he put the bag of groceries on the kitchen counter, a small boy in a large and uncaring world.

Fortunately, Arthur had two advantages, without which he could not have managed.

First, he had learned to take care of himself. Each night he did his homework, took a bath, laid out clothes for the next day, and put himself to bed. In the morning he made breakfast, dressed, and packed his own lunch, usually a peanut butter sandwich, a banana or apple, and cookies. He would buy a carton of milk for three cents at the school cafeteria.

Arthur bought groceries every few days. He also made dinner each night, although his mother did not eat much of it, regardless of what he had prepared. The food was not fancy, mostly reheated canned goods and fruit, and at first he usually burned it. But it was better than nothing, and as Arthur's cooking skills improved—a major breakthrough was learning to keep the heat low—more and more of what he prepared was not only edible, but actually tasty.

His proudest moment as a cook was when he recreated his favorite dish by himself. There were flaws. The bigger potatoes were still crunchy because he had not cut them in half, simply throwing them into the boiling water with the smaller ones at the same time. He had also let the milk boil by mistake when warming it, and thus it had foamed up and separated a little. But the dish turned out well enough, and it was better the second time. His success gave him the confidence to read his mother's cookbooks and try other experiments.

Since Arthur was only ten, self-reliance took him only so far. Arthur and his mother had gotten by initially in the new apartment on the meager dollars earned from the auction of most of their property, held the day they moved from the farm to Belfast. But this money had finally run out, and Arthur's mother was now unable to earn more. Food, rent and utilities were ongoing needs that had to be met, and the meager social security check she received as Horace's widow didn't begin to cover the bills.

This is where Arthur's second advantage became important.

Aunt Esther Mclachlan, a quiet woman of practical bent, would drop by once or twice a week, sometimes with a bag of homemade doughnuts clutched in one hand as she negotiated the wooden stairs. She rarely said much as she spent each visit cleaning the kitchen and bath, sweeping and dusting the rest of the apartment, and changing the sheets while Arthur did his schoolwork, munching on a doughnut. At first she helped Arthur with the laundry, showing him how to sort the clothes and measure soap, and how to work the coin-operated washer and dryer in the basement. But she stopped when he showed he did not need supervision.

Once a week, she would help her sister take a bath. Then, after Maude had been put to bed, Aunt Esther would make herself a cup of tea, check Arthur's homework if he asked, make a final inspection tour of the apartment, and then take her leave. Arthur always found twenty dollars on the kitchen table after these visits. Of course he thanked Aunt Esther for her kindness each time she came by.

"You and your mother are family, Arthur," she would reply, as if no other explanation were required. It would be years before it dawned on him that his aunt must have also paid their rent and utilities.

Still, for all his self-reliance, and despite the help he received from Aunt Esther, it was not a pleasant existence. While he was busy in the evenings, it was bearable; he did not have to think about it very much. But it was often difficult late at night, after Aunt Esther had gone home and he had gotten into bed.

Listening to Red Sox games with Puppa, and how Momma used to be, and collecting eggs in the morning, and picking corn and cucumbers and digging potatoes from our garden, and Momma's whistling Rose of Culloden, seeing Hag each Sunday...

The memories made him smile and made him sad at the same time. He would stare at the ceiling, listening to his mother snore.

On these nights, sleep would come hard.

ii

November, 1959

Something wasn't right.

Arthur awoke, shivering. He looked at the clock on the bedside table. A little after two. What had awakened him? Then he realized he could see his breath in the moonlight streaming through the window. *Why was it so cold in the apartment?*

He heard no snoring.

"Momma?" he called. There was no answer. He hopped out of bed and pulled on his sweater. He hurried from his room, saw his mother's bedroom door was open. He looked in. "Momma?" Again, no answer. With growing alarm, he turned on the light. Her bed was empty, her bathrobe and slippers in a heap on the floor where she had left them upon going to bed earlier.

Arthur turned, looked across the sitting room. His heart seemed to stop. The front door was open, a cold wind blowing in. *"Momma!"* he called, dashing through the door and onto the landing at the top of the stairs. Still no answer. *"MOMMA!"* he called again, frantic.

A cat meowed in the cold, mocking him.

He ran back to his room, hurriedly pulled on trousers, stuffed his feet into his sneakers, then threw on his coat and a stocking cap and headed for the door. He grabbed his mother's coat off the tree by the door, pulled the door shut behind him and careened down the stairs, almost slipping on the frost on the way down. *"MOMMA!"* he called. *"WHERE ARE YOUUU?"*

His question was answered a moment later.

From the alley came the faint sounds of someone humming softly, almost like a small child. The tune was *Rose of Culloden.*

He walked around the bottom of the stairs and into the alley, and caught his breath in both sadness and relief. "Oh, Momma," he breathed.

His mother sat in the alley, barefoot and shivering. She hummed the ancient ballad with difficulty, her lips starting to stiffen from the cold. Arthur had no idea how long she had been outside, but he knew it had been long enough for her to be in serious danger.

"Momma, it's all right," Arthur said, kneeling by her. He draped her coat over her shoulders, and then put his stocking cap on her head. He tried to lift her to her feet, but she would not move. "Momma, we've got to get you inside, it's cold out here and you'll freeze!" He rubbed her feet with his bare hands. They were so cold as to be painful. The toes were immovable.

"No Artie, I'm fine, you don't need to worry," she assured him, smiling. "Your father's forgiven us…"

Arthur looked around involuntarily, neck hair rising, half-expecting to see his father, smiling, emerge from the shadows. He stared at her in dawning horror.

"Momma, you've got to come inside," he said. "Come on now!" But she would not budge. He began to cry in frustration. "Please, *GET UP!*"

A window went up down the alley; an angry male voice yelled, *"Can't a body get any sleep around here?"*

Arthur looked toward the voice, saw a dark head and shoulders protruding from a second floor window across the alley. "Mister, we need help!" Arthur called.

"Who's that needs help?" The voice replied, less angry. Other lights in windows along the alley began to come on.

"Me and my mother, Mister! We live in the apartment upstairs here and she's sick, real sick! If you have a telephone, call a doctor, please!"

The man was silent a moment. "Ayuh, I will then," he said. The window slid shut.

iii

Esther and Arthur accompanied the ambulance to the hospital, where Esther signed the necessary paperwork to have her sister admitted. She was placed in the intensive care unit, and the next day had surgery to remove two frostbitten toes. After leaving the recovery room, she had been sedated and then placed in the hospital mental ward. Arthur and his aunt returned home after his mother had been settled.

Arthur spent the next day at the apartment, packing his things. He moved in with Aunt Esther, in her large house on Congress Street, that afternoon.

A week later, his mother was transferred to a mental hospital in Augusta. She died there two years later.

. . .

PART III: THE ROAD
CHAPTER 10
i

Dixon, California
October 5, 1969

Arthur and Ginger Jake, the truck driver who had picked Arthur up two hours earlier, entered the diner just off the interstate in Dixon and got coffee and pie, both of which Arthur thought were delicious, especially since he had not eaten in 24 hours. When they were done, Jake stood, reaching for his wallet. "Well, I do have to get along, Preach," he said. "Thanks for the company. Got a load of fruit to pick up, and then back to Frisco. You take care, Lovey," he called to the waitress.

"See you again soon, Ginger Jake!" she called back.

"Jake, let me get the tab," Arthur said. "You gave me a ride all this way. It's the least I can do."

But Jake wouldn't hear of it, so Arthur walked outside with him, shook his hand, thanked him again and, a few moments later, watched Jake's tail lights disappear.

Now, realizing he was alone in a small town somewhere in Central California with almost no money, no place to stay, and no clear idea on where he was going next except east, Arthur looked around, taking stock.

To the north and west, farmland rolled away beyond the interstate. To the east, the local road led toward what had to be the town of Dixon. It was also hot, a lot hotter than San Francisco.

Arthur glanced back at the diner. *Another cup of coffee'd hit the spot.* He went back inside and headed to the men's room, where he washed up. The cut on his forehead had scabbed, and he carefully washed around it. The yellow and blue streak below his eye was also not getting any worse, he noticed.

"Back so soon?" the waitress said when he had taken a seat at the counter. She wore a tan uniform and her hair was a nondescript brown. A dusting of ancient acne haunted her right cheek, partially hidden by poorly applied makeup. She was maybe thirty-five, but trying to look younger.

"Just coffee," he said.

"Coming up," she said. She fetched the pot and a heavy white ceramic mug and poured. "Cream and sugar?"

"Cream."

She brought him a small plate with a half dozen creams. He poured two into the coffee, stirred, and sipped.

He sipped again, added another cream, figuring he could use the calories. "Top you off?" the waitress said.

"You bet, thanks."

As he finished his second cup, a man, carrying a well-filled rucksack, entered the diner. He sat several seats down the counter. He had a full white beard hovering over an expansive chest and girth to match, and wore overalls, a flannel shirt, a baseball cap, and work boots. The waitress poured him coffee, and he ordered the daily special, meatloaf.

Arthur's stomach growled; he liked meatloaf. He realized he was still hungry; the pie had done little to alleviate it. He checked the prices on the menu in front of him. The meatloaf plate was $2.25.

Deciding he could not afford that, Arthur ordered a tuna salad sandwich and chips for a dollar. As he ate, he began to think about options. He eyed the waitress.

'Lovey', Ginger Jake called her.

When he finished the sandwich and chips, still hungry, he rolled the tip of his finger over the remaining crumbs and licked the finger clean, then asked for a refill on the coffee. "Thanks," he said, smiling as she poured. "Great coffee."

"Just passing through?" Lovey asked.

"Guess so." He added more cream. "'Lovey', is that what folks call you?"

"Yes. You came in with Ginger Jake before, didn't you?"

"Ayuh," Arthur said. "My name's Preach."

She eyed his black eye and cut forehead. "Looks like you had a tough time recently."

He smiled ruefully. "I got mugged in San Francisco."

Her face immediately filled with a concern that was almost motherly. "I'm so sorry. You know, people ask me why I stay here in this little town when San Francisco's only an hour away. I tell them I like it here just fine, thank you very much. You can leave your doors unlocked at night and not worry, and folks here are nice as pie. So where are you going?"

"East."

"How far? Reno? Denver?"

"All the way to Maine."

"Maine? My gracious, you are a long way from home. Why'd you get off here?"

"Only as far as Jake was going."

"Well, there'll be other rides," Lovey said. "Truckers come here all the time, going east and west. You'll get a ride quick."

Arthur smiled, and decided the time was right to pop the question. "Say, Lovey, could I ask you a favor?"

Lovey looked at him uncertainly. "Well, I guess so. What?"

"When I got mugged last night, they took all my money except for like fifteen bucks. So I was wondering if maybe I could do a little work around here for a meal and a place to sleep tonight."

She started to shake her head, alarmed. "I don't think—"

He hurried on. "I'll sweep, mop the floor, wash the dishes, anything you need doing. I'm willing to work, is what I'm saying. Not askin' for any handouts. And I'll sleep anywhere. In the storeroom, you name it, just as long as it's out of the weather. How about it?"

Her smile had gradually disappeared. "No, I'm sorry," she said. "We don't have anything for you here. And you'd have to ask the manager anyway. He isn't here right now."

Arthur nodded. "Okay. Well, is there anything like a…a church or Salvation Army mission or something like that in town?"

"There's churches, of course. But they don't…and no, there's no Salvation Army mission here, either. Just a motel in town, ten bucks a night. Say, you want to settle up now?"

He smiled.

That sure went well.

"Sure, I understand." He gave her two dollars. On impulse he said, "And keep the change. More coffee, please?"

She hesitated a moment, then poured him another cup. "You gonna drink all the coffee we got or what?" she said.

"Menu says free refills."

She sniffed once in disapproval, then walked to the other end of the counter and busied herself with wiping it down.

A few minutes later, the man with the beard finished his meatloaf and paid. He nodded to Arthur. "I hear you say you need a flop?" he said.

"Ayuh," Arthur replied, suddenly hopeful. "Don't have any money. Well, much, anyway. But I can work some."

"Try the jungle east of town."

"Jungle?"

"Yeah. Other side of the SP tracks, near the warehouses."

Arthur looked at him, uncomprehending.

"Jungle," the man said. "Hobo jungle. Anyone's there, they might help you. Listen, I'm headed that direction. I'll show you where it's at if you want."

"Well, thanks, real nice of you. Name's Preach."

"I'm Chevrolet. Friends call me Chevy." He picked up his rucksack and noted Arthur's almost empty duffel. "That little bindle all you got?"

"Ayuh."

Chevrolet smiled and shook his head. "Travelin' light. Well, I started out that way too," he said. "But when you get old like me, you need your comforts. Come on, we'll get you fixed up."

"Who's we?"

"Depends on who's around. Come on, if you're comin'. And listen, you gotta work on your ghost story. What you used back there on that gal didn't get you anyplace."

Arthur, mystified, said nothing but followed.

. . .

CHAPTER 11
i

Hobo Jungle, Dixon, California
October 5, 1969

"Well, if it ain't Chevrolet himself!" The speaker was a balding man with a dark beard, likewise clothed in overalls and heavy work boots. He wore a red bandanna around his throat.

"Walkabout, how the hell are you?" Chevrolet roared.

Chevrolet and Arthur had walked through Dixon to the railroad tracks east of town and turned southwest, following the tracks. As they approached a small patch of woods two hundred yards south of the tracks, Arthur had noticed a faint wisp of smoke rising above the treetops, and as they got closer, the tantalizing smell of cooking food reached his nostrils. His stomach had begun to growl and he had realized his mouth was watering. Now, standing in the middle of the patch of woods, the cooking smell was overpowering, heavenly.

Walkabout and Chevrolet embraced heartily, slapping each other on the back. "Anyone else around?" Chevrolet asked.

"Yep. Bob."

"Damn, he's still alive?"

"Yep. We been travelin' together some. Headin' west. There's also a fella I ain't met before, name of Sky Pilot. He's been called to Jesus, so watch out, especially when he's *elevated*, if you know what I mean. They're down at the creek washin' up. Saw Bama a couple days ago, but he's headin' to Oregon."

Chevrolet said, "That bastard's owed me a sawbuck since '63, and I keep missin' him!"

"That's because he can smell you coming, you old fart," someone behind them said softly.

Chevrolet turned and smiled. "Bob, how the hell you doin'?" he said.

Bob was the thinnest man Arthur had ever seen. Well over six feet, he could not have weighed a hundred and thirty pounds. He coughed a couple of times, and wiped his mouth on the back of his sleeve. "Oh, about the same, Chevy."

"Cancer ain't got ya yet, I see."

"It's tryin', but I'm still hangin' in there."

"I keep tellin' him to get himself to a clinic, but he won't listen to me," Walkabout said. "Talk some sense into him, Chevy, will ya?"

"Who's this?" Bob said, nodding to Arthur.

"New buddy of mine," Chevrolet said.

Arthur smiled, a little uncertainly, and nodded. "Hi, guys. Name's Preach. Headin' east—San Francisco to Maine."

"You hungry?" Walkabout said.

"I could eat," Arthur allowed.

"Come on," Walkabout said. "We got some stew cookin'. You got a bowl or something? An old tin can'll do."

Arthur shook his head. "Nope. Sorry."

"Well, let's see," Walkabout said. He looked around, found a can off in the bushes. He handed it to Arthur. "Here you go," he said. "Wipe this out and you're good to go. Rust won't hurt you none." Walkabout smiled. "Some folks call this a gunboat."

Arthur picked a few large leaves and wiped it out. "Guess it's clean enough," he said.

Walkabout led them to a small clearing. A fire burned, above which hung a large pot, suspended from a tripod. He looked into the pot and was surprised to see a hearty broth filled with vegetables and potatoes, and what appeared to be a hambone. The smell was maddening.

"There's a head of garlic in there," Walkabout said. "Even some meat, if you scoop deep enough. Hope you like it."

Arthur scooped the can as deep as he could without burning himself. Walkabout was right; a few scraps of ham and a piece of a hot dog were in the can along with the vegetables. He brought the can to his lips, blew on it to cool it a little, then sipped the broth.

Too hungry to restrain himself, Arthur then gulped a big mouthful, inhaling sharply over the hot stew to cool it in his mouth, burning his tongue but not caring for his hunger. He had never had such good stew.

"Nice thing about a jungle in farm country," Chevrolet said. "You can always find fresh vegetables."

"I'd say you were hungry all right," Bob said. Walkabout and Chevrolet laughed as Arthur nodded, chewing.

"Too hungry to thank the Lord for His blessing, too, I see," said another voice. Arthur looked up.

A wizened little man with a Mediterranean complexion and green eyes entered the clearing, holding a stack of wet clothes in his hands.

"Hey, Pilot," Walkabout said.

"Who is your sinner friend here?"

"Preach," Walkabout said. "Other one's Chevrolet."

"Nice to meet you," Arthur said.

"Likewise," Chevrolet said.

"Preach," Sky Pilot said, nodding thoughtfully. "Have you accepted Jesus Christ as your Lord and savior?

"You bet we have, brother," Chevrolet said at once. "Washed in the same blood of the lamb as you."

"Oh, me too," Arthur said at once, nodding vigorously. He indicated the can of stew. "And praise the Lord for his bounty!"

"Amen," Sky Pilot said. "Amen, brothers. Welcome." Sky Pilot began draping the wet clothes over some bushes beside the clearing.

Chevrolet took a large can from his duffel bag and dipped himself some of the stew. He sat down next to Arthur and whispered, "Glad you're quick on the uptake."

Arthur grinned. "What's *elevated* mean?"

Chevrolet whispered, "Likes his booze." He pulled two plastic spoons from his overall pocket and handed one to Arthur. "Try this."

Arthur smiled and shook his head. "Man, Chevrolet. You guys are…well, I appreciate it. I do. Thanks."

"Rules of the road, Preach," Chevrolet said. "We help each other out. Leastwise, most of us do. 'Course, nowadays you gotta be careful going into jungles. It ain't like it used to be. The road ain't always a nice place, Preach. Some of the people you're gonna meet out there…you think they're all gonna be decent folks? Hell no, I tell you what. You are going to meet some roarin' assholes, take it from me. And you'll do and see things you never even *thought* about."

"Well, I gotta get back to Maine," Arthur said.

"You got any money?"

"A few bucks," Arthur said.

"You got family?"

"Nope. Family's all dead."

"So what were you thinkin', some 'Lord'll provide' kinda deal?"

Arthur shrugged. "Something like that, I guess."

Chevy chuckled. "Damn, Preach, you are a holy roller, ain't you? How old are you?"

"Twenty."

"Well, I gotta hand it to you. Robbed and broke, and—" Chevrolet eyed his tunic—"been to Nam?"

"Ayuh, just got back."

"Been shot at and lived to tell the tale, and now hitch-hikin' across the whole damned country. You done some livin' in twenty years, ain't you?"

Arthur nodded. "The past few days, anyway."

Chevrolet laughed again. "Well, don't you worry, Preach," he said. "I think you'll come out all right, once this trip you're on is over. You'll be different, but you'll be all right. Now look, you better eat that stew while it's still hot and not listen to me rattle on."

Arthur began devouring his stew with slurping abandon, Chevrolet eating more slowly, savoring each bite.

He had perhaps a third of a can left when he noticed Arthur watching him eat. "You still hungry, Preach? Here." Chevrolet handed him the can.

Arthur shook his head. "I can't."

"Course you can. And you will. Come on now, I just had a plate of meatloaf back in that hash house by the highway, and I ain't hungry no more."

"Well..."

"No well about it."

"Okay. Thanks, Chevrolet. I'll pay you back someday, I swear." Arthur took the offered can and gobbled down the rest of the stew.

ii

At dusk Walkabout built up the fire, and Chevrolet took out a harmonica and began to blow some old tunes.

Sky Pilot took a can of Sterno and a sock out of his bindle. He scooped the Sterno into the sock, and began to squeeze the sock so a pink liquid dribbled into his gunboat. He dumped the solid from the sock into the fire. He then poured some water into the can and, to Arthur's stunned amazement, gulped a mouthful.

"Won't drinkin' that stuff kill you?" Arthur asked.

"Probably someday, but not just yet," Sky Pilot said.

"You drink *Sterno?*"

"Naaa, just the alcohol in it," Chevrolet said, grinning. "It's called a pink lady."

"Yes," Sky Pilot said. "A sinful name for a sinful drink, suitable for a sinful man such as myself." He took another sip, and stared at the fire. After a moment he said, "Have you ever considered sin?"

"All the time," Walkabout said, grinning. "Why you think I always got a hard-on?"

"I have come to the conclusion," Sky Pilot said, ignoring the jape, "that my appreciation of alcohol is not the sin. Take away the alcohol, and I am still a sinner. You see, my *addiction* is the sin." He gulped his pink lady. "We all have our addictions."

"Well, I ain't addicted to nothin'," Chevrolet said.

Sky Pilot took another sip of his pink lady. After a moment he said, "Would you say you are a proud man, Chevrolet?"

"I am," Chevrolet said. "Nothing wrong with that."

Sky Pilot smiled. Softly, he said, "Chevrolet, you suffer from the worst addiction of all."

Bob coughed in the silence.

After a moment, Chevrolet's expression turned flat and he stood. "You talk too much, Sky," he said. "I'm turnin' in." He left the glow of the fire.

iii

Arthur awoke the next morning, slightly chilled. He sat up, wrapping the blanket Chevrolet had loaned him around his shoulders. Red streaks lit up the sky. The fire had reduced to ashes, although a few coals still glowed orange in the gray powder. Snores filled the clearing.

Stir up this fire a little, make myself useful. He gathered some kindling, nursed the fire to life, and soon had a decent blaze going. The flames licked the bottom of the stew pot.

"You're up early."

Arthur whirled around. "Jeez, Bob, didn't know you were up. Make some noise one time, will ya?"

"Been sitting here watching the morning come. You got that fire going real easy. I admire that. I can never get a fire going myself." He cleared his throat, and then coughed.

"I could show you how."

"That's okay. It wouldn't do any good." Bob shivered and moved closer to the fire. He coughed against his sleeve, and inhaled wetly. "Can't seem to get warm these days."

"How long you been up?"

"All night, pretty much. I never sleep. Not much anyway. I can't breathe too good. That, and…the worry."

"Bob, why don't you check yourself into a hospital? They'll help you. At least move somewhere warm. Arizona, maybe."

"Nope. I'm a lousy patient. Hate being looked after. And I hate Arizona, too. Worse than Texas." He started coughing again, and this time the spasm took control. Within moments, his wracking cough had him doubled over, gasping for air, body convulsed with his effort to breathe.

"What do you need? Somethin' I can do?"

Bob waved Arthur's concern away as his coughing mercifully began to subside. When he had regained control he shook his head. "I'm too far gone, Preach," he croaked. "I won't see spring."

Arthur didn't know what to say to that. After a few moments, he said, "Stew's lookin' like it's hot. You want some?"

"I could probably take a little."

"Well, get your gunboat," Arthur said. "I'll dish you up some."

iv

"Where you and Bob headed, Walkabout?" Chevrolet asked after he had finished his portion of the leftover stew. Bob and Walkabout had washed up at the creek after breakfast and were retying their bindles. Sky Pilot was still out from the night before, having gone through several cans of Sterno.

Walkabout said, "Probably jungle up here today, and catch the westbound tomorrow morning. That sound okay to you, Bob?"

Bob coughed a couple of times. "Guess so," he said.

"How 'bout you, Preach?" Chevrolet said.

"Gonna keep headin' east," Arthur said.

"Goin' that way myself. You want some company?"

"Serious?" Arthur said.

Chevrolet laughed. "Sure. Somebody's gotta keep ya outa trouble."

Arthur nodded. "I'd be real pleased to have some company."

v

"Well, see ya on down the road," Walkabout called. He saluted Arthur and Bob waved, then Bob hunched over and brought his hand to his mouth, shoulders convulsing as a coughing spasm shook through him.

"Ya'll take care now," Chevrolet called over his shoulder as he and Arthur left the woods. "All right, then, Preach," he said, "if we're gonna travel together, we gotta get you a kit. Where's your gunboat?"

"Right here," Arthur said.

"You got a blanket, too."

"Yours."

"You can use it, long as we're travelin' together."

"Thanks."

"Now, you need a water jug and a hat."

"I don't need a canteen."

Chevrolet laughed. "Oh you best believe you do, ridin' trains. You get on an express, you might not have a chance to get water for days. Never get on a train without water. At least a gallon."

"Where am I supposed to get a canteen?"

"A plastic jug will do. We'll go hunt one up in town. We got time. Eastbound's not due til one."

An hour later they were back by the tracks. Arthur had stuffed in his duffel bag a one-gallon plastic cider jug which he'd filled with water from a gas station hose, some twine, and some plastic utensils. Perched on his head was a beat up purple sombrero with the words *"Viva Mexico"* stitched around the brim in silver thread. He had scrounged it from a trashcan behind a dingy Mexican restaurant.

"That is about the silliest damned hat I've ever seen," Chevrolet said, laughing. "But it'll keep the sun off ya 'til you find something better."

Arthur also had a few books of matches tucked in his pockets, taken from a box by the cash register at the grocery where Chevrolet had bought cigarettes, a half-pint of cheap bourbon, and some candy bars.

"Where do you get your money?" Arthur asked.

"Social security checks," he said. "Got a post office box in Denver. Bank account, too. I stop by every few months to pick up the checks and cash 'em. Not much money, but I don't need much. And sometimes I work a little. Dig ditches, pick fruit."

"If you don't mind my asking," Arthur said, "I'm guessing Chevrolet is a nickname?"

"Now why would you think that?" he asked, grinning. "Actually, 'Chevrolet' is my given name. Chevrolet Ford."

"Come on," Arthur said.

"Gospel," Chevy said. "That is indeed the name on my birth certificate, I swear before all that's holy. The old man had a sense of humor, you see. It took some getting used to, growing up, but now I kinda like it. And there's worse nicknames than 'Chevy.' Now come on, let's go catch a train."

103

They found a patch of woods and scrub growth along the tracks about a half-mile north of the jungle. Chevrolet dropped his bindle in the bushes, then went out and stood by the tracks, staring off to the northeast.

"What were you doing?" Arthur asked when he returned.

"Checkin' that there ain't no signs or switches along the tracks. You don't want to rack yourself up on something if you're running to get on a moving freight."

"Why don't we just sneak on when it's stopped?"

"The bulls watch. Or worse, they'll let you get on, then just when the train starts to move they'll hop in the car with you, pull out some heat, and make you jump off once it gets movin' forty or fifty miles an hour."

"Seriously?"

"Some of 'em ain't nice people, Preach. Of course, most'll let ya ride if you give 'em a fiver or somethin'. But all in all, I prefer to get on a train when it's movin'." Chevrolet cocked an ear. "Well, there she is. Listen."

Far away to the southwest, Arthur heard a whistle.

"She'll be here in a few minutes, stop down the tracks at the industrial park, then pull out. Ought to still be goin' slow enough to get on when it passes here."

Sure enough, the train came into sight a minute later. It stopped at the park loading dock. After a few pallets were loaded, the train's whistle blew, and it began to move.

"Get ready," Chevrolet said. "When I say 'move,' start runnin' and follow me." Arthur nodded.

The train slowly picked up speed, drawing closer and closer. The front unit grew big, huge, gigantic and then it was a colossus as it creaked by ten feet from them, but they were well hidden in the brush away from the eyes of the crew. The second unit passed, and then the freight cars, clattering by one by one by one. Chevrolet peeked out of the bushes, eyes flicking down the tracks, looking for an open boxcar door. He spotted one. "Move!" he yelled, and burst from the bushes, Arthur hard behind.

The open boxcar was still several cars down as Chevrolet, surprisingly agile, began to trot alongside the moving train. His timing was perfect as the open door drew almost abreast of him. He quickly tossed his bindle into the car, then grabbed the steel handle of the door and in one smooth motion, allowing the moving train to do most of the work, flipped himself into the car. Arthur increased his speed and ran alongside the open door.

"Come on, toss in your duffel!" Chevrolet yelled. Arthur did so.

The train was going perceptibly faster now, and Arthur suddenly realized he was losing ground—an inch at a time, but losing just the same.

"Hop on in, come on, you can do it!" Chevrolet yelled.

"I can't!"

"Gimme your hand!" Chevrolet braced himself, sticking out his hand.

Arthur grabbed and Chevrolet pulled, one massive tug dragging Arthur halfway into the car. Arthur kicked, shoved, and tried to help Chevrolet as best he could. Chevrolet continued to pull. *"Lift your legs up, Preach, come on, I got ya, you're almost in!"*

Arthur did so, holding his legs straight out, and this made it just easier enough to allow Chevrolet, with one last yank, to pull him into the boxcar.

Arthur lay panting, the dust, dirt and debris tickling his nose and threatening to make him start sneezing. He lifted his head a little, trying to regain control of the beating of his racing heart.

Made it.

Chevrolet lay beside him, huffing and puffing as well. After a few moments, he sat up. "Gotta tell ya,

Preach, if we're gonna travel together, you're gonna have to work on your boardin' technique."

Arthur shook his head and laughed, still amazed at what he had done. "You made it look so easy. How'd you do that?"

"I've had a lot of practice."

"People ever get hurt doin' what we just did?"

Chevrolet nodded cheerfully. "Oh yeah. Saw a man lose his grip once and slip under the train. Saw one piece of him land by the roadbed. Don't know what happened to the rest. That's called greasin' the tracks."

"Good Lord, Chevrolet. That coulda happened to me."

"Well, it didn't, did it? Come on, let's get outa sight. Don't want to call attention to yourself when you're ridin the rails."

The train headed east, toward Sacramento, the Sierras, and Reno.

.   .   .

PART IV: MAINE
CHAPTER 12
i

Waldo County, Maine
July, 1965

"Go home!" Clement and Dick Osgood yelled at a passing car with New Jersey plates.

Arthur and Hag sat with them on the front steps of a gift shop in Searsport, watching the bumper-to-bumper traffic on Route 1 roll by. School was out, tinny rock 'n' roll poured from Hag's transistor radio, and it was a midsummer day, glorious as only Maine midsummer days can be—crystal blue sky, brilliant sun, on the breeze the smell of the nearby sea.

Just about every passing car had New York or Massachusetts tags. Some were from even further south—Virginia, North Carolina. A Cadillac with Florida tags passed, headed north.

"Turn around!" Clement and Dick yelled, and Arthur and Hag grinned. Catcalling the tourists was a game they had begun to play a week or so earlier.

Arthur, like the others, was dressed in sneakers, faded blue jeans and a flannel shirt. He had turned sixteen in June.

"They got beaches down south, don't know why they gotta come up here," Clement said. The song on the radio ended.

"That's 'Help' by the Beatles, comin' at ya from the mid-coast's tower of power KLBR the Lobster, home of the latest and greatest HITS they keep comin' here on the Lobster and I'm Ed LeBeck, the swingin'est Canuck this side of Saskatoon with the NUMBER ONE record on the Lobster—'Satisfaction' by the Stones, going out from Rene to Darryl before he ships out with the Marines to Vietnam next week and take it away Stones!!!"

"Gotta love the Stones," Dick said. "But man, I hate the Beatles."

"Queers, you ask me," Clement said. "Little suits and all."

Another car from Florida passed, pulling a trailer. "Go home, ya morons!" Clement yelled.

"Oh shit, here comes Loudermilk," Hag said as Oscar Loudermilk, now in the uniform of a Searsport cop, appeared around the corner. The boys immediately began looking as innocent as possible.

Loudermilk had finally graduated from Crosby High School, and had become a Searsport town constable the year before. It had been six years since the incident at the quarry.

Loudermilk stopped in front of them. "Howdy, boys," he said, smirking.

"How are you, Officer Loudermilk?" Clement and Dick said in chorus, smiling sweetly.

"Doin' fine, just fine. That is, until I heard you wise asses yelling at tourists."

"Yellin'? We weren't yellin'," Clement said.

"Now don't you be lyin' to me, Clemmie," Loudermilk said lazily. "I heard it with my own ears."

Clement started to say something, and Loudermilk's hand moved slightly toward his billy.

"Careful, Clement," Arthur said.

Clement remained silent. He glared at Loudermilk, eyes flat as gunmetal.

Loudermilk chuckled, his hand relaxing. "Artie, you always were the smartest one in this bunch." He began to lecture. "See, it's like this, boys. Searsport's a nice little town. We got a museum here, restaurants, inns and motels, the flea market, gift shops, you name it. All for the tourists. They spend a lot of money here. Summer folks are real important, so we try to treat 'em right."

The boys said nothing.

Loudermilk continued. "We don't hassle the tourists here, you got me? If folks hassle the tourists, they may decide to spend next summer someplace else. And then all the folks here who depend on the tourists for money to get 'em through the winter aren't going to be happy. Is this starting to make sense to you?" No one replied. "Well—*is it?*"

"We get the message," Arthur said. "Officer Loudermilk."

Loudermilk smiled again. "Well good, Artie," he said. "Since you're so smart and all, how about you explain it to them again?"

"I'll do that," Arthur said.

Loudermilk ended it. "Good. Now, you lads just move it along, before I get annoyed."

Arthur stood. *Lads.* It was galling, but he said nothing in response. "Come on guys, let's go."

Dick's car was parked around the corner on the Mt. Ephraim road. As they drove off, Arthur, who had called shotgun, watched Loudermilk shrink behind them in the mirror until he disappeared.

"What a fuckin' jerk," Dick said.

Dick was a year older than the others; he would be a senior at Crosby in the fall. He and Arthur had shared a class together during Arthur's freshman year.

Against the expectations of just about everyone who knew them, they had hit it off: Dick, seemingly born to get into trouble, and Arthur, so responsible for his years that at Crosby he was sometimes referred to as "the young fogey." It was as if their very differences formed the basis of the bond.

Clement said, "Yeah. Well, fuck it, let's go swimmin,' huh?"

"Now you're talking," Dick said.

Clement was not referring to the quarry. That option had vanished a year ago when a local kid drowned there jumping off The Cliff, and the county had sealed it off behind a high chain link fence. Instead, they had taken to going swimming at the dam at the south end of Swan Lake.

"Maybe some girls'll be there," Arthur said.

"God, I hope so," Hag said. "Maybe they'll be wearing bikinis. Just thinking about it makes my pants feel tighter!"

"Sure Hag, like anyone would notice," Arthur said.

"Bang! Zoom! Right in the kisser!" Clement screamed, and they all started laughing.

ii

The dam was at the junction of the Swan Lake Road and route 131, in what was jokingly referred to as downtown Swanville.

The Swan Lake Grocery (*Best by a Dam Site* read the sign over the front door) was the only business, and the largest of the half dozen or so buildings in the hamlet. It was a small, dark store, hard by the dam. The merchandise leaned heavily toward cheap fishing tackle, magazines and paperbacks, sun tan lotion, beer and sodas. Basic canned goods were also available, as were such staples as bread, milk, and eggs, usually. A single ancient gas pump stood out front, noisily dispensing Texaco regular at a quarter a gallon whenever it was turned on.

Dick parked and the guys got out, looking for cars they recognized among the others parked around the dam. Betty Tibbets' Rambler was there, and Arthur's interest perked up. He glanced toward the dam, hoping to get a glimpse of Betty's sister, Sharon. Hag noticed, and laughed. "Maybe you'll get lucky today, huh, Preach?"

Arthur grinned, embarrassed. "Maybe." Sharon Tibbets was fifteen, a year behind Arthur in school. Her father owned a clothing store in Belfast. They had shared a biology class at Crosby a year ago. Arthur had been careful most of the past spring to smile at her a lot in class, and whenever he passed her in the halls. So far, his signals had been acknowledged but not returned.

Shrieks and giggles floated over the dam as the boys walked across the road and onto the gravel beach to the right of the dam. Betty and Sharon, accompanied by a girl Arthur had seen around school but did not know, were splashing each other in the green, waist-deep water. "Hi, Dick!" Betty called. "Come on in swimmin'!"

"Hi yourself!" Dick called to Betty. In a lower voice, he said, "That's Wilma Philbrick," indicating the third girl. "Look at those jugs, would you?"

Dick was the acknowledged ladies' man of the group. He was good at small talk, and was always up on the latest trends. He was wearing cologne before the rest of the boys at Crosby had discovered deodorant, and was one of the few male teenagers in Belfast who had learned to dance. He was also the only one among them with a steady income, having just gotten a summer job at the Belfast chicken plant packing drumsticks, thighs, and breasts into 'Pik-o'-the-Chik' packages for sale in local markets. He was to start the following Monday. "How's the water—wet?" he called.

Wilma giggled at Dick's sally. "Real wet!"

"Godfrey mighty," Dick whispered as his eyes feasted on the girls' pale bodies, wet hair and swimsuits. He began to take off his shirt.

"You don't have a swimsuit," Clement said. "You goin' swimmin' in your jeans?"

"Jeans'll dry," Dick said. "You think I'm not swimmin', you're crazy." The other guys, following Dick's example, began taking off their shirts and shoes. They joined the girls in the water.

"Hi," Arthur said when he was able to catch Sharon's eye. Sharon, in sharp contrast to her sister and Wilma, was almost boyishly slender with sharp features and green eyes. She was the only one wearing a two-piece suit.

"Hello, Preach," she replied. "How's your summer been so far?" Faint freckles dusted her nose and cheekbones, no doubt from the sun. Arthur knew they would fade in the fall. His always did.

"Fine. Yours?"

"Okay. Helping daddy in the store sometimes." She ran her fingers through her long dark hair, tucking it behind her ears.

"He paying you anything?"

"Dollar an hour. Not much, but it beats babysitting." An impish grin crossed her face. "Race you to the float!" With that she was off, slithering across the surface of the lake in a competent crawl toward the float, in deeper water twenty-five yards away.

Arthur hesitated only a moment, then was off as well. The water was warm on the surface under the July sun, but frigid a foot down.

He was a strong swimmer and had no trouble catching up, but he slowed just enough the last few yards to make sure Sharon got to the ladder first. She giggled prettily as he arrived a split second behind her, his hand brushing her smooth arm, cool as limestone from the water. "Too bad," she said. "Now you owe me a soda."

"Didn't know we were racing for stakes," Arthur said, treading water beside her. Where was he going to get the money to buy her a soda, he wondered. He'd have to borrow fifteen cents from Hag.

"I never race for free. Come on, let's get on the float."

They climbed onto the float and lay on their backs beside each other, allowing the sun to dry them off. "Nice day," Arthur said.

"Yes, it is." She propped herself on both elbows and watched the others splashing each other near the beach. Arthur rolled onto his side and propped himself on an elbow, looking at her. He watched a drop of water trickle from the bottom of her ribcage down her smooth midriff, and pool in her navel. "So how long have you and Hag been friends?" Sharon asked after a few moments.

"As long as I can remember," Arthur said. "Since before I—before my father died."

"I'm sorry," she said.

"That's all right. It was almost ten years ago." He said, as casually as possible, "Say, would you like to go out sometime?"

Sharon touched his arm. "That would be nice," she said. "Call me."

Pleased, he smiled. "I will." Then, to his horror, he realized he was becoming aroused. Embarrassed, he thought frantically about what to do. "Race you to shore!" he said, and dived into the water.

She followed him, but he won easily. He was waiting for her on the beach. The cold water had solved his problem in short order. "Now we're even on the soda," he laughed as she emerged from the water.

"You cheated!" she said, giggling.

"But I'll buy you one anyway," he said, then heard himself saying, "Because I want to, not because I have to."

She eyed him, then smiled. "Maybe next Saturday night?"

"Ay—Ayuh. Saturday night it is." And just like that, he had made a date with Sharon Tibbets. They arranged to double date with Dick, who had lined up a date with Wilma.

iii

That night after supper, Arthur raised the key issue as he helped his aunt clear the table. "Aunt Esther, I'm going out Saturday and wanted to know if there was something I could do to earn a little money? Fifteen dollars ought to do it." Esther had stopped giving Arthur money the day he moved into her house, almost six years before.

"Who are you going out with?" She asked, scraping scraps into a small bowl to dump on the compost heap.

"Girl I know from school, Sharon Tibbets. I'm double-dating with Dick Osgood."

"Good family," she allowed. "I knew her grandfather."

"So is there something I can do between now and Saturday?"

"Well, I suppose we can find something," Aunt Esther said. "Mow the lawn, trim the hedge, wash the second floor windows, weed the garden—that ought to do it."

"Okay, thanks," Arthur said. "I'll start in the morning." He pointed to the dishes. "So, do you want to wash or dry?"

But Aunt Esther continued. "Tell me, Arthur, you're sixteen now, almost grown. Have you thought about getting a job this summer?"

"No," he admitted.

"You should think about it," Aunt Esther said. "A young man your age needs regular money—more than you can earn doing chores around the house."

Arthur was silent.

"I expect you'll be driving soon. Have you thought about a car? You'll probably need one."

Actually, Arthur had been driving without a license on the sly for almost a year now; Dick had taught him the previous summer. "We've been getting by all right without one so far," Arthur said cautiously. Although the conversation was moving in an unexpectedly promising direction, it never paid to seem too eager with Aunt Esther.

She nodded. "True, Arthur, but I've been thinking lately that it would be good for us to have a car. I'm not going to start driving again at my age." She had just turned eighty. "But if you got your license, and saved your money this summer, I might be willing to buy us one."

"You would?" Arthur said. "Really?"

"Yes. Really." She smiled. "Of course, I'd expect you to take me on errands and such. Walking back from downtown is getting harder for me these days. I don't know why the town fathers didn't found the place on the flat somewhere." Arthur laughed. Belfast's oldest neighborhoods were on steep hills rising sharply from the main commercial district by the harbor.

"Let's start on the dishes," Esther said. "Do you want to wash or dry?"

"I'll dry," Arthur said. He reached for the dish towel. He would start looking right away.

.　.　.

CHAPTER 13
i

Waldo County, Maine
July 1965

"Hi, Dickie!" Wilma Philbrick called as she hurried awkwardly down the front walk of her parents' house to Dick's car. Arthur could hear her stockings rubbing together under her tight green dress. The dress and her high heels made running impossible. She pulled open the door, and slid her large bottom across the front bench seat toward Dick until she was pressed up against him. She leaned closer and tickled the back of his neck with her painted fingernails, her heavily permed hair a brown helmet around her plump, pancaked features. "I missed you!" she giggled. The heavy scent of perfume filled the car.

"I missed you, too!" Dick said. He gestured to Arthur in the back seat. "Wilma, you remember Art from the other day. Everyone calls him Preach."

Wilma smiled, nodded. "You're from the lake the other day. Sharon's friend. But why do they call you Preach?" She giggled. "Hope you're not going to give us a sermon!"

Dick laughed as he turned onto Pearl Street. "Don't worry, Preach doesn't preach. He just doesn't sin! Nossir, Preach doesn't smoke, doesn't drink, doesn't swear. Nor does he lie, cheat, or steal!"

"My goodness, what do you for fun, then, Preach?" Wilma asked, all wide-eyed and innocent.

Desperate, Arthur flashed Wilma what he hoped was a wickedly charming grin. He leaned forward, glanced around mysteriously. He arched an eyebrow, and lowered his voice. "Well now, Wilma, that's for me to know and you to find out." He winked, and sat back. He hoped this display seemed less silly to her than it did to him.

It must have. "Oooohhh," Wilma said. "Now I *am* interested! Better be nice to me, Dickie. If you're not, maybe I'll ask Preachee here to walk me to my door."

"You tryin' to steal my girl, Preach?" Dick said.

"No way, got my own girl," Arthur replied.

When they pulled into the Tibbets' driveway, Arthur got out, smoothed his hair down, and walked to the door. Sharon opened the door before he could knock. Her father was standing behind her.

Sharon's long dark hair was parted in the middle and fell below her shoulders. She wore very little makeup, and a simple blouse, skirt, and flats. "Hello, Art," Sharon said.

"Sharon." Arthur offered his hand to her father. "Mr. Tibbets, I'm Arthur West."

"How are you, Arthur?" Mr. Tibbets said. His handshake was dry, firm. He was a short, stocky man with wavy, salt and pepper hair. He wore well-polished loafers, slacks, a pressed white shirt and a soft wool sweater. "So where are you taking my daughter tonight, Arthur?"

"Going to the movies downtown, then to Jordan's in Searsport."

"We'll be back by midnight, Daddy," Sharon said.

Mr. Tibbets shook his head emphatically. "Oh no, young lady! Eleven."

Sharon rolled her eyes. "Daddy, please? Midnight's not that late and eleven will barely give us time to get back from Jordan's. Midnight? Pleee-ease?"

Mr. Tibbets was silent a moment, weighing the situation.

"It won't be a problem, Mr. Tibbets," Arthur said. "I'll make sure she's back safe and sound by midnight. Or...whatever time you decide."

Mr. Tibbets looked at Arthur, weighing him now. He decided. "All right, midnight then. But not one second later." He looked at his daughter. "I'll be waiting up, honey."

"Thank you Daddy," she said, rewarding him with a smile and a kiss on the cheek. As they walked to the car, Sharon whispered, "Thanks." They were off to the theatre moments later.

"Good Lord, what was all the yakkin' about?" Wilma asked when they had pulled out of sight. "Thought we were never going to leave." She opened her purse, pulled out a pack of Kents and lit up, exhaling the smoke expertly through her flared nostrils, leaving a ring of lipstick around the filter. She turned, waved the Kents around. "Anybody want one?"

Arthur and Sharon both declined. Dick said, "I believe I will indulge. Light one for me, will you, babe?"

When they entered the theatre, Sharon and Arthur started down toward the front. He was relieved they had decided to go to a movie; he could just sit there and be quiet and not have to worry about making small talk.

"Hey, where you going?" Dick said. "Let's sit here." He indicated the back row; there were already several couples there, waiting for the lights to dim.

Arthur, knowing full well why couples sat in the back row at the movies, looked at Sharon.

She smiled. "Why not?" she said.

Shortly after they had taken their seats, the lights darkened and the movie started. It was called *Dr. No*. It soon became apparent, however, that Dick and Wilma were not interested in the movie so much as in each other; they began necking almost as soon as the theatre went dark. Arthur, embarrassed, looked at Sharon, but she kept her eyes on the screen, so he turned his attention to the front as well and was soon absorbed in the movie. Dick and Wilma continued to neck.

Arthur's eyes widened when the female lead emerged, stunningly, from the sea in a white bikini. A thought occurred to him. He leaned over to Sharon and whispered, "You remind me of her, a little."

"Oh I do not and you know it," Sharon whispered back. She was right, of course, but she was also clearly flattered, as Arthur found out a moment later when, astonishingly, he felt Sharon's hand slowly entwine with his own. He glanced at her, suddenly feeling a shortness of breath and a growing tightness through his stomach and chest. She smiled at him, and returned her eyes to the screen.

ii

After the movie, they made a brief stop at Jordan's. Then Dick drove to the north end of the lake and turned into a fire lane. He parked in a meadow so they faced the moon, high in the sky to the south. He cut the headlights, killed the engine and turned on the radio, adjusting the volume until the Supremes' *Back in My Arms Again* was barely audible. "Well, here we are," he said. "Privacy at last."

Wilma giggled as she lit a cigarette. "And just what did you two guys have in mind, parking here?"

Dick chuckled. "You know I pack chicken pieces at the plant." He leaned toward Wilma. "Want to see how I handle breasts?"

Wilma shrieked with laughter, slapping Dick on the arm. "Now you just stop it, you devil!"

Arthur, hot with embarrassment, could feel Sharon looking at him with a bemused smile.

Dick chuckled. "Aaarrrggghhh, methinks the fair maiden'll be needin' her whistle wetted first." He reached beneath his seat, and pulled out a mostly full bottle of bourbon.

"You've got whiskey?" Sharon said. At this point, all Arthur wanted to do was disappear, quietly and completely.

"You bet," Dick said. He unscrewed the cap, took a swallow, shivered. "Brrr, that's t—tasty! Want a snort?" He offered her the bottle.

"No, I better not," Sharon said. "If my father smelled that on my breath he'd kill me!"

"None for me, thanks," Arthur said.

"You were right about your friend," Wilma giggled. "He doesn't sin a-tall, does he?" She took the bottle from Dick and swallowed loudly. "But that's okay, all the more for us, right, Dickie?" The two of them drank for several more minutes, making small talk, ignoring Arthur and Sharon.

Sharon looked at Arthur, smiled, and took his hand again. "Want to go for a walk? Look at the stars?"

Arthur was delighted with the opportunity to leave the car. "Okay, I guess. Lot of them tonight. Let's go. We're going to go for a walk," Arthur said. Neither Dick nor Wilma objected.

They got out of the car and walked across the field until they could no longer hear the radio or their companions' conversation, aside from the occasional shrill giggle. "Sorry about all this," Arthur said.

"I don't mind at all," Sharon said. She turned to him and kissed him chastely on the lips. A moment later Arthur responded, putting his arms around her. When they separated, she said, "Let's sit down."

The stars were brilliant, filling the sky with uncountable pinpoints. Arthur gestured to the northwestern sky behind them. "That's the Big Dipper," he said. "See how it's shaped? Did you know one of the stars in the handle is actually a pair of stars? Now follow the line the two stars on the front edge of the dipper make. See that star out there? That's the North Star, called Polaris. Right there, see? If you know how to find the North Star, you'll never get lost."

"That's the North Star?" Sharon asked. "I thought it would be brighter than that."

"Nope. The important thing about it isn't its brightness, but that it's always right there, in the same place, almost dead on north. All the other stars rotate around it during the year. Of course, the stars aren't really rotating. It just looks that way. We're rotating. Earth, I mean." *Stop babbling,* he told himself.

But Sharon seemed impressed. "Cool," she said. "Where'd you learn about the stars?"

"Did an astronomy project in school, and kind of got interested." Arthur looked at her in the moonlight, smiled, dared to say, "Can I kiss you again?"

"Of course." And he did.

Arthur heard the sound of car doors opening and closing, and turned. Two dark shapes opened the rear doors and got in the back seat, a giggle drifting from the car a moment later. "I guess we probably shouldn't bother them now," Sharon said after a moment.

"Ayuh," Arthur agreed.

As they watched the stars, behind them the car began to gently rock. Sharon glanced toward it, looked at Arthur, and suddenly began to giggle, smothering the noise with her hands as best she could. Arthur began to chuckle, too.

"I'm sorry, I can't help it," Sharon said. "This is the weirdest situation. If Daddy knew about this, he'd kill me." She started laughing again. "And probably you, too."

"Just what I needed to hear," Arthur said, smiling. "Speaking of Daddy, we've got to get you home. Don't want you to turn into a pumpkin."

"I know," Sharon said. The car continued to rock and she smiled again in the moonlight. "But, I think we're going to have to give them a little more time."

Arthur wanted to kiss her again, but decided against it. He contented himself with keeping his arm around her and they sat silently, waiting. A minute or two later, the rocking slowed, finally stopped. "Give them a few more minutes," Arthur said. "When we start back to the car, make some noise. And walk slowly."

"You betcha," Sharon said.

But when they approached the car five minutes later, to Arthur's horror, both Wilma and Dick were sprawled in the back seat asleep, their clothes in a state of considerable disarray.

Sharon began to laugh again. "Arthur West, you really know how to show a girl a good time." When they finished chuckling, Sharon said, "So how are we going to get out of here? Can you drive?"

"I don't have my license yet, but I can get us home. We need to get them dressed before we leave, though. You take Wilma and I'll take Dick."

Sharon nodded.

With some difficulty, they got Dick and Wilma dressed; fortunately, they had not entirely disrobed. When finished, they leaned them against each other, snoring, in the back seat. Neither Dick nor Wilma did more than stir slightly during these operations. Arthur found the almost empty liquor bottle. "Man," he said, "they almost finished it. Look at this."

"Better get rid of it, don't you think?" Sharon said. Arthur nodded, and then threw the bottle as far into the field as he could.

They got into the front seat; Dick, luckily, had left the key in the ignition. Sharon sniffed, grimaced. "You can still smell the alcohol in the car."

"We'll leave the windows down. Fresh air might help wake them up, too." They rolled down the windows, then, ready at last, Arthur gingerly drove out of the field.

Ten minutes later they pulled into the parking lot of the Swan Lake Grocery. The store was closed. "How're they doing?" Arthur asked.

Sharon looked into the back seat. "Still asleep." She sniffed. "Car doesn't smell so bad now." She looked at the dashboard clock. "Yikes, eleven-thirty. We better get going!"

They arrived at Sharon's house at five minutes before midnight. Sharon sighed. "Well. Here we are."

"Ayuh." He looked at her and smiled, and they leaned gently toward each other. Their lips met; this time, the kiss was considerably less chaste. When they parted, Arthur said, "I don't suppose you want to go out again, do you?"

Sharon nodded. "Sure I do. Call me, all right?"

"Really?"

She laughed. "Really. I had a good time. I did."

He smiled, nodded. "Come on, I'll walk you to your door."

As they stepped onto the porch the door opened. Mr. Tibbets looked at his watch. "Congratulations, you just made it."

"I know, Daddy, we were keeping track of what time it was. Good night, Pr—uh, Art."

"Good night, Sharon." Then, he couldn't help it. He started laughing again. Sharon tried her best to stifle a giggle, but couldn't help herself either. She hurried into the house and Arthur heard her running up the stairs.

Mr. Tibbets smiled. "Well, you must have had a good time. Good night, son." He offered his hand. "Arthur, is it? Arthur West?"

"Yes sir. Good night." Arthur shook hands, and hastily left the porch.

He parked Dick's car in front of Wilma's a few minutes later, woke Dick up, and then walked home, ten minutes away.

.   .   .

CHAPTER 14
i

Waldo County, Maine
August 1965

Arthur's job search did not start well. Over the course of several days, he was turned down for one reason or another at several Belfast businesses. Even the chicken plant had stopped hiring. Aunt Esther suggested he broaden his search beyond Belfast proper.

Her advice proved to be sound. Two days later, Arthur saw in the *Bangor Daily News* that the Searsport FoodMart was looking for a stock boy. Best of all, the ad said, "pt/ft, no experience necessary, advancement potential."

ii

The store manager, Mr. Laverdiere, was impressed. "You biked here from Belfast, young fella?"

"Yessir. Five miles. Got here in thirty-five minutes."

"Thirty-five minutes? Imagine that." Laverdiere was bespectacled, pink, balding. "Let's talk in the office."

Fifteen minutes later, Arthur had a job. He would be a stock boy, bagger and general helper to start, at $2.00 an hour. If that worked out, he would advance to cashier trainee and also get a raise. And if that worked out, the exalted position of deli counter man might be available later in the summer, with another raise. He would work thirty hours a week, morning to midafternoon. Overtime might be available, too, if they were really busy. "Most weeks you'll be taking home about fifty a week after taxes and social security," Laverdiere said.

"Good enough, Mr. Laverdiere," Arthur said. They shook on the deal, and Arthur filled out an employment application. He would start the following Monday.

"A good start, Arthur," his aunt said when she heard Arthur's news. "Of course, you'd be cheap at twice the wages he's offering you." She smiled. "But work hard and do your best. If you do, raises will take care of themselves."

Arthur nodded. "So, when can we get our car?"

She smiled again. "After you've gotten a paycheck or two, then we can see."

iii

Arthur was at the store before eight the following Monday. Laverdiere showed him how to punch in and where to keep his timecard, then put him to work uncovering the produce and misting it to make it look fresh. About the time this task was finished, the Harris Bakery truck arrived, and Arthur spent the next few minutes carrying trays of baked goods into the store, which he put on the shelves under Laverdiere's direction.

The Penobscot Creamery truck then arrived, so Laverdiere had Arthur go out back and carry in crates of milk, cream, and other dairy products. These went into the cold case, which Arthur started to load through the glass doors opening into the store itself. Laverdiere stopped him, and told him to load the case from the back, accessible

124

from the storage room. "Got to keep the older milk in the front," he said. "Want to sell that before the new milk."

At eight twenty-five came a knock on the door. "Get that, will you, Arthur?" Laverdiere said. "That'll be Nelson."

Arthur unlocked the door, opened it. "You must be the new stock boy," the man said, coming into the store. "Good to meet you. Name's Nelson Darling. I run the deli counter." Nelson was a tall, lanky man with brown hair combed straight back. He wore black horn-rimmed glasses, and when he smiled he revealed brilliantly white, even teeth.

"Nice to meet you, Mr. Darling," Arthur said, shaking hands.

"Just plain Nelson, if you please. Nobody calls me 'mister.'"

"Nelson," Laverdiere called from behind the checkout counter, "you didn't see LaVerne outside, did you?"

Nelson shook his head. "Nope. Ain't seen her since closing yesterday. She'll be along, though. Always is, don't you know." He hung his coat on a peg behind the deli counter, and glanced at Laverdiere casually. "How's the missus?" he asked.

Laverdiere said, "Doin' fine, Nelson, thank you."

At eight forty-five a large, sturdily-built woman, in her early forties, with a blonde beehive and red lipstick, knocked at the front door. Laverdiere came to the door himself. "Hello, LaVerne," he said, opening the door and smiling.

"Hello, Riley," the woman said, smiling back and entering. "Sorry I'm a little late."

"No problem," Laverdiere said. "This is Arthur, the new stock boy."

"Pleased to meet you, Arthur," LaVerne said, smiling broadly. She offered a hand. "I'm LaVerne Cook, the cashier."

"Nice to meet you, Mrs. Cook," he said. "What should I do now, Mr. Laverdiere?" he asked.

"You could go sweep the stock room."

"I'll show him, Riley," LaVerne said. "Got to punch in anyway. Come on, Art. Mind if I call you Art?"

"Nope," Arthur said. He followed her into the stock room.

"First off, Art, it isn't 'missus,'" LaVerne whispered as they entered the stock room. "Not married at the moment. I'd just as soon be called LaVerne."

"Sure...LaVerne." Arthur was not used to calling adults by their first names.

LaVerne punched in, and then showed Arthur where the broom and other cleaning supplies were. From out front, Laverdiere called, "Showtime, people! Nine o'clock. I'm openin' the doors now."

"You can help me at the cash register," Laverne said. "Do you know how to bag?"

"Never done it before," Arthur said. "What about sweeping the stockroom floor?"

She waved that away. "Customer service is always first. Besides, they don't see the stockroom. And bagging isn't complicated. But first, you better wash your hands. We've had complaints. Bathroom's off the stockroom."

A few minutes later, Arthur was bagging groceries for his first customer. As LaVerne had said, bagging was not complicated. Heavy items like cans and potatoes went in the bottom of a bag, and soft and breakable products like bread and eggs went on top. Don't overfill.

Customers did have their idiosyncrasies, however. One wanted groceries packed by meal—breakfast in one bag, and supper items like hamburger and potatoes in another. Arthur didn't know where to put the denture adhesive and wart remover the woman bought, so he put them in a separate bag as well.

Arthur got a fifteen-minute break at eleven o'clock, which he took behind the store, sitting on the back stoop in the sun. When he returned, Laverdiere had him relieve Nelson behind the deli counter so he could take his break. "Don't worry about slicing anything," Nelson said. "Just give people what they want from what's already sliced. There's enough, don't ya know. Weigh it on the scale there."

"Okay," Arthur said. He had only one customer before Nelson returned at eleven-thirty. "You'll have to show me how to use the slicer," Arthur said. "If I've got a shot at counter man, I'll need to know."

"Shot at counter man?" Nelson said, looking at him quizzically. "Who told you that?"

"Mr. Laverdiere," Arthur said.

"He did, eh?" Nelson said, glancing toward Laverdiere. "Well, well."

Arthur had the distinct feeling he had said something wrong. "I think he was just using that as an example of how I could advance if I worked hard," he added.

"No doubt," Nelson said, smiling as he loaded a five-pound block of American cheese into the slicer.

iv

The store closed at noon for lunch. Laverdiere locked the front door and put a sign in the window that said BE BACK AT 12:30. Arthur hadn't brought a lunch; he'd remember to bring something on Wednesday.

Arthur sat outside, enjoying the afternoon. He assessed his first day so far. *Not too bad,* he thought. The work was not difficult, and the people seemed nice. He had definitely lucked out. He was pretty sure working here beat slaughtering chickens.

Laverdiere came outside. "Arthur, I need to talk to you. Would you come into my office a minute?"

"Sure, sir."

Once settled, Laverdiere said, "Arthur, what did you say to Nelson this morning about being a deli counter man?"

"Well—didn't exactly say that," Arthur said, suddenly nervous. "Just asked him to show me how to use the slicer, since if I had a shot at the job, I'd need to know. Remember, you said I might. Just making conversation, Mr. Laverdiere."

Laverdiere sighed. "Arthur, please don't discuss conversations you and I have about work with other employees."

Alarmed, Arthur said, "Mr. Laverdiere, I'm sorry, I didn't know there was any—"

"Arthur, it's all right, don't be upset," Laverdiere said. "See, Nelson didn't know I'd said anything to you about working behind the deli counter." He lowered his voice. "Nelson likes to think he's irreplaceable."

"I'm sorry, Mr. Laverdiere," Arthur said. "I'll be more careful."

Laverdiere beamed. "Good man. I'll let you get back to your lunch break now."

At 12:30 the store reopened, and Arthur resumed bagging groceries for the remainder of the afternoon. As he bagged, he thought. Nelson had obviously said something to Laverdiere about their conversation earlier. *Why?* He thought it unlikely that Nelson saw him as a threat to his job. He wished there were someone he could talk to about it.

At 4 p.m. Laverdiere said, "Four, Arthur. Quitting time for you. I'll see you on Wednesday."

"Okay, Mr. Laverdiere, thanks." Arthur finished bagging the groceries of his last customer for the day, and then went to the back room. He hung up his FoodMart apron and punched out.

As he started for the back door, he heard LaVerne behind him. "Art?"

"Ayuh, LaVerne?" Arthur said, turning.

"Don't worry about that flap with Riley and Nelson this morning. Those two fuss and fight all the time. Too bad you got in the middle of it." She smiled. "See you Wednesday, okay?"

"Okay," he said. Arthur left, mounted his bike, and started pedaling home. As he pedaled, he wondered how LaVerne had known about the conversation he had had with Nelson. *And with Laverdiere?* Arthur pondered these questions as he biked south.

v

Saturday evening at quitting time, Arthur got his first paycheck, forty-nine dollars and seventy-two cents. He tucked the check in his pocket, then punched out. As he walked his bike out the back door to start home, Laverdiere stopped him. "Arthur, you did good work this week. You've been dependable and you learn fast."

"Thanks, Mr. L," Arthur said.

Laverdiere reached in his pocket and took out his key chain. He unhooked a key, and then handed it to Arthur. "Key to the store. Think you can open up Monday?"

Arthur smiled. "I think I can do that. Thanks, Mr. L. I appreciate it. Won't let you down."

"I know you won't, Art. Have a good Sunday, and I'll see you Monday morning."

vi

Arthur showed up at 7:30 Monday morning to open up, and it pleased Laverdiere to no end that when he arrived at 8:15, Arthur had already misted the vegetables, unloaded the Harris bakery truck, and was sweeping the floor. He had also disposed of a mouse found in one of the store traps. "Arthur, you've got potential written all over you," Laverdiere said. "Keep up the good work."

Arthur was delighted, of course. "Thanks, Mr. L." He smiled as Laverdiere went back into his office. He couldn't wait to tell Aunt Esther.

As Arthur swept, he noticed the floor around the edges, under the shelves and counters, was caked with years of dirt, grease and grime, forming a thin border where the daily sweeping and weekly mopping rarely if ever reached. Then an idea occurred to him. He decided to scrub the floor that very evening after work. Laverdiere would no doubt be pleased, and maybe that raise he had mentioned might happen.

That afternoon, Arthur punched out and left, but rather than going home, he pulled into Jordan's parking lot and parked his bike behind the restaurant to wait until the FoodMart closed.

vii

When the clock in the restaurant said 6:15, Arthur got on his bike and rode back to the store. He unlocked the door and entered, feeling slightly like an intruder although he knew he had no reason to.

The only sound he noticed at first was the humming of the electrical power to the cold case. He started to the back of the store to find a scrub brush, bucket and some floor cleaner. He opened the door to the storage room, then stopped, alarmed. He heard murmured conversation.

Someone else must have decided to work late. He frowned; now his surprise was ruined. He started to leave, but then noticed the door to Laverdiere's office was slightly ajar. Laverdiere and LaVerne were talking.

"Well I don't see why not," LaVerne said. "The one I have is a rust bucket, Riley."

"I can't afford one, Vernie. I can barely afford my own car."

"Oh come on," she said, smiling, touching his arm. "Mustangs are great cars."

"It's a better car than the one I have myself."

LaVerne sighed. "Well, at least buy me something. I need a new one, Riley. Please?" She looked longingly at him.

Laverdiere grunted. "Oh hell," he said. "I'll see what I can do. Not promising, though."

"Oh thank you," she said, smiling. She kissed him on the cheek. "You come over the evening you buy it," she said. "I'll make that sausage and peppers dish you like, and after, I'll have something special for you for dessert."

Riley chuckled. "I'll hold you to that," and embraced her. At this point Arthur, stunned, quietly took his leave.

viii

On Wednesday, Arthur could hardly bear to look at Laverdiere. It embarrassed him to realize that he had not had the slightest inkling of what had been going on. This was a startling thought, immediately followed by a thought even more startling: *did everyone have secrets? Did he really know anyone well at all?* He could no longer say.

As the day wore on, Arthur's newfound awareness did allow him to pick up on one change since the day before. LaVerne and Nelson were, apparently, no longer speaking. Instead, Nelson made a great show of his work, noticeably ignoring LaVerne throughout the day, even going so far as to turn his back on her whenever she came within comfortable conversational range. LaVerne made no effort to dissuade Nelson from this behavior. Indeed, she acted as though she almost expected it.

Arthur, of course, said nothing about any of this to anyone. The war for his approval did not begin in earnest until Friday.

ix

"Hello, Arthur," Laverdiere said as Arthur let himself into the store on Friday morning. It was not quite eight o'clock. "Wanted to have a word with you, if I could." Arthur followed Laverdiere into his office.

"Arthur, you may have noticed that LaVerne and Nelson are not speaking to each other lately. Have any idea why that is?"

"No sir. Not any of my business."

"Good," he said. "Has Nelson ever threatened you?"

Arthur was surprised at the question. "No sir. Except for that misunderstanding my first day about the slicer, everything's been fine."

Laverdiere nodded thoughtfully. "All right. Arthur. But listen. If Nelson ever talks to you about something or someone at the store, let me know, okay? Will you do that?"

Arthur, mystified, said, "Sure."

"Good." Laverdiere stood. "I continue to be impressed with you, Arthur. You've been a fine, trustworthy employee, so far. An assistant manager's position might be yours for the asking in a few more months, if you continue working here."

"Thank you, Mr. L." Arthur left and started sweeping the floor. It took him almost a half-hour to realize that he had been offered a bribe, and threatened, in the same sentence.

x

"I need to talk with you," LaVerne whispered during a lull in business. "Meet me at Jordan's for lunch, okay?"

"LaVerne—"

"Shhh, Riley's coming."

Against his better judgment, Arthur went to Jordan's at noon; LaVerne arrived a few minutes later. "Want a cheeseburger?" she said.

"Thanks, already ordered lunch," he said.

They sat down at a picnic table. Arthur's fried clams arrived a moment later, and he began to eat as LaVerne talked. "You may have noticed Nelson and I aren't speaking," she said.

"None of my business," he said.

"I appreciate that," she said. "But when you're working in a place with such a small staff, like we are, it's important that you be aware of what's going on. Won't make mistakes that way, don't you know."

Arthur smiled. "That's what Nelson says. 'Don't you know.'"

LaVerne smiled. "You're pretty observant, aren't you, Art?" She chuckled, and then lit a Salem. After a moment, she said, "I guess you've figured out that there'd been something between us, right?"

"None of my business," Arthur said, although he had begun to suspect as much.

"I don't mind. You need to know. It'll help you understand." She dragged on her Salem again, flicked the ash into the grass. "Nelson and I started seeing each other shortly after the new year. We had fun together. Everything was fine until about two months ago. Then..." she stubbed out her Salem, and lit another. "Then, I started seeing someone else."

Arthur nodded, but said nothing. *What was there to say?*

"Anyway, the other night, we met and I told him I couldn't see him anymore. So now he's not speaking to me." LaVerne stubbed out her Salem, and stood. "So, if Nelson says anything to you about the situation, now you'll understand what it's all about."

133

"Thanks for filling me in on the, uh, lay of the land," Arthur said.

LaVerne smiled. "You know, you are a fine young man, Art. You'll make a girl very happy someday."

LaVerne bent down and kissed him on the cheek. He blushed while struggling to keep from recoiling at the stench of menthol cigarette smoke on her breath. "See you later." LaVerne started back to the FoodMart.

xi

Nelson quit that afternoon. The departure was quiet. After visiting Laverdiere in his office, he collected his personal things, said, "Good luck, Art," and left.

Five minutes later, Laverdiere called Arthur into his office, and when Arthur came out ten minutes later, he was the new deli counter man. He would start behind the counter on Monday morning.

. . .

CHAPTER 15
i

Waldo County, Maine
September 1965

Arthur—

Deep in sleep, he heard someone calling his name. "Arthur!"

It was Aunt Esther. He looked at the clock—nine. It was the Saturday before Labor Day. School would start on Tuesday. "Whaa-uutt?" he called, annoyed. His aunt usually let him sleep in on Saturdays.

"Better get up. I need to show you something."

Great.

"Okay okay, give me a minute." He sat up, rubbed his eyes, and scratched himself. He stumbled out of bed to the bathroom.

When he walked downstairs, his aunt sat in the kitchen, sipping a cup of tea. "Good morning," she said, smiling.

"Morning," Arthur said. He poured a cup of coffee, added milk, sipped. Aunt Esther may have been a tea drinker, but she knew how to make good coffee. "Thanks," he said. "Good." He sipped again. "So what did you want to show me?"

She smiled. "You might want to take a look outside. In the driveway."

Arthur, with dawning comprehension, smiled broadly and hurried to the front door. He opened it, stepped onto the porch and walked to the end nearest the driveway. "Wicked," he whispered.

A 1959 Chevrolet Bel Air sat in the driveway. It was a hardtop, the roof white, the body cinnamon brown. The tail fins were magnificent—massive and unignorable, like the car itself.

"We needed a car," Esther said. "This one was available. Plenty of room, very low mileage, and a V-8 engine. It's in excellent condition. I had a mechanic go over it bumper to bumper. Should do us very well."

"Aunt Esther..." He looked at her, smiled, hugged her. "Don't know what to say. Thank you." He felt hotly embarrassed about his earlier annoyance.

"Go on now," Esther said, blushing a little but allowing herself to return the hug slightly. "The car isn't yours. It's mine. Which I'll let you drive, now that you have your license, as long as you don't get us arrested or killed."

"Thank you." He kissed her on the top of her head—he realized he was taller than she now—and walked

135

to the car in his bare feet, went around to the driver's side, and opened the door. "You have the keys?"

Esther nodded.

Arthur grinned. "Then let's take her out for a spin. What do you say? Can we?"

Fifteen minutes later they were on Route 1 headed toward Rockland. Just past Lincolnville, where the speed limit went up to 60 before coming into Camden, Arthur opened it up and watched the scenery sail effortlessly by, and *wasn't it fine, though?*

ii

Arthur arrived at the FoodMart at noon, pulled up in front, and parked. He could not have been more proud.

"Jesus, Art," LaVerne said, looking out the window. "If that isn't the biggest car I've ever seen. Yours?"

"Family's. But I'm going to do most of the driving, my Aunt tells me. LaVerne, she runs like a dream. We just got her this morning."

She laughed. "Riley, look at Art's new car!"

Laverdiere, at the cashier's stand—he had been working the register a lot lately, Art realized—nodded. "I see, LaVerne."

Arthur punched in, put on his white apron, and went behind the deli counter to get ready for the lunch crowd. A few minutes later, Loudermilk came in, the first time he had been in the store since Arthur had begun working there.

Loudermilk ordered a roast beef sandwich with Swiss, on rye.

Arthur quietly made the sandwich. He wrapped it in pink butcher paper, wrote '$2' on it with a grease pencil and handed it to Loudermilk. "Thanks, son," Loudermilk said. He winked. "See you next time."

Loudermilk then took a cream soda from the soda case just inside the front door, and left the store. Arthur bolted from behind the deli counter. *He didn't pay!*

"Arthur—no," Laverdiere said. Arthur stopped and looked at him.

"Mr. L, Loudermilk just—"

"I know." Laverdiere peered owlishly from behind his spectacles. "Arthur…" He paused a moment, then lowered his voice. "Officer Loudermilk comes in for a sandwich and soda once in a while."

"And doesn't pay?" Arthur was appalled.

"Yes." Laverdiere smiled apologetically, took off his glasses, and massaged his temples. "You know we usually take deliveries out back. Panel trucks and such are fine, but some trucks are too big to fit in the alley, so they have to unload out front. Not supposed to do that—town ordinance. Blocks traffic on Route 1. So, giving him a free lunch a couple times a month keeps our deliverymen from getting tickets. It's just a cost of doing business, like rent or electricity."

Arthur was inexplicably enraged, but only nodded.

Laverdiere sensed Arthur's disapproval. "Arthur, I don't like it myself, but…" He continued, "we do what we must. Understand?"

Arthur understood. "You're the boss, Mr. L."

iii

After work, Arthur collected his paycheck, closed up the store, punched out, and drove back to Belfast. Aunt Esther had gone to bed, but left a note for him on the kitchen table. *Sharon called. Please call her back.*

Sharon answered. "Hi. I'm bored. Home by myself."

"Where's everybody?" Arthur asked.

"Orono. Betty's getting settled in at the University and the folks are helping her. They're staying the night. Want to come over?"

iv

He knocked on her door fifteen minutes later.

"Hi," Sharon said, opening it. She looked very pretty, Arthur thought, slim and clean in shorts, bare feet and a t-shirt. Her hair was back in a ponytail. "Want to watch TV or something? *Secret Agent* is on. Ever seen it?"

"Once or twice," he said. "Pretty good show, I guess."

"Want a Doctor Pepper?"

"Sure." A few minutes later they were ensconced at opposite ends of the living room sofa. "Come outside and see my car," Arthur said after a few minutes. "Just got it this morning. Really boss."

But Sharon did not seem interested. "During a commercial, maybe," she said. She drained her Coke. "I'm going to go get another one, be right back," and she left the room. When she returned she sat down again, but this time in the center of the sofa, only a foot or so from Arthur. She smiled at him, and he smiled back. He finished his DP. She said, "Would you like a sip of mine?"

"Ayuh," Arthur said. She slipped closer to him, offered him the edge of the glass. He leaned forward and took a sip as she tilted the glass slightly, then took it from his lips.

Their eyes met, held. The time seemed right, so Arthur leaned forward, Sharon leaned toward him in response, and he kissed her gently. Her lips parted, and she delicately touched his lips with her tongue. He responded, and soon they were lying together on the sofa, legs intertwined, hands exploring.

v

"We'd better stop," Sharon whispered. Arthur had lost track of time, but *Secret Agent* was over.

"Guess so," Arthur said, not wanting to, but knowing she was right. They all knew of girls who *went to live with relatives,* only to return mysteriously the following school year.

"Sorry," Sharon said, sitting up and tucking in her T-shirt again. "I know you must think I'm...I mean, I don't have any protection and...I guess you don't either, do you?"

"Nope," he said. "But it's all right."

"And my folks...they said they were staying in Orono tonight, but..."

"Sharon, don't worry about it," Arthur said. "I'm kind of...didn't mean to, uh, force myself on you or anything."

Sharon giggled. "Hey, I invited you over here. I liked it. I like you." She kissed him again, her lips lingering on his.

Arthur nodded, and swallowed twice, wondering if he was ready for this.

"So, you want to see my car?" he said.

"Sure!" Sharon said. She took his hand, and they went outside.

vi

Two weeks into the first quarter of the fall term, Arthur, Hag and Clement were sitting with Dick in the school cafeteria, eating lunch. Arthur was recounting the Loudermilk free lunch incident. "Just like that fucker," Clement said. "Expecting a free lunch."

Wilma Philbrick approached their table, carrying her lunch tray. She smiled slightly at Arthur, nodded to Hag and Clement. "Dickie," she said, "I need to talk to you."

Dick stood, winking at Arthur. "Hey guys, duty calls. Later." He got up, followed Wilma to an unoccupied table in a corner of the cafeteria. They began talking quietly, occasionally leaning close to each other, whispering.

vii

The following Friday night, Arthur, Clement and Dick were sitting in Arthur's car, parked in the field off the fire road at the north end of Swan Lake. Dick had gotten a case of beer, and he and Clement were knocking them back. Dick took a last swallow from his third beer, crushed the can, threw it out the open window.

"Guys, I have an announcement."

Arthur laughed. "Uh oh," he said. "This sounds important."

Clement looked at him expectantly. "Well?" Clement said.

Dick popped the tab on another one. "Me and Wilma are getting married."

"Getting *married?*" Arthur said.

"Wilma Philbrick?" Clement said.

"Yup," Dick said, grinning.

Clement started guffawing. "Yeah, right. Like you're going to marry that fucking cow!"

Dick stopped grinning and turned toward the back seat, stared coldly at Clement. "Shut up."

Clement snorted derisively. "Oooohhh, you and Wilma Philbrick! Jesus H. Christ. Sure!" He guffawed again.

Dick kicked open the car door, leapt out, yanked open the rear door, and gestured for Clement to get out. "Come on, you fuck. Get out of the car and make another comment about Wilma. *Come on."*

"Hey Dick," Arthur said. "Settle down. Clement didn't mean nothin'. Did you, Clement?"

Clement looked at Dick, grew serious, and shook his head. "No, man, I didn't mean nothin'. You're one of my best friends, Dick. Come on, man. I'm sorry. Let's have another beer."

Dick lowered his fists, and exhaled deeply. "Okay. Just keep your mouth shut about Wilma, Clement. You hear?"

Clement nodded. "Sure man," he said. "I won't do it again. Come on. We square?"

"All right, then," Dick said, nodding. He got back into the car.

"So when did you pop the question?" Arthur asked.

"Well, I didn't, exactly. Parents worked it out, hers and mine."

"Your parents worked it out?" Clement said. "What the fuck does that mean?"

Arthur, however, needed no explanations. "When's it due?"

Dick looked at him, nodded. "We figure April," he said.

"Ohhh! You got a kid on the way!" Clement said, the light dawning.

"Ayuh," Dick said. "A bun in the oven, like they say." He took a big swallow of beer, laughed nervously. "Ain't that something? Soon there's going to be another little Dickie or Wilma running around!"

"And you're going to keep it?" Arthur said.

"Ayuh," Dick said. "Wilma wanted to…go away, you know, but…" He shook his head. "Our folks said 'Hell no' to that." Dick laughed shortly. "I've got to quit school and go to work now. So, I'm startin' full time at the chicken plant next week. Of course, Wilma's got to drop out, too. She can't go to class pregnant. After she has the baby she can go back and finish up, her folks say. We're also renting a place. Going to move in as soon as we get married. In a week, maybe two." Dick turned to Arthur. "Want you to be my best man, Art."

"Well…thanks, Dick. Sure."

"Damn, man…" Clement said. "I'm really sorry. Didn't know."

"It's okay, Clement," Dick said, laughing shortly. "It'll work out. Being married is gonna be *great*." He took another big swallow of beer, eyes wide as he stared out the front window toward the lake. "Just great."

viii

141

A few days later, Arthur looked out the window of the store and watched as LaVerne pulled up and parked out front in a new Ford Mustang. She came in and smiled at Laverdiere behind the cash register. "Nice car," he said.

"Yes it is, Riley," she said, grinning broadly. She winked at him.

·　　·　　·

PART V: THE ROAD
CHAPTER 16
i

Reno, Nevada
October 6-7, 1969

Arthur and Chevrolet left the train in the Reno yards, and found their way to a cheap motel along a nondescript boulevard north of town. The lights of downtown glowed to the south.

Two single beds and a matching desk and chair occupied the room, the furniture chipped and barked, clearly suffering from hard use. A television sat on a low dresser. The room smelled of stale cigarette smoke. Arthur poked his head into the bathroom. A shower stall stood in the corner, water dripping from the head.

"Not exactly the lap of luxury, but I guess a shower'll feel pretty good," Chevrolet said.

Arthur clicked on the television and hopped onto his bed; the springs creaked. "So how you planning on getting money here? Gonna get a job or something?"

Chevrolet laughed. "Preach, we're in Reno."

Arthur looked blankly at him.

"Reno, Nevada. Gamblin', you idiot," Chevrolet laughed. "Gonna hit the crap tables. How 'bout you? Coupla years in the army—musta learned how."

"Nope," Arthur said. "Not craps. I played poker, though. Some."

"They got poker tables here."

"Chevy, first, I don't think relying on my poker-playing skills is a great game plan. Second, how am I gonna play poker with no money?"

"How good are you? You usually win when you played?"

Arthur thought about that a few moments. "I guess so, over the long run. But you never know what's gonna happen. Might end up playing with people a lot better than me, or—"

Chevrolet waved the objection away. "What kind of stakes you play for?"

"Quarter-half, mostly."

"Think you can play for one to three dollar stakes?"

"Probably. But Chevy, I already told you, no money."

Chevrolet pulled another twenty from his pocket and dropped it on Arthur's chest. "That enough of a stake?"

"Serious?"

"Sure. You play poker, I'll play craps."

"Well, Chevy—twenty's kind of skimpy, but I guess if I'm careful it'll be enough. I do have a ten to go with it. I'll have to play pretty tight at first, though."

Chevrolet handed him another ten. "Forty's gonna have to do, Preach. Let's get cleaned up and head on downtown."

ii

They entered Monty Carlo's Hotel and Casino at nine-thirty after walking the two miles into downtown. Arthur was dressed in some of Chevrolet's clean clothes, although they were more than a little large.

The place was a sea of flashing lights and noise from the acre of slot machines in the main room, virtually every one in use. Waitresses in miniskirts, heels and low-cut blouses wandered through the crowd taking drink orders. "Never play the slots, Preach," Chevrolet said. "Strictly for losers."

"Where are the poker tables?"

He pointed across the casino. "Poker room's over there. Now remember what I told ya. Don't try to bluff at the one-three tables. Someone will call you. Always."

"Got ya, no problem."

"Okay. And don't forget to toke the dealer when you win. They won't take as big a rake that way."

"Chevy, just relax, okay? I'll be all right." He started toward the poker room. He joined a game after a brief wait for a seat to open up.

The game was seven card stud. Ante was a nickel; the first card required a bet of at least fifty cents. After that, the bet had to be one, two or three dollars.

Arthur waited until his second hole card landed in front of him before picking them up. He struggled to maintain a straight face. Two aces stared at him.

All right.

His first up card was a seven.

A Mexican guy next to him had a king showing and started the betting with fifty cents.

In the next round, Arthur was astounded to catch a third ace, and on his sixth card he caught a seven, giving him a full house. The pot had grown to more than fifty dollars. The Mexican guy clearly had something working with a pair of kings showing, and bet three dollars.

Trying to suppress his excitement, Arthur said, "your three and up three."

"And three more," the Mexican said. By this time everyone else had folded.

Arthur called.

"Boat," the Mexican said. "Kings over queens."

Arthur grinned broadly. "Sorry, my friend. Aces over sevens."

"Well played," the Mexican guy said.

"Thanks," Arthur said. "Some luck there, clearly."

As another player left the game, the dealer pushed most of the chips toward Arthur, but about five dollars' worth disappeared into a slot. Arthur gave the dealer a one dollar chip. *Things have started well,* he thought.

A balding man with a thickening waistline, wearing a maroon blazer and white shoes, took the empty place at the table. "Hey, how's everybody doin' tonight?" he said, grinning and nodding around the table. He bought a hundred dollars' worth of chips and ordered a double bourbon, water on the side, clearly not his first of the evening. "Send some good cards my way, honey," he said, winking at the dealer and tossing her a five-dollar chip.

On the next hand, Arthur folded without making a bet. "Folding already?" the drunk said. "Damn son, get yourself some *cojones!"*

"Oh I got them," Arthur said, grinning. "Just no cards."

The thirtyish woman to his right smiled. Arthur smiled back. "Are you from around here?" she asked.

"Nope," he said. "Just passin' through. You?"

"River City, Iowa. A girlfriend and me are on vacation. Name's Marie Hoye."

Marie had done her hair, wearing it up, but not severely so. Nice earrings and makeup. She also wore a gold necklace, a large pendant with a green stone picking up the color of her blouse, which was open a couple of buttons down, revealing just a wink of a pale green, lacy bra. He noticed her eyes were green as well. She was trending a little toward *zaftig,* but carried it well. Arthur noticed that her ring finger showed the unmistakable mark of a ring long worn, but not this night.

"Nice to meet you. Art West."

"Are you staying here, Art?"

"Nope. I'm at—uh, another place, down the strip."

"Oh." Marie started to say something else, but stopped. Arthur turned his mind back to the game.

Arthur folded a lot over the next half hour, conserving his money while studying the play of the others, especially the drunk, who Arthur knew was likely to be a major loser as the evening wore on. Sure enough, as he consumed double bourbons, the quality of his play, wild to begin with, continued to deteriorate.

Even more important, after a few hands, Arthur began to notice tells. He had learned through painful experience in the army that all poker players had unconscious, repetitive habits while playing—drumming fingers, changing their tone of voice, shifting their body weight, nodding. Further, these habits were all (invariably and astonishingly) tied to the hands the players held. Arthur thus noticed that the drunk rubbed his chin when he got a card he wanted, but not when he didn't. He filed this away for future use.

Arthur began to bet more aggressively. After another half hour he had recovered his string of small losses, and now had about sixty dollars in front of him. The whole time, the man in the maroon blazer continued to consume double bourbons, his play becoming loose to the point of recklessness.

Marie was also feeling no pain, although in contrast to the drunk, with each Tom Collins her play grew tighter. She also grew steadily more annoyed at the drunk. "Good for you," she said across the table when the drunk won a rare hand and slapped the table in whooping glee. "You finally won something!"

"You bet, baby," the man said, grinning. "How 'bout you? When you gonna win one?"

Marie glared at him, but did not reply. She whispered to Arthur, "Jerk."

"Take it easy," Arthur said, whispering. "He's just drunk is all."

"Hey, hard on, you talkin' about me or what?" the drunk said across the table.

Arthur said, "Talkin' to the lady here."

"Take it easy, man," the Mexican guy said to the drunk. "Let's just play cards."

"Just don't like people talkin' about me, is all," the drunk said.

Marie ordered another Tom Collins.

Arthur's showdown with the drunk came two hands later. The pot grew quite large, as everyone appeared to have something working in the early going. However, by the sixth card Arthur and the drunk were the only players left in the hand. The pot was well over a hundred dollars.

The drunk had a pair of nines showing, and on the sixth card, Arthur caught a second three. This gave him two pair; he had a queen in the hole to go with the one showing. A queen-high flush was also possible, as he also had four diamonds, and only one other diamond had come out around the table.

They each bet, then were dealt their hole cards. Arthur looked at his card.

The drunk peeked at his hole card. He did not rub his chin. "Bet three."

Arthur looked again at his seventh card. The ace of diamonds stared back at him. *Bingo,* he thought. He had his flush.

"Checking to make sure your card's still there, hard on?" the drunk said.

"I am," Arthur said. "And it'll cost you three more to see it, too."

Barest hesitation. "Okay, fine. Your three and three more," the drunk said.

"Back at ya," Arthur said.

"Hard on, I'm gonna give you a break and just call," the drunk said. "Whatcha got?"

Arthur turned over his hole cards. "Ace high flush."

"Fuck!" the man exploded, throwing his cards across the table.

"Sir, please refrain from that kind of behavior," the dealer said, pushing the pile of chips toward Arthur, who was grinning broadly.

"Why don't you go fuck yourself," the drunk said. The dealer signaled across the room.

"You're very rude," Marie said. "And also a bad loser."

"Here's a sawbuck," the drunk said, tossing a twenty across the table. "Blow me, why don't ya?"

A burly man in a suit appeared behind the drunk. "Sir, you need to call it a night," he said. "Come on, I'll help you back to your room."

The drunk started to protest, but the burly man took him firmly by the arm, and both led and pushed him away from the table. The drunk muttered a steady stream of obscenities but did not resist. A second attendant picked up the drunk's chips and followed him and his escort out of the poker room.

The Mexican guy shook his head. "Man, what an asshole."

"So how much you win, Art?" Marie said. She lightly placed her hand on his shoulder.

"Don't know," Arthur said, smiling. "Think I got a hundred and fifty here."

"I got about fifty of his money myself," the Mexican said. "Too bad he left. He was makin' us all rich."

Marie laughed. "Got that right. And he went off and left his twenty, too." She picked up the bill and put it in her purse.

Arthur figured at this point that he was ahead enough. "Well, Marie," he said, standing, "I think I'm gonna call it a night."

"So soon?" she said, lowering her eyes again. She smiled at him.

He smiled politely. "I'm shovin' off early tomorrow." He smiled again. "Got a train to catch." *If she only knew,* he thought.

"Okay," Marie said. "Well, good luck. And listen, if you're ever in River City Iowa...I'm in the phonebook. Hoye. With an E." She blushed. She reached in her purse, and handed him a handkerchief with the initials MH in the corner. "You can return it to me. If you want." She was suddenly embarrassed. "God, look at me. I'm so sorry."

Arthur smiled, flattered. He put the handkerchief in his pocket "Thanks. I'll remember." He left the poker room, cashing in at the teller near the door. He was surprised to learn that he had won almost two hundred dollars.

iii

He found the craps tables a minute or so later. Roars were coming from around one of them, and Chevrolet was the center of attention. Arthur shouldered his way through the crowd. Chevrolet was standing at one end of the table preparing to shoot. A large pile of chips sat in front of him, and Arthur grinned. He yelled, "Hey, looks like you're doing all right!"

"You betcha, Preach my man! Look at this—must be five hundred, easy! Ridin' a streak like you wouldn't believe!"

"All right!" Arthur said. "Here's some more." He peeled off two twenties. "Your stake, plus half the cost of the room."

"Damn!" Chevrolet roared, pocketing the money. "Now I got cash comin' from everywhere!" The crowd around the table guffawed.

149

"Shoot, sir," the stickman said.

"Okay, here we go, come *on*, baby!" Chevrolet roared, tossing the dice toward the end of the table. A three came up.

The crowd groaned. "Don't worry, that ain't nothin', that ain't nothin'!" he roared again. "Bet fifty!"

All the players placed their bets, and Chevrolet rolled again. This time a twelve came up. He groaned, and turned to Arthur. "Listen man, you're queerin' my streak here. Take off, will ya?"

Arthur laughed. "Chevy, what are you talkin' about? I don't have a thing—"

"Just *beat it,* I said!" Chevrolet yelled, suddenly angry. *"You're jinxin' me!"*

"Okay, man, okay," Arthur said, confused. "I'm gone. I'll see you back at the motel."

"Sure, sure, I'll see you there," Chevrolet said, softening. "Don't worry, Preach, you've just changed the vibe, that's all. Tell you what, when I'm done here we'll go get us a steak dinner, what do you—"

"Sir, are you shooting?" the stickman said, rapping the table.

"Just watch!" Chevrolet said, turning from Arthur. He slid a pile of chips across the green felt. "Fifty to win," he said. Others were betting now. "Now don't y'all abandon me, you hear?" he yelled to the other players.

Arthur had no idea what was going on, except that Chevrolet wanted him to leave, so he did so. A few moments later shouts of exultation went up from the table behind him, Chevrolet's stentorian voice loud above all the rest.

Arthur smiled.

Leaving must have worked.

He left the casino and began walking north, back toward the motel.

Twenty minutes later he found a cheap clothing store that was still open, and bought three sets of underwear, socks, a couple of flannel shirts and work pants, a brimmed hat, and a lined jacket and gloves.

Then, within sight of the motel, he went into a hamburger joint and bought burgers, fries, and a couple of chocolate shakes.

When he let himself into the motel room, he figured he still had about fifty dollars left. While not exactly a princely sum, he was in far better condition now than he had been twenty-four hours earlier.

Then he noticed the purple sombrero on the floor by the bed. He grinned, pulled on his new hat, and picked up the sombrero.

Vaya con Dios, amigo.

He took it outside and stuffed it into a dumpster behind the motel. He returned to the room and flopped down on his bed. As he began to munch his French fries, the door opened and Chevrolet walked in, grinning broadly. "Well, Preach, quite an evening, I'd say. How'd you do?"

"Great," Arthur said. "Won two hundred bucks. Here, I got you a cheeseburger and a shake."

"Well damn, that's real nice of ya," Chevrolet said.

"Fries too. They're still warm. I was too hungry to wait for that steak dinner."

Chevrolet grinned broadly. "Oh yeah. Well, we can do that some other time."

"So how much did you win?" Arthur said. "You were way ahead there at one point."

"Oh yeah, more than six hundred. It was great!"

"Well, that's terrific, Chevy. What're you gonna do with all the money?"

"Oh I don't know. Buy stocks and bonds, I guess." He laughed. "What're you doin' with yours?"

Arthur told him of his purchases. "I'll hit a sporting goods store tomorrow. Buy a sleeping bag, maybe. Like you say, it'll be getting cold in those boxcars soon." He grinned. "I can give you back your blanket."

"Sleeping bag's a good idea." Chevrolet turned on the television. "Let's see what's going on in TV land, huh?"

They watched television quietly for a few minutes.

"You okay?" Arthur asked at one point—Chevrolet was uncharacteristically silent.

"Yep, I'm okay," Chevrolet said.

"Sure? You're awful quiet."

"Yeah, I said. Can't I be quiet one time?"

"Okay, no problem."

Finally, Chevrolet said, "Dammit, Preach, I gotta be straight with you." He sighed. "I didn't win no six hundred bucks. That was all a lot of bullshit I was feedin' ya."

Arthur said, "But Chevy, you had a whole pile of chips in front of you when—"

"Yeah, I know," he said. "Lost it all over the next half hour, too. Streak ended when you showed up, and—"

"Chevy, I didn't have anything to do with your streak."

Chevrolet waved his defensiveness away. "Hell, I know that," he said, "I ain't an idiot, you know. But the fever had me, Preach. That's why I yelled at ya. Wasn't thinkin' clearly." He sighed. "Anyway, the dice got real cold real fast...stayed cold even after you left...so I passed the dice and instead of keepin' it simple and just bettin' on the pass line—or leavin' while I still had some money left, imagine that—I got more and more complicated in my bets until even I didn't know what the hell I was doin'. I was makin' don't pass line bets, don't come bets, any damn kinda bets. Hell, toward the end I was makin' one roll bets. Once you start makin' those, especially if you ain't hot, you're a goner, sure. And old lady fortune let me win just enough to keep me hangin' in there 'til I was finally cleaned out. Damn!"

"Chevy, I—"

"No need to say anything, Preach," Chevrolet said. "I ain't never been able to quit when I'm ahead for some reason. When old Sky Pilot back in Dixon was goin' on about sin and addiction, hell, he sure had me pegged. Preach, you are lookin' at the biggest damned gamblin' addict you'll ever see."

"You got *any* of your winnings left?"

"Nope. Not a nickel. Not even the forty bucks you gimme. Thanks, by the way. Sorry I didn't make better use of it."

"I owed ya, Chevy."

Chevrolet snorted. "You didn't owe me nothin'. Hell, you still don't. You'da done the same for me, after all. Look what you did just now—bought me supper! I didn't even have to ask. You just done it."

"Well, now what?" Arthur said.

"Hell, I don't know," Chevrolet said. "Keep on pushin' east, I guess. I'll check out my post office box once we get to Denver, probably a check or two in it now. We catch an express, we'll be in Denver in a coupla days."

"Too bad about the money," Arthur said. He grinned. "You coulda rode in a Pullman instead of a boxcar."

Chevrolet laughed. "Easy come, easy go, Preach. I've lost lots more'n six hundred bucks in my time. Anyway, I had to be straight with ya. I ain't never lied to a partner in more than twenty years on the road, and didn't want to start now. So what are you gonna do?"

"Push east, too. Want to get back to Maine."

"Where 'bouts in Maine?"

"Belfast. Penobscot Bay, mid-coast. My aunt owns a house on Congress Street there. Actually, it's—" Then he stopped, figuring there was no sense in telling Chevrolet his troubles. He had his own.

"I've been to Portland, but never further up the coast," Chevrolet said. "Hell, maybe I'll look you up one day."

"Sure, man, that'd be fine."

Arthur fell asleep an hour or so later, in the gray glow of the flickering television.

iv

Arthur awoke as light streamed in the front window. He sat up and looked around. Chevrolet's bed was empty. The door to the bathroom was open, but no sound came out. "Chevy?" Arthur called.

No answer.

Arthur stood in his new boxer shorts, and stuck his head in the bathroom. Empty. He looked around the room, and noticed that Chevrolet's bindle was gone. Then, a little embarrassed, he quickly searched his own possessions. Nothing was missing.

Feeling even more embarrassed, Arthur sat on the edge of his bed. Then he noticed the folded piece of grease-stained hamburger bag with "Preach" written on the outside. It lay on Chevrolet's white bedspread.

Preach—

> *I decided to lite out on my own after all. I thought you needed help at first to keep out of trouble but last night I realised (that word doesnt look right but what the hell) you did not need help no more at least from me, so I am out of here. Take her easy and rember to quit when your ahead.*
>
> *Your buddie Chevrolet*
>
> *p.s.—keep the blanket, you'll need it I have another one. Chevy*

Arthur caught an eastbound freight late that evening.

• • •

PART VI: MAINE
CHAPTER 17
i

Waldo County, Maine
October 1965

Dick and Wilma kissed lustily while everyone in the audience clapped. Dick wore a black suit and highly polished black boots. Wilma wore a pale yellow, full-length dress. Her hair had been freshly permed and she clutched a bouquet of flowers. They were at Wilma's parents' house.

Arthur stood beside Dick in his only suit, having performed his duties as best man a few minutes earlier. Wilma turned to Arthur, giggled, and said, "Looks like I get to kiss you next, Preachee." She did so, leaving a smear of lipstick on Arthur's cheek. Sharon reached over and took Arthur's right hand.

"Okay, everybody," Dick called, "me and Wilma want all of you to come to our new place for a party!"

ii

Dick had rented a doublewide in a clearing in a patch of scrub forest called Toad's End, off the Oak Hill Road north of town. Arthur and Sharon were among the last to get there. Dick had put a stack of 45s on the record player. As usual, he rarely sat out a record. All the girls, even Sharon, wanted to dance with him, which surprised Arthur.

I've got to learn to dance, he thought. And, if he practiced with Sharon, it would be an opportunity to spend time with her, something he very much looked forward to these days.

By nightfall, when the tail lights of their parents' cars had disappeared down the dirt driveway, Dick yelled, "Jesus, I thought they'd never leave!" and ran into the back of the trailer. He came back a few moments later with two fifths of Smirnoff's Vodka. "Let me at that punch bowl!" A cheer went up from the assembled guests, none of whom was of voting age, as Dick poured an entire bottle of vodka into the punch. "Gentlemen!" Dick roared. "Charge your glasses!"

All the guys filled cups of punch. Even Arthur scooped up some of the punch.

"What about the girls?" Sharon called.

"What the hell. Ladies, *charge your glasses too!*" Dick bellowed.

Sharon and the other girls all scooped up cups of punch. Arthur was surprised to see Sharon joining in so enthusiastically.

"A toast to my lovely bride!" Dick yelled, and chugged the cup of punch in three quick swallows. Most of the others tried to emulate him, but only Wilma finished her cup in equally quick fashion. Arthur sipped his drink, and then put the punch cup down. Sharon took several swallows, turned and smiled at Arthur.

"Now it's my turn!" Wilma said, "and so…I want all of you to charge your glasses too!" She refilled her glass with a flourish, spilling some of it on the orange shag rug as she brought it up to her lips. When everyone had refilled, she said, "To my new husband! And may he only dance with me from *now on!*" She drank off this cup of punch in quick fashion.

"Not too likely!" Dick yelled, guffawing, and finished his cup. "I will, however, save this dance for you right now!" He reached over and grabbed Wilma and began pumping her around the crowded room, she shrieking with laughter.

When the record finished, Wilma said, "Gotta sit down, Dickie, put me down for a minute!"

Dick unceremoniously deposited the laughing Wilma in a chair and returned to the punch bowl. "Time for refueling!" he yelled, and scooped up another cup of punch.

"Me too, Dickie!" Wilma called, and he got her another cup as well. She stood and they linked arms, and each somewhat unsteadily drank punch from the other's cup, accidentally spilling about as much on each other as they were able to swallow. The guests applauded.

"Starting to run low on punch," Dick announced, and poured the second bottle of vodka into the punch bowl. He went into the kitchen and returned with a bottle of ginger ale and a carton of Hawaiian Punch, both of which also went into the punch bowl. The guests cheered with each pouring. "Now we're set!" he yelled, dipping himself another cup of punch.

Land of a Thousand Dances began to play, and Jeanette Morrison called, "Dance with me again, Dick! You're such a good dancer!"

"You be careful, Jeanette," Wilma yelled. "He's mine now!"

"Now now, there's plenty of me to go around!" Dick yelled. He grabbed Jeanette's hand, and led her to the center of the shag rug.

Jeanette was a good dancer in her own right, and even though Dick was starting to show the effects of a half dozen glasses of punch, he was still able to keep up with her. They went through the pony, mashed potato, alligator, the watusi, fly, twist, swim and the jerk in short order. They shifted effortlessly, gracefully from step to step as each was mentioned in the song's lyrics, mirroring each other's moves in fluid harmony. The guests cheered and applauded.

Wilma, sitting in her chair, stared quietly. She was no longer smiling.

The record ended, and Dick and Jeanette giggled, nodding appreciatively at each other's skills. Jeanette hugged Dick, who hugged her back. "You're a great dancer!" Dick said, kissing her on the cheek.

"So are you, Dick," Jeanette said. "I'd dance with you all night if I could!" *Under the Boardwalk* began before Dick and Jeanette had separated from their hug. Jeanette looked at Dick and smiled, and began to dance slowly with him. Dick hesitated the barest fraction of a second, and then began to respond to the slow rhythm Jeanette had established.

Wilma stood, a little unsteady on her feet now, and strode across the dance floor. She smiled sweetly as she tapped Jeanette on the shoulder. "Want to cut in," she said.

Jeanette smiled. "Sure, Wilma. Sorry." She started to separate from Dick.

But Dick kept Jeanette's hand in his own and said, "It's okay, honey, we'll dance next." He leaned toward Wilma to kiss her.

"Wanna cut in *now!*"

Dick straightened up, and now he was no longer smiling. "Fine, Wilma. But next dance, okay? Babe?"

"Dance with Wilma, Dick. It's all right," Jeanette said, extricating her hand from his.

"Damn right it's all right. He's *my* husband," Wilma said, a touch of anger in her voice. She must have heard it herself, as she became contrite. "Can dance with him any time I want." A few of the other guests shuffled nervously.

"Look, honey," Dick said, "maybe we should sit a couple out."

"I see," she said. "You dance with her and not with your own *wife.*" Dick didn't answer. Wilma, suddenly enraged, tossed her cup of punch at Dick, the liquid striking him in the chest.

The party grew quiet; Jeanette's eyes widened. Dick looked down at his wet shirt and tie, stupefied for a moment, then slowly raised his head and stared at Wilma, as if seeing her, really *seeing* her, for the first time.

"Ohhhhh shit," he breathed.

Wilma seemed to sense that she had gone too far. She said in a small voice, "I just want to dance with you, Dickie."

Dick continued to stare at her, open-mouthed. He then snorted. "Oh yeah, right." With that, he stalked to the door and went outside into the darkness, slamming the door behind him.

Silence filled the room as *Under the Boardwalk* ended. A moment later, *The Bird Is the Word* began.

Wilma's single sob was followed by an agonized wail. *"DIIHH-KEEE! PLEEEZE!"*

Arthur and Sharon left then with the rest of the guests.

iii

The next evening at work, at closing, Laverdiere took all the cash out of the til and went into his office, shutting the door. Arthur shrugged; *some new procedure.* A few minutes later, Laverdiere came out with a small canvas bag. He put on his coat. "Gonna go drop off the day's cash at the bank," he said. "Lock up, and I'll see you tomorrow, Arthur."

iv

November 1965

"Hi Preachee! Hi, Clement!"

Wilma opened the door to the trailer. She smiled and waved them in, the drink in her hand slopping just a little. "Dick went on a beer run. He'll be back in a few minutes. Come on in, come on in."

"We just wanted to say hi, we hadn't seen Dick in a while," Arthur said. It was a month after the wedding.

Wilma was showing now, close to four months into the pregnancy, although in truth it was not easy to tell. Never petite, she had ballooned since the wedding, and rolls of fat were visible, even under the maternity clothes she had begun to wear. "You're looking great," Arthur said.

"I feel so fat," Wilma said.

159

"So this is the place," Clement said as he stepped into the trailer.

"I hope you'll forgive the mess," Wilma said.

The main room was a wreck. Dirty dishes were piled on the table. The shag rug was covered with numerous stains. An ashtray on the end table was filled to overflowing, and next to it sat an almost empty bottle of Smirnoff. The trailer smelled of stale smoke and bacon.

"Dickie said he'd do some cleaning this afternoon," Wilma said.

"Maybe we shouldn't stay," Arthur said.

"No, it's okay," Wilma said. "He was happy you called. No one's been to visit since…" She picked up a pile of dirty clothes on the sofa and put them in a green trash bag near the door. "Got to go to the laundromat," she said. "When he gets back with the car. Please, sit down."

"Thanks," Clement said. They sat.

"So how are you feeling?" Arthur asked. "Baby all right so far?"

"So the doc says," Wilma said. "Starting to move a little; I can feel it wiggling now and again. And I'm not throwing up or anything. You and Sharon getting along all right?"

"Oh yeah," Arthur said. "Just fine."

"Cigarette?" Clement asked, offering her one. She accepted, and they lit up.

"Jesus, that's good," Wilma said, exhaling the smoke. "Been tryin' to cut back on the smoking and the drinking, but sometimes you've just got to relax. Too much to do around here all the time."

Dick pulled into the clearing. He bounced in a moment later with a case of Narragansett under one arm. A large bag of potato chips stuck out of the top of the grocery bag in the other. "Hey guys, great to see you!" he said. Dick's moustache had come in now. His hair was also getting longer. He had begun to grow it now that he was no longer subject to the Crosby dress code, which banned hair over the ears or shirt collar. "Want a beer, Clement?" he asked. Clement nodded.

"Got a Doctor Pepper?" Arthur asked.

"Of course," Dick said. "Wilma, didn't you offer Preach a DP?"

"No, I forgot. Sorry."

"Would you get one for him now? Please?"

Wilma took another swallow of her drink, then silently left the living room. Dick tossed Clement a beer.

Wilma returned with the DP for Arthur. "Thanks, Wilma," he said.

"You're welcome," she said. "I'm going into Belfast now to do laundry. Remember, Dickee, you said you'd clean up a little around here."

"Yeah yeah," Dick said. "I'll take care of it." He popped the top off a beer.

"We can come back later," Arthur said.

"You sit right there and be quiet," Dick laughed. "Housekeeping can wait."

Wilma carried the bag of dirty clothes out to the car, and a moment later she pulled out of the driveway.

"So how's married life?" Arthur said.

"Great!" Dick said. "Got a new job at the plant. Inspecting chicken parts now, instead of just packing them. Better job. Getting three-fifty an hour. Forty hours a week, I'm taking home about a hundred and ten after taxes."

"Not bad!" Clement said.

"Ayuh," Dick said. He took another big swallow of beer. "And being married's great! Wilma's great! Hell, everything's great!"

"Great!" Arthur said. They all laughed.

"Who needs school, anyway?" Dick said. "I'd just be sitting there listening to the teachers drone on. Now, I'm making some real bread. On my own, got my own place. I'm telling you, you can't beat it." He opened another beer.

"It's nice, being married. Different." He brightened. "Hey, let's see what's on TV, okay? Clement, you ready for another beer? You want some chips?" He tossed Clement the potato chips and flipped on the TV, turning to *Wide World of Sports,* just starting.

v

Wilma came home two hours later. By this time Dick and Clement were feeling no pain, having consumed a six-pack of beers each. She entered the trailer as Clement and Dick guffawed at a joke Dick had heard at work.

Wilma looked around the trailer and glared at Dick. "Thanks for doing what I asked you!"

Dick stopped laughing, but winked at Clement. "Nice to see you too, honey," he said.

Clement tittered.

Wilma dropped the bag of laundry on the rug and stalked into the kitchen. Moments later, the sound of banging pots and pans echoed through the trailer.

"My lovely wife. Cleaning up, loudly, for my benefit," Dick explained. Clement tittered again.

Arthur had had about as much of this as he could take. He looked at his watch. "Listen, man, I've got to be going. It's been great seeing you."

"Hey, don't leave!" Dick said. "Don't mind her, she's just being a bitch, as usual." The noise in the kitchen stopped.

Wilma stalked into the living room. "Richard Osgood, what did you just call me?" she said.

"Nothin', honey," Dick said. "I didn't call you nothin'."

"You called me a *bitch!*" she said, her voice beginning to shake.

"Dick," Arthur said, standing, "I'm heading out. Let's go, Clement."

"'Kay," Clement said, standing.

But then Dick got to his feet, swaying a little. "Now look what you've done," he said. "Friends come over for the first time since the wedding—and you pick a fight and *chase 'em away.*"

"Why didn't you clean up the trailer like I asked?" Wilma said. "You live like a pig, Dick! *A pig!*"

"Yeah, and it looks like I married one, too!" he bellowed.

"Bastard!" Wilma snarled, lunging at Dick, fingernails extended. Dick threw his beer can at her; fortunately, it was empty. It bounced off her shoulder, doing no damage but enraging her further.

Arthur and Clement hurried outside, shutting the door as a staccato of slaps, thumps, grunts and yells began, followed by the sounds of furniture tipping over and glass breaking, the trailer actually shaking from the force of the struggle.

"Jesus," Clement said, sliding into the front seat of Arthur's car. "They really gettin' it on, ain't they?"

Arthur started the car, put it in gear and started to pull away, but then stopped. As the engine idled, he turned, looked back over his shoulder at the shaking trailer, incoherent bellows from inside forming a bass under a treble of shrieks, the whole a raucous harmony of rage. "Clement, this sounds pretty serious," Arthur said. He turned off the engine and started from the car.

"You crazy?" Clement said, but Arthur was already hurrying to the trailer.

He reentered in time to see Wilma come at Dick with a rolling pin. Dick roared something incomprehensible and managed just in time to pick up a cushion from the sofa that he used to fend off Wilma's uncoordinated swings. *"Bitch!"* he yelled. *"I'll get you for this!"*

Wilma swung the rolling pin again, eyes filled with fury, but overbalanced and spun into the end table, which collapsed beneath her weight as she fell to the living room floor, showering herself and the rug with cigarette butts and ash. She struggled to get up.

Arthur saw his chance. He grabbed Dick from behind and began pulling him toward the door. Dick was too drunk to struggle effectively against the unexpected assault. "It's Preach, Dick," Arthur whispered into his ear, hoping the quiet voice would help calm him. "Come on man, you gotta get out of here before one of you gets hurt!"

"Don't care!" he bellowed.

"Think about the baby, man. The *baby.*"

That got him. He suddenly quit struggling, and then nodded. With that, he allowed Arthur to pull him from the trailer into the dooryard. Wilma did not follow.

Silence filled the dooryard, the only sound Dick's raspy breathing. After a moment, they began to hear low, wracking sobs from inside the trailer.

Dick shrugged Arthur's hands off his shoulders. He turned and looked at Arthur, then at the trailer. Next he looked at Clement, sitting drunken and wide-eyed in the front seat of Arthur's Chevrolet. He looked back at the trailer, then at his hands. He rubbed his head absently, and then turned and looked at Arthur. His face seemed to crumble. He groaned, and cradled his head in his hands. "What am I gonna do, man?"

Arthur sat down next to him, put his hand on his shoulder. "I don't know, man," he said. They sat there in silence, Wilma's sobs filling the clearing.

vi

At school the next day, Clement and Arthur sat together during lunch. Arthur saw Hag in the cafeteria line, caught his eye, and motioned him over to join them. But, as he had been doing lately, Hag glanced away and went to sit with another group of boys across the cafeteria.

Arthur knew he had been snubbed, and thought he knew why. Hag's folks had taken him to a revival meeting one Saturday night a couple of months earlier. Hag, ashamed, told Arthur afterward he had gone just to laugh at the religious nuts, but had ended up tearfully accepting Jesus as his savior instead, even joining several dozen of the newly converted who came to the front of the hall to be baptized.

Clement and Dick had hooted with sardonic laughter when they heard this, but to Arthur, the conversion appeared genuine.

Arthur's suspicions were confirmed that evening at home, when the telephone rang.

"Hey, Preach." It was Hag. "Listen, I wanted to apologize for not coming over to sit with you today. It isn't you, okay?" He lowered his voice. "It's…well, it's Clement."

"What about him?"

"The drinking, Preach. And…other stuff. Do you think…" Hag trailed off.

"Do I think what?" Arthur said.

"Let's just say I think you'd be wise not to hang out with him anymore."

Arthur was silent a moment. "Why wouldn't I? Clement and me go back almost as far as you and I do. Thought he was your friend, too."

"I know, I know," Hag said. "That's what's tough about this for me. But Preach, I gotta tell ya, I'm kind of worried about him now. These rumors…"

"What rumors?"

"You haven't heard? About him being…you know…"

"Being what?"

"A…a queer," Hag whispered. "Preach, it's a *sin.*"

Arthur laughed out loud. "What are you talking about? Clement is not a queer!"

"Maybe, maybe not," Hag said. "But…a lot of people think he is. It wouldn't look good for a guy to be hanging out with him, all I'm saying. Everyone at school might get to thinking that…about you. I'm praying for him, but…it might not be enough. You should pray for him, too."

Arthur could hardly believe what he was hearing.

"I mean, I've already stopped hanging out with Dick," Hag continued. "After that scene at the wedding and all."

"So Clement's not your friend anymore, Hag?" Arthur said.

"Preach, you're smart and you could do great things with your life. Become manager of a big Foodmart, if you stick with the company. Be somebody. Me, I want to become a pastor. Have my own church someday. We think big, Preach, but if we keep hanging around with guys who cause trouble, we could end up in big trouble ourselves."

Arthur said nothing.

Hag was silent for a few moments. "So," he finally said. "Hope you understand. Didn't want you to think I was upset with *you* or anything today, is all."

"Sure, Hag. See you tomorrow." Appalled, Arthur hung up and returned to his room.

•   •   •

CHAPTER 18
i

Waldo County, Maine
April 1966

Arthur was visiting the trailer in Toad's End the evening Wilma's labor began. They were sitting in the living room watching *The Man from U.N.C.L.E.* Wilma and Dick were both drinking beer, as usual, when Wilma suddenly sat up straight and looked at Dick strangely. "Dickie?"

"Now what?" he said.

"I think my water just broke."

Dick looked over at her. "You sure?"

Arthur did not have the faintest idea what they were talking about. *Something to do with babies,* he guessed.

She stood, felt the chair seat. "Soaking." She began to laugh nervously. "Oh my God, Dickie, it's started. We better get to the hospital."

"Jesus, okay." Dick chugged the rest of his beer and stood. "Where's your bag?"

"Under the bed." Dick went into the bedroom.

"Anything I can do?" Arthur asked.

"Call our folks," Wilma said. "Their numbers are on the wall by the phone. Have them meet us at County General." She clutched her stomach. "Just felt my first contraction, Dickie," she called. "Better hurry!"

"Hold on, for Christ's sake!" he called from the bedroom. He came out a few moments later with the suitcase. "Let's go," he said curtly. They started for the door.

"Want me to lock up after I call?" Arthur said.

"No need, Preach," Dick laughed. "Nothing in this dump worth stealing. Come on, Wilma, let's get this kid born." They went outside to Dick's Dodge, and a moment later drove off.

Arthur called both sets of parents as asked, then called Sharon. "Hey."

"Hi," Sharon said. "Miss you. Wish you were here."

"Miss you, too. I'm over at Dick's," he said. "Guess what? Wilma just went into labor."

"She *did?*" Sharon squealed. "What happened? Tell me all about it!"

Arthur related what had occurred. "That's about it," he finished. "Sharon, what does it mean when your water breaks?"

Sharon laughed prettily. "Boys don't know anything, I swear. Probably think babies come from the supermarket." She explained.

"Oh," Arthur said, oddly repulsed. "Interesting. Well, I've got to go. See you tomorrow at school. Want to study together tomorrow afternoon?"

"You bet," Sharon said. She whispered, "Mom'll be at her garden club and Daddy won't be home until suppertime, so come on over."

A wave of lust shot through him, settled in the pit of his stomach, grew there. "You betcha."

"Love you," she said.

He paused, croaked, "See you tomorrow. Bye." He hung up, turned out the lights, shut the trailer door and drove home, thinking about tomorrow. And Sharon.

ii

Sharon and Arthur had gotten progressively bolder, and now rarely found themselves alone without indulging in sexual play considerably beyond the tentative kisses and gropings they had exchanged in the fall. The relationship still had not been consummated, but their explorations were bringing them closer each time they set out.

Sharon had proven to be an eager participant in these little journeys, and her willingness to engage in them—even initiate them—was a revelation to Arthur. He had not understood until now that most girls were at least as interested in sexual matters as were boys. In a display of the good sense with which even his Aunt Esther acknowledged he had been blessed, Arthur had taken to carrying a condom in his wallet.

And so it was with considerable anticipation that Arthur knocked on Sharon's door the next afternoon. She opened it immediately and he entered; she shut the door, locked it, turned and threw her arms around him. "Oh, I missed you!" she murmured, kissing him hungrily. She wore a pair of very short cutoff jeans and a tight t-shirt; she was obviously braless. She had put on a little makeup and wore her hair in the twin ponytails that Arthur had once mentioned he liked.

"I missed you too," he said, eagerly returning her kisses.

"Come on, we can study later," she said. She took his hand and led him toward the stairs. Arthur needed no prodding. He allowed himself to be pulled upward, knowing what lay ahead. Sharon led him into her bedroom and shut the door. She opened the window, the better to hear a parental car arriving home unexpectedly, she had explained on their first foray upstairs a month or so ago. She turned toward him, pulling down her shorts and taking off her t-shirt as Arthur watched. She stepped to the edge of the bed and reclined gracefully on it, leaving on only her panties, part of their agreed upon arrangement to keep what had happened to Wilma and Dick from happening to them. At last, comfortable, she nodded. "Come on. Hurry," she whispered.

Arthur, by this time thoroughly aroused, kicked off his shoes, yanked off his shirt and jeans, and hungrily slid across the comforter until he covered her, he too leaving on only Fruit-of-the-Looms. They were soon lost to everything except exquisite sensation.

On these occasions in the past, an hour or so of such petting would be followed by a mutual climax attained through use of their hands on each other, a method of gratification at which both had become adept. However, Sharon astonished Arthur this afternoon by proposing something else altogether. "I will if you will," she said, grinning mischievously. Her hand wandered down his stomach, fingers teasing him at the edge of his underpants.

"O—Okay," Arthur said, rolling onto his back. A moment later, she kissed his stomach, then rolled down the waistband of his underpants and eagerly took him into her mouth. He could not restrain himself any longer and gasped, coming almost instantly, but she, momentarily surprised, recovered quickly, and it was soon over.

Arthur caught his breath for a few moments, then with a low growl grabbed Sharon and rolled her onto her back. He pulled her to the edge of the bed, roughly pulled her panties to one side, and eagerly fulfilled his end of the bargain, Sharon grabbing the back of his head, pulling him against her as she cried out, finishing almost as quickly as had Arthur. "Oh, I love you," she gasped after a moment, relaxing her grip on his hair. "Love you love you *love you*," she whispered.

Arthur climbed back up onto the bed beside her, and they lay together listening to their breathing as their hearts gradually slowed. She put her arms around him and hugged him tenderly, stroking his shoulder and kissing him on his forehead and eyes and cheeks. She took one of his hands and placed it on her breast. "That was incredible," she whispered. "I had no idea."

"I think I saw God," Arthur said, and they both giggled. They lay silent for a time. "So…Do you think you might be ready soon?" he asked.

"Getting there," she said. "Are you?"

"I think so," he said. "Any time."

"I've never done this before, you know," she said.

He decided to be honest with her. "Neither have I."

She said, "Seriously?"

"Ayuh."

"You." She snuggled closer to him and kissed him on the cheek again. "Soon, Art. We'll know when it's time. It's best not to rush these things."

"I don't mind," he said, not being entirely truthful. A few minutes later, they dressed and went back downstairs, and when Sharon's mother returned from her garden club meeting a half hour later, the two of them were deeply immersed in the complexities of Mendelian genetics.

iii

Arthur called Dick several days later. "So how's the proud papa?" he said. "Mom and baby doing fine, I guess?"

"Not so hot," Dick said.

Arthur grew serious. "Hey, man, what's wrong?"

"There's something wrong with the baby, Preach."

A hard ball formed in the pit of Arthur's stomach. "What?"

"Looks funny."

"What do you mean?"

"I don't know, exactly. Just looks funny, like an idiot, kind of. Eyes wide apart, nose kind of turned up funny like. Cries all the time. A little boy, but..." Dick's voice became anguished. "Oh Jesus, Preach, he's a mess. Might even be a...a *reetard*." Dick sighed. "I am definitely not ready for this."

Arthur was silent a moment. "How's Wilma?"

"Not so hot. Doc thinks she drank too much while she was pregnant. Says he's seen this in babies before, and every time the mothers drank too much."

"What does drinking have to do with it?"

"Beats me. I'm no doc. Anyway, Wilma feels guilty or something, I dunno."

"Is she home?" Arthur asked.

"Nope. Staying at the hospital with the baby. He's in intensive care while they run some tests. She won't come home, Preach, won't even let me spell her. Says she isn't leaving until the baby can come home. Showers there, eats there. I bring clothes to her each morning."

"I'm sorry, man. Anything I can do?"

"Ayuh. Get me outa here." Dick hung up.

iv

Arthur knocked on the door of Dick's trailer after school a few days later. There was no answer, even though Dick's car was in the dooryard. *He must be outside somewhere.* Arthur walked around to the rear of the trailer.

171

It was then when he heard a radio, turned down low, the music emanating from one of the windows. He grinned and started to say something, then stopped.

In addition to the radio, he heard other sounds from inside—a male and female voice—low, inarticulate, only occasionally a word forming.

Arthur recognized the female voice. *Jeanette Morrison.*

He stole back to the front of the trailer, started the car, and drove away, the engine barely idling until he was well out of hearing range. He pondered his discovery as he drove back to Belfast.

v

Arthur was sweeping at the FoodMart a few evenings later when the telephone in Laverdiere's office rang. Ordinarily, he would let it ring—the store was closed—but it continued for ten rings, and then started up again a few seconds later. He put his broom down and went into the office. "FoodMart, Searsport," he said. "We are closed now."

"Riley boy, is that you?" a laughing male voice said. He had a heavy Boston accent.

"No," Arthur said. "Mr. Laverdiere isn't here right now."

"Well now, that's too bad. Can you leave a message for him?"

"Sure." He picked up a pencil. "Shoot."

"Tell him Paul Mancuso, from the Boston office, called. Can you do that for me?"

"Of course, Mr. Mancuso."

"Tell Riley boy he'd better call me."

"Can I have your number?"

"He has it." Mancuso hung up.

vi

"Hello, Arthur," Sharon's father said that evening, opening the door. Mr. Tibbets was dressed impeccably, as usual, wearing pressed slacks, a cream-colored silk shirt, loafers, and a tan cardigan.

"Hello Mr. Tibbets," Arthur said. Sharon had invited him to dinner. Betty was home on spring break and had brought her new boyfriend over.

"Glad you could join us," Tibbets said. "Betty's young man is here. I think Sharon didn't want to feel left out." He whispered, "Sharon seems quite taken with you."

Arthur blushed. "Well…I'm quite taken with her," he allowed.

"I know you are, Arthur. Believe it or not, I remember how it was when I was your age. Come on in, meet Stuart."

Arthur followed Tibbets into the living room. Sharon, Betty and their mother sat talking with a young man wearing a green army uniform. The man stood, smiling as he crossed to Arthur. "Hello, Art," he said, grinning. "Stu Emery."

"It's nice to meet you," Arthur said. "So you go to the university, Stuart?"

"Please, call me Stu. Yes, but not for too much longer," he said. "I graduate in a couple of months. Then I go on active duty." Stuart was tall and muscular. His hair was short, almost but not quite a crew cut. Deep brown eyes and a sharp, Romanesque nose dominated his pleasant features.

"Hi Art," Sharon said. "You remember Betty."

"Of course I do," Arthur said, smiling at Sharon's older sister.

Betty smiled back. College agreed with her, Arthur noticed. Casually dressed in jeans and a cotton turtleneck, she had lost weight and was letting her hair grow, now shoulder length, thick, and parted in the middle. She seemed several years older than when she had left for Orono, a mere eight months before. "Sharon tells me you two have become quite the item since I've been away," she said.

"Well…" Arthur said, smiling. Everyone laughed gently.

"Can I get you a Doctor Pepper, Arthur?" Mr. Tibbets said. He winked at Arthur. "After you told Sharon you were coming, she insisted I buy some."

"Daddy!" Sharon said, blushing, as Mr. Tibbets left for the kitchen. Betty and Stuart laughed.

"So you were saying, Stuart?" Mrs. Tibbets said.

"Well," Stuart said, "after I graduate I'll get commissioned, then I'm to report to Fort Benning—that's in Georgia—for twelve weeks of officer training at the infantry school there. Then, I don't know. Probably a stateside assignment for a while, but I'm pretty sure I'll be going to Vietnam soon." He smiled. "I volunteered, anyway. Hope I get there before it's all over. If not this year, next."

"Vietnam," Mrs. Tibbets said. She sighed. "I do so worry. Do you think we're doing the right thing there, Stuart?"

"Oh, Mom, don't get him started!" Betty said, rolling her eyes.

"Come on, Betty," Stuart said, grinning, "it's a legitimate question." He turned to Mrs. Tibbets. "Absolutely," he said. "The reds are trying to take over South Vietnam, and we guaranteed we'd protect the south when the country split after the French left. We can't let the communists win. If they do, then there'll be no stopping them. They'll use South Vietnam as a springboard to take over all the rest of Southeast Asia, then maybe even go for Burma and India. Maybe even further. It's like dominos— one falls and all the rest go, too. That's what they told us in ROTC."

"Well, I suppose," Mrs. Tibbets said. "But I hate the thought of our young men dying for some little country most of us can't find on a map. I know I couldn't find it," she laughed. "At least until lately."

Stuart laughed too. "I know," he said. "But I think our guys in Vietnam understand what they're doing."

"I hope so," Mr. Tibbets said, returning with Arthur's Doctor Pepper. "Because I sure don't."

"Stuart was just telling me about how if South Vietnam falls all the rest of the countries there will fall too," Mrs. Tibbets said.

"I've heard that," Mr. Tibbets said. "The so-called Domino Theory." He made quotation marks with his fingers. "Can't say as I think much of that idea."

"You don't think Thailand and Laos and Cambodia would be in danger if South Vietnam falls?" Stuart said.

"In danger of what?" Mr. Tibbets said.

"Of being taken over by the communists."

Mr. Tibbets laughed. "They might be, Stuart, but I can't see as how that should matter to us."

"But we can't let the communists win!" Stuart cried.

"Stuart, I'm as anticommunist as anyone, but we've gotten ourselves into a serious war over there without a clear idea of how we're going to win it, or even what we want to win in the first place."

"I—but—" Stuart started, face reddening.

"Dear, I think maybe you men should talk about—"

Mr. Tibbets held up a hand to cut her off. He chuckled. "Stuart, it's all right. We're just having a conversation. Why don't you come in the backyard and help me cook the steaks? Arthur, you want to join us?"

Arthur looked at Sharon, who smiled and nodded slightly. "Sure," Arthur said, pleased to be included. Arthur followed them into the back yard, where the grill was already fired up, the coals glowing under a nice coating of ash. Large baking potatoes wrapped in aluminum foil lay

175

around the edges of the grill, and on the picnic table sat a platter of steaks covered with cellophane.

"Coals look pretty much ready to go, wouldn't you say, Arthur?" Tibbets said.

"Look good to me," Arthur said, although he had never grilled before.

Tibbets put the steaks on the grill, seasoning them as they began to sizzle. He asked, "So Stuart, you support the military buildup in Vietnam, do you?"

"Yes sir," Stuart said. "These war protesters and all…I don't know. Most of them probably mean well, but some of them are just trying to tear the country down. Some are cowards, too, going to Canada so they won't have to serve their country. And all of them are giving aid and comfort to North Vietnam, you ask me. No telling what effect they're having on troop morale."

Tibbets nodded, considering this a moment. "Stuart, I was a marine in the Pacific during World War II. Guadalcanal, Okinawa. Got back probably about the time you were born. So I like to think of myself as a patriotic American, too. As much of a one as you, wouldn't you say?"

"Of course, sir," Stuart hastily said. "I didn't m—"

"No, no, I understand," Tibbets said, waving him silent. "No offense taken. But Stuart, I've got to tell you, I've got questions about this war. A lot of people do, more every day. I don't think asking questions is giving aid and comfort to North Vietnam. I just don't see why we've sent three hundred thousand men over there, with more going over every month and no end in sight."

"Three hundred *thousand?*" Arthur said. "There's that many American troops there now?" He had had no idea.

"Yes," Tibbets said. "And Johnson wants to send more. Arthur, *you* could end up fighting there."

"Oh, I can't be drafted until I'm eighteen," Arthur began confidently, "and that's..." He stopped. "Well, that's about...fourteen months away, now that I think about it." He thought a moment. "You think we'll still be fighting there then?"

Tibbets nodded. "I do. Even if Johnson started pulling troops out tomorrow, it would take months to get all of them home. And he's given no sign of doing any such thing. In fact, quite the opposite." He looked at his watch, then the steaks. "A couple minutes more, and we'll turn these, what do you say?"

"But what would you do instead of fighting, Mr. Tibbets?" Stuart asked. "Just let the reds take over? We can't just abandon South Vietnam now. What about our credibility?"

"Johnson's taken to saying that lately," Tibbets agreed. "I don't know, though. How many American lives is our so-called credibility worth? And Stuart, don't all those coups bother you? I've lost count how many, at least three or four. Diem getting assassinated—which we might have had a hand in. Then that Buddhist monk burning himself to death. Awful. I don't know how he did it, choosing to die that way, but he must have really believed in his cause, don't you think?"

Stuart was quiet a moment. Then he shrugged. "I don't know," he said. "I guess. Maybe."

"What do all your friends think?"

"Most of my ROTC friends agree with me, that we should fight," Stuart said. "Of course, most of the others are too busy drinking beer and socializing to care much, one way or the other." Stuart thought a moment. "Oh, there've been a few protests in the last year or so," he admitted. "A half a dozen protesters waving signs and chanting, you know. I read in the student paper that a few professors are starting to lecture against the war. A couple of them even held something they called a teach-in, where

177

they talk about the war instead of march around with signs." Stuart shook his head. "I don't understand it. What do they know about it, a couple of scientists? They ought to stick to teaching and leave the war to the experts. Next thing you know, they'll be telling us we all ought to smoke pot."

"I see," Tibbets said, nodding. He glanced at Arthur, and winked. "Stuart, you are a remarkable young man," he said. He turned the steaks.

Stuart blushed, but was clearly pleased. "Thank you, sir." Arthur smiled at this exchange.

"Arthur, you've been awfully quiet," Tibbets said. "What do you think about all this?"

Arthur was afraid this would happen. If the truth were known, he knew nothing about Vietnam or the war or politics, or about much of anything else beyond the confines of Penobscot Bay and Waldo County. But he knew he was expected to say something. "Well," he ventured, "we probably ought to fight communism, I guess. Don't you think?" He realized that this remark was not much of a contribution to the discussion.

But Stuart apparently thought it was. "Absolutely right, Art," he said, nodding vigorously. "We've got to fight communism. And it's better to fight it twelve thousand miles away than have to fight it here at home."

"Yes, I suppose," Tibbets said. "Well, I think these steaks are done. It's about time for supper."

vii

That night, when Arthur got home, Aunt Esther was still up, in the living room having a late cup of tea. She was watching the news. "Did you have a good time at Sharon's?" she asked.

He nodded and sat down. "Aunt Esther," he said after a moment, "where's Vietnam?"

．　．　．

CHAPTER 19

i

Waldo County, Maine
May 1966

Arthur pulled up in front of Sharon's house and parked. He looked at his hair in the rear-view mirror; he had spent a half hour on the part alone. After fussing with it a moment longer, he decided his hair looked acceptable, mostly because it was too late to do anything about it now anyway. Next, he cupped his hand in front of his mouth and smelled his breath—clean after repeated brushings, copious doses of mouthwash, and a dozen toothpicks.

Arthur got out of the car and retrieved his white dinner jacket from the hook above the backseat. It was pressed and clean, still fresh from the rental shop in Bangor.

As he put it on, he thought how grateful he was that Aunt Esther had had experience with formal wear, as she had to help him in several crucial stages. He was glad the bow tie only needed fastening around his neck, not tying—at least he had been able to put that on without assistance, contributing something to preparing for the evening. He picked up the corsage from the front seat, and then, feeling very sophisticated in his rented finery, walked up to Sharon's door and knocked. It was junior prom night.

Mrs. Tibbets answered, and smiled broadly. "Why Arthur, please come in. Sharon will be down in a few minutes. My, but don't you look handsome!"

Arthur blushed, entering the house. "Hello, Mrs. Tibbets."

Mr. Tibbets sat in the living room, reading the *Bangor Daily News.* "Hello, Arthur."

"Mr. Tibbets. How're the Sox doing?"

He scoffed. "Shaping up to be an awful year, but don't get me started." He put down the paper. "You certainly look good in that tux, Arthur."

"First time I've ever had one on." He smiled. "I had to get my aunt to help me with the French cuffs. Couldn't figure them out. Didn't know you folded them double before you put the cufflinks in. I thought there were two sets of button holes or something."

Mr. Tibbets laughed. "Hell, son, I own a clothing store. You should have asked me."

Arthur nodded. "I should have. Didn't think of it."

"Well, remember next time. Ahhh, here's Sharon." He stood.

Arthur turned, and smiled.

"Hi, Art," Sharon said. She came downstairs in a pale blue, ankle length gown, two strands of pearls around her throat, her hair up in a mounded perm. Betty followed behind, smiling broadly.

"Jeez, Sharon—" Arthur searched frantically for something to say. Finally, he had the wit to stammer, "You—you look gorgeous."

"Doesn't she, though?" Betty said. "Of course it took a while, I can tell you."

"Betty!" Sharon said, but both of the girls giggled.

"Here's your corsage," Arthur said. He handed it to Sharon, the purple orchid and baby's breath artfully arranged and tied with ribbon, encased in a box with a clear plastic top.

Sharon took it, and smiled expectantly at Arthur, who looked back at her, mystified. "Well?" she asked. "Aren't you going to pin it on?"

"Oh—well, sure," he said. "Didn't know, uh..." He took the corsage back and removed the lid of the box. He withdrew the corsage, and pulled out the long, lethal-looking pin. He approached her tentatively. "So, where do I..."

"Right about there," she said, indicating a spot on her gown just above her left breast. Her eyes twinkled playfully, and Arthur blushed, although he tried not to. His mouth and hands had been on that very spot, as well as the terrain surrounding it, yesterday afternoon. "Try not to stick me," Sharon warned.

"Do my best," Arthur mumbled. He suddenly felt as though his fingers were hot dogs as he tried to place the corsage in the proper spot and pin it without doing any physical damage. After several embarrassing moments, he managed to get the corsage affixed, but when he stepped back and surveyed his handiwork, he knew it was not going to do. The corsage hung there swinging, upside down.

Mrs. Tibbets came to the rescue. "You men," she laughed. "No one ever teaches you anything. Here, Arthur, let me do that for you." She unpinned the corsage, and in a matter of seconds it was placed properly, providing just the right accent to Sharon's gown.

"Thanks," Arthur said. "I can see I've got a lot to learn about going formal."

"You kids better get going," Mr. Tibbets said. "Prom starts at eight, right?"

"Okay, Daddy," Sharon said. She gave her father a kiss on the cheek, and hugged her mother and sister. Arthur shook hands all the way around, although Mrs. Tibbets also insisted on a kiss.

"What's curfew time, Mr. Tibbets?" Arthur asked as they walked to the door.

Tibbets smiled. "I'll leave that to your judgment, Arthur. Just take care of my daughter."

Arthur nodded. "Thank you. I will." They left, got in Arthur's car and pulled away from the curb.

"You," Sharon said, sliding across the seat and pressing up against Arthur. "I about fainted when you asked about curfew."

181

"Hey, I get along great with your dad, don't want to blow it now. Besides, it turned out all right, didn't it?"

"Yes it did," she said. She kissed him on the cheek, and put her hand on his thigh. "I love you, Art."

"I know," he said. "So let's have a good time tonight and make it an evening we'll always remember."

"You can be sure of that," she said softly, leaning her head on his shoulder. The rest of the ride passed in contented silence.

ii

The prom's theme was Time Travel. As they checked in at the door they passed through a huge inverted U, bedecked with aluminum foil, crepe paper, and papier-mache turrets and abutments, labeled *Time Tunnel—the Past is the Future.* "Pretty neat," Arthur said.

"It did turn out nice," Sharon said. The gym walls were covered with murals on huge sheets of brown paper, depicting modes of travel from the past. The murals started with cavemen on foot, and then progressed through the horse, the invention of the wheel, the internal combustion engine and the automobile, then flight, then rocket ships, until finally, at the end, was a mural labeled "Welcome to the Future in the Year 2017!" The mural featured a big, highly stylized question mark. Aluminum foil stars, comets, planets and moons hung from the gym ceiling, and a rotating mirror ball flashed colored light around the dimly lit gym.

The chaperones, mostly teachers, had gotten into the spirit of the event, and were all in costume. These included the football coach in a caveman outfit, the Latin teacher in a Roman lady's gown, a history teacher in a union army uniform, and an English teacher dressed as Captain Ahab, complete with harpoon and stovepipe hat—although he still had both legs. Even the principal was gamely wandering around, dressed like Mr. Spock—

pointed ears and all—from *Star Trek,* the new science fiction show.

Arthur looked around for friends, saw Hag with a girl he hadn't seen before, both standing next to the punch bowl and hors d'oeuvres. Arthur and Sharon walked over to say hello. Hag smiled broadly. "Hey, Preach." He introduced his date.

Then Arthur said, "Hey look, there's Clement." Hag glanced toward Clement, then, with a meaningful look at Arthur, drifted away.

Clement was wearing a blue velvet dinner jacket with black trim and a madras cummerbund. His hair was slicked back and heavy with Brillcreem. He was alone.

"Hey Preach," Clement said.

"No date?" Arthur asked.

"No, didn't get around to asking anyone in time," Clement said. "But thought I'd come anyway. How you been?" He nodded to Sharon, who nodded silently back.

"Just great," Arthur said. "Glad you're here, man. Look around. There might be a few women who came by themselves too. You never know."

"I'll keep an eye peeled. See you later." Clement wandered off toward the punch bowl.

The band started playing *You Really Got Me.* "Oh I love that song," Sharon said. "Let's dance!"

"Okay," Arthur said, and they walked back onto the now crowded dance floor, joining the throng of students gyrating to the power chords pouring from the twin speakers bracketing the drummer. Arthur saw Jeanette Morrison, dancing with wild abandon with a guy he did not know. Jeanette was a far better dancer than her partner, and the guy tried manfully to keep up, but without much success.

When done covering the Kinks, the band shifted smoothly into *Satisfaction,* followed by *Just like Me,* then *Twist and Shout.* Finally they slowed it down with *Heart of*

183

Stone. Sharon clasped Arthur around the waist, leaning her head on his shoulder as they rocked more or less in time to the music, catching their breaths. "Good band," she said.

"It is," he said.

The band finished the last song, then announced they were taking a short break. "Want to go outside for some fresh air?" Sharon asked.

"Sure," Arthur said. They went outside; the night was very clear, the stars visible even with the school's outdoor lights on. He looked toward the parking lot, and smiled. "Hey, Shar', look. It's Dick." Dick leaned against Arthur's car, smoking a cigarette. He noticed Arthur at the same moment Arthur noticed him, and waved. "Let's go say hi," Arthur said, and before Sharon could say anything he was pulling her along behind him. "Hey man," he said.

"Woo woo, Preach, look at you," Dick said, grinning. "Don't you look sharp!"

"You ought to see Clement," Arthur said. "You know we're supposed to wear these stupid things to proms. How you been? What are you doing here?"

"Just hanging out, Preach," Dick said. "To see what I can see. Bored." He smiled at Sharon. "So, you enjoying your prom?"

Arthur nodded.

"Want to make it a little more fun?" Dick asked. He opened his jacket, revealing the bottle he had stashed there.

"I'll pass, thanks," Arthur said.

"I'll take a little sip," Sharon said. Arthur looked at her, surprised. "Well, it's only one drink," she said. "Won't kill me, silly."

Arthur shrugged. "Hey, enjoy yourself," he said. "That's why we're here."

They got into the front seat of Arthur's car, Sharon in the middle. Dick pulled out the bottle and unscrewed the top, passing it to her. She looked around outside a moment, then quickly tilted the bottle skyward, taking a big swallow. She began to cough immediately, slapping her chest.

Dick chuckled. "Kind of strong the first time, ain't it?"

"Kind of strong any time," she croaked. "Thanks, that was tasty." Then she said, "Say guys, um...would you like to try something else?"

"Like what?" Arthur said.

She reached into her purse, and pulled out a thin, hand-rolled cigarette. "Look what I've got."

"Jeez, Shar', is that pot?" Arthur said, stunned.

"Yep," she giggled.

"Godfrey mighty, where'd you get that?" Dick asked.

"Betty. You can get it at the university easy, she says. Lots of students are smoking it now, even some of the professors. She tried it a month or so ago and really liked it. So I tried some myself. It's really neat."

"You *tried it?*" Arthur asked.

"Sure. Try it yourself, you'll see. It's great. So— you want me to light this?"

Dick hesitated. "Well, no, probably I better not," he said. "Drinking's one thing, you know, but...it's illegal and uh...and I'm worried about...getting hooked." Dick opened the car door. "Listen, I've got to go. I'll see you." He left, hurrying back to his own car parked across the field.

"Well, that's a surprise," Sharon said. "Thought Dick was up for anything." She smiled, rotating the joint between her fingers. "Means all the more for us now."

"Are you sure you want to do this?" Arthur said. "What if we get caught, Shar'? Dick's right, this is illegal."

"Artie, listen. Do you trust me, honey?"

"Of course."

"Then try it. Smoke this joint with me. I guarantee you'll like it. And you're not going to get hooked," she laughed.

Arthur looked at her, then at his fingernails, then out the window, thinking, *I need to loosen up and not be so...* "What the heck," he finally said. "How do you light the thing anyway?"

Fifteen minutes later they went back inside the gym, Arthur's throat scratchy from the coughing fit he had had as they finished the last of the joint. "You okay?" Sharon asked.

"Fine," Arthur croaked, clearing his throat. The band began to play again—*96 Tears*—and Arthur smiled as he noticed the big question mark on the wall.

"Get some punch?" Sharon said.

"Huh? Oh, sure," Arthur said. He allowed Sharon to lead him across the crowded dance floor, Arthur smiling at everyone as he moved toward the punch bowl, now sparkling in the reflected light from the glowing, rotating orb above the dance floor. Jeanette continued to keep her poor dance partner busy.

Mr. Spock stood by the bowl, smiling at all the students. "Hello, Mr. West," Spock said, pointed ears seeming to reach for the ceiling, light from the orb catching the tips just so.

"Live long and prosper," Arthur replied, giggling. Sharon giggled too. Everything seemed to sparkle, as if covered with glass.

"Very good, Mr. West," Spock said. "Miss Tibbets. Enjoying yourselves, I see."

What did he mean by that?

"Uh...yessir, we are. Nice party. Prom."

"Yes it is," Spock said. "Mr. West, my compliments to your class's decorating committee. They did a fine job."

"Thank you, sir."

Sharon nodded and smiled. "I thought so too, sir." Arthur noticed Sharon appeared and sounded perfectly normal. Could it be that only he had gotten high and she had not? "They must have worked very hard on it," she finished.

"It shows," Spock said.

What shows? Arthur wondered. *That we're high?*

"Well, carry on. I have to check in with Mr. Scott in engineering." Spock started to circulate again, but then turned to Arthur. "And Mr. West?"

"Yes—yessir?" Arthur said, suddenly worried. *I'm flying on this stuff. He's gotta know. Must be able to tell. Here it comes. Oh God jail...*

Spock, deadpan, flashed the Vulcan sign of greeting. "Live long and prosper yourself."

"Uh...yessir, I will. Thank you." Spock moved off into the crowd.

Sharon giggled. "Wow. Was that a strange conversation, or is it just me?"

"His ears sure looked real, didn't they?" Arthur said. "Let's have some punch." He dipped into the purple liquid in the bowl and filled two wax paper cups, handing one to Sharon. He sipped his, and a wave of sweetness engulfed him, but it tasted and felt delicious against the dry roughness in the back of his throat. "Mmmm, good," he said.

"Isn't it, though," Sharon said. She grinned at him. "So how you doing?" she whispered.

"My dear, I am doing...spectacularly!" he finished, bowing to her with a flourish.

Sharon giggled again. "Well good. Let's dance some more!" She led him onto the dance floor just in time for *Louie Louie.*

As they danced, Jeanette Morrison took up a spot on the dance floor nearby, still with the bad dancer. The guy was trying, but did not appear to be having a very good time. Finally, he stopped and said something to Jeanette, then walked off the floor. Jeanette stopped dancing a moment, watched him go, then shrugged and began dancing alone.

When *Louie Louie* ended, Jeanette went to the table where the guy sat and said something. He shook his head and looked away from her, sipping his punch. Jeanette, appearing slightly miffed, shrugged and headed for the gym door.

"—Jeanette Morrison?" Sharon asked.

"Huh? Oh, ayuh," Arthur said. "Looks like she's trying to find someone who can dance as good as she can. It sure isn't the guy she's with, I can tell you. I've been watching." At this point the guy Jeanette had been dancing with tossed back his punch, got up and stalked for the gym door. "Let's sit down for a while," Arthur said. "You want some more punch?"

"Sure," Sharon said. She leaned over to him, whispered, "Or we could go sit in your car if you like."

Arthur smiled. "You have another one of those things?"

"Oh no, just that one," she giggled. "I was actually thinking of…something else."

Arthur's stomach lurched, and his heart began to pound. "O—okay. Let's go." Hand in hand, they went outside, heading for the Bel Air.

But then something of a commotion got started across the parking lot. Several people were gesticulating and arguing loudly. With dawning comprehension, Arthur realized one of those involved was Dick. Then he realized the other two were Jeanette and her date. Suddenly Jeanette's date threw a right cross at Dick, who threw up his hands to parry but with only partial success. The other guy leaped toward Dick, who grappled with him a moment before both of them fell to the ground behind Dick's car. Jeanette stood to one side, shouting something.

"Oh man," Arthur said. "Look at that!" He let go of Sharon's hand and dashed across the parking lot, she following along behind.

Arthur got to the fight just as Dick rolled over on top of the other guy, swearing and swinging for all he was worth. *"Call me a chicken plucker again, you bastard!"*

"Leave me alone!" the guy on the ground yelled, trying to fend off Dick's blows but not attempting to land any himself. "Stop it! *Jeanette, make him stop!"*

Arthur grabbed Dick from behind and pulled him off his now thoroughly beaten opponent. Dick kept struggling. "Lemme alone! Gonna kill him. *Let me be I said!"*

"Dick, it's Preach," Arthur said soothingly. "Cut it out. You've *won.* " But Dick continued to struggle, swearing loudly in turn at the guy on the ground, at Arthur, and even at Jeanette a time or two.

"Better get out of here, pal!" Arthur said to the guy on the ground.

The guy jumped up and ran off into the darkness. Dick tried to break free of Arthur's grip and chase him.

"Richard, settle down!" Jeanette said sharply. "Stop it now! Do you hear me?"

Dick looked at her, shook his head sharply, and stopped struggling. Arthur gradually released his grip. "I'm okay," he said to Arthur. He breathed deeply. He turned to Jeanette, then spoke softly, soothingly. "Baby, I—"

"Don't 'baby' me," Jeanette said. "I told you I was going to be here with Will. And I asked you to stay away. I just wanted to come to the prom. Will's nothing, Dick. Nothing! He can't even box step!" She stamped her foot, put her hands on her hips and glared at Dick. "Why'd you have to come here and make trouble?"

Dick spread his hands. "But baby, I—"

"Oh, you're impossible!" Jeanette said. She turned and stalked back toward the school.

Arthur watched her go, and then turned to Dick. "So what was all that about?"

Dick looked at Arthur and smiled bitterly, then shook his head in disbelief. "Jesus, Preach, grow up. What the hell do you think it was all about?" He got in his car, started the engine, and drove off.

"Well," Sharon said after a moment. "I guess we know how much Dick—"

"Look, just cut it out!" Arthur said, turning on her. "Lay off him, will you?"

Sharon looked at him with hurt, open-mouthed amazement.

Arthur immediately calmed himself. "Sorry, honey. I'm sorry. Look, I just don't feel like talking about it right now."

"Sure," Sharon said. "I'm sorry, too, honey. Please, let's not fight," she whispered. "I love you and don't want to fight. I couldn't bear it if—"

"I know, I know," he said, cutting her off. He would give Dick a day or two to calm down, and then give him a call. "Come on," he said, taking her hand. "Let's go back inside and get some punch."

iii

Arthur pulled the Bel Air up in front of Sharon's house at dawn Sunday morning. The effects of the pot had worn off by then, and both were tired but otherwise none the worse for wear. "Well, here we are," Arthur said. "Thank you."

Sharon smiled, leaned against his shoulder. "For what?"

"For coming with me tonight. For being my girlfriend. For putting up with me snapping at you about Dick and all. For…everything." He put his arm around her and kissed her on her forehead.

"I love you, Art," she replied. "I better go in. Daddy's probably watching us." She kissed him chastely on the cheek. "Come on, walk me to the door."

They got out of the car, holding hands as they came up the walk. They stepped onto the porch. Sharon turned to him, came into his arms, hugged him fiercely. "Don't ever leave me, Art," she whispered. "Don't ever leave me."

"Sharon, I—" But then the door opened.

Tibbets stood there. "Young man," he said, glowering, "if you brought my daughter home at dawn any other night but prom night I'd be plenty upset." A twinkle appeared in his eye. "But you get dispensation this time."

Arthur nodded. "Thank you, sir. You notice I got her back here safe, sound and sober."

"Lucky for you!" Tibbets laughed. Then he offered his hand. "You're a fine young man, Arthur."

Arthur took the hand. "Thank you, sir. Good night. Or—good morning. Or—well, you know what I mean. See you later, Sharon." He turned and went back to his car. He was home and asleep fifteen minutes later.

.   .   .

CHAPTER 20
i

Waldo County, Maine
June 1966

A week after the prom, Arthur knocked on the trailer door; Dick answered a moment later. "Hey, man. Come on in." Arthur went inside, and he and Dick sat in the living room. From the back of the trailer, Arthur heard the baby crying.

After a moment, Dick said, "Listen, Preach, I'm sorry about what I said to you at the prom. I was all hot about that little asshole Will, and didn't know what I was saying. We square?"

"Don't worry about it, man, of course. Where's Wilma?"

"With Justin." Dick shut his eyes wearily, and shook his head. "I've gotta warn you, she's different now. And the kid, he's out of the hospital and all, but...I don't know. He's not so good." He laughed bitterly. "Bet you're glad you came over, ain't you?"

They sat down. The trailer was considerably cleaner than the last time he had been here, he noticed. The rug had been shampooed; the stains that had been there were noticeably less distinct. The place had also been swept, and there were no dirty dishes or other debris scattered around. The ashtray beside the sofa was clean, now only a single cigarette burning in it. And the bacon smell was gone.

Dick returned with the DP. "Thanks," Arthur said. "So when do I get to see the baby?"

"You sure you want to?" Dick said.

"Sure, why not?"

"Okay. Wilma?" Dick called. "Preach is here. Wants to see Justin."

"All right, honey," she replied. "Just let me finish changing him."

"Don't let on like anything's wrong," Dick whispered.

Arthur nodded.

A few moments later Wilma, more massive than ever, came into the living room carrying Justin, wrapped in a white wool blanket. "Arthur, it's so nice to see you again," Wilma said, smiling. "Here's Justin, our bouncing baby boy." She smiled gently at the baby, whispered to him, "Aren't you our bouncing baby boy, yes you *are.*"

Arthur stood and crossed to her, and peered into the face peeping vacantly out of the blanket wrap. "Well well, look at you!" he whispered, smiling at Justin's tiny, wide-eyed, somehow odd features. "What a cute baby," he said.

"Yes," Wilma said. "Justin Osgood, our little gift from God, yes you are!" she cooed.

Justin began to cry again, weakly and thinly but insistently. "What do you think is wrong now?" Dick asked, coming over and peering down at him helplessly.

"We might need to be fed again, mightn't we?" Wilma said, smiling and cooing again to Justin rather than addressing Dick. "We just changed our diapers, yes we did, and we just had our nap, didn't we? So I guess getting fed is about the only thing left, yes it is!" She said, "Arthur, you'll excuse us please—we've got to go get our yumyums now, don't we, precious?" She disappeared into the back of the trailer. A few moments later, Justin quieted down.

Dick rolled his eyes skyward and mouthed *thank you,* hands clasped as if in prayer.

"Been tough for you, I guess?" Arthur asked.

"You don't know," Dick said. He stubbed out his cigarette and lit another. "Kid never seems to stop crying. Like he's hurting all the time or something. Wilma and me try, but…"

"Sorry."

"It's all right. Nothin' you can do." Justin began crying again. "Oh Jesus," Dick breathed, "I can't take this anymore. Come on, let's go into town." He stood. "Honey?" he called. "We're going into town. You need anything?"

"Baby shampoo and Ivory," she called back. "Justin needs a bath."

"Okay," he said. They left and got into Dick's car. Dick pulled away from the trailer and sighed with relief. "Sometimes I can't stand it," he said. "Think I'm going crazy or something. Like I've got to get away someplace. How'd I get myself into this mess? Take it from me, Preach, make sure you use rubbers when you screw."

"I'll keep that in mind," Arthur laughed.

Dick accelerated expertly down the narrow road toward town. After a few minutes he said, "I don't know what's happened to Wilma. You catch that 'gift from God' crap? Says that all the time now. And whenever Justin's asleep, she's reading her Bible. And lately she's started talking about going back to church."

"Quite a change," Arthur said.

"You ain't kidding. Quit drinking and smoking too. And now she wants me to do the same." Dick chuckled bitterly. "I can't quit smoking. I tried. And as for drinking, forget it." Dick shook his head. "Preach, sometimes, I..." He trailed off.

"You what?" Arthur asked.

"I don't know," Dick said. "Feel like...I'm trapped or something, you know? I think about splitting. I do. San Francisco or some place. Just away from here. Or even Europe. Amsterdam, maybe. I hear it's nice there."

Arthur looked at him and said carefully, "So that's why you're seeing Jeanette, I guess? You're trapped?"

Dick glanced at him, and shrugged. "It just kind of happened. Didn't mean for it to. But Preach, she was throwing herself at me every time she saw me. Even came on to me at the wedding reception. You saw, man. I mean, *shit,* you know? I tried for months to stay away from her, but what was I supposed to do, just keep ignoring her?"

"So when did it start?" Arthur asked.

"Only a month or so ago. She came over one afternoon when Wilma was still at the hospital with Justin. Just to see how we were doing, she said. Well, we were alone, had a couple of drinks, put on some dance records, and one thing led to another. One minute we were dancing, and the next..." Dick slowed for the stoplight at the edge of town.

"Not proud of it," he continued, "but that's what happened." He looked at Arthur. "I know I ought to stop seeing her, but..." He leaned forward conspiratorially and grinned. "But Preach, she fucks as good as she dances. You wouldn't believe. She'll do anything, Man. *Anything.* What am I supposed to do, just stop seeing her now?"

Arthur said nothing, shrugging.

"Oh right, I forgot," Dick sneered, "you're Preach, not a mere sinner like the rest of us. Like you'd take a pass on her if she came on to you."

Arthur started to protest, but then stopped. After a moment, he shrugged again and grinned. "Well, I'd...think about it."

Dick chortled. "I bet you would."

ii

Arthur was puttering round in the back room at the FoodMart a few days later when he heard Laverdiere talking. "Yes, Paulie, I know. I haven't forgotten...Of course I'll take care of it. I've been good for it so far, right? Look, there's no need for that...Okay, fine. *Fine,* I said. Just give me three days...Okay, two. Yes. Good bye."

Laverdiere hung up more vigorously than necessary and left his office. He glanced at Arthur. "Don't you have anything better to do than hang around out here?"

iii

Several evenings later, Arthur showed up at the Tibbets' door. It was seven o'clock. Betty answered. "Hi, Art. Glad you could come."

"Thanks for inviting me." Betty was cooking dinner for Stuart. It was his last night of leave in Maine, and she had invited Arthur and Sharon to join them.

"Thanks for coming," Betty said. "Come on in. Stu's out back with Sharon. I'm getting the salad together. You know the way." She returned to the kitchen, and Arthur walked through the living room to the back yard.

"Hey buddy," Stuart said, standing as Arthur appeared. He was wearing his green dress uniform, but the

ROTC insignia were gone. He now wore gold bars on his epaulets, and had crossed rifles on the lapels of his tunic.

"Hi Stu," Arthur said. "Or should I say, 'Lieutenant'?"

"Stu's fine," he laughed. "But yeah, I got my commission. Finally. Leave tomorrow for Connecticut for a couple of days to see the folks, then Benning. I'm glad you could come tonight, Art."

"Glad I'm here. Hi Shar'," Arthur said.

"Hi," she said, winking at him. "Your usual?"

"Of course."

Sharon got up. "I'll just be a minute." She brushed her hip against him, grinning as she passed.

"Boy, they're a couple of pretty sisters, aren't they?" Stuart said after Sharon had gone inside.

"You know it," Arthur said.

Stuart whispered, "I love Betty, Art. In fact, tonight I'm..." But then Sharon returned, and he stopped.

"Here you go," Sharon said, handing Arthur his DP. She kissed him on the cheek.

Betty came out a minute later, clapping her hands. "For better or worse, dinner is ready! Come on inside."

Betty had made spaghetti and meat sauce and salad. Water glasses sat at everyone's place, and a bottle of red wine sat in the middle of the table next to a basket of rolls. "Mom doesn't know about the wine," Betty laughed, "but I figure if Italian kids drink it, all of us can!"

"Great," Sharon said. "I'll have some, please."

Betty poured some into Sharon's glass. Betty looked at Arthur, who hesitated a moment, then nodded. "Special occasion, I guess."

When all had wine, Stuart stood. "I want to propose a toast." He turned to Betty. "To the most beautiful girl in Maine!"

"Hear hear," Arthur said, smiling at Sharon as he nodded, sipping.

"Thank you, Stuart," Betty said. "That's very sweet. Let's have some dinner, okay? I'm starving. Shar', start the salad around, would you?"

After a moment, Stuart sat down. "So, Art, how's school coming along?"

"Not bad," he said. "I'll be a senior in September. Turned seventeen two weeks ago."

"What are you going to do when you graduate?"

"Well, I don't know," Arthur said. "Probably start working full time at the FoodMart in Searsport. I'm in line for the assistant manager's job, the boss says. I'd be making decent money, and I've been saving for the last year, too. So, when I graduate and if I get that promotion, it might be time to think about settling down, you know?"

"Have you thought about going to college, Arthur?" Betty said.

"Nope. Don't think college is for me, Betty."

"Now don't be silly," she said, putting down her fork. "You're smart, Arthur. Forgive me for saying this, but you working as an assistant manager at the Searsport FoodMart is a terrible waste. I mean, do you really think that's the best you can—" She stopped, then reddened a little. "Sorry. Didn't mean to get on my high horse. It's your life, of course."

Arthur laughed. "It's okay. I just don't see myself in college is all."

Betty returned to her salad, but after a moment spoke again. "Art, if money's a problem, there's always scholarships. You shouldn't have too much trouble getting one. And your aunt would surely help with tuition, right?"

Arthur nodded. "She would. It's not the money."

"But there's something else to consider, too," Betty continued. "This war in Vietnam. Have you thought about it?"

"Oh God," Stuart said, rolling his eyes. "Here we go."

"Now you stop it, Stuart Emery," Betty said, smiling. She turned back to Arthur. "Arthur, you need to think about this seriously. You're going to get drafted, probably when you turn eighteen or a little after, unless you get a deferment, which you can get if you're in college. So going straight to college when you graduate from Crosby means you won't have to worry about going to Vietnam. At least for four years, and by then it'll be 1971. It's bound to be over by then."

Arthur shrugged. "Well, maybe I ought to go, you know? Do my bit? Lots of other guys are."

Betty stared at Arthur in disbelief. "Arthur, are you crazy? Our troops are getting killed over there. Hundreds, every week. Not to mention thousands of Vietnamese. Do you really want to go and risk that? Most of the guys I know at school would do anything to keep from going."

Stuart laughed. "Present company excluded, of course. Now Betty, don't go trying to convert Arthur into some kind of protester or something!"

"I think it's kind of noble, wanting to fight for your country," Sharon said.

"Oh my God, Sharon," Betty said, shaking her head in disbelief. "There's nothing noble about Vietnam."

Arthur smiled. "Well, I don't know how noble it is, but..." He trailed off. "My family's always served—my father, my grandfather, his father before him, going back at least to the civil war. Even before that, in Scotland, my...my mother told me. Figure I ought to as well, I guess, if I'm called up."

Betty looked at Arthur a moment, then lowered her head and closed her eyes. Softly, she said, "I hope you think this through before you make your decision. You're a pretty decent guy, Art." She smiled and continued, "Shar' would probably like to make sure you're around for a while."

"Betty!" Sharon said, blushing.

"As you might gather," Stuart laughed, "me and Betty kind of disagree about the war." He smiled at Betty, tipped his glass of wine toward her. "But hey, if we agreed on everything it'd sure be boring! And that's why I love her."

Betty smiled at Stuart. "Oh you do not, Stuart Emery, and you know it," she said, then turned to Arthur before Stuart could respond. "You want to get the spaghetti started around, Arthur?"

They ate heartily; Betty was a quite good cook, Arthur decided. To cheers and applause from Stuart and Sharon, Betty produced a second bottle when the first was finished. Arthur refrained from refilling his wine glass, discreetly switching to water.

They sat around the table after dinner, talking quietly. Then, with an air of finality, Stuart drained his third glass of wine and stood. "Ladies, Art, I have an announcement to make."

"Uh oh," Arthur said, chuckling. "Don't like the sound of this!"

"At ease, Private!" Stuart barked, smiling. "This is a serious moment here!" He appeared a little flushed.

"I am all ears, Lieutenant, *Sir!*" Arthur said.

"Thank you," Stuart said. He stood tall and proud in his officer's uniform and looked at Betty, eyes glistening. "As all of you know, I am off to Fort Benning, Georgia in a few days for three months of infantry officer training." He paused expectantly.

"And?" Sharon said.

"Aaaand," he continued, "at the end of that time, I expect to have a brief leave. Although I am from Darien, Connecticut, I'm going to spend most of my leave here." He looked at Betty and smiled. "In Belfast, Maine. With the most beautiful, charming, and wonderful woman I've ever known." He reached into his tunic pocket, and pulled out a small box and held it gently. "And who I hope will

199

consent to be my wife." He looked at Betty, smiling broadly, and extended the box.

"Betty, will you marry me?" he said.

Betty stared at Stuart, open-mouthed, then glanced at Sharon and Arthur. She did not take the box. "Stuart, I—I don't know what to say."

"It's very easy," he replied, extending his hand further toward her, again offering the box. "Just say, 'yes, Stuart, I'll marry you.'" He smiled again, but Arthur noticed something was changing in his eyes; they were not as joyful as they were a few moments ago.

Still trying to keep it light, Stuart said, "I know, I'm not down on my knees!" He stepped from his place at the table, still smiling, although it was beginning to look a little forced.

"Stuart, I—" Betty said. She was unable to continue.

"No no, don't say anything," Stuart said. He took the two or three steps necessary to reach her side, then went gracefully down to one knee and held the box out to her with both hands. He opened it; a gold ring was revealed, the single small stone glinting faintly. "Betty—say you'll marry me. Please."

Betty was silent a moment, looking at the ring. Her eyes began to moisten.

"I know it's not much of an engagement ring," Stuart said, "but it's the best I can do right now. Marry me, and I promise I'll get you a bigger one when I can afford it."

"Oh, Stuart." She averted her eyes.

"What's wrong, honey?" Stuart said.

A moment later, she spoke softly. "Stuart, it's not the ring. It could be five carats and it wouldn't matter." She touched him on the arm. "You're very sweet and I'm deeply honored and touched that you've asked me to marry you. I'll always remember it, and when I do I'll think of one of the kindest, most decent men I've ever known. But I—I can't marry you. I'm sorry." She threw down her napkin, stood and hurried from the room.

"Ohhhhh boy. I'd better go," Sharon said, hurrying after her.

Stuart and Arthur listened to the sounds of the sisters running upstairs, then a door slamming on the second floor. Stuart, ashen faced, snapped the ring box shut and slowly stood. He returned the box to his tunic pocket. He sighed deeply, poured another glass of wine, killing the bottle, and drank it off in two or three quick gulps. "Well, Art," he said, placing the glass back on the table. He laughed shortly. "I sure made a goddamn fool of myself, didn't I?"

Arthur shook his head. "You asked a girl to marry you and got turned down, Stu. Doesn't make you a fool. It just happens, that's all." He clapped Stuart on the shoulder. "Hey, it's her loss, if you ask me."

"Thanks." He coughed, then picked up one of the napkins, and blew his nose. "Damn. Damn *damn DAMN*. Don't know how I could have been so stupid." He walked into the living room, Arthur following, and picked up his garrison cap, lying on the end of the sofa. "I'd better shove off. I've got a train to catch tomorrow. Say good night to the girls, will you?" Arthur nodded. "So long." As he walked out, he stopped and turned, considered Arthur a moment. "You're a good man, Art."

"Thanks, Stu. So are you."

"Thank you for that." He left the house and drove away.

Sharon came down. "Has Stuart gone?" Arthur nodded.

"Okay." She ran back upstairs, and a couple of minutes later she came back down again, Betty following. Betty's eyes were red, and she clutched a handkerchief.

Arthur smiled gently at her. "Well, I learned one thing tonight. I won't ask someone to marry me in front of a bunch of people unless I know I'm not going to get turned down."

Betty smiled. "I'm sorry."

"How long have you two been seeing each other?" Arthur said.

"We started going out last fall," Betty said. "I met him at a fraternity party. He was nice. Very sweet. We got to be friends. We don't agree on much, but we could talk about most things. Except Vietnam. We began to argue about it. *A lot.* Once we were having dinner and got into a big fight and I stormed out and we didn't speak for a week. Finally he bought me a big bouquet of roses and we made up. But I decided then that we could never work as a permanent thing. We're too different. I thought he realized that, too. Damn," she said. "*Damn damn DAMN.* Don't know how I could have been so stupid."

. . .

CHAPTER 21
i

June 1966
Waldo County, Maine

Arthur and Sharon held each other in the back seat of Arthur's car. The movie had ended over an hour ago, and they had driven quickly to the meadow on the north end of the lake.

Their necking had a furious, desperate quality about it, as if what they had was in danger of coming to an end.

Arthur sensed the strange quality of the mood first, but it was Sharon who escalated things to new levels.

As they finished undressing each other to their agreed upon barrier, his hands roamed up her torso to her breasts. But instead of arching them upward to meet his hands as she usually did, she covered his hands with her own and guided them back down and placed them on her panties. "I'm ready now," she whispered, kissing him hungrily.

"Are you sure?" Arthur asked.

"Yes, hurry."

Arthur, shaking, gently pulled her panties down her slender legs, she lifting her hips to make it easier for him. Quickly he covered her body with his own.

If either had had more experience, the loss of virginity of the other would have been accomplished with little difficulty. However, since neither knew quite what to do except in general terms, the act required a bit more fumbling than either had expected, but as does everyone, they managed to figure it out. And thankfully, Arthur did remember to put on his condom.

When he withdrew after several minutes, he sat back up, smiling, and started to say something. But then, to his horror, he saw Sharon's eyes clenched shut, and tears streaking her cheeks as she bit her lower lip. "Shar'?" he whispered.

"W—what?" she said, voice trembling.

"Are you okay?"

"Yes. No. I don't know. Oh Arthur, it hurts!"

"Well...I'm sorry," he said. "I'd heard it might, but..."

"No Arthur, it really hurts. It aches. I can hardly stand it." She tried to sit up, a sharp intake of breath indicating her pain as she did so. "Oh God, I hope I haven't..." She stopped short and started to sob, her keening low and insistent.

"Hope you haven't what?" Arthur said, starting to worry. *What if he had really hurt her somehow?* he thought. Not knowing what else to do, he reached into the front seat for her clothes. "Here, you better start getting dressed."

"Do you have any Kleenex?" She struggled to control her breathing as she pulled on her panties.

"No, I'm sorry," Arthur said, helpless, making a mental note to start keeping a box in the car. "What would you like me to do, Shar'? I can take you to the emergency room if you like. Right now."

"I don't know," she said, still crying. "God, I can hardly move. Please, help me get dressed, okay? Oh Arthur, I'm frightened!"

"It's okay," he said miserably. "If it doesn't stop soon, I'll…I'll take you to the hospital, don't worry."

"O—okay," she said. "We probably ought to think about doing that, Arthur. It really hurts, I'm not kidding."

This was not something Arthur had planned for. "Okay. Okay. Let's get you dressed. I'll take you to County General. I'm sorry, Shar'. I'm really sorry."

"It's all right," she said. Painfully, she opened the rear passenger door and hobbled into the front seat and finished dressing, quietly sobbing. Arthur joined her, feeling empty and embarrassed, and started the car. They were on the way back to Belfast a minute or two later.

Arthur rolled down his window as they drove, thinking some fresh air might help. But Sharon asked him to roll it back up; she was cold. He did so. As they drove silently, all Arthur heard was Sharon's sniffles as she stared outside, watching the black countryside roll by.

What a mess, Arthur thought. *And what if she's really hurt?* And what would he tell her folks and Aunt Esther?

As they approached the Passagassawakeag Bridge ten or so minutes later, Arthur said, "Well, here we are. Do you still want to go to the emergency room?"

Sharon was silent a moment, then said, "I'm actually starting to feel a little better. Why don't we just drive around for a few more minutes and let's see."

"Okay," Arthur said, uncertain that this was the best idea. But he continued out the Route 1 bypass, circling Belfast and heading south.

By the time they got to Lincolnville, Sharon had stopped sniffling and seemed to be doing considerably better. "Well," Arthur ventured, "they say you always remember your first time."

Sharon smiled weakly. "I can see why."

"How are you feeling?"

"Better. I think you can take me home. I should be all right."

"Are you sure you're okay?"

"I think I'm okay, Artie. Really."

"Oh." After a moment, Arthur said, "Listen, do you think we...did it...the right way?"

Sharon smiled, and even chuckled a little, which Arthur took as a good sign. "Of course. You did just fine; it was me, that's all."

"It was me too," he added. "It'll be better next time, I bet. If you...want to, I mean."

"We'll see." They drove back to Belfast.

ii

The next morning, Arthur walked out to the car, on his way to the midday shift at the FoodMart. As he opened the car door, he idly glanced at the back seat, and blanched.

A reddish brown stain about the size of a silver dollar occupied the exact center of the back seat.

iii

"Looks like you got a problem."

"It's why I'm here," Arthur said. He was on his lunch break and had driven to a repair shop on the north end of Searsport. He indicated the stain. "Can you get it out?"

"Well—don't really know," the service station attendant said. "What is it?"

"Blood."

The attendant looked at Arthur and, with dawning comprehension, began to smile. "Do tell," he said.

"Was out hunting last evening," Arthur said. "Shot a couple of rabbits and tossed them on the back seat. They bled on the upholstery."

"Rabbits."

"It's true."

"Didn't say it wasn't," the attendant said, grinning. "Well, I guess we can probably get it out. Let me go talk to the boss, get you a quote." The attendant walked into the gas station, and Arthur watched him through the picture window in front as he talked to another man. The attendant gestured toward Arthur, both looked at him, and both began to laugh. They came out a moment later.

The second man said, "Shooting rabbits, huh?"

"Ayuh," Arthur said, reddening.

"And you need us to get the blood out of the seat?"

Enough. "How much?"

"Guess twenty dollars ought to do it."

"Twenty?" Arthur said. "That's a little steep, ain't it?"

"Twenty. Take it or leave it." The second man smiled.

Arthur frowned, scratched his head, and thought for a moment. "You'll get it all out?"

"Don't worry, your Momma won't be able to tell you'd had a rabbit back there." Both men chuckled again.

"All right," Arthur said, furious. He pulled out his wallet, showed them a twenty. "I've got the cash right here. I'll be back at eight tonight to pick it up. Just fix it."

"It'll be ready," the second man said.

"Good." Arthur started to walk off.

"Oh, and son?" the second man said.

"Ayuh?" Arthur said, turning.

"Next time you go rabbit hunting, be sure and put a rubber sheet over the back seat."

The attendant began to guffaw.

Arthur stalked off, their laughter ringing in his hot ears.

iv

Arthur got back to the FoodMart at about one o'clock and let himself in. The front door was locked, the CLOSED sign up in the window. He thought it odd. Mr. L usually opened back up at half-past. But Laverdiere was nowhere in sight. LaVerne was also not in. "Hello?" Arthur called. "Mr. L?" There was no answer.

Arthur crossed the store to the back room and flipped on the light and looked around. Laverdiere's office door was shut. Arthur crossed to it and knocked. "Mr. L?"

"Come in, Arthur."

Arthur opened the door. "Mr. L? You okay?"

"Oh yes, Arthur, I am just fine and dandy, thank you very much." Laverdiere sat behind his desk, a half-full pint of Southern Comfort before him along with a paper cup. "Would you care for a drink, Arthur? I know you're underage, but hey, man to man, who's going to know but us, hmmm?"

"No thanks, Mr. L. Say, shouldn't we be opening up the store now? It's almost one and we open up at twelve-thirty usually."

"We're taking the afternoon off today, Arthur. I am still the boss, after all."

"Well sir, do you think that's a good idea?"

"I think it's a great idea, Arthur."

Arthur was silent a moment. "Well…all right. What would you like me to do, then?"

"Have a seat."

"Mr. L, I—"

"Please." Laverdiere gestured to the chair in front of his desk. "Please. Have a seat."

Arthur sat.

"You are a pretty perceptive young man, Arthur. Aren't you?"

"Hadn't thought about it," Arthur said carefully.

"Well, I think you are." Laverdiere poured himself another inch or so of Southern Comfort and sipped appreciatively. "Sure you don't want to join me?"

"I'm sure, thanks."

"All right. Arthur, I fired LaVerne an hour ago."

"Oh?" Arthur was not surprised.

"That's it? *Oh?*" Laverdiere said.

"Not my decision to make, Mr. L."

"You and she are friends, aren't you?" Laverdiere said. "I thought certain you'd be upset."

"We're work friends," Arthur said. "Not real friends."

"Have lunch together a lot, do you?"

"Nope. Not in months."

"Did she ever tell you anything about her personal life?"

"Well…I know she dated Nelson."

"Bingo," Laverdiere said. "She did date Nelson. She did, indeed. She tell you anything else?"

"About what?"

Laverdiere took another sip of his drink. "Hell, boy, let's cut the crap, okay? About her and me, dammit!"

"Nope," Arthur said carefully. "She never mentioned anything between her and you specifically. Said she'd been dating another man, though."

"Oh she did, did she?" Laverdiere said. "Well, that other man was me, Arthur." He took another sip of his drink. "Yes, me. The boss. Screwing the help. Not supposed to do that, are we? Nope, I should say not. If regional found out, I'd be out of here tomorrow. Against company policy."

Arthur said nothing, just wanting the conversation to end.

"I couldn't help it, Arthur. God help me, I couldn't help it. I was a married man with two sons and a dog. I was a den leader in the cub scouts. Went to church. I thought I was happy. But...there was something about her. I saw it from the day she started work here. It was quite a state of mind I'd gotten myself into," he said. "Of course she expected me to marry her. Don't blame her none. But I couldn't."

"Mr. L," Arthur ventured, "It's kind of weird, you talking about this with me."

Laverdiere laughed shortly. He took another swallow of Southern Comfort. "Arthur, since you've got her perspective on this, you ought to have mine, don't you think? So you just sit right there, please."

Arthur said nothing. *Better just to let him talk.* After a moment, Laverdiere continued.

"She can be so damned stubborn!" Laverdiere shook his head bitterly. "I tried to talk with her, make her understand my position—a married man, her boss. But she wouldn't listen. Wouldn't even respond. Finally, she said since we were obviously going no place, she was leaving me. That's when something snapped, and I fired her." Laverdiere buried his face in his hands on his desk. "Oh Jesus, how could I have done such a thing? And now— well, never mind. Not your worry."

Arthur took the opportunity to look at his watch. "I'm sorry, Mr. L," he said, and stood. "Look, we really ought to open up. You go on home now and I'll watch things. Take the afternoon off. We won't get all that much business now anyway. Lunch time is over and it'll be quiet until suppertime. What do you say?"

Laverdiere said nothing, but nodded. Arthur screwed the cap back on the bottle of Southern Comfort and returned it to Laverdiere's desk drawer. He patted his boss on the shoulder, then went out to the front of the store. He put on his apron and unlocked the front door, smiling apologetically to the elderly lady waiting outside. "Would you be wanting anything from the deli today, ma'am?" he asked.

"Nope. Just for the store to be open when it's supposed to be," she said, brushing by him.

.   .   .

CHAPTER 22
i

Waldo County, Maine
October 1966

Outside Arthur's window it was dark, and frost had formed on the panes for the first time since last winter. He was sitting at his desk finishing up the last of his English lit—a test on *Beowulf* was coming up on Monday—when he heard the telephone ring downstairs.

It was Wilma Osgood. "Preachee," she said in an uncharacteristically quiet voice, "is Dick over there?"

"Nope. Haven't seen him. What's the trouble?"

"He's…He's gone, Preachee. Disappeared. Left yesterday morning for his job, same as usual, but didn't come home last night. I wasn't too worried at first. But after a couple hours I called the plant, and the line supervisor said Dick had punched out at quitting time, picked up his paycheck and left. Now it's been a day, and…and nothing."

"Have you called his folks' house?"

"Yes. Nothing there either. They haven't seen him in weeks. Dick and his father don't get along." Wilma's voice began to shake. "Oh, Preachee, what if he's hurt?"

"Now calm down, Wilma, you would have heard something by now if that was so. Have you called the police yet?"

"Not yet."

"You probably should. Look, you do that and I'll call around a little. Someone might know something."

Arthur called several classmates, but got nowhere. Next he called Clement and got his father.

"Clement ain't around," Mr. Paul said.

"Any idea when he'll be back, Mr. Paul?"

"Nope. Out with that new friend of his, I expect."

"New friend?"

"Some college boy."

"Okay," Arthur said, mystified. "When he gets home, ask him to call me, would you?"

"I ain't his messenger boy. Call back and ask him yourself." Mr. Paul hung up.

There was only one person left he could think of to call regarding Dick's whereabouts.

The telephone was picked up on the first ring. "Hello?" a breathless female voice said.

"Jeanette Morrison, please."

"Who is this?"

"Arthur West, a classmate at Crosby. Jeanette?"

"No, this is her mother." The voice became tired, almost world weary. "Have you seen Jeanette today, Arthur?"

Arthur said, "No. Not since yesterday. At school."

"You saw her at school? What time yesterday?"

Arthur thought a moment. "At lunch. Mrs. Morrison, is there a problem?"

Mrs. Morrison sighed. "Arthur, Jeanette did not come home from school yesterday. I've been calling everyone I could think of, trying to find her. She's just disappeared."

"Well, Mrs. Morrison, I'm calling for the same reason, sounds like. Friend of mine's disappeared too. Thought Jeanette might know where he was."

"Who is it?"

"A fellow named Dick Osgood."

"Oh yes. Jeanette's mentioned him. A good dancer, she told me. Didn't he get married a year or so ago?"

"That's him."

"And he's missing too?"

"Ayuh. Didn't come home from work yesterday afternoon. Of course, Wilma—that's his wife—is pretty worried."

"Of course." Mrs. Morrison was silent for several moments. Then she said, "Might I ask you...Arthur, is it?"

"Yes ma'am," he said.

"This will probably sound strange, Arthur, but how well do you know this Osgood fellow?"

And with electric, startling clarity, it all came together. *How could he have missed it?*

"Pretty well," he said carefully. "We're friends. You know."

"And how well does this Osgood fellow know Jeanette, Arthur?"

Arthur was silent.

"I see," Mrs. Morrison said. "My God." She sighed deeply. "I'd suspected she was involved in..." Her voice trailed off. "Well Arthur," she continued, "I think we both have a pretty good idea where Jeanette may have gotten off to, don't we?"

"Yes ma'am," Arthur said.

"Thank you for calling, Arthur. I'm going to suggest to the police that they speak with you. I'm sure you can understand."

Miserable, Arthur said, "Yes ma'am. Good night." He hung up and left the kitchen.

As he passed the entrance to the living room, Aunt Esther looked up from her crocheting. "What's the trouble, Arthur?"

"There's a problem," he said, and sat down. Esther put down her crocheting.

ii

The police interviewed Arthur the next day. A check of bank records showed that Dick had cashed his paycheck the night he disappeared. He had also cleaned out his and Wilma's checking account—a little over a hundred dollars—for good measure. Finally, a Crosby student reported seeing Dick sitting in his car across the street from the main entrance to the school shortly after lunch the day Jeanette disappeared. That was the last sighting of either of them the police were able to pinpoint.

The Belfast police sent a description of the duo and car to all the New England state police departments. A brief article about the disappearance appeared in the *Republican Journal* the next week. However, Jeanette and Dick were both of age, and as the week following the disappearance stretched into two, then three, then into a month, the trail became as cold as the story. By Thanksgiving, the pair's disappearance was no longer a topic of conversation even at Crosby.

"Good riddance to bad rubbish," Aunt Esther said, the last time Arthur mentioned the disappearance. "Leaving his wife and baby for that little tart."

"Wilma and Justin have moved back in with her family," Arthur said. "They'll be all right."

"Thank goodness for that."

"Aunt Esther, why do you think they ran off?"

Aunt Esther scoffed. "You know the answer to that, Arthur."

He smiled. "Guess I do."

"Not to put too fine a point on it," Aunt Esther said, "you young men would do well to keep your pants zipped around the girls."

"Aunt Esther!" Arthur blushed—recent meetings with Sharon had come to mind—but he grinned at the same time.

In spite of herself, she grinned at him, and even blushed a little herself. "I'm sorry, Arthur. Didn't mean to be crude."

Arthur smiled and chuckled. "That's all right," he said. He went back to his homework.

iii

It was too cold now for Arthur and Sharon to carry out their trysts outside, so they had to meet on the infrequent occasions when her parents or Aunt Esther were away. And, after almost getting caught at Sharon's house one evening in early December, both realized some other arrangements would have to be made.

This is when Sharon hit upon the idea of using Betty's place in Orono.

"Hi guys," Betty said, opening the door the following Saturday. She looked great, Arthur thought. Her hair had gotten very long since he had last seen her, to her waist now, and she had slimmed down almost to the size of her sister. She wore tight blue jeans and a long-sleeved, form-fitting brown knit top that left little to the imagination. Arthur tried not to notice.

"Hi, ducks," Sharon said, kissing Betty on the cheek. "Thanks for letting us come over."

"Sure," Betty said. They came inside. "Have a seat. I'll get us some drinks." She disappeared into the kitchen, and Arthur and Sharon sat on the sofa.

Arthur looked around absently: brick and board shelves with books and records. Posters covered the walls—Peter, Paul and Mary, Dylan, The Byrds. Betty returned with the drinks.

Arthur sipped his DP, then noticed a letter sitting on the end table. He could tell from the handwriting that it was from Stuart.

"Yes, Stuart writes to me," she said, noticing where Arthur's attention had turned.

"Sorry. Didn't mean to snoop."

"That's all right, don't worry about it. He's doing okay, he says. Says he's got orders for Vietnam. Leaves after the New Year. Wants me to come down to visit him over Christmas." She snorted. "Sure, like I'm going to spend Christmas break visiting Fort fucking Benning."

Arthur smiled. "Guess he hasn't given up on you yet."

"He should. If he thinks I'm interested in getting involved now, with him *wanting* to go to Vietnam, he's even crazier than I thought. He's basically being used. He's in favor of everything I'm opposed to. I can't abide it."

"Seems to me he's just a guy who loves his country, Betty. And loves you too, it sounds like."

"Loves his country," she sneered. "What's to love? Genocide, slavery, raping the environment? Fuck that. And as for loving me, well, I'm not interested, thank you very much. Besides, I've gotten involved with someone else anyway."

"Ohhh, how interesting," Sharon said. "And who might that be?"

Betty smiled. "An instructor in the philosophy department. He just finished grad school and is joining the faculty next semester."

"You're dating a *teacher?*" Sharon said.

Betty laughed. "Shar', this is college, not high school. Jeez. Besides, Mark's not a teacher. He's an *instructor*. Tenure track. Anyway, I met him at a teach-in right after school started. He's very angry about the war and he's trying to organize the students into resisting the draft. There's millions of us, he says, and if we all refuse induction, who're they going to get to do the fighting? Factory workers and day laborers?" She scoffed. "Farm boys? Sure, they'll really take care of things over there." Betty sat down and smiled at them, sipping her drink. "Mark is so committed. I'll introduce you to him sometime. So," she said, "what brings you two to visit?"

Sharon smiled. "Arthur and I were wondering if we could...drop by once in a while. Say, on weekends. Maybe after school sometimes."

"You can drop by any time you want, Shar'. You know that."

Sharon tried again. "Mom's usually home in the afternoons, and so's Arthur's aunt, and it's too cold to spend any time outside, and..."

"Oh!" Betty said. She smiled broadly, finally getting it. "My, my, little sister's all grown up. Who'd have ever believed it?"

"We really appreciate it," Arthur said, blushing.

"No problem. *Preach.*" Betty was clearly enjoying his embarrassment. She sipped her drink again. "Would the two of you be wanting some privacy...like now?"

Sharon smiled, and Arthur blushed. "The thought had occurred to us," he allowed. Sharon took Arthur's hand.

Betty chuckled, looked at her wristwatch and stood. "My, just look at the time. I've got to go meet a friend. I'll be gone for...oh, at least an hour. A good hour." She pulled on a wool sweater, then put on her coat, hat and gloves. "If you leave before I get back, just pull the door shut. It locks automatically. And don't worry about my roommates. They went to Boston for the weekend." She kissed Sharon on the cheek. "Have fun!" and she was gone.

"See?" Sharon said. "I told you it would be all right."

Arthur grinned and reached for her. "Come here, you saucy wench. I've got a surprise for you."

"Oh! You nasty boy, stop!" Sharon giggled, and pretended to try to escape, but he caught her and carried her, struggling prettily, into Betty's bedroom and shut the door.

The DP sat unfinished, next to Stuart's letter on the end table.

iv

They left Betty's apartment later that afternoon. "I love you," Sharon said, squeezing his arm and pressing the side of her head against his shoulder as they crossed the street to Arthur's car.

"Want to get a soda before we head home?" Arthur said, gesturing to a luncheonette on the corner. Sharon nodded.

After they were seated and had ordered, Sharon said, "Arthur, can I ask you something?"

"Of course."

She leaned forward and whispered, "Do you know you never say you love me?"

"I hadn't noticed." *Best be careful here,* he told himself.

"Well? Do you?"

"Sure, Shar', I love you. I guess." He added hastily, "No, not 'guess'. I know. I love you. Absolutely." Arthur nodded vigorously.

Sharon was silent a moment, then leaned back. "Okay," she said. "I just wanted to make sure."

"Why?"

"Why? Arthur, I love you so much. If something bad happened or..."

"Hey, don't worry. It's all right. Nothing bad is going to happen."

"Arthur, do you think we…we might get married?"
He must have looked shocked, because she added hastily,
"I don't mean right now. Or even next year. But someday.
Do you think?"

"Well…" Arthur stopped and thought for a moment.
"I guess we might. Someday. We're awfully young now
though, aren't we? I mean, we haven't even finished high
school yet and…"

"I know, I didn't mean—"

"I understand. But do you want to end up like Dick
and Wilma?"

She laughed. "Oh of course not, silly. I was just
trying to see where…how we were going to end up, is all.
I've been thinking about it a lot lately." She smiled again.
"I do love you, you know."

"I know," he said, trying to keep the impatience from
his voice. *She told him that constantly.*

He glanced up as the door to the luncheonette opened.
He smiled. "Hey, look, it's Clement."

"Great," Sharon whispered, rolling her eyes.

Clement and a man who looked to be in his twenties
came in, talking and laughing together. Then Clement
noticed Arthur, and he stopped laughing.

Arthur waved.

Clement hesitated a fraction of a second, then
shrugged and came over. His friend followed, staying
behind him. "Hey man," Clement said. He did not sit down
in the booth. "We just came in for a Coke. Can't really
stay." He nodded at Sharon.

"Oh." Arthur smiled at Clement's friend. "I'm Arthur
West. Friend of Clement's."

"Hello, Arthur," the man said. "I'm Ted Crockett."
Ted offered his hand, which Arthur took. Ted had bleached
a lock of his hair.

"So do you go to school here?"

"Yes. I'm a design major. In the fine arts school."

218

"What do you design?"

Ted laughed. "Well—all kinds of things, actually. I'm concentrating on furniture right now."

"Ted's trying to get me to come to college here next fall," Clement said. "Says I've got real talent."

"Really?" Arthur said. "I didn't know."

"Clement's eye for composition and line and the relationship of forms is phenomenal," Ted said. "He'd do very well here."

Silence followed.

"Preach, I've got to go," Clement said. "Good to see you again. I'll call you later."

"Sure, Clement. See you around. Nice meeting you, Ted."

"Likewise," Ted said. They left the luncheonette.

"Lord help us," Sharon said, distaste evident in her tone. "That Ted guy's a queer, betcha ten bucks."

Arthur said, "Now just how did you come to that conclusion? Seemed okay to me. Just artsy, is all."

Sharon looked at Arthur in disbelief. "Seriously? Trust me. We girls are more attuned to these things than guys are." She leaned forward, whispered, "But doesn't it make you kind of wonder about Clement?"

"Now that's enough," he snapped. "I know you don't like him, but there's no need to get nasty about it like that." *First Hag, now Sharon,* Arthur thought.

Sharon looked at him as if he'd struck her, then lowered her eyes. "I'm sorry, Arthur," she whispered.

Exasperated but trying not to show it, Arthur reached across the table and took her hand. Gently, he said, "It's all right. I'm sorry. Shouldn't have snapped at you."

She nodded. "I'm sorry I upset you," she said quietly.

They paid for their sodas and left a few minutes later.

. . .

CHAPTER 23
i

Waldo County, Maine
December 1966

Arthur arrived at the FoodMart at 7:30 the following Monday morning. As he went through the store's opening routine, he found himself thinking about Clement.

Was Sharon right? Was Clement a queer? That was the big question, of course. And Hag had also raised the issue. It had never occurred to him before, but now that he considered it, he had to admit their assessments were not unreasonable. First, Arthur realized that Clement, now seventeen, had never been on a date with a girl, or had ever even mentioned being attracted to one.

But this Ted guy was something else, Arthur told himself. Did Sharon have him pegged correctly? A "design" major, rich, dyed blonde hair, hanging out with Clement who was several years younger, trying to get Clement to come to the university…

Because he's talented or…

Was any of this conclusive? Of course not, and Arthur found himself feeling a little embarrassed. What business was it of his what Clement did, anyway? He'd known Clement since they were little kids. Even if he *was* queer, did that really make any difference?

After thinking about it a bit, Arthur decided that, while maybe it should have…*it didn't.* Clement was his friend, and that was what mattered. Arthur shrugged, and went back to work.

When his preparations for the next day were finished, he tidied up and then looked at his watch. 8:30. Laverdiere was usually in by now. But he no longer had any illusions about his boss.

It had become an open question about when Laverdiere would arrive. And beyond that, he had been acting more and more weird lately; he hadn't seemed right for months.

The bottle of Southern Comfort had become a common fixture in the office, and he had sure been taking a lot of sick days lately. More than once Arthur had had to man the store by himself. Clearly, something more was going on than the breakup with LaVerne.

It suddenly dawned on him that the store was not as busy as it used to be. When he first started working there, he never would have been able to run things by himself; there were just too many customers. When he started, there was Laverdiere, Nelson, LaVerne, and himself.

Now, there were days when he was here alone, and rarely on those days did he have too many customers to handle efficiently. Of course, this meant sales must have dropped off...and Arthur suddenly had an insight that he realized had been percolating for months.

Laverdiere was in trouble with regional.

This led Arthur to another, even more troubling thought. Did that mean he, Arthur, was also in trouble? At this disquieting idea, Arthur checked his watch. Eleven 'til nine, and he realized he probably was going to have another day running the place by himself. He sighed, and went into the back room to punch in. He turned on the light.

He stopped and stared, his jaw dropping open.

Laverdiere, his office door open, was slumped in his chair. His head was a mess. The chair was covered with blood, the pistol he had used to shoot himself on the floor below his right hand. An almost empty bottle of Southern Comfort, a mute sentinel, was on the desk.

Arthur took a couple of steps toward Laverdiere, but then stopped. His heart was pounding, but he was outwardly calm.

Probably shouldn't touch anything, he thought. *But what...?*

Then he knew.

Call the cops.

ii

The Searsport police, including the chief and Loudermilk, had shown up within minutes of his call. After a brief investigation—interviewing Arthur and looking around—the chief called the county coroner. The body was zipped into a large black plastic bag, loaded on a gurney, and taken to the morgue at County General. Loudermilk was then dispatched to inform Laverdiere's family.

Once the chief finished questioning Arthur about what he knew, Arthur realized he had probably better call the FoodMart state office in Augusta. He found the weekend number in Laverdiere's Rolodex and called, being careful to avoid the blood on the desk and floor. The state manager, Mr. Forrest, was at the store in a little over an hour.

Arthur sat in the storeroom and watched Forrest talk with the police outside Laverdiere's office. A couple of times Forrest turned and looked at Arthur—making him profoundly nervous, he had to admit—then turned back.

Finally, they finished talking. The police left except for the cleanup team, and Forrest walked over to Arthur. He offered his hand. "Arthur, I want to thank you for your presence of mind in this awful situation. You did very well, and we in the FoodMart family are fortunate to have a young man like you as part of it. People who keep calm and don't panic in emergencies are always valuable."

"Just did what anyone would have done, sir."

Forrest smiled. "No, you didn't, Arthur, trust me on this one. You kept your head and did just the right thing. That quality is rare. Some people would have run out of the store screaming. Look, I'd like to get your perspective on this thing. Let's go get a Coke."

"Maybe a Doctor Pepper?"

Forrest smiled. "I think I can manage a Doctor Pepper." They walked down the street to Jordan's.

iii

"Arthur," Forrest said once the drinks had arrived, "have you given any thought to your future?"

"I guess," Arthur said. "You know. Some."

"Have you made any decisions?"

"I graduate from high school in June. Mr. Laverdi—" He stopped. "Sorry. Seems awkward to talk about him."

"That's all right," Forrest said.

"Mr. Laverdiere had been talking about making me an assistant manager. I was definitely interested in that. I've got a girlfriend and we're pretty serious. Maybe even marrying serious, you know? Being an assistant manager right out of high school would be a good start, don't you think?"

"Any thought about college?"

He shook his head. "I don't think it's for me, Mr. Forrest. I'm no college boy. Besides, I like working at the FoodMart. And if I'm gonna get married I'll need to support my wife. Can't ask her to marry me if I don't have a job."

"I see." Forrest sipped his cup of coffee. "How are your grades at school?"

"Decent," Arthur said. "B's, mostly. Sometimes an A or two creeps in there." He smiled. "But sometimes a C or two does, too."

"Honor roll?"

"A coupla times." He smiled. "Trig's getting the best of me this quarter, though."

Forrest laughed. "Trig was tough for me, too." He leaned forward. "Arthur, I'm glad to hear Mr. Laverdiere was considering making you assistant manager. I think in this, at least, he made a wise decision."

"Thank you, sir."

"However."

Arthur stood. "It's all right," he said. "I understand. Clean sweep and all that. Do you have a pen? I'll give you my address and you can send me my last pay—"

Forrest laughed. "Please, sit down, Arthur. I'm not going to let you go."

"Oh." Arthur sat down.

"In fact, quite the opposite. I have a proposition for you. After you've heard what I have to say, I'd like you to go home and discuss it with your folks."

"Actually, Mr. Forrest, I live with my aunt in Belfast. My mother and father are both deceased."

"Oh my Lord, I'm sorry," Mr. Forrest said.

"It's all right," Arthur said. "It was a long time ago."

Forrest nodded. "Well, my sympathies anyway. At any rate, Arthur, here's my proposition. How would you like to be an assistant manager right now, and the manager of this store the day you graduate from high school?"

Arthur grinned broadly. "I—I—Mr. Forrest, are you serious?"

"I am."

"But I'm not even eighteen yet."

"I know, but you will be when you graduate, right?"

Arthur nodded.

"Okay then. Arthur, you're an impressive young man. There's always a place at FoodMart for people who know what they're doing. What do you say?"

"What sort of salary could I expect?"

"Well, you'd be part time until June, of course, and we'd bring in a manager to give you some on-the-job training and help you run the place until you graduate." But then Forrest mentioned a figure.

"Wow," Arthur said. "Nine thousand a year?"

"That's your full time pay, of course," Forrest continued, "but we'd pay you at an equivalent hourly rate till June. Plus profit sharing, once you're full time. We also offer two weeks' vacation—paid, of course—and a health care plan. Just what you need if you're thinking about getting married. A two-week honeymoon, wouldn't that be nice? And health care afterward, to take care of your wife and any little ones that may happen to come along."

Arthur smiled broadly. "Boy, Mr. Forrest. I hardly know what to say. That's very generous. I do have a question, though?"

"Yes?"

"What about Mr. Laverdiere? I feel kind of bad about...just moving in and all. So soon. I mean..."

"I understand. Look, Arthur, about Mr. Laverdiere. It had become a difficult situation." Forrest sighed. "I probably shouldn't be telling you this but...well, you have a right to know, I guess. I'll rely on your discretion."

Arthur nodded. "Of course."

"Arthur, he was probably going to be fired. Things were not going well at the store. You must have been aware?"

"It had occurred to me."

"We'd received complaints. Not opening on time. Closing early. Hard to get waited on. Spoiled chicken. It was not a pretty picture. Of course, sales had dropped off as a result. But even more disturbing, in recent months, some discrepancies in the books have appeared. Thousands of dollars are just...missing. We had just told him we were sending in a team of auditors and for him to have all records available for the past year."

"Maybe that's why he...did it?" Arthur asked. Suddenly it all made sense. *The new procedures for handling cash. How he paid for the new Mustang for Laverne. The strange telephone calls.*

Forrest nodded. "That's a fair conclusion, yes. How long had he been drinking on the job?"

Arthur was caught off guard by the question, but knew not to dissemble. "Several months, I guess. Look, Mr. Forrest, there were some pretty tough things going on in his life. The drinking was only part of it. And the phone calls from Mr. Mancuso must have upset him. I hope you won't get into all this with Mrs. Laverdiere?"

"No, of course not, Arthur. I'll make sure she and the children get his company insurance policy. I just wanted to make sure you knew the situation, is all." Then Forrest said, "But, who is this Mancuso person you mentioned?"

"The man from corporate in Boston who called him. Several times. Was he part of the auditing team?"

Forrest took out his notebook. "Tell me about Mancuso."

Arthur did so.

Forrest put away his notebook when Arthur finished. "Thank you for mentioning this," he said. "Arthur, I have no idea who Paul Mancuso is, but I can assure you, we are going to check this out."

Forrest finished his cup of coffee, put a two-dollar bill on the table, and stood. "Arthur, you have a bright future with us, if you want it. You take a week off and think about what I've said. It's a big decision. Then call me and let me know what you want to do. I'll respect whatever you decide." He handed Arthur his card.

"Thank you, sir. I'll let you know."

iv

All the local stations covered Laverdiere's suicide—any sort of violent death was rare in the county—but it was not until a few days later that a possible motive became public.

Laverdiere had been embezzling money from the Searsport store. Then, in a desperate effort to recoup the funds he had stolen, he had begun gambling. However, he did not do well, and lost even more money. This led to borrowing from a Boston loan shark, which led to even more money being embezzled to pay that debt.

The story closed with Mr. Forrest assuring everyone that the Searsport store was back in business. "We have a new management team taking over this coming Monday, and we expect no further problems. I hope all our customers will continue to enjoy the extra value and extra savings that come with being a part of the FoodMart family."

Arthur began as assistant manager ten days later.

.　　.　　.

DREAM

The company slogged on through the paddies, keeping well away from the roads now, until finally reaching a thin band of jungle and undergrowth. As Mike platoon reached the trees, the company turned right and paralleled the woodline.

When Lima platoon reached the woods, LT signaled for them to halt, Arthur watching as the rest of the company moved further down the woodline. The ground inside it was slightly higher than the surrounding paddies, and appeared to be dry, mostly. LT called the squad leaders to the CP.

"We're halting here for the rest of the afternoon," *he said. "Get your squads into the woods and dry out. Relax, eat some chow. Be ready to move at dusk. Brigade thinks the gooks are using the river here to move around at night. So, we're setting up platoon-sized ambushes all along it, about five hundred meters apart."*

Arthur, Brown, and Garcia nodded. Then Brown asked, "LT, you think Blue Berry'll make it?"

"Probably," LT said. "He was alive when they loaded him on the dustoff. That's a good sign. Most guys who get on the dustoff alive make it." He cut it off. "Okay, back to your squads. And try to catch some Z's now. Might be a long night."

At dusk the platoon moved into the site, the only dry spot on this side of the river within five hundred meters big enough to hold the whole platoon.

Arthur's squad, along with Garcia's machine guns, had the kill zone along the murky river, thirty feet across and placidly flowing from the left. Thick brush lined the opposite bank. LT, Thrasher, and the rest of the platoon CP set up about five meters behind the kill zone. Sergeant Brown's squad, on rear security, set up just inside the back woodline, facing back across the paddies where they had labored so hard earlier that day.

Arthur's squad set up in two holes, with he, Pappy and Turnip in the hole to the left. Lurch, Bear and Nose were in the hole to Arthur's right. Garcia and his machine gun crews flanked both of Arthur's squad holes. The holes were about five yards apart.

Although the ground was dry on the surface, digging adequate fighting positions proved difficult. They struck water a mere twelve inches down, and the deeper they dug the more water accumulated. Soon giving up, they resorted to scraping up earth from around the holes and piling it in front of their positions, tamping it down with their entrenching tools. A few of the men stripped branches off the trees and put them in the bottom of the holes, giving them something other than mud beneath their feet.

The men put their claymores out along the very edge of the river, at first aiming them toward the thick brush on the opposite bank. Arthur put a stop to this; he told them to aim them at the surface of the river. "The river's the kill zone, not those bushes," he said.

Once the claymores were properly aimed, they placed the mines' firing mechanisms on the berms in front of the foxholes, taking care to place them in the same order from left to right as the mines themselves. Finally, they placed their rifles and grenades on the berms.

As darkness fell, the rain continued and the men settled down for the long night ahead. Formal watches had begun at 2100 hundred, as usual.

Arthur always took first watch, so at 2230 he handed the radio handset off to Pappy and then quietly crawled to a spot just behind the fighting position. He was off for the next three hours, and he prepared to make the most of it. He sat on his poncho liner and took off his boots and rubbed the dampness off his feet, allowing the night air to complete the drying, then put his boots back on. He placed his helmet on its side at one end of the poncho liner and lay down, his head resting in it. He pulled the poncho liner over him and sighed deeply, finally comfortable. In moments he was dropping off.

Something scampered across his feet.

Arthur instantly sat up. He looked around. Nothing. Had he imagined it?

No way.

He sat listening for a couple more minutes, then lay back down again. Again, he started to drift off.

It happened again.

This time, Arthur opened his eyes, but did not move.

There. Again he felt tiny feet scampering over his legs, and this time heard the sound of little claws skittering over the nylon of the liner.

Arthur pulled the poncho liner tightly around him, tucking it in around his feet at the bottom and pulling it over his head. He made sure he was thoroughly sealed inside a poncho liner cocoon, then lay still, waiting. A few moments later, another rat scurried over him, but made no effort to get inside the poncho liner or otherwise disturb him.

Arthur began to relax. They're just passin' through. Don't mean nothin'. Too tired to worry about it.

Blood warm rain continued to fall.

PART VII: THE ROAD
CHAPTER 24
i

Wells, Nevada
October 8, 1969

The freight pulled out of the Reno yards and clattered eastward across the Great Basin. Arthur wore his jacket and two shirts and wrapped himself in Chevrolet's blanket against the rushing wind. Once out of the yards, it had gotten cold quickly and the steel boxcar he had boarded did not make it any warmer.

He tried to sleep, taking care to lie with his feet toward the front of the train. Chevrolet had given him this piece of wisdom about freight-hopping their first night out. "If you sleep wrong-end to, a full-out emergency stop could kill ya," Chevrolet had told him. "Train'll stop but you won't. You slam head first into the end of a boxcar one time and see if you don't get one hell of a headache."

Arthur smiled. He missed Chevy already.

The night wore on, the emptiness of the desert implied by the mountains on the horizon—a jagged line, with clouds of stars above but only blackness below.

Arthur's luck ran out shortly after he fell asleep at dawn.

ii

"Rise and shine, asshole!"

The phrase hit his consciousness as a boot cracked into his ribs. Arthur gasped and tried to jump to his feet, but a second kick sent him sprawling.

Arthur rolled over and looked up. Two large men in tan uniforms holding clubs stood over him. The train was stopped, he had no idea where. He could see a few small buildings through the open boxcar door.

"Now just what in the *hell* are you doin' on my train, boy?" one of them said. The bull was bald as a parsnip.

"Ridin'," Arthur panted, clutching his side.

"Not anymore," Baldy said. "Not on this train, anyway."

"Okay okay, I'm gone." Arthur sat up and reached for his duffel. He started to move toward the open boxcar door, but Baldy pushed him back down again.

"Who *told* you to get up?" he barked.

Arthur said, "Listen, guys, we can work something out, can't we?"

The bulls said nothing, but Arthur thought he detected a glimmer of interest.

Arthur continued, "I've got a little bread on me. Would a ten spot buy me a ride to the end of the division?"

The bulls looked at each other and Baldy began to laugh. "A ten spot won't buy you the sweat off my balls!"

"Ten apiece?"

No answer.

"That's all I got, guys. Really."

The bulls looked at each other again. "Show me," Baldy said. "And don't try nothin'."

Arthur nodded. "You got it. The money's here," he said, gesturing to his left front pants pocket. "I'll get it now."

"Nice and slow," Baldy said.

Arthur reached in and withdrew the money. He had lied, of course; he had stashed most of his money in his jungle boot, at Chevy's suggestion.

He withdrew the money and showed it. "See? Like I said. There's twenty bucks here. Take it all."

Baldy took it. The train began to move.

"So what do you think?" the other bull said to Baldy. "That enough to get him a ride to Salt Lake City?"

"Nah," Baldy said. "He pisses me off, just lookin' at him."

Arthur started to worry seriously now. The bulls meant to wait until the train was moving at full speed, and then make him jump.

But the other bull was getting nervous. "Joey, we're getting up to speed. We need to toss him. Like *now,* you know? I ain't about to kill nobody."

"We got time," Joey said.

Arthur said hastily, "Look, Joey, I might be able to find a little more cash if you let me check out my bindle." He leaned for it, picked it up and stood. "Now, let's see—"

He threw the bindle at Joey and darted for the boxcar door.

"Why, you little—" the other bull swung his billy. Arthur managed to dodge it, but then Joey swung a backhand toward his head. Arthur dodged again but not as effectively; Joey's billy caught Arthur's shoulder and he yelled and fell to his knees.

Oh God I'm gonna die, he thought. *Is this how it ends?*

Then he felt huge hands grabbing him and then he was flying and yelling all at once. He landed on the gravel beside the track, the wind bursting out of him at the impact, and he rolled, gasping, down the embankment, slamming to a halt against a pile of gravel. His bindle followed a moment later, landing with a thud thirty yards further up the track.

Arthur gasped for breath, tried to stand but could only reach his knees.

Joey was yelling, shaking his fist. *"BETTER NOT CATCH YOU..."*

His words became inaudible, and Arthur gave him the finger as the train sped away.

When the train had disappeared, Arthur sat down on the pile of pebbles and caught his breath, then checked himself for injuries. He had picked up a few scrapes and his knee hurt a little, but he was okay. He knew he had been lucky. If the train had been going much faster, he might have been seriously hurt. He shivered.

Could have greased the tracks.

He limped up the tracks to his bindle. He opened it and inspected. All his stuff was okay, including his jug of water, sufficiently padded by his clothing to have survived the impact.

He took a sip of the water and looked around.

There was nothing but desert and sagebrush to the north, shimmering as the desolation disappeared in the distance. Low barren hills were to the east and south. But the town was just to the southwest, about a quarter mile away.

iii

A few minutes later, he stood at the corner of Humboldt Avenue and Seventh, in what a water tower indicated was Wells, Nevada, "GATEWAY TO THE WEST!" He had no idea where Wells was in relation to anywhere else, except that it must be a good ways east of Reno.

He found a small coffee shop on Sixth and ordered breakfast. "Passing through?" the waitress asked when she brought him his order.

"Ayuh," Arthur said, buttering a piece of toast. "Is there a place where I could get a map?"

"What are you looking for?"

"A major highway, headed east."

"You don't need a map for that. Sixth turns into US 40 outside of town. That goes east." She gestured down the street. "Leastwise as far as Pequop. Not that I've ever been there. And the interstate's about a mile south of here. I-80. Goes all the way to New York, I hear." She smiled bitterly. "Never been there, either."

Arthur got picked up two hours later at Highway 40.

iv

"We always pick up hitchhikers, man," the driver said. His shoulder-length black hair was parted in the middle, and tied back with a red bandanna. He wore jeans and a red-checkered flannel shirt, unbuttoned, tail out. He was tanned and barefoot. "Life's like a circle, you know? Someday I'll need a ride and the karma'll come back."

The panel van was a white Ford Econoline. The driver and a young, slightly plump but very pretty Asian woman with thick, lustrous hair occupied the only two seats.

Arthur quickly focused on the people around him, seated on the floor in the back of the van.

Amidst bags, boxes, and bedrolls, plus an electric guitar, amp and a bag of cables, were four people—a young, scowling woman with a baby at her breast, and a boy about ten years old, sitting next to the most beautiful woman he had ever seen.

She was older than the others—well into her thirties—and elegant, with classic features, huge jade eyes that threatened to drown him, and perfect skin the color of cream tinted with just a little coffee. Her auburn hair was worn in a French braid. Her skirt was ankle-length; her feet were bare, smooth and lovely. The only flaw he saw was a tiny scab on her upper lip, which only made the rest of her all the more perfect.

She smiled at him, perfect teeth behind almost perfect lips, and Arthur smiled back, embarrassed, then tore his eyes away with difficulty. "Well, I appreciate it, man," he said, sitting on his bindle and returning his attention to the driver. "Where you headed?" He resisted the urge to look at the woman again. *What was she doing with these people?*

"Utah, at the moment," the man said. "Lookin' for that perfect spot, you know? We'll know it when we find it."

"Cool," Arthur said. "Thanks for picking me up. I was waiting there for like an hour. I'm Art. People call me Preach."

"Name's Freddie," the driver said. He gestured to the Asian woman. "This here's Laurel. She's my girlfriend." Laurel nodded absently. "In the back's Brenda, Eric—that's the kid—and Sarah and Brig, the little one."

Brenda, the beauty, smiled. Sarah just scowled.

"Hi," Arthur said, grateful for the excuse to look at her again. "I'm Preach."

"So you said," Brenda said. She smiled again, bemused. "Eric is my son."

Eric grinned evilly. He wore a bandana, tied as a headband around his unkempt, blonde hair. "I got a pocketknife," he said.

"Cool," Arthur said.

"Want to see?" Eric said, eyes gleaming. "It's really sharp."

"That's okay," Arthur said.

"Quit botherin' the man, Eric," Laurel said.

"I'm not botherin' him, Aunt Laurie," Eric said. He turned to Arthur. "Am I botherin' you, mister?"

"It's all right," Arthur said, smiling. "Just don't need to see your pocketknife. And you shouldn't take it out unless you need to use it."

Brenda mouthed a *thank you* to him. "Eric, you heard Preach now," she said.

"You never let me have any fun," Eric said.

"Hush now," Brenda said. "Just hush." She glanced at Arthur, devastating him with a smile and a delicately arched eyebrow. "I'm sorry. Eric forgets his manners."

"That's—uh—all right," he stammered.

"Are you a preacher?" Eric asked.

"No," Arthur said. "It's just a nickname."

"How'd you get it?"

"That's what they called me when I was a kid." Arthur turned to the breast-feeding woman. "You must be Sarah."

Sarah glared at him, saying nothing. She finally nodded. Brig stirred a little as he suckled. Arthur smiled uncertainly.

Ooooookay.

Brenda smiled again. "Sarah," she said. "The man's just being nice."

"Look at his eye," Sarah said, continuing to glare. "He doesn't look very nice to me."

Good grief. "I got mugged in San Francisco a few days ago," Arthur said. "Some guys jumped me in Golden Gate Park. Gave me a black eye. Robbed me."

"If you say so," Sarah said.

"Bummer," Freddie said. "You okay now?"

"Mostly."

Laurel turned around. "Do you have any grass?" she asked. "We're dying for some grass."

"Nope, sorry. No grass."

"Shit." Laurel looked at Freddie. "Freddie, you've got to get us some grass. We ran out like two days ago."

"I know, babe," he said. "We'll be in Salt Lake City in the morning."

"In the morning?" Laurel said. "But Salt Lake City's only like three hours away, tops!"

"It's gonna be dark soon," Freddie said. "I don't want to be wandering around a strange city trying to score at night. We can wait til morning. There's a campground up ahead. Anyway, if we can't score there in the morning, we can go to Provo. There's a university there. Gotta be some heads, even if most of them are Mormons," he laughed.

"I hope so," Laurel said. "I'm dyin' here."

"Freddie, I gotta pee," Eric announced.

"Oh, for God's sake," Sarah said.

"Jesus, Eric!" Freddie said. "You had your chance in Wells, man. Why didn't you go when we gassed up?"

"Freddie, you know how kids are," Brenda said. "Maybe we can pull over somewhere?"

"He's just going to have to wait," Freddie said. "You hear me, Eric? You gotta wait, man."

"I gotta go!" Eric said. "Fred-deeee, I gotta *go!*"

"Shhh, Eric," Brenda said.

A moment later, Laurel said quietly, "Really, Freddie, can't we stop by the side of the road or something? It won't take long."

Freddie continued to drive.

"Freddie?" Brenda said.

"Jee-zus," Freddie said, and began to slow down. He pulled over to the side of the road. There was nothing but sagebrush and sand in every direction. Freddie turned and surveyed the back of the van. "Does anyone else have to take a leak?" He looked at each of them in turn. "Last chance. Come on, speak up now."

No one said anything.

"All right then," Freddie finally said. "Eric, get out there and pee, man. And hurry up."

Eric jumped out the back of the van and headed for a clump of sagebrush a few feet off the shoulder.

Freddie, muttering, pulled a pack of Winstons out of his shirt pocket and lit up, drumming his fingers on the steering wheel. Laurel turned on the radio and found some music.

Eric hopped back in the van. "Okay, I'm done," he said.

"Finally," Freddie said. He put the van in gear, gunned the engine and pulled back onto the empty highway.

Arthur said, "So where are you guys headed in Utah?"

"I dunno. I've heard about a place south of Provo, off US 6. Near Price. We can ask about it tomorrow when we score some grass."

"They just better have some," Laurel said. "I'm not stayin' someplace where no one tokes up. I mean, get real."

A few minutes later, Arthur saw a young black man up ahead, carrying a backpack, thumb out. He held a cardboard sign reading "SLC." Arthur said, "Uh oh, looks like another hitch-hiker."

Freddie snorted, accelerating. "I ain't givin' a ride to a nigger," Freddie said.

Arthur, stunned, said nothing. He had not expected this. He looked around. Brenda caught his eye, rolled her eyes, and shook her head in disgust.

Arthur had never met a black person until he joined the army, they being almost nonexistent in Maine. And he had seen racism in the army, of course, where he had first heard the word *nigger,* muttered occasionally by an acquaintance or two. So it was jarring and even uncomfortable to hear the word used here, especially by someone unexpected.

But, Arthur put aside his vague feelings of discomfort. He thought a moment about saying something, but he needed the ride. *Just avoid talking about it,* he told himself.

Everyday People began on the radio.

By this time, Brig had fallen asleep. Sarah gently detached him, and slipped her breast back inside her shift. She glared at Arthur again. "What're you looking at?"

Arthur blushed. "Sorry. Didn't mean to stare."

"You never seen someone breastfeed a baby before?"

"Sure. Just not lately."

His affirmative answer caught her off guard. After a moment, she said, "Well, it's perfectly natural. You don't have to stare."

238

"Freddie?" Eric said.

"Now what?"

"I gotta go number two."

Freddie looked at Laurel, who started to giggle.

After a moment Freddie started to laugh too. "Of course you do, Eric. Of course you do, my man." He began looking for a place to pull over.

.   .   .

CHAPTER 25
i
Megiddo Ranch, Price, Utah
October 10, 1969

The man wore a straw cowboy hat and aviator shades. Jeans, a black t-shirt, black cowboy boots and a shotgun completed his outfit. He had begun walking toward the gate to the ranch the moment Freddie's van appeared on the horizon. The sign over the entrance said "MEGIDDO RANCH PRIVATE PROPERTY.

Freddie and Arthur got out of the van. "Mornin'," Freddie said, smiling.

"Something I can help you with?" the man said. He held the shotgun loosely in his right hand, barrel pointed mostly but not entirely at the ground. It was a Remington pump, seven shots.

We should have stayed in the van, Arthur thought.

"Umm... well... just passin' through," Freddie said. "We heard this was a good place. You know."

The man looked at him. "No, I don't know. You heard what?"

"Uhhh... a coupla chicks back in Provo. They sold us a lid. They told us this was a commune or somethin'. We might like it. We're looking for a place. You know."

"Uh huh," the man said. "Well, you boys best turn your van around and get on out of here."

"What?" Freddie said. "We can't—"

"Mom, I've gotta pee again!" Eric said. Arthur heard Brenda murmur something to him.

The man was now wary. "Wait—there's more of you in there?" he asked. "Kids? Women?"

Arthur said, "Yeah, but we're leaving, man, no worries. Come on Freddie, let's—"

Look," Freddie said. "Kid's gotta pee, and I do, too. Can't you give us like five minutes? Maybe let us fill up our water jugs?"

Brenda called from the back. "Freddie, what's going on? Is there a bathroom here?"

The man glanced at the sound of her voice. He seemed to think for a second, then said, "Okay. Come on out. I'll show you where the can is."

"Thanks, man, thanks," Freddie said. "Really. Damn kid does nothin' but piss." He opened the side doors. "Come on everybody, we're takin' a break." Brenda and Eric got out, followed by Laurel and then Sarah, clutching Brig to her breast.

The man looked the women over for a few seconds, eyes lingering a second or two on Brenda and Laurel.

In a swift movement, he swung the shotgun up. Arthur dove for the ground as the sound of the shotgun blast echoed off the van. The blast brought a gasp from Freddie and Sarah. Brig began to cry.

"Jeezus!" Arthur heard Freddie shout after a moment that lingered forever. "What'd you do *that* for?"

Arthur glanced up. The shotgun was pointed to the sky. Arthur stood, breathing deeply to calm his heart. The man smiled at him, grim satisfaction playing at the corners of his mouth as he pumped the shotgun, chambering another shell.

As Arthur brushed himself off, several things occurred. A second man holding a bolt action hunting rifle darted toward them from a large barn. Next, a group of young women ran into the yard from a single-story building near the barn. They stopped, stared, and began to whisper among themselves. Several more emerged from a two-story clapboard house across from the barn. Last, a shade in a front window of the house went up, stayed up several seconds, then lowered.

"What's going on, Tex?" the man from the barn said. He glanced at Arthur and the rest of the group. "Who are these people?"

"Just passin' through, Harold," Tex said. "They ain't stayin'. They want to use the shitter. Take 'em to the one in the barn. I'm gonna go tell Blue Hawk what's going on." Tex turned and started toward the ranch house.

"Who the fuck is Blue Hawk?" Freddie said.

"Don't worry about it," Harold said, grinning. He nodded to the women. "And don't mind Tex. He's a bit free and easy with the shotgun. He just wanted to get some help. I've been trying to convince Blue Hawk we need some walkie-talkies. Come on, I'll show ya where the can is." Harold started toward the barn, and after a moment, Brenda followed, Eric in tow. Freddie and Arthur and the rest followed. Most of the women who had run outside went back into the building.

After Arthur finished, he stepped outside and looked around. Harold was absently smoking a cigarette. "So how many people live here, man?" Arthur asked Harold.

"Some," Harold said, grinning lazily.

"Who were all those women? What are they doing here?"

"Never you mind right now," Harold said.

Arthur said nothing further.

Something isn't right.

Freddie and the others emerged from the barn as they finished.

Tex exited the ranch house and walked toward them, the shotgun slung over his shoulder now. "Okay, it's all cool," he said. "Blue Hawk's gonna let you stay tonight."

"Aaalll righty then," Harold said, laughing. "Let's get you folks settled in. Come on." Harold took them to the smaller of the two bunkhouses.

Several bunk beds occupied the otherwise empty room. Thin mattresses lay rolled up on bare springs at the end of each bunk. A picnic table sat in a corner.

"A bathroom and shower are in there," Harold pointed, indicating a door in the end of the bunkhouse. "Y'all hang loose. One of us'll be back in a bit." Harold left and Freddie began to unroll one of the mattresses. The others followed suit.

A few minutes later, Tex returned. "Blue Hawk wants to talk with you soon, but can't right now. He says a girl will bring food for you. Nothing fancy but..."

"When's he gonna want to see us?" Freddie asked.

"Maybe tomorrow." Tex left.

Laurel threw her backpack onto one of the lower bunks. "So, while we're waiting for His Majesty to see us, I'm going to take a shower." She looked at Freddie, sniffed in his direction and smiled. "You could use one too, babe." She winked.

Freddie laughed. "Okay," he said. He followed her into the bathroom and they shut the door, Laurel and then Freddie giggling as the door closed.

ii

A little before dusk, Arthur was sitting on the porch. Not only was it cooler there than inside; he also thought, for no particular reason he could put his finger on other than a vague sense of disquiet, that it was best that someone keep an eye out.

He watched a young woman approach from the house, carrying a cardboard box. She stopped in front of Arthur and smiled. "Blue Hawk told me to bring y'all some dinner."

"Thanks," Arthur said, smiling back at her. "We could use it." The girl, about his age, looked worn, although once she might have passed for pretty.

"Nothing fancy," the girl said. "Just vegetable stew and bread. Paper plates and plastic forks are in there, too."

"Thank you," Arthur said.

The girl went into the bunkhouse. Arthur listened to the sounds of the food being put out on the table. "Hey Preach, soup's on!" Freddie called out to him.

"I'll be in in a minute," Arthur called back.

A couple of minutes later, the girl emerged. Arthur smiled. "I'm Arthur. People call me Preach."

She ignored him and started back to the house, but then stopped and turned. She appraised him a moment. "I'm Susan."

"Nice to meet you."

Susan glanced around a moment. "So what's going on?" she asked quietly.

Arthur, puzzled, said, "Well, these people I'm with picked me up hitching in—"

"No," Susan said. "I mean, in the *world.*"

Arthur looked at her, confused.

"We have no TV, radio, newspapers. I've been here a year. I have no idea. I've tried to stay detached like Blue Hawk wants, but I can't help it. Please, can you tell me? Did Humphrey win the election?"

"What? No. Nixon did."

"Oh my God. Really?"

"Really."

"Fuck. Are we still in Vietnam?"

"Yes, but a few troops came home this summer. I think it might be starting to wind down. Did you hear about the moon landing?"

"Moon landing? Really? We landed on the *moon?*" Susan was clearly delighted.

"In July. You really have been out of touch, haven't you?"

She nodded. "Blue Hawk says it's best we keep away from the outside world. Corrupting." She smiled, looking around nervously. "But I can't help it. I'm curious." She laughed again. "The moon? For real?"

Arthur chuckled. "For real. There's movies and everything of them jumping around." He decided to plow ahead. "Now let me ask you—what's going on *here?*"

Susan became wary. "What do you mean?"

"I mean, how'd you end up here. Blue Hawk?"

"Oh, you don't want to hear about that."

"I do. Please."

Susan looked around, then lowered her voice. "Okay, but you have to promise not to tell anyone I told you."

"I promise."

Susan had met Blue Hawk a year ago, in the Haight. She had been sharing a crash pad with several other girls, doing and selling a lot of drugs-crank and PCP, beside the usual grass and acid—and panhandling to make rent. "I met him one afternoon in Golden Gate Park," Susan said. "You know Golden Gate Park?"

Arthur nodded. "I know Golden Gate Park."

Blue Hawk had seen her sitting by a pond. He had started talking, and she somehow knew, instantly, that this man was someone she should follow, especially when he told her he could give her what she needed. "And he was *right,*" she said, a gleam of certainty in her eye. Later, he told her he had been immediately drawn to her.

Blue Hawk was calm, she said, reassuring, a bit aloof but friendly, with deep eyes, but also with a depth of character, understanding, and wisdom she had never experienced before. "It was like—like—magic or something," she said. "He knew me. I mean, he like—*knew me.*"

Arthur nodded, trying to keep her talking.

She brought Blue Hawk back to the crash pad and he spent the night there, taking her gently but with power sometime in the night, when she awoke to find him next to her under her blanket, stroking her thigh, he hard and insistent, and she, after a moment, sleepily willing.

Unfortunately, in the morning, it became clear that the other girls had very different impressions of Blue Hawk. Each told her privately that she had to get him out of the place. *Immediately.*

"Well, I couldn't see it," Susan said, shaking her head. "I mean, they were all scared, but I didn't know what they were talking about. I still don't."

Susan took all this negativity as a sign that she should leave the crash pad, so, even though the other girls, alarmed, tried to talk her out of it, she packed her few belongings and followed Blue Hawk out to a beat up old Jeep. They drove all night, arriving at the ranch the next day.

"Okay," Arthur said. "So who owns the place? Blue Hawk?"

Susan laughed out loud. "Oh no, he doesn't own anything. He teaches us that possessions are the work of the devil. We need to detach from this life."

"So who does own it, then?"

"Well, there's this man named Wendell. He lives in the barn. He has a room there. It's nice, all fixed up."

Blue Hawk had met Wendell in the Summer of Love, in LA. Blue Hawk had apparently had the same effect on Wendell that he had had on Susan, as Wendell

245

soon invited Blue Hawk to move to the ranch. After a while, Blue Hawk began taking road trips to various western cities, almost always returning after a week or ten days with young women, although Tex and Harold had joined him just before Susan herself came. Wendell seemed not to mind.

"At least, he never said no," Susan said.

Then Harold appeared around the corner of the bunkhouse. Susan blanched. "Shouldn't you be getting back to the house, girl?" he said. It was not a suggestion.

"Yes, yes, I should." She stood and hurried off before Arthur could say anything more.

Harold watched her go, and then glanced at Arthur, grinning.

"You might want to be a little less curious, my friend." He walked back toward the house in the gloaming, leaving Arthur with much to mull over. He went inside to get some dinner.

"What was all that about?" Freddie asked. "Saw you talkin' with that girl."

"Oh nothin'. He winked at Freddie. "I was kinda puttin' the moves on her, you know."

Freddie laughed. "Any of that chow left?" Arthur asked.

There was. It was vegetarian. Bad vegetarian. There were lots of leftovers.

iii

After eating, Arthur cleaned up the supper remains and said, "Gonna get some fresh air." He stepped out onto the porch.

The warmth of the day still radiated from the adobe walls of the bunk house. But the glow of the sun was fading, and the evening was rapidly becoming cool. When the last of the sun disappeared, the night suddenly lit up, the dark punctured by uncountable pinpoints, filling the sky.

Even in Maine, the stars aren't like this.

Then he glanced at the barn.

After a moment, he walked toward it quietly.

As he approached he saw nothing out of the ordinary, just a dark building, with a rusting but still serviceable metal roof, and gray, old wood siding. Then, on the lower level, he noticed a soft light glowing from a window toward the rear. As he softly walked closer, he noticed that the window shade was drawn almost but not quite all the way down. Then he heard noises from inside. He stopped and listened intently.

Grunts, soft whispers, moans of what sounded almost like pain, bed springs creaking.

Knowing what he was likely to see, he carefully looked into the room through the inch or so of space between the window sill and the bottom of the shade.

An old man lay on a plain, uncovered mattress, two girls straddling him together, he impaling one while the two girls faced each other, tongues probing each other's mouths, the old man's face a strange mix of ecstasy and what could only be described as regret. The girl being impaled was Susan. The other shifted her hips back so the old man's face was between her thighs.

Arthur now knew what kept Wendell cooperative.

Appalled, but at the same time aroused, he backed away from the window and began quietly to retrace his steps across the yard, toward the bunkhouse. Halfway there, a voice said, "What are you doing out here?"

It was Tex, with his ever-present shotgun.

"Just out for a little fresh air," Arthur said, trying to sound as casual as possible. "It's hot in the bunkhouse. Cooler out here."

Tex nodded, appraising him.

Arthur said, "And lots of stars." He gestured upward.

"Okay," Tex said after a moment. "Best get back to the bunkhouse. It doesn't do to wander around here after dark. Coyotes."

"I hear that," Arthur said.

Tex started to walk away, then stopped. "Oh—I came to tell y'all that Blue Hawk wants to talk to you tomorrow. You, the other guy, and the kid and his mother. Not the baby's mother, the other one." Without waiting for an answer, Tex headed back to the main house.

Inside the bunkhouse, Brenda and Eric sat on their bunks near the door. Everyone else had settled down for the night. When Arthur sat down on his bunk, Brenda leaned forward, looking around to make sure she wasn't being noticed. She softly said, "We should talk soon." Arthur nodded.

.   .   .

CHAPTER 26
i
Megiddo Ranch, Price, Utah
October 12, 1969

Blue Hawk was a small, almost scrawny man, with a shock of dark long hair hanging low over his forehead. He sat on a cushion in the center of the furnitureless room, barefoot, wearing jeans and a light blue cotton work shirt. He was brown from the sun. Utterly nondescript in appearance, Arthur thought, except for his eyes. They were bottomless, so dark it was hard to distinguish pupil from iris. Blue Hawk's smile did not extend upward to them.

Tex sat beside him. A dozen young women, Susan among them, sat against the wall behind Blue Hawk: in the room, but not part of the conversation. Harold, still holding his rifle, lounged by the room entrance.

"Welcome," Blue Hawk said, nodding to them. His voice was vaguely southern. He gestured to the pillows arrayed in front of him. "Please. Sit."

Brenda, Arthur and Freddie sat on the cushions. Eric remained standing. Blue Hawk looked at him, then snapped his fingers at the women behind him without turning to look at them. One leapt to her feet and hurried to Blue Hawk. "Another cushion for our young guest," he said.

The woman nodded and hurried from the room. She returned a moment later and placed another cushion next to Brenda, then returned to her place against the wall. Blue Hawk kept his eyes on Brenda as Eric sat.

"Thank you," Brenda said. "What do you say, Eric?"

"Thank you," Eric said.

"You're welcome," Blue Hawk replied, continuing to appraise Brenda.

After a long moment, Freddie said, "So. Here we are."

Blue Hawk nodded. "Yes."

"So, like, what did you want to talk to us about?"

Blue Hawk said, "Who speaks for your group?"

"Well," Freddie said, scratching his head. "I guess that would be me." Blue Hawk looked at Arthur, who nodded.

After another moment, Blue Hawk began. "Why do you think you were sent here to Megiddo?"

"Sent here?" Freddie said. "We weren't sent here, we—"

"I know about the girls in Provo. But events don't happen at random. The concept of random coincidence is merely a device people use as cover for not knowing the reason for the serendipity." Behind him, several of the girls nodded emphatically.

"Well, I hadn't thought much about it," Freddie admitted.

"And you?" Blue Hawk nodded at Arthur.

"Me neither," Arthur said.

"And you?" Blue Hawk said to Brenda.

"My son and I are looking for a safe and comforting place," she said. "I'm not sure we've found it here, though."

"Why?"

Brenda took a deep breath. She began, "Perhaps you could tell me what arrangements are made for children here. Schooling, accommodations, and so forth."

Blue Hawk nodded. "We are a collective," Blue Hawk said. "Actually more than that. We are a nation. A world." He gestured dismissively in the direction of the ranch gate. "We have left the world out there behind. And so, we have decided it best that any children here be raised and educated collectively. The collective of mothers—ten mothers, twenty mothers, their unified consciousness—is vastly better than the single mother. An atom is not a whole without protons, neutrons and electrons. Just so, our society here. Our world."

"So, if I understand you," Brenda said, "children are raised by the group here?"

"Yes. That is our vision."

Brenda shook her head. "I'm sorry, that's not going to happen with my son and me. I won't be separated from my son. I will raise him. No one else. And what about his education?"

Blue Hawk stared hard at her, but Brenda did not avert her eyes, meeting his gaze.

After a moment, Blue Hawk smiled again and shrugged. "While we prefer to educate our children here, perhaps we can make an exception in Eric's case. There is an elementary school in Price."

Several of the women behind him gasped.

250

Blue Hawk turned and fixed them with a hard gaze over his shoulder. They all immediately fell silent, and turned their eyes down to the floor.

"Now then," Blue Hawk continued, turning back to Arthur and Freddie. "We are looking for specific skills."

"What kind of skills?" Arthur asked.

"We expect everyone in our community to put their skills to work for the group. Men have some skills, women have others. What about you, Freddie? That's your name, yes?"

"Yeah," Freddie said.

"Do you have any skills? Something useful. Weapons, for example. Firearms. Fighting skills. We have important work coming. Soon. We must be ready."

Freddie said, "Well, I wasn't in the army. In fact, I'm even a draft dodger. I hit the road when I got my draft—"

Blue Hawk cut him off with a dismissive hand wave. He looked at Arthur. "Were you in the army?"

"Why do you ask?"

"You have the eyes."

Eyes? That was a first. Arthur nodded. "I just got out."

"You must have some firearms training, then."

"Some," Arthur said. "Basic training."

"I take it from the jungle boots that you were in Vietnam?"

"Ayuh."

"Did you kill anybody?"

That question again. But this time, it did not appear to have been asked out of idle curiosity. For some reason, he thought it best to conceal his combat experience. "No. I was just a clerk. Lots of paperwork. I spent my tour filling out reports."

Blue Hawk seemed disappointed. "All right," he said. "We could use you, regardless. We can talk later about it."

"And what is it you do?" Brenda asked. One of the young women behind Blue Hawk gasped.

Blue Hawk stared hard at Brenda. *He isn't used to being questioned,* Arthur thought.

"I am a seer," Blue Hawk said after a moment. "I have visions. Some say I can see the future. Unfortunately, what I see isn't good."

Brenda said, "What do you see?"

Blue Hawk appeared to be reflecting on the question. The women behind him edged closer and became attentive. When they had resettled themselves, he spoke.

"Cosmology teaches us that there are multiple universes, maybe an infinite number, coexisting simultaneously in the same point of time and space. Sitting here right now, we are in one universe. Or—are we? Might we not be in two? Or more? Intersecting momentarily?"

The girls behind Blue Hawk nodded in understanding.

"Maybe intersecting is a regular occurrence. Perhaps each of us is a separate universe. Perhaps each molecule. And life itself may be an illusion. Just a brief comingling of molecules with a force, maybe the dark force some scientists think exists. Animated by something beyond our comprehension but that can be seen occasionally by a few of us. Across time and space. And the infinite."

Freddie nodded. "Heavy."

Give me a break, Arthur thought.

"All our emotions, all our senses, all our perceptions, are mere illusions, put up for the benefit of making existence at least somewhat manageable. But none of it is real. We are just energy made solid for a brief period. We must see behind the cardboard masks everyone wears, to perceive the ultimate reality. Take love. Here, we believe physical love is the ultimate good," he said.

"Without physical love, nothing else matters. Honesty, sadness, joy, hate—they don't matter. Sex is the ultimate physical manifestation of the infinite. Read the Bible. You think those psalms are about heavenly love? Some of the most erotic poetry ever written, and it's been transmuted into something dry and sterile."

Arthur glanced at Brenda as Blue Hawk held forth. Brenda was listening carefully, but her face was pale. She grasped Eric's hand firmly.

"That's our vision here. Love. It bonds us as a community, but it also bonds us to humanity through its ultimate purpose. Which is the production of children and a new society. Ultimately, love will help us survive what is coming."

"And what's coming?" Arthur asked.

"A terrible war. Here. Soon." Blue Hawk must have noticed Arthur's stunned look. He continued, smiling slightly. "This is no mystery to the fascist state and its alphabet agencies. The FBI, the CIA, the NSA." Blue Hawk continued, "the ABC, the DEF, the GHI, and so on. All of them. They all know about it. This is why we don't have a telephone here. Too easy to tap, listen in."

And for the next fifteen minutes, Blue Hawk expounded on his vision.

The black man had been brought to these shores 350 years ago, Blue Hawk said, a huge mistake of the then-metastasizing cancer of global capitalism. Unfortunately, they were not temperamentally suited to civilization and while exposure to the white race had gradually taught most of them to hide their savagery under a veneer of civilized behavior, the veneer often was pierced, as one could see any day in any big city where they congregated: crime, murder rates, unemployment, alcoholism and deadly drug use, vast numbers of them on welfare, growing bastardy, and other pathologies.

Most of them, Blue Hawk went on, thus were incapable of living under any sort of peaceful vision of reconciliation such as the dupe King espoused, and of course had no desire to try—which was why tougher, more ruthless men in the black power movement had King assassinated by a pathetic white man who failed to see he was being used.

"Wait, black men had King killed?" Brenda said.

"Yes. Of course," Blue Hawk said.

"I must have missed hearing about the evidence of that," she said.

"Of course you missed it," Blue Hawk said. "There *is* no evidence. That there is no evidence is the proof, you see. These people are extremely careful to hide their tracks."

Brenda nodded. "I see. Please go on."

The riots resulting from King's assassination eighteen months ago were only the initial harbinger of the coming war, in which millions would soon die. Blue Hawk intended for his disciples to survive this war by living in isolation, avoiding contact with outsiders. And, after the war was over, they would begin repopulating the earth with white children.

"I realize many will fail to see the truth of this vision," Blue Hawk said. "But I know as sure as I am sitting here that it is inevitable. And now you know about it. You see now, I hope, that you were not brought here to Megiddo by accident. Brenda, you are clearly fertile. Your group has at least one other child among you. You can contribute your children, and more to come, to rebuilding the white race. Not right away, but soon, after the war starts and with the arrival of Armageddon, as the Bible prophesizes. Oh yes, there is truth in the Bible, as there is in all of the Ur texts—the Baghavad Gita, the Koran, the

Torah. All of you can contribute your essence to helping renew our world in a new civilization of Beauty. And truth. And love." Blue Hawk smiled at them. He nodded expectantly.

Arthur, dumbfounded, struggled to say something. "Why would you need people with weapons training for your new society, Blue Hawk?"

"We of course need the means to defend ourselves. But also, we may, regrettably, need to take certain actions to precipitate the war," he said. "Something to tip the scales, launch the great conflict. People with weapons training can...do what's necessary. Do you understand?"

"I think so," Arthur said, hoping he didn't. He had heard enough. "Blue Hawk, I've never heard anything like this before. That is quite a vision. Astounding, in fact. But...it's a lot to absorb at once. Maybe you could give us time to talk it over. We can let you know in the morning."

"I dunno man, sounds good to me," Freddie laughed. "I never had no use for niggers anyway. Fuck 'em." He grinned, and Blue Hawk chuckled, nodding in agreement.

Arthur looked at Freddie, astonished. *Holy crap, he's buying into this.*

Brenda stood. "Thank you, Blue Hawk. Preach is right, there is a lot to think about here. Come on, Eric, we need to go back to the bunkhouse."

"Probably a good idea," Arthur said, also rising. "We should go, Freddie. We need to talk with the others. It's a big decision."

"Oh yeah, the others. Sure." Freddie stood.

Blue Hawk stood. "The storm is coming, my new friends, and remember—we are part of it. Nothing can stop it. Choose wisely. Mankind will be your judge." He exited. His women and Tex all followed.

As they walked back to the dorm, Brenda quickened her step and caught up with Arthur a few steps ahead. She leaned close and whispered to him, "Blue Hawk is crazier than a shit house rat."

Arthur nodded. "Tell me about it."

ii

He started awake sometime in the night with a hand across his mouth. For a second he began to struggle, but Brenda leaned in close and breathed into his ear, "Shhhhh," and after a moment he relaxed and nodded. She removed her hand from his mouth and he sat up quietly.

Brenda knelt beside his cot, her small bag of things slung over her shoulder, Eric standing next to her in the dark. He also carried a small bag.

Arthur started to whisper, but she silenced him with an impatient wave of her hand. The light snoring of the others continued, undisturbed.

Brenda held a finger to her lips, pantomiming *no talking*. She gestured for him to collect his stuff and come outside. She made the letters V-A-N with her fingers and pointed to the door and mouthed the words *We. Must. Leave.*

Arthur nodded.

She took Eric by the hand, putting her finger to his lips, and they crossed to the door and slipped outside.

Arthur, alert to any noise from the others, quietly packed up the few things he had taken from his bindle. As he packed, he thought about what he had heard.

It had been a stunning conversation. The others had all decided to stay. Laurel had shrugged. "I don't care," she had said. "You do drive me crazy, Freddie, but if you want to stay here for a while it's okay by me."

Freddie had laughed. "My girl," he said.

Sarah had also agreed. "Brig needs a break from riding in a hot van all day. I can take care of him here. We can stay for a while, anyway."

Brenda had then indicated enthusiastically that she wanted to stay, too, which astonished Arthur. But she saw the question in his eyes, she shook her head slightly. So Arthur also pretended to go along. He planned, however, to leave at the first opportunity—which now seemed to have arrived.

Arthur, carrying his boots, crossed to the door, while the snores of the others continued.

Outside, by the faint light of the new moon, he put on his boots and then walked quietly toward the van. He stopped twenty yards from it.

Brenda and Eric were against the side of the van, Harold standing in front of them with his rifle unslung, back to Arthur.

Arthur stood silently. After a few seconds, he realized that while Harold hadn't heard him approach, Brenda had indeed seen him.

Harold muttered something, and Brenda spoke a little louder. "Harold, no one needs to know about this now, do they?" she asked. She stepped toward him, gently reaching for his hand. "I could be very grateful for a little discretion." Arthur began to move quietly toward them.

"Yeah?" Harold chuckled softly. "How grateful?" He stepped closer to her.

Brenda moved her hand to Harold's groin. "Very," she breathed, leaning in toward him.

"Oh yeah, baby," Harold chuckled, his free hand moving to Brenda's breast as he lowered his head to kiss her.

Arthur was close enough now.

He leaped forward and threw his right arm around Harold's neck, using the sentry takedown he had learned in infantry training. He applied a choke hold as he dragged Harold down from behind, the hold cutting off blood flow to his brain. Harold dropped his rifle and flailed his arms, but the exertion simply made him use up what oxygen was already in his system. Within a few seconds, he went limp.

Arthur hissed, *"Get some rope and a scarf out of the van. Hurry!"*

"Wow Preach," Eric said, "that was so *cool!* You took that guy out all by yours—"

Brenda shushed him. "Eric, get in the van, honey."

A moment later Brenda emerged with a scarf and several quarter-inch mic cables.

Arthur flipped the still unconscious Harold onto his belly, and then tied his hands behind him. He wrapped the scarf around Harold's mouth and got it tied securely in place just as he started to move, the scarf cutting off the barest beginnings of a yell. Arthur sat on Harold's thighs and tied his ankles while Brenda held his head down, then used the last cable to pull them up toward his waist, wrapping the cable around Harold's wrists; he was now thoroughly trussed up and unable to move. Harold grunted, still trying to make noise.

Arthur reapplied a choke hold but did not close it. "Shut up, Harold," he hissed, "or I'll shut you up again, and this time you might not wake up."

Harold stopped struggling and nodded.

"What do we do with him?" Brenda asked.

"Nothing, just get in the van," Arthur said, grabbing Harold's rifle.

Harold started to struggle against his bonds but was unable to do anything else.

At the van, Arthur, figuring Brenda had the keys, climbed into the passenger seat, pointing the rifle back at the barn and house. Brenda said, "Give me the pliers in the glovebox."

"What—"

"Do it!" she hissed.

"Okay okay," he said, and after a second, found the pliers.

He handed them to her and she gave him two paper clips she had removed from her bag. "Here, straighten these out."

Arthur started to ask what she was going to do, but then thought better of it.

By the time he was done, she had loosened the casing holding the ignition assembly and removed it from the dash board. "Give me a paper clip." He did so.

After fiddling with it a moment, she said, "Give me the other one." He did so.

"Okay, get ready." She made another connection, then touched the wires together. The engine caught almost immediately. "Now, let's get the hell out of here," she said.

Arthur looked at her in frank admiration.

She put the van in gear, then turned toward the gate and, driving as quietly as possible, exited the ranch.

Fifteen minutes later, they reached the paved road again, turned left, and accelerated to 65, passing a sign that said "Green River 58 miles."

"Mom, are we okay now?" Eric asked. "Preach, is everything okay?"

"I think we're safe now," Brenda said, looking in the rear view mirror. Arthur turned and looked behind them.

Nothing but black night, the new moon, and a million stars.

"I think we're all right, Eric," Arthur said.

They drove on in silence for a few minutes. Then Brenda said, "That man was a monster."

"Ayuh," Arthur said. "Scariest guy I ever met."

After a moment, she added, "We should do something."

They found a gas station in Green River. It was closed, but there was a pay phone out front. Brenda drove the van into the shadows beside the station and stopped, leaving the engine idling.

Arthur got out and dialed the operator. "State police, please."

.   .   .

CHAPTER 27
i
Denver, Colorado
October 13, 1969

At 4:30 that morning, Arthur and Brenda had gotten off I-80, figuring that using a more circuitous route to Denver would be less predictable in the event Blue Hawk sent Tex and Harold after them. They had also decided to abandon the van, in case it had been reported stolen, and take a bus to Denver.

Brenda parked the van on a dark street a block from the bus station in Delta, a town an hour south of Grand Junction. She killed the engine, and they searched the van for anything useful, finding a bottle of cheap wine and a twenty dollar bill in a bag of music equipment.

The next bus was to Pueblo, leaving in an hour, so they bought tickets, reaching the city without incident early that afternoon. They slept most of the six-hour trip. They then caught a bus up I-25 to Denver, arriving about 8 pm.

Brenda did not like the looks of the neighborhood surrounding the terminal. So, they caught a cab, and Brenda had the driver take them to the nearest Holiday Inn.

ii
They checked in, Brenda paying with a credit card for two adjacent rooms with a door between. "Thanks for the room," Arthur said as she handed him his key. "You sure I can't give you some money?"

Brenda laughed. "Believe me, it's no problem," she said. "This is one of my ex's credit cards. I figure I can use it for a while longer before word gets around it's cancelled."

"Well, let me buy you dinner, then. We can spend Freddie's twenty bucks. There's a pizza joint next door."

"Lots of pepperoni and mushrooms!" Eric said.

"Sure, Preach, pizza works," Brenda said. "And thank you. Again."

"You're welcome. I'll go right away. It's getting late."

By the time he returned with the pizza, Brenda had already opened the bottle of wine. She handed Arthur a glass. "Won't you join me?"

"Sure," Arthur said. He sipped it. All wine tasted like varying degrees of vinegar to him, but this was sweeter than most. "What is this?"

"Moscato," Brenda said, making a face. "Cheap moscato. Too sweet for me, but it beats no wine at all. My ex was a psycho, but he knew good wine. What kind of pizza did you get?"

"Pepperoni and mushroom like Eric wanted, but I got extra cheese too. They never put enough cheese on." As they served themselves, Arthur asked, "How'd you end up with Freddie and them? I mean, you seem like you're...I dunno, different."

She laughed. "Older, you mean?"

Arthur grinned. "Something like that."

She sighed. "I was in a very bad marriage. Abuse, both psychological and physical. Beginning shortly after we were married."

That explains the scab on her lip, Arthur thought.

"I thought having a kid might make it stop, so we had Eric about a year later. It didn't work. I left him just a couple weeks ago. Laurel and I were friends, in a yoga class together. I called her the night I left, looking for a place to stay, and she said she was splitting LA with her boyfriend and did I want a ride? So here I am. I am forty-two, actually."

Arthur was flabbergasted. "Wow. You look like, I dunno—a lot younger," he finished awkwardly.

"Thank you," she said. "It's both a curse and a blessing. Good heredity, I guess. My mother was drop dead gorgeous."

So are you, he thought. "Where are you headed to?"

"I'm not sure, someplace east. Anyplace my ex isn't. I'm going to disappear for a while. More wine?"

"Maybe just a little." She poured him a half-glass. "Where did you learn to hotwire a car?" he asked.

She laughed. "I grew up with brothers who were car freaks. But what about you? What's your story?"

"Not much to tell. I grew up in Maine. Finished high school, had a pretty decent job, but then I got drafted. Went to Vietnam about a year ago, got back a week before I met you guys. On my way back to Maine now. Sort of. That's about it."

"How old are you, if I might ask?"

"Twenty-four," Arthur lied.

"Wow," she said. "I'm almost twice as old as you."

"I should look as good as you when I'm forty-two."

"I thank you, sir," she smiled.

They ate and talked more, Eric eating half the pizza himself. "Where do you keep all that food you eat, Eric?" Arthur asked.

"I don't know, Preach, I just eat it and then I poop it out the next day."

"Eric! That is disgusting!" Brenda said sharply, but Arthur just laughed.

"It's all right," he said. "Me too, little buddy." Eric laughed.

Brenda laughed too, embarrassed. "You guys," she said. "More wine?"

"No, I'm good. Thanks."

"Okay." Brenda poured the rest of the wine into her plastic bathroom cup.

"Well, Eric," she said after a few moments, "I think you could use a bath. What do you say?"

"Oh, Mom, do I have to?"

"Yes sir, and when you are done, I'm going to take one, so you'd best get started."

"A shower sounds like a good idea," Arthur said as Eric started for the bathroom. "I'll see you guys in the morning, then."

iii

Brenda knocked on the door between the rooms at about ten. "Can I come in?" she asked. She was wearing a shift, her feet bare, her hair still wet from her bath.

"Of course," he said. She came in and sat in the chair in front of the desk.

"Thanks. Sorry to bother you. I couldn't sleep."

"It's no bother," Preach said. Her legs were crossed so that an expanse of lovely, smooth thigh was exposed.

"I mean, I can leave if you want—"

"Oh no!" Arthur said, a little too quickly. "No, that's fine, nice to talk."

Brenda smiled. "Eric finally fell asleep. We watched TV for a while. *Red Skelton*. He hadn't watched any since we've been on the road." She smiled. "He calls it 'Red Skeleton.'"

"I caught up on the late news myself. Just finished."

"Anything exciting?"

"Not really. The Russians did some space mission, I dunno."

"I hate the news. Last year was awful. Riots, Bobby and King getting killed. Tet. This year has been a little better. Troops are starting to come home now. That's something."

"Ayuh."

"What was it like for you?"

Arthur shrugged. "Mostly dirt, boredom and exhaustion. With some terror thrown in once in a while. And blood. Not mine, thankfully." *And rats.*

She nodded. "I'm so sorry." She came over and sat beside him, took his hand. "Are you all right?"

Arthur looked at her. Then, unable to control himself, he leaned toward her suddenly and tried to kiss her.

"What—" Brenda recoiled. "Preach, I—"

Arthur was immediately embarrassed. He pulled back. "Brenda, I'm so sorry. I don't know why—"

"It's okay," she said. "I wasn't trying to…you know. I just wanted to…you seemed like you could use a hug, is all. The war and all. Do you sleep okay?"

"Mostly."

Except for the dreams.

"Okay, that's good." She stood. "Anyway, I just wanted to thank you again for helping us get away from that awful place. Blue Hawk and them. Ugh. But I—I probably ought to be getting back to Eric."

Arthur decided to try one more time. Hating himself, he said, "Are you…sure? I mean, he's only next door, and…" He gestured to the double bed and smiled. "It's getting cold outside."

Brenda shook her head. "Preach, I'm sorry, but no. You're a nice guy and even kind of good looking. But, look, I'm twice your age. Almost, anyway. I know, it shouldn't make a difference, but it does. To me." She apparently decided to give him something. She smiled. "If I were younger, sure."

"Okay."

"I mean, I'm old enough to be your mo—"

"It's all right." *Jeezus.*

Brenda smiled again, very maternally. "Okay, fine. We're still friends, though?"

Before Arthur could answer, Eric started yelling. "Mom! Mommy! *Where are you?*"

"Oh Lord," Brenda said. "I'm coming baby, I'm coming," she called. "I'm sorry, Preach," she said. The door closed.

Arthur stared at the door for a moment, flushed. He took a few deep breaths. Then, knowing he wouldn't be able to sleep until he settled down, he went into the bathroom and jerked off, flushing the tissue away after. That helped. He was asleep a short time later.

iv

Brenda and Eric were gone the next morning when Arthur knocked. He noticed the folded sheet of paper, a corner of which showed under the door.

Preach, I'm sorry. I decided it's probably best that Eric and I move on. Thank you again, I'll always remember your kindness. B

Arthur got a ride east an hour later.

. . .

PART VIII: MAINE
CHAPTER 28
i

Waldo County, Maine
January 1967

Arthur arrived at the FoodMart late on a Friday afternoon; he had taken Aunt Esther to see her doctor.

Mr. Higgins was inspecting the wine shelves, his ever-present clipboard and pencil in hand. He saw Arthur come in and beckoned him over. "Hello, Arthur," he said. "I hope your aunt is okay?"

Although Esther hadn't complained, Arthur had noticed she was having trouble standing after she had been sitting a while. She was also becoming more forgetful. She dismissed these problems as mere symptoms of old age, but Arthur had convinced her to see her doctor.

"Yes sir, thanks," Arthur said. "The doc checked her out, gave her a prescription for aches and pains. We just picked it up and I took her home. He says she's just tired, needs to take it a little easy." Arthur grinned. "'Too many birthdays', the doc told her."

Higgins nodded. "Well, I hope she'll be fine," he said. Forrest had transferred Higgins from the Camden Foodmart to give Arthur a hand until he got comfortable. He was perhaps thirty-five, with a wife and a young daughter. His hair was cut in a flat-top, and his heavy horn-rimmed glasses perched above a fresh pimple on his right nostril.

Higgins turned to the wine. "Now look at this, Arthur, and tell me what you see."

"Ummm...bottles of wine?"

"Yes," Higgins said. "But what kinds?"

"Well, I see red. Chianti's red, right? And white. Oh, and I think the Mateus is pink." This was the extent of Arthur's knowledge of wine.

Higgins snorted. "It's called rose," he said, carefully pronouncing both syllables.

Arthur offered, "We do have a few other wines. And here's a local one." He pointed.

Higgins laughed. "Oh yes, blueberry. *Blueberry!* Good lord, does no one in this town drink decent wine?"

"All this does sell, sir." He smiled. "Well, the blueberry, mostly to the tourists."

"Yes, I bet," Higgins laughed. "But just the same, we're going to go a little more high end in the wine department. We need to talk to the wine sales rep. When is he due in?"

Before Arthur could tell him that they didn't have one, Officer Loudermilk came into the store, accompanying Mr. Laverdiere's widow. Higgins walked over to them. "Afternoon, Officer. Mrs. Laverdiere."

"Hello, Mr. Higgins," Loudermilk said. He smiled and nodded to Arthur. "Hi, Art."

"Officer," Arthur said, barely nodding.

"We just came in for a chicken," Loudermilk said. "Dinner tonight. June's roasting one. My favorite!"

"You came to the right place," Higgins said. "Right over here, Ma'am." He escorted them to the meat counter. "Renato," Higgins said to the new meat and deli man Arthur had hired, "pick out a nice plump one for the lady."

"*Si,* Mr. Higgins." Renato gestured to them.

In one of the stranger twists of fate Arthur had seen in his short life, Laverdiere's death had apparently had a profound impact on Loudermilk. For some reason, during the course of the investigation, Mrs. Laverdiere had become enamored with him, and he with her. Amazingly, the relationship had caused what appeared to be a complete transformation in the man. Loudermilk had become polite, solicitous, and pleasant to Arthur, and even Clement— perhaps the strangest change of all. Not that Arthur believed it; something about it didn't ring true to him.

Mrs. Laverdiere picked out the roaster she wanted while Loudermilk ordered a sandwich at the deli counter. Arthur went to man the cash register when they were getting ready to leave.

"That will be $2.49 for the roaster, Mrs. Laverdiere." As usual, he did not charge Loudermilk for his sandwich, merely putting it into the same bag.

"How much is the sandwich?" Loudermilk asked.

"No charge, Officer," Arthur said.

"No, I can't do that," Loudermilk said. "What do I owe you?"

Arthur looked at him. "That would be $1.50."

Loudermilk gave him a ten. "Keep it." He smiled. "I've run up a tab the past year or two."

Arthur nodded. "Ayuh, you have." Grudgingly, he said, "Thank you."

Loudermilk smiled. "I owe you for a few more. Next time."

Arthur said nothing, but nodded again.

"Have a blessed day," Loudermilk said. He offered his arm to Mrs. Laverdiere. "June? May I?"

Mrs. Laverdiere giggled. "You may, sir," and took his arm. Loudermilk and Mrs. Laverdiere left the store. As they did, Loudermilk turned and, behind Mrs. Laverdiere's back, caught Arthur's eye, smirked, and winked.

ii

Several nights later, as Arthur finished his homework, there was a knock at the door. Aunt Esther looked up. She was sitting in her rocker, crocheting. Jigs, one of her cats, sat in her lap, purring. The other, Maggie, lay before the glowing fire. "I'll get it," Arthur said.

Arthur opened the door. "Hi, Art," Stuart said.

"Wow, Stu, how are you?" Arthur said, recovering quickly. He shook Stuart's offered hand. "Hey, come on in, I sure didn't expect to see you."

Stuart laughed as he came in. "I bet. It's nice to see you. Been awhile." Stuart took off his winter coat and garrison cap. Arthur hung it in the entry hall closet.

Arthur showed Stuart to the living room and introduced him to Aunt Esther. After the formalities, Esther went into the kitchen to make some hot chocolate.

"So," Arthur said, once they were seated. "When do you leave for Vietnam?"

"Next week," Stuart said. "I'm flying to Oakland, California, then to Nam. I should be with my unit a few days after that."

"Do you know what unit you'll be with?"

"No," he said, "other than infantry, of course. I'll probably be a platoon leader. I could be anywhere, except probably not Eye Corps. That's marines, mostly. Up along the DMZ."

"Eye Corps?"

"Yeah, First Corps. Like the Roman numeral."

"Gotcha." They made small talk another couple of minutes until Esther returned with the chocolate.

"Just instant," she said. "Arthur, I've added milk to the grocery list."

"I'll get some tomorrow," he said.

"I'll leave you boys to talk. Stuart, you be careful over there, now."

"I will, ma'am, thank you."

She headed back to the kitchen.

Stuart sipped his chocolate appreciatively. "Ahh good," he said. "Hits the spot."

"I guess you won't be experiencing much winter, the next year," Arthur ventured.

Stuart laughed. "No, probably not." He took another sip. "So...how's it going with Sharon?"

"Good. We're getting pretty serious. She wants to get married in the next year or so but I—" He stopped. "Sorry."

"Oh it's okay," Stuart replied. "And funny you should mention that. It's kinda why I came back to Belfast. Art, I—I still want to marry Betty. I know, I know, lost cause, right? But I figured, how serious could she think I was, if I gave up so easy that I'd take a first 'no' for an answer?" He laughed ruefully. "I was hoping she'd see me again while I'm here. No such luck, though. Yet."

Arthur nodded. "Ayuh, she's pretty dead set against the war now. So I doubt she'll agree to see you."

"I know. I've tried writing, too, but she doesn't answer. But look, uh...maybe you could help me a little."

"How so?"

"Maybe I could write to you instead? You could tell me how things are going, how she is, that sort of thing? Not spying on her, just so that when I come back, I'll have some idea of the lay of the land, so to speak."

After a moment, Arthur nodded. "I could do that. I mean, I'm not going to follow her around or anything."

Stuart looked horrified. "Oh no, please don't. No. That's not what I'm asking. I just want to know how she's doing is all. Don't tell me anything you don't think you should."

"With that stipulation, okay then, sure," Arthur said. "In fact, I'd like to hear from you. And I'll write back when I can. I guess getting mail is a good thing for you guys, right?"

"Oh yeah," Stuart said. "Letters are always good for morale."

iii

Arthur got his first letter from Stuart in late February. A photo was enclosed.

20 Feb 67

Hey Art,

I got to Vietnam okay; I arrived on 4 Feb. Saw some shelling as we were coming into Bien Hoa AFB, explosions going off below. It was late at night and you could see the big orange blasts really well against the black background of (I guess) the jungle. It finally brought home to me what was going on here. It takes seeing it in real life to really appreciate it.

They sent me to Long Binh to a processing center there for new officers (and also for those just leaving—I've got 349 days to go!). It's not too far from Saigon. A huge army base with two hospitals, tons of other logistical support units, even a stockade which is known as "the LBJ" for "Long Binh Jail." (Hah!)

You'd think a base this big would be safe, but just two nights after I got there, a bunch of sappers (gook engineers) got inside the base and blew up a huge pile of 8-inch artillery shells. You wouldn't believe the noise and how the ground shook. The explosion sure woke me up, in more ways than one!

Anyway, I shipped out a day later and am now in the 25th Infantry (Tropic Lightning) Division. After a week of in-country training, I got assigned to B (Bravo) Company, 2nd Battalion, 22nd Infantry. I'm 1st Platoon Leader. The captain's a real hard ass, but a good soldier, so I'm working hard to do a good job.

We're based in Tay Ninh Province near the town of Dau Tieng, right by the Michelin Rubber Plantation. This is in III Corps, maybe 40 miles NW of Saigon.

The battalion (the "two double deuce" we call it) is a mechanized infantry unit. We ride around in armored personnel carriers, called "tracks". My platoon has 5 tracks, but one or another of them is almost always down for repairs, so on any given day I usually have 4. Sometimes 3!

We spend most of our nights guarding artillery bases out in the field, then doing mine-sweeping duty on the local roads in the mornings (the gooks put out mines at night). We patrol, and provide armor support to leg infantry and ARVNs during the day.

I've enclosed a photo, looking very warrior-like (hah)!

The Polaroid showed Stu, grinning and bare-chested, next to a boxlike armored vehicle. He was pointing to a mark on the side of the vehicle, with a white circle

271

around it, and the word "OUCH!" written above it. Arthur put the photo on his dresser.

The spot I'm pointing to is where a gook RPG hit the side of the track a few days before I got here. The guys laugh about it, but it makes you think.

The countryside is beautiful here. You wouldn't believe how green it is. And the people are nice, mostly. Kind of scared of us, though, sometimes. There are lots of pretty women, very delicate. They giggle a lot! The mamasans try to sell you stuff, including pot (grrr) whenever you stop near a vill. I haven't seen any of the men use it, but I suspect some do. I better not catch any of them smoking that stuff.

How's Betty? Well, I hope.

All the best,

Stu

iv

Arthur and Sharon lay together naked and panting, hearts thudding enough that Arthur could feel the bed faintly shaking. They were at Betty's apartment. Sharon rolled over and snuggled up against Arthur and rested her head on his chest. He put his arm around her, but after a moment she rolled away. "Ughh, too sweaty," she chuckled.

He laughed. "Hey, you were dripping sweat on me there when you were on top."

"I was not!" Sharon said. "Girls don't sweat. They glow."

"Oh suuure," Arthur said, rolling his eyes.

Sharon laughed and then moved her pillow over so a corner of it was on Arthur's chest, then lay against him again, head on the pillow, her leg draped over his. "Ahhh, yes, that's better." She sighed contentedly. "Artie?"

He knew from her tone what was coming next. "What?"

"When do you think we might—you know—make it official?"

"I don't know," Arthur said, beginning his rationale once again. "I've got five more months of high school and you're still a junior, so I'd think not for what, 18 months or so? Maybe Sum—Fall—of next year?"

"So looong," she pouted. "I don't want to wait that long."

"Now Shar', we've talked about this. Several times. I've got to finish high school, and you should, too."

"I wouldn't need to, once you finish and get your new job. Things are going well for you at the FoodMart, aren't they? Higgins likes you?"

"Well, sure, but I'm still only part time. And I won't be fully running the store until the summer."

Sharon sat up, faced him, and said, "Artie, you do still want to get married, don't you?"

"Of course," he said. "Sure, why wouldn't I?"

"I mean...you know."

"No. What?"

"I mean...well, I was afraid you'd not want to get married anymore, since..."

"You mean, 'Why buy the cow when you can get the milk for free?'" Arthur said, grinning.

Sharon blushed. "Now you stop that, Arthur West!" and she playfully slapped him on the thigh and started giggling again.

"You better watch it, you naughty girl!" He pretended to grab for her.

She pretended to try to get away.

v

March 4, 1967
Dear Stu,

Sorry I haven't replied sooner, not much of a correspondent. But here I am.

I guess you are settled into your unit now. Eleven months to go! Your unit is an easy number to remember: three 2s. Wow, tracks. That was one of yours in the Polaroid? It doesn't look like the ones you see in World War II movies. I hope you are doing well.

Everything is good here. I'm in my last quarter of school; I made the honor roll last time. Yay me! Trying to really work the grades before graduation. If I do decide to go to college it will be good to raise them some. Have you ever taken the SATs? Any advice?

Me and Sharon are dating pretty hot n heavy now (smile) and will probably get married in '68. You'll be home by then so expect a wedding invite. We will invite Betty too, of course.

I'm not sure if you'll want to hear this, but Betty has gotten even more involved in the anti-war movement since when you were here. She's an organizer. Traveling to places like Portland and Boston to help set up protests, sit-ins, things like that. She's trying to organize a war protest up Orono on the university campus for April some time. In good news, I don't think she's seeing anybody now. There was some instructor she was seeing but I think that's over with, or so Sharon says. She's still living with a couple of roommates. I'll see if I can get a picture for you if you want one.

If you like, I'll ask my Aunt Esther to send you some homemade cookies? Let me know.

Well, that's about it. Keep your head down and I'll see you in eleven months.
Best,
Art

Arthur received no reply.

Belfast, Maine
April 1967

The phone call came at eleven o'clock, the evening of April 13. Esther had been in bed for two hours. Arthur had just gone to bed. He jumped up and ran downstairs to answer it, hoping the call would not wake up his aunt. "Hello?"

"Hello. My name is Robert Emery. I'm Stuart Emery's father. I'd like to speak to Arthur West, please."

"Yes, I'm Arthur West."

"Mr. West, I'm—" Mr. Emery paused. "Excuse me." After a moment, he continued, "Stuart asked me to call." Terrible pain filled Mr. Emery's voice.

"Yes sir? And please, call me Arthur." An ache began in Arthur's gut.

"Arthur, I'm sorry to be the bearer of bad tidings, but Stuart has been wounded. Badly. He's back in the States now, but he may—may not live."

Arthur swallowed once or twice, suddenly feeling as if he might throw up. *Jesus, Stu was his friend,* he thought, as if this made it somehow impossible for Stuart to have been injured. "Oh Lord," he said. "I'm so sorry to hear, sir. What happened, if I may ask?"

Emery spoke in the flat, emotionless tone of someone barely keeping his emotions under control.

Some kind of bomb had gone off when Stuart was out on patrol, destroying one of their tracks and killing most of the men in it. Stuart had survived, miraculously. Once he had been stabilized, he had been flown back to the States.

Although Stuart was from Connecticut, he was in an intensive care ward in the VA hospital in Togus for now. "It's the only VA hospital with an ICU bed in New England," Emery finished. "He's here until a bed opens up at the VA hospital in Boston. They specialize in—in care and rehab for severely wounded men there."

"Mr. Emery, would it be okay to visit Stu? I'm only an hour from Togus."

Emery said, "Yes, that's why I called. He wants to see you. I spoke with him earlier today. He also wants to see a girl you may know. Betty Tibbets?"

"I know her. I'll ask. Sir, how can I reach you?"

Emery gave Arthur the number and address of his hotel.

.   .   .

CHAPTER 29
i

Togus, Maine
April 1967

"Mr. West?"

A nurse approached Arthur, who was sitting with Sharon and Betty in the main lobby of the VA medical center in Togus. They all looked up expectantly. Arthur nodded. "Yes?"

"You're here to see Lieutenant Emery?"

"Yes ma'am," Arthur said.

The nurse nodded and sat down next to them. "Lieutenant Emery may not be able to spend more than a few minutes with you. He is usually asleep, but he is awake at the moment. He's been putting off taking his medications so he could see you and be able to talk. Does he know these ladies are here as well?"

"I mentioned to his father this morning that they'd be coming."

Betty nodded. Sharon was ashen-faced, drawn.

"His father will explain further," the nurse said. "He's rarely left the ICU since his son arrived." She stood and gestured toward the elevators. "Please follow me."

The three of them stood, but Sharon then sat down. "Artie…"

"What?"

"I…I don't think I can do this. You go on, though."

Arthur looked at her. "Seriously?"

"I'm sorry. I just can't. I mean…" She trailed off. "Please. I'll wait here."

"It's all right, Shar'," Betty said. "Preach and I will go. I understand. Come on, Preach."

"Okay," Arthur said. He and Betty followed the nurse toward the elevators.

"She's never been very strong," Betty whispered.

ii

"Stu has mentioned you," his father said, shaking Betty's hand after Arthur had introduced her.

"I hope kindly," Betty said, smiling but clearly embarrassed.

"I can assure you, he is very *very* glad you are here." Emery smiled. "And so am I."

"I'm sorry to meet you under these circumstances."

Emery nodded. "Shall we?" He gestured down the hall.

Outside the door, Emery took a deep breath, exhaling with finality. "All right. We'll have no more than fifteen minutes." He handed face masks to them and put on his own. "It's important for infection. He's got some burns. They're healing, but…"

"I understand," Betty said. They entered the room.

Stuart lay in his bed, his torso raised to a quarter sitting position. Machines surrounded him, tubes leading to his remaining arm—his left, nearest the window, oddly undamaged—and what remained of his legs. The right side of his face had been severely burned, the puckered skin healing but still red and angry. The hair on that side of his head was gone, his scalp also red and heavily scabbed. His right eye was covered with a bandage. He breathed shallowly, wincing as he did so.

"Stu?" his father said. "Some visitors."

Stuart opened his one eye and turned his head slightly to the right, the exertion obviously difficult. He saw Arthur and smiled. Then he saw Betty and his face started to light up, but the pain of doing so made him wince again. "Hi guys," he whispered. "Thank you...coming. Hello, Betty. ...love you."

Betty smiled gently. "Hello, Stuart." She walked around to the other side of the bed and sat in the chair by the window and grasped his hand. She chuckled gently. "It looks like you forgot to duck."

Stuart smiled again, this time showing less pain. "I know," he whispered. "Art, how the...heck are you?"

"I'm fine, Stu," Arthur said. "Thanks for sending me that Polaroid. I'm keeping it forever. You're a hero, buddy."

"Hah. Hardly. Just a...a casualty. There's been thousands of us." He gestured to a tube with a plunger on the end of it. "Betty, would you...pass me that? I've been putting... off as much as I can. Damn stuff...puts me to sleep but... need a little boost."

She passed him the plunger and he squeezed it. "Ahhh good," he sighed after a moment. "Works great, takes the edge right off. I only took half a dose; I should be...good til you have to leave."

Arthur, horrified but trying not to show it, asked, "Can we...can we get you anything?"

"No, I'm good, thanks. Dad here's taking care of me."

After a few awkward moments, Betty said, "Stu, if you don't want to talk about it, that's okay. I completely understand. But...could I ask—"

Stuart nodded, knowing the question. "It's all right," he whispered. "There's not really much... tell. I can't remember much at all after...the explosion."

The mine sweep the morning of March 21 started out routinely enough. Stu's platoon of tracks—there were three of them—and a truck carrying the engineers and their equipment left the nameless little firebase where they had spent the night on perimeter security. They were a mile from the nearest village, which hosted a small RuffPuff detachment.

"What's that?" Betty asked.

"Regional Forces/Popular Forces," Stuart said. "Local militia, basically... although half of 'em... probably VC." He took a few labored breaths, then continued, haltingly but speaking clearly.

The sweep was meant to clear the road from the fire base to the vill. "We were doing everything right," Stuart said. "Security was out, fire teams...on both flanks and front and rear... vehicles...tracking just like they were supposed to."

"Tracking?" Betty asked.

Tracking was an important driving skill, Stuart explained. Each driver kept his vehicle's tracks exactly in the track marks made by the vehicle before him as they moved slowly down the road at the pace of the engineers in front, since, obviously, those particular spots on the road were guaranteed to be clear. Stu's track was the second in line. Next was the engineers' truck. The third track brought up the rear.

About a half mile into the sweep, the road took a sharp turn to the left. A paddy was along the raised berm of the road, and approximately 25 yards beyond the paddy was a wood line along a meandering stream. Midway

279

through the curve was a large crater beside the road, mostly filled with water, one edge intruding into the road so it was narrower at this point.

The engineers, the lead track, and then Stuart's, made it past the crater with no problem. The truck, however, was driven by a new guy, and he managed to hang up the front wheel over the edge of the crater, made more slippery and soft by the churning action of the treads from the tracks in front of him.

"I halted the column," Stu said, "and ordered...lead track to remain in...place...while I had my driver back our track up...to the truck. I was...going to tow it past the crater. The driver...tracked back. He didn't leave...track...marks by an *inch.*

"I was just...starting to pull the...tow cable from the truck to hook...the rear of my...when there was this flash of light...and I...thrown through the air."

Stuart stopped. He took a number of deep breaths. Betty said, "Stuart, are you tired? Do you want us to leave so you can rest?"

"No," he said. "Give me a..."

"Son, we can come back in a bit, let you—"

*"No...*I said!" Stuart exclaimed, then groaned at the exertion speaking above a whisper cost him. He squeezed the plunger again. "Anyway," he continued when he could, "that was the last... thing I remember. Til I woke up in...hospital.

"I was told later it must have been...command detonated. A big mine, maybe a...250-pounder, unexploded bomb...something. The gooks...must've buried it in...the crater. Wrecked the engineers truck...and my track, killed...driver and gunner. If I hadn't gotten out...to hook up the...the tow cable, I'd have been...killed, too.

"So they put me...on a dustoff and I got...Dau Tieng," Stuart said. "They had a plane waiting for me…flew me straight away to the hospital…Long Binh. Chaplain there told me I'm lucky… alive." Stuart laughed shortly, then gasped. "Right…Some luck. I mean—look at me. A fucking…*mess.*"

Arthur started to say something, but then stopped. *What is there to say?*

"So they…patched me up best they…could, and…when I could travel, put me…a flight to The World. And here I am…what's left of me. Jesus fucking…*Christ.*"

Arthur found himself unable to speak. Stuart's father turned away and wiped his eyes with a handkerchief.

Betty nodded, still holding Stuart's hand. Then, to Arthur's astonishment, she leaned forward, lowered her mask, and kissed him on the forehead. "There now," she whispered. "There now. I'm here. Don't you worry about a thing."

Arthur had to look away.

Stuart whispered "…love you, Betty." He drifted off, the second boost finally returning him to merciful oblivion.

The nurse came in. "I'm sorry, but it's time to go. Lieutenant Emery needs his rest."

iii

"I feel so guilty," Betty said as they drove toward Belfast, past the old Lake St. George camps along Route 3. It was the first thing any of them had said since leaving the hospital a half hour earlier.

"Why?" Arthur said.

"I should have answered his letters. And I didn't. And now I've got to live with that."

After a moment, Arthur said, "It was kind, what you did back there. Trying to help him, encourage him." Arthur reached down and squeezed her hand. She squeezed back and smiled at him.

"Do you think he'd mind if I came back?" She asked. "I can arrange time. Not every day but—"

281

"Of course he won't mind," Arthur said. "Betty, he loves you. And I can see why."

"Still?"

"Ayep. He told me." Arthur told her of Stu's visit a few days before he left for Vietnam.

"Oh God," Betty said. "I should have seen him then. How could I have been so ugly? The war isn't his fault." She dabbed at her eyes with a handkerchief. "Christ, what a bitch I've been." After a moment, she added, "He didn't deserve this."

"I know," Arthur said.

And yet it had happened anyway.

Sharon had been silent during this exchange. Then she said, "Look, could we please stop talking about it? It's just depressing." Arthur glanced back at her.

"Okay, Shar'," Betty sighed.

"I mean… it's too bad that—"

"Stop talking," Betty said. "Please. You said you wanted to stop talking about it. So stop. Jesus."

.   .   .

CHAPTER 30
i

Waldo County, Maine
April 1967

The Saturday after visiting Stuart, Arthur arrived at the FoodMart and found Higgins in a foul mood. "Arthur, we have a problem. We are trying to sell groceries in a town with absolutely no taste!"

After Higgins had launched his effort to sell more high-end wines, which so far had been a miserable failure, his next step had been to add some new deli items. They had added some kind of pork called Pancetta—Italian bacon, Higgins patiently explained—and something even weirder, basically an Italian type of baloney called Mortadella, which had globs of fat in it. Plus some cheeses: Asiago, Brie, Camembert. Arthur could not tell the difference between the latter two. Higgins had even added a goat cheese, the very idea of which Arthur found revolting.

"The FoodMart in Camden does a lot of business in these very items," Higgins had said. "No reason they won't sell here too."

"Except, Mr. Higgins, Searsport is not Camden," Arthur tried to explain. "Camden is richer, with more tourists from New York and Boston. Searsport is more of a working man's town. Those things sell in Camden because people there are used to having them around. And can afford them. Not here. We're a Laughing Cow and olive loaf kind of place. Not Brie and...Mortabella."

"Della," Higgins said. "Morta*della*. Well, we'll just have to educate the local palates."

Arthur gave up. "I guess we can give it a shot." He was starting to look forward to the day Higgins returned to Camden.

"Good! Now then, I want to—" At this point a lobsterman Arthur recognized came in. Higgins greeted the man, who grunted and walked to the beer case.

The lobsterman took a six-pack of Schlitz from the cold case, then came to the deli counter. Renato was off for the day, so Arthur walked over to fill in. The lobsterman nodded. "How's Esther?" he asked.

"She's fine, sir, thanks. What can I get you?" The lobsterman ordered a baloney and American cheese on white bread, with lettuce and Miracle Whip. "Maybe a few pickles. Hold the tomato."

As Arthur made it, he asked, "Can I interest you in trying some Asiago on that sandwich?"

"What in the bejesus is that?" the lobsterman asked.

"Italian cheese."

The lobsterman snorted. "No. Godfrey mighty."

Arthur, trying to keep a straight face, wrapped the sandwich, and the lobsterman picked up a bag of potato chips, paid, and left.

Esther got quite a laugh out of the story that evening. "You know, Arthur, I like most cheese but I've never had Asiago. Maybe bring some home for us?"

Arthur laughed. "You betcha, Aunt Esther."

He tried some the next morning. Surprisingly, it was all right.

ii

The following Saturday was the first warm day since November, so Arthur took advantage of it to eat his lunch—mortadella and Asiago on a Kaiser—at one of the picnic tables outside Jordan's. A few minutes before he was due back inside, Loudermilk pulled up in June Laverdiere's car and got out. He was not in uniform.

Just great, Arthur thought.

"Afternoon, Artie," Loudermilk said as he approached. He sat down without asking. "I want to give you something." He handed Arthur a couple of booklets. "I can't force you to read them or anything like that, but I hope you do. Salvation is a gift. But you have to accept it first. Eternity is a long time to burn, Artie."

Arthur looked briefly at them. They were religious tracts, the size of a pocket notebook, 30 or so pages long, mostly consisting of cartoons with balloon texts like in a comic book, but there were also a lot of Bible verses scattered throughout. "Thanks. I'll look them over." He tried to keep a straight face.

"You might want to give the second one to your friend. Clement."

Arthur looked at the second one. After a moment, he said, "Why should I give this one to Clement?"

Oscar smiled thinly. "In a small town, you hear things. Like, about Clement's new friend, by way of an example. All I'm saying is, Clement might want to seek the Lord before it's too late. It'd go very bad for him if he got caught doing anything... uh...sinful. You should talk to him."

Arthur, remembering the quarry, had sense enough not to say what he was really thinking. "I've known Clement all my life," he said. "I don't know what you're talking about."

"Whatever you say, Artie," Loudermilk said, standing, and smiling again, not so pleasantly this time. "Anyway, keep the tracts. And, while I'm at it, take a look at the first one. Think about it. Have a blessed day, son." He walked back to the car, waved, smirked, and drove away.

After Oscar was out of sight, Arthur looked at the first tract. It focused on "crazed teenagers, rumbling and twisting across America, smoking deadly marijuana and listening to satanic rock music." Arthur chuckled at the unintentionally humorous drawings of leering boys chasing after scantily clad, bosomy teenage girls, while a "negro" rock band played. The Biblical verses were straight Old Testament, with a little Revelation mixed in.

The second tract, the one Loudermilk wanted him to give to Clement, was even more lurid. It told the story of a "sodomite" who, as the story unfolded, became more and more a captive of his "sinful urges." It finally ended with him and others "of his kind" being marched, naked, screaming and tearful, into a lake of fire for all eternity, grinning demons prodding them on with pitchforks.

Arthur had gotten the message. *Loudermilk was watching.* He threw both tracts into the harbor.

iii

"Let me get this straight," Clement said. "Loudermilk gave you some of those stupid tracts the bible

285

thumpers at school leave layin' around?" They were drinking sodas at Johnson's.

Arthur nodded. He described them briefly.

"Damn," Clement said, snickering. "I wish you'd kept them. The ones I've seen at school are wicked funny. I don't think I've seen those two, though."

Arthur grinned. "They were pretty bad. I wasn't going to keep them." He leaned forward. "Loudermilk asked me to give you one of them." He whispered, "The one about queers."

Clement was suddenly on alert. "What? Why would he do that?"

Arthur decided to press on. "I don't know. Why would he?"

"He thinks I'm a fucking queer?"

Arthur said, "I guess so."

Clement looked closely at him. "Wait a minute. Do you think I'm a fucking queer?"

"Of course not," Arthur said. "I've known you my whole life. I think I'd know something like that about you if it was true." Then, he continued, "But even if it was true—I'm not saying it is!" he added as Clement started to get angry. "Not saying it is. But even if it was true, you're my best friend and it wouldn't matter to me. Honest."

Clement leaned back and stared at Arthur. "Shit, that's just great. You think I'm a queer!"

"I just said I didn't!"

"Yeah, right. Well, go fuck yourself, Preach! Just keep the fuck away from me anymore. Jesus!" Clement jumped to his feet and stalked out.

"Now you be careful with your language in here, Clement Paul!" the counterman yelled as Clement slammed the door behind him.

That went well.

Arthur paid for the sodas and left, worried he might have lost a friend.

But he hadn't. Clement called him later that evening. "I'm sorry I got mad at you this afternoon, Preach."

"It's okay. Don't worry about it."

"And—I appreciate what you said, too. About it...not making a difference to you. If I *was* a...you know."

"I meant it."

"I know you did. Not sayin' I am, you understand."

"Ayuh."

"But, if I was, it's good to know you wouldn't hate me."

"Never, buddy."

"Okay. Thanks, and I'm sorry again." Clement hung up.

iv

June 1967

A few days after Arthur's birthday, he filled out a brief form registering for the draft, as he was required to do. He dropped it in the mail and promptly forgot about it.

At his graduation from Crosby, Arthur walked across the stage and received his diploma, to the polite applause of the audience, after which he drove his Aunt home. He had made honor roll again his last quarter, and this brought his grades up enough that he graduated in the top 15 percent of his class.

Clement had not bothered to show up. "Fuck it, they can mail the diploma to me," he had told Arthur.

Arthur and Sharon skipped the prom, instead driving to Orono for their own celebration. Betty had given Sharon a key to the apartment. Betty was usually not there now. She had been going to Togus several times a week since April.

"She stays in his room, holds his hand, helps him with his bedpan, stuff like that," Sharon told him. "I don't see how she does it. I couldn't do it. I mean, bedpans? That's what they have nurses for."

"It's good of her to do that," Arthur said. "Given her feelings about Vietnam and all."

"I guess," Sharon said. "He's asleep most of the time. He's in constant pain. They have to keep him pretty doped up." She grasped his hand. "I just can't imagine."

v

One morning a couple of weeks later, shortly after Arthur opened the store, Mr. Forrest walked in, along with a photographer. "Good news, Arthur. As of today you're the new manager of the Searsport, Maine, FoodMart. Congratulations." He shook Arthur's hand. The photographer took a picture.

Arthur was almost speechless. "I—I—thank you, Mr. Forrest," he stammered. "Wow. I'll try not to let you down."

"I know you won't, Arthur," Forrest laughed. "You're the youngest store manager in the company. I think the youngest in the company's history."

"Is Mr. Higgins still going to be here? You know, to backstop me?"

"Oh, no, you're in charge now. He's back at the store in Camden. You have full authority now. Hire, fire, ordering, everything. Of course, if you ever want advice, here's my card, but otherwise, I'm sure you'll do a great job." Arthur posed dutifully for the company photographer.

Renato had watched all this, amused. When Forrest left, he smiled. "Mr. Art, you are *jefe* now," he said, smiling.

Arthur tried out a little of his high school Spanish. *"Si, Renato. Estoy el jefe. Para ahora."*

Renato laughed. "You do fine, Mr. Art."

On Monday morning, Arthur posted the *WINE SALE* signs he had made the night before in the front window and opened for business. It was indeed a good day.

July 1967

"Betty's spending a lot of time in Togus," Arthur said. "I haven't seen her in weeks." He and Sharon were at Betty's apartment.

"I'm sorry," Sharon said. "I should have told you. She's in Boston for a few days, and she's talking about moving there. Stuart's dad gave up on the VA, and got him into Massachusetts General. The place has top docs from all over the world, Betty told me. He's paying for a lot of it."

"Really?"

"Yes." Sharon rolled over on top of Arthur, straddling him. "Although why she'd want to move down there is beyond me." She grinned. "I like my men to be..." She giggled. "Lively. Like you." She grinned mischievously, slid down his body, and then engulfed him.

September 1967

By the end of the summer, business at the store was thriving. Arthur's summer-long wine sale had paid off handsomely; the better wines Higgins had insisted they stock had all sold with a 20 percent markdown, and soon Arthur had returned to carrying mostly American jug wine again.

Higgins was right about one thing, though; some folks did like the new wines, so Arthur did not completely eliminate them. Rather, to keep them moving, he made the sale price permanent, so the store only made a few cents on each bottle. But, to his surprise, the customers who bought the more expensive wines also spent more in the store than they had before.

"They're what we call a loss leader, Aunt Esther," he explained one evening. He did not tell her that Forrest had just explained this concept to him earlier that day when he brought up the odd phenomenon. "I carry the more expensive wines because a few customers like them. It gets them in the store, and then they buy other things, see? Almost no one comes in and just buys a bottle of wine."

"It sounds like you are doing well, Arthur," his aunt said. She returned to her crocheting.

Arthur also had Renato begin to offer a weekly free sample—*FREE FOOD FRIDAYS*—of some of the high-end meats and cheeses they were now selling. To Arthur's surprise, sales of these went up dramatically, more than making up for the cost of the free samples.

Arthur also stopped closing the store for a half-hour at noon, and it was soon common to see a line of customers at lunch, waiting at the deli counter. The line increased when Arthur began offering coleslaw, potato and macaroni salads made by a family business in Winterport. And when he added locally made tuna, chicken and, finally, lobster salads to the deli menu, Arthur soon had to hire another person to help Renato deal with the lunch crowd.

As a last step, Arthur began opening at 8 a.m., not at 9, as had been traditional. Renato agreed to come in early to open, and Arthur gave him a raise, which Renato appreciated, having a wife and children. Then, Renato suggested putting a couple of small tables and chairs near the deli counter, and having coffee and fresh, locally-made doughnuts available in the morning. Arthur agreed. The new amenity was a hit; Searsport's mayor had taken to holding court there a couple of mornings each week. And the income the tables generated more than made up for Renato's raise.

Forrest was impressed. "Arthur, you're doing a fine job," he told him on an early fall visit.

"Thanks, sir, I appreciate that a lot," Arthur said. "We've been working hard. And Renato is a great member of the team. It was his idea, the coffee and doughnuts."

"That's wonderful," Forrest said. "I've got to tell you, we were thinking about closing the store. Things hadn't been going well with Laverdiere, as you know, and Higgins is a good man, but he was just a caretaker. Anyway, there were some skeptics about you at corporate, but I was never one of them. I'm glad they listened to me. And they are, too."

"Just doing my job, sir," Arthur said, beaming.

"Keep up the good work, Arthur, and one day you'll be running this company," Forrest laughed, shaking Arthur's hand as he left.

A week later, Renato told Arthur he had been drafted.

viii

"I go in one month," Renato said when he told Arthur the news. "But...I will quit here in two weeks. I am sorry, but it is necessary I take time to spend with my wife and children."

"Of course, Renato," Arthur said. "Will they be okay while you are gone?"

"Oh *si*, Mr. Art. My wife...her *abuela?*"

"Grandmother."

"Si, she lives with us and will take care of her."

"Okay," Arthur said. "I'll miss you, Renato." They shook hands.

On Renato's last day, Arthur gave him an extra week's pay. As he watched him get into his beat up Ford, Arthur realized Renato was the first person he knew who had been drafted.

He wondered if he was next. But as the weeks went by and with no draft notice having arrived, by October he had put the worry from his mind.

ix

October 1967

Arthur and Esther sat in the living room, watching the news. The lead story was about a huge demonstration at the Pentagon.

"Look at that," Esther said as crowds of shouting young people surged against ranks of soldiers clutching rifles. "We're fighting each other now over this damned war."

"Well, shouldn't we be trying to help South Vietnam? Keep them from being taken over?" Arthur asked.

"I don't know," Esther said. "I worry, Arthur. I worry about the country, about all those young men over there fighting and dying—hundreds a month now. And most of all, I..." She fell silent. After a moment she put down her crocheting and looked away from him, her hand to her mouth.

Arthur, alarmed, said, "Aunt Esther?"

"Most of all, Arthur, I worry about you. You're eligible for the draft. You haven't been called yet, but if this continues..."

"Oh I'll be okay," he said. "I'm just 18. They're only drafting older guys now."

"Maybe so, for now," Esther said. "But this war doesn't show any signs of—"

"Aunt Esther, look!" He pointed to the television. "That's Sharon's sister!"

"We're here trying to stop this insane war!" Betty yelled at the correspondent over the crowd noise. *"My fiancé was almost killed there!"* She was radiant, earnest, and beautiful with her passion, long dark hair, and perfect figure. Arthur smiled.

No wonder she's on TV.

"Are you worried about the communists taking over in South Vietnam?" the correspondent asked.

"It's not our country!" she shouted over the chants behind her. *"We have no business over there supporting a corrupt and dictatorial regime!"*

When Betty's appearance ended, Arthur ran to the phone to call Sharon.

"Really? Wow. She told me she was going. Neat!" Betty had moved to Boston as planned in August.

"She said her fiancé was almost killed there. Is she marrying Stu?"

Sharon sighed. "Yes, unfortunately. He proposed again, just a couple of days ago. When she told him she was going to the Pentagon. For him."

x

November 1967

Just before Thanksgiving, some hikers found Oscar Loudermilk's body in the woods near the old quarry, a hundred yards or so from June Laverdiere's car, which he had apparently been driving. He was in civilian clothes. He had been shot in the head.

Oscar's death was the first murder in Waldo County anyone could remember. That, combined with his status as a police officer, sparked more than the usual interest in the Augusta and Portland media. The reaction in the county, however, was decidedly mixed.

Loudermilk's family did not consider the local investigation to have been adequate, and demanded an FBI investigation, or at least one by the state authorities. Oddly, they seemed more angry than grief-stricken.

June Laverdiere was the most distraught, sobbing brokenly at his funeral. Arthur could understand. She and Loudermilk had been a well-known couple in their church since his apparent conversion. "And of course he's the second man she's loved who ended up shot to death," Arthur noted, talking about it with Sharon one evening.

Sharon nodded. "The next guy she dates better be careful." Then she giggled. "I'm so bad," she said, blushing.

"Yes you are, you naughty girl," Arthur chuckled. "Seriously, though, Laverdiere was a sad man in a tough situation and I'm sorry about him. But I'll not miss Oscar Loudermilk."

Clement reacted as Arthur expected. "I'm glad he's dead, the son of a bitch."

"What do you really think, Clement?" Arthur said, trying to get a smile out of him.

"You heard me," Clement said. "And I didn't kill him either, if that's what you're thinking."

Arthur looked at him. "Um…didn't think you did."

"Good." Clement was silent a moment. "Anyway, enough about that asshole. You want to go catch a flick? There's a new one in town. *Cool Hand Luke*. Paul Newman."

This was the first time Clement had suggested they do something together in close to a year. "Sure," he said. "But what about your buddy? Ted?"

"He's splitting," Clement said. "He's quitting the university and moving back to Portland after the holidays."

.　.　.

CHAPTER 31
i

Waldo County, Maine
February 1968

It was after a particularly delicious love-making session with Sharon—she was wilder than she had ever been before—that Arthur decided. *It was time.*

"Oh baby baby baby," Sharon said, panting beside him. "That was unbelievable."

Arthur nodded. "Man, was it ever."

Sharon smiled. "I love you, Arthur West."

"I know." Arthur rolled onto his side and, propping his head up with his right hand, looked at her fondly. He said, "Listen to me. I've been thinking."

294

"Uh oh," Sharon said, smiling again. But, sensing his mood, she grew serious. "What?"

"Why should we wait til September to get married? Why not get married in June, right after you graduate?"

Sharon sat up, amazed. "Oh Arthur—yes, yes, *yes!*" She fell on him and began frantically kissing him. "Oh thank you, thank you, you couldn't have given me a better present!"

He continued, "I mean, I'm running the store now, it's going well, my salary is good enough to live well on, I'm in the profit-sharing plan, and—"

"Yes, whatever!" Sharon laughed. "I don't care about all that, but fine, if that's important to you. It just doesn't matter. So let's get this done, start making plans. June it is. Oh I can hardly wait, I'm going to have Betty as my bridesmaid and—"

Arthur laughed and said, "And I'll get Clement to be best man—"

Sharon abruptly stopped smiling. "Oh Arthur, do you have to? I mean…seriously? Him?"

Arthur, sensing he had broken the mood, tried to retrieve it. "Sure, hon', we can talk about it later. We have lots of time to plan."

ii

March 1968

The letter arrived on March 25.

ORDER TO REPORT FOR INDUCTION
March 23, 1968
The President of the United States
TO: Arthur Leon West
       5007 Congress Street
       Belfast, Maine 04915

GREETING:

You are hereby ordered for induction into the Armed Forces of the United States, and to report at <u>Greyhound Bus Lines, Inc. 530 Coldbrook Road, Bangor Maine</u> on <u>April 28 1968 at 5:30 a.m. (Standard time, in the morning)</u> for forwarding to an Armed Forces Induction Station.

When you arrive at the bus station, check in with the leader, Clarence W. Cameron.

iii

"You're not really going to go, are you?" Clement asked over sodas at Johnson's the next afternoon.

"I guess I don't have much choice," Arthur said.

"Listen, you always have choices. First off, you can try to get the draft board to reconsider. I hear people with connections can get out of it, not get drafted at all. You must know someone on the Board."

"I doubt it," Arthur said. In truth, he hadn't even known there was a local draft board.

"I bet your aunt does. She probably knows everybody on it."

"I guess she might. I could talk to her about it." He considered this a moment or two. "But the question is, should I?"

Clement scoffed. "What do you mean, 'Should I?' Are you fucking kidding me? You want to go over there and get your ass shot?"

"No, of course not," Arthur said. "But…"

"But what?"

"Is it right I try to pull strings?" Arthur felt stupid even bringing the subject up.

"Is it right? Is it *right?* The whole fucking war isn't right. Jesus Christ, wake the fuck up. Hell, if it was me and I hadn't already gotten out of it, I'd get my ass to Canada.

You ought to think about that too, my friend." He finished his Coke. "Buddy, don't do this, I'm telling you. If you never listen to me again, listen to me now."

Arthur leaned forward. "You got out of going? How? I mean, you registered, right?"

Clement laughed, and leaned forward. He whispered, "well, yeah, but I went in and told 'em I was...you know..." He mouthed the word *'queer'*. He chuckled. "Hell, might as well use it if everyone thinks I am anyway, right?"

Arthur was stunned. "You told 'em you were...a queer?" he whispered.

"Well, I kinda implied it. One of them on the Board had heard the rumors. So I didn't have to do much convincing." He smiled. "Maybe you could...do the same thing? I mean, everyone knows we're friends and all, it wouldn't be hard."

Arthur laughed. "Uh, no, buddy, sorry, I'm not doing that."

"Hey, it beats getting your ass shot, Preach." Clement stood. "Look, I gotta go. You might give it some thought, man. I'll catch you later."

Arthur, open-mouthed, watched Clement leave.

iii

"I know several people on the Board," Aunt Esther told him that night over supper.

"Well, what do you think?" Arthur asked. "Clement says I should appeal. He did, and got out of it." He did not tell her how.

Esther sighed. "Ahhh me." She considered this. "Arthur, I love you more than I can express to you. I always have. Nothing would make me happier than for you not to go to Vietnam. I'd do anything to keep you here. But it's not up to me. It's up to you. You have to decide. If you want me to talk to someone on the board, I will. I can't guarantee it would work, but I think it probably would."

She smiled. "I was sweethearts with George Seekins many years ago. I think he still has feelings for me." She blushed a little.

Arthur laughed. "I'm sure he does."

"But I can understand why you are thinking about it. It's not easy for some people to have strings pulled for them. There's something unfair about it, some folks think, I guess. You've never sought favoritism that I know of, for any reason, and it's one of the things that I admire about you. I don't think it would even have occurred to you if Clement hadn't mentioned it."

"No, it hadn't," he said.

"That speaks well of you, Arthur."

He said nothing.

She smiled. "But, if you do go, it's potentially your life on the line, so I can see how that would make a difference. So you think about it a few days. Then tell me what you want to do. I'll talk to George if you decide you want me to."

"I will." They finished dinner in silence.

iv

"You're going to fight it, aren't you?" Sharon asked. Arthur did not reply. "I mean, *aren't* you?"

"I don't know." They were at Betty's old apartment. Since she had moved to Boston, Arthur had started paying Betty's share of the rent, forty dollars a month, in order to have a place to go with Sharon.

"What do you mean you don't know? Are you crazy? Did you see what happened to Stuart?"

"Of course," Arthur said. "I saw."

"So, what's the issue?"

"I just think that…"

"Think what? *What?*"

"Taking advantage of the fact that my aunt knows someone on the draft board isn't right, and—"

"Oh for God's sake." Sharon jumped up, naked, and walked across the room in the dark. She stood to the side of the window, looking out into the gloaming. The days were starting to get longer now after a dark, cold winter.

"I'm not saying I won't do it," Arthur said. "But I'm not sure I'd feel right about it, either, is all."

"Why? Thousands of guys would love to have the chance you have here."

"Maybe. But I guess that's kind of the point, too. Why should I get special treatment?"

"Aaaggghhhh!" Sharon growled. "Jesus, you are sure living up to your nickname."

"Hey, I can't help it," Arthur said hotly. "If it makes you angry, I'm sorry!"

Sharon turned away from him, and stared out the window.

Arthur stood and started to get dressed. "We probably should go," he said.

"What's really going on here, Arthur?" Sharon asked.

"What do you mean?"

"Why do you really want to go into the army?"

"I don't want to," he said. "I may have to, is the point."

"No, no, you just told me your aunt could get you out of it. You don't have to." She turned and faced him. "I'm beginning to wonder if you want to marry me at all."

Oh Lord, Arthur thought. *Not this again.* He glared at her. "Of course I do," he said angrily. "Why would you even think that? I wouldn't have said we should move up the date if I didn't."

Sharon scoffed, but said nothing.

He thought of something else. "In fact, if you want, we can get married right now, tonight. Or at least before I leave." He caught himself. "If I leave."

"There," Sharon said in triumph. "You just said you were going. Catching yourself lying to yourself doesn't cut it, Artie."

Arthur sighed. "I haven't made up my mind yet, I was just saying, is all. But marrying you is not the problem here, I promise. We can get married now. My report date isn't until late April, so if I go, we could do it. And I want to."

She looked at him carefully, then crossed to the bed and picked up her panties. "Arthur, I need to think about this." She started to dress.

"Hey, I thought you were all hot to get married," Arthur said. "Wanting me to move up the date and all. Now you say you need to think about it?"

"Yes," she said. "This changes everything, you going into the army. Arthur, I couldn't stand it if…" She sighed. "If something happened to you. Like what happened to Stuart. We'd be married, and…"

Finally, he understood. "And you wouldn't want to be married to a…a cripple."

She sighed. "Come on, get dressed. I need to get home."

v

Several days later, he made his decision. He told his Aunt. She sighed as she looked up from her crocheting. "Are you sure?"

"Yes. I'm going."

"All right. You are a man now, and you need to make your own decisions."

"Of course. But thank you for offering to help," he said. He looked at his aunt. "I love you, Aunt Esther," he said, crossing to her.

She hugged him fiercely as he leaned down to kiss her cheek. "You're the son I never had, Arthur. Now you come home, do you understand?"

"Yes. And I will."

vi

"You're a fucking idiot," Clement said.

vii

Sharon started to tear up. "How—how can you go off and *leave me*? How? If you loved me, you wouldn't be doing this!"

"You know I'm serious about us getting married *now,* don't you?" Arthur said.

Sharon was having none of it. "No." Weeping, she continued, "I told you before. Arthur, you need to think about this carefully. I don't think you are."

"Sharon, now come on, you know I want to marry you. It's not a question of that. I've told you over and over. I just have to go. I wouldn't feel right about it if I didn't."

"Anybody else would feel right about it!" she said, mocking him. "But oh no, not you!"

"Maybe," he said. "I may be stupid, I don't know. But I have to go. I'd feel guilty the rest of my life if I—"

"At least you'd be alive!" She stood. "Well, you go ahead and go then. Just go. But know this. I may not be here when you get back. *If* you get back." She stalked out of Johnson's.

viii

Aunt Esther drove him to Bangor on the appointed morning. She waited with him until the bus to Portland arrived. She had made a thermos of her excellent coffee. They sat quietly, waiting. Time felt heavy, momentous, as the seconds vanished.

"So you talked to Mr. Forrest about the store?"

Arthur sipped his coffee and smiled. "Yes, Aunt Esther. Mr. Higgins is taking over again."

"Oh of course, I remember. You told me already. I'm sorry, I don't remember things as well as I used to."

Arthur squeezed her hand. "I know. It's okay. But I've taken care of everything."

"Did you see your little friend Sharon yesterday?"

301

"Yes, I did."

Actually, he had not; she did not want to see him. "Arthur, I think it best that I not," she had told him over the phone. "It will just make me upset. I hope you understand. I'll write to you, though, I promise. And I guess you'll be home on leave at some point. I'll see you then." And she had hung up. Arthur had started to call her back, but then decided against it. He realized that his freedom as a civilian may not be the only thing he was giving up with his decision to go.

When the bus arrived, Arthur was the last of the half-dozen draftees to board. His aunt walked with him to the bus door and hugged him desperately. "Now you be careful, Arthur." She smiled.

Arthur teared up a little, in spite of himself. "I will," he managed to say.

"I love you," she said.

"I know," Arthur said. "I love you, too, Aunt Esther."

"Let's go, West," the leader of his group said.

Arthur gave her one last hug. She felt so frail in his arms. He turned and boarded the bus. He found a seat, the door pulled shut, and the driver put the bus in gear and pulled away. Arthur watched his aunt get into the driver's seat of the Chevy. He turned away, and by the time the bus had reached I-95, he had fallen asleep, the sky just starting to turn pink off to the southeast.

· · ·

CHAPTER 32
i

Bangor, Maine
September 1968

Five months later, a bus pulled up in front of the Greyhound station on the Coldbrook Road late in the afternoon of a mid-September day. Arthur stared out the window, searching for the familiar Chevrolet Bel-Air, and yes, there it was, parked near the station entrance. Aunt Esther stood beside it, along with Mrs. Hall.

"Bangor," the driver announced over the intercom. "Fifteen minute stop. Next stop, Brewer." Arthur got up, put on his garrison cap, walked to the front of the bus and dismounted.

He retrieved his duffel from the cargo bay, and turned just in time to meet Aunt Esther approaching him with a large smile and open arms. He grinned back. "Hey, Aunt of mine!" He grabbed her and swept her off the ground, and gently lowered her back to earth. *She weighs almost nothing,* he thought.

"Arthur, it's wonderful to see you," she said, kissing him on the cheek. "I've missed you so." She patted him on the shoulder. "My, you have filled out. You were a skinny teenager when you left, but look at you now. They must have kept you busy. And well fed."

He laughed. "'Keeping busy' doesn't begin to describe the last five months. And army chow is actually not bad, mostly. And there's plenty of it." He smiled at Mrs. Hall and gave her a hug as well. "Hello, Mrs. Hall, it's nice to see you again. Thank you for coming."

"I'm happy to be here, Arthur," she said. "It's good to see you, too."

"I asked Sylvia to drive," Aunt Esther said. "I was feeling a little tired. Come on, let's get you home. I have a chicken to put in the oven. With stuffing and mashed potatoes."

"That sounds great, Auntie, thank you." He stowed the duffel in the trunk of the Chevy, helped Esther into the passenger seat, and climbed in the back as Mrs. Hall pulled away.

"I see you have a little rank now," Aunt Esther said, turning to look at him. She indicated the single chevron on his sleeves. "What's that?"

"I made PFC a week ago, at the end of infantry training. That's Private First Class."

"That's wonderful!" Esther said. "Five months in and you've already gotten promoted."

"Ayuh," he said. "It's not that big a step but it does mean more money. A lot more percentage-wise, compared to what I got when I first was in. My first month's pay was ninety dollars. Three dollars a day. A PFC makes almost thirty dollars more."

"Is that all?" Mrs. Hall asked. "That sure doesn't sound like much."

"And it isn't," Arthur laughed. "But remember, I get free food, clothing, medical care and a place to live. And, I don't spend my money on much. We got a few weekend passes, but I'd just go into Columbia, split the cost of a hotel room with one of the guys, maybe eat out Saturday night, go to a movie. I try to save a little each month. I've already got almost two hundred in my pocket."

"Did you open a bank account?" Mrs. Hall asked.

"No," Arthur said. "I kept the money in the company safe. I was keeping it in my footlocker, but one of the guys got some money stolen out of his—he'd left it unlocked—so I thought I probably ought to safeguard it."

"That's awful, soldiers stealing money from other soldiers," Mrs. Hall said.

Arthur nodded. "It is."

Aunt Esther smiled at Arthur. "We need to get home. I have a chicken to put in the oven. With stuffing and mashed potatoes."

"Yes, thanks, Aunt Esther," Arthur said.

After a moment, Mrs. Hall said, "Henry Junior is a freshman in college now. It's very different with him. He's costing us a lot of money," she laughed. "What with tuition, room, board, books, a little spending money, it sure adds up."

"Where's he going?"

"As you may remember, he felt the call of the Lord a couple of years ago."

"I remember," Arthur said.

"He has decided to become a minister, amazingly enough. He is a freshman at a bible college in Rumford."

"Too bad he's not here, I was hoping to see him before...before I left," Arthur said.

"I'll tell him you're home on leave," Mrs. Hall said. "He might be able to take a day and come see you while you're home."

"Great," Arthur said. "Please say 'hi' for me. I hope he can come."

"You bet. Henry Senior will want to see you as well." Mrs. Hall sped up to pass an 18-wheeler in front of her.

"I'd like to see Mr. Hall," Arthur said. "How is he?"

"Not well, Arthur," Mrs. Hall said. "He was diagnosed with lung cancer three months ago. All that smoking finally caught up with him." She sighed. "Don't start smoking, Arthur. It's a nasty, expensive habit, and it can kill you."

"I won't," Arthur said, although in truth, he had tried smoking during basic. He figured so many of the guys smoked, there had to be something to it. But he had not developed a taste for it.

"Any idea how the store is doing, Aunt Esther?" he asked.

"Oh, well enough, I guess," she said. "I'm sure they miss you. I have a housekeeper who comes in now, three days a week. She does the shopping for me. I'm not as spry as I used to be, Arthur." She smiled. "But I can still cook. In fact, when we get home, I have a chicken to put in the oven. With stuffing and mashed potatoes."

"Yes," Arthur said. "I can't wait."

After a minute or two, Esther seemed to doze, and Mrs. Hall was concentrating on her driving, so Arthur sat back as they drove south down Rt.1A toward Belfast. He quietly watched the scenery go by: farmhouses and businesses he had seen along the highway since he was a child. But these previously familiar landmarks seemed different now, as if not a part of his life, but rather, monuments in a strange land, marking another time and place—familiar, and yet not a part of his own memory or experience any longer, as if he were watching a film.

Everything is different.

Then his thoughts turned to Sharon. He was eager, and also somewhat reluctant, to talk with her.

She had written to him about ten days after he left the previous April. That letter, in reply to one he had sent her, was the first piece of mail he had received after arriving at Fort Jackson.

Sharon was unexpectedly contrite. She apologized for not seeing him before he left. She was missing him, and she hoped—she had drawn a little winky-face beside the word—that the photograph she had included, taken with her new Polaroid camera, would keep him company until she could be with him again.

He smiled. The photograph had been of her leaning back on a bed, one eyebrow arched, wearing a halter top and a very short skirt and high heels, the skirt short enough to reveal the tops of her stockings and the tabs of the garter belt holding them up. She was smiling alluringly. She had drawn a heart at the bottom and wrote "missing you" under it, followed by several X's.

At first, as May turned into June, he had received a weekly letter from her, each letter becoming more explicit about what they would do when he got home, and containing a photograph, each progressively more explicit than the previous one, until soon she was sending photos in which she was nearly naked.

This made Arthur the envy of the barracks, as one evening during a rare hour of free time, one of his squad mates saw one of the photos. Word soon spread, and several of the guys began asking if they could see the photo as well as the others. Arthur declined.

Then, shortly after he finished basic and reported for infantry training, the letters stopped. He hadn't heard from her since mid-July. Arthur wrote a couple of times, but got no response.

ii

After supper, Arthur offered to help with the dishes, but Aunt Esther declined. "No, Arthur, you are home on vacation and you shouldn't be expected to do any work while you're here. Why don't you call some of your friends while I clean up?"

Arthur nodded. "Are you sure?"

"Absolutely," Aunt Esther said. "Now *shoo!*" She motioned him away.

Arthur chuckled. "Yes ma'am," he said, then went to the living room and sat in the easy chair by the telephone. He called the Tibbets house. Betty answered.

"Art!" she said. "How nice to hear from you. Are you home?"

"Ayuh, just got in this afternoon. I'm staying with my Aunt, of course. Nice to hear your voice, Betty."

"Yes, well, I do hope you'll be able to come over for dinner while you're home. In fact, wait just a sec." She held the phone against her body and Arthur heard muffled conversation. She came back on. "Yes, please do come for dinner. How about tomorrow? My parents and Stu both want to see you!"

"That would be great," Arthur said. "Umm…is Sharon there?"

"No," Betty said after a moment. "I think she's at work. She got a job a month or so ago at the new McDonalds out near the bypass." She lowered her voice. "I'll tell you more when I can, but don't bring Sharon up tomorrow night. There are issues."

"Okay," he said. "But please let her know I'm in town."

"I'll tell her when I speak to her," Betty said. "See you tomorrow."

iii

"Arthur, it's great to see you again," Mr. Tibbets said, offering his hand as he opened the door. "My God, you look great. You've really filled out."

"Thank you, sir," he said. "Army chow and lots of exercise, I guess."

"The food must be better than the Marine Corps chow I remember," Tibbets laughed. "Come on in." Arthur followed him into the living room.

"Dinner smells wonderful," Arthur said.

"Mrs. T is making roast pork, one of her specialties. Well, let me get Betty. *Betty! Stu!*" he yelled. *"Arthur's here!"*

"We'll be right there," Betty called from the kitchen.

"Have a seat, Arthur," Tibbets said. "Can I get you something?" He smiled. "Your usual?"

Arthur hadn't had a Doctor Pepper since the spring. "Yes, sir. Thank you."

"Coming right up," he said.

A minute or so later, Stuart, in his wheel chair, appeared in the entrance to the living room, Betty pushing him. "Hello, Arthur," he whispered hoarsely, smiling. "It's good to see you."

"It's good to see you too, Stu," Arthur said, offering his left hand. Stuart took it, squeezed firmly.

Arthur pretended not to notice Stuart's missing limbs. The right side of his face was still scarred, and the scalp on that side was pink and mottled, the hair apparently gone for good. He wore an eye patch over his right eye.

"I know what you're thinking," Stuart said. "There's something different about this guy."

Arthur smiled. "Well...maybe a little. I'm glad you're out of the hospital, my friend."

"Me too, but it's just a short break. I've got more surgery scheduled in October, and of course lots of PT. At some point the VA's going to fit me up with a new arm. But for now, the docs in Boston think I deserve a couple weeks off, so they let me come for a visit with the in-laws."

Tibbets came in with the soda and handed it to Arthur. He placed a bottle of wine and two glasses on a coaster on the coffee table.

"So I hear you two got married," Arthur said.

"Oh yes," Betty said. She smiled, and winked at Stuart. "Thankfully, not everything's damaged." Arthur and Stuart laughed.

Tibbets laughed too, in spite of himself. "Okay," he said. "I think that's my cue to go help Mrs. T in the kitchen." He disappeared.

Betty poured Stuart a glass of wine. He took it and drank it all at once. She poured him another. "Thanks, sweetheart." He sipped this one. He looked at Art. "Wine, good for what ails you. Helps with the aches and pains."

Arthur nodded. "So what have you two been doing?"

Betty sighed. "I hope this doesn't upset you. Stu and I are very involved in the anti-war movement."

"Oh I knew that," Arthur said. "About you, anyway."

"Me too now," Stuart said. "Of course it took getting my ass blown to pieces for me to wake up. But, here I am. As soon as I physically can, I'm going to start showing up at demonstrations. Make speeches. Get arrested. Run for Congress, maybe. Right now all I can do is help with phone calls, dictate letters, arrange meetings, that sort of thing. Betty here's been doing some traveling, though."

"I was in Chicago last month," she said proudly.

"Oh?" Arthur said. He looked at her.

"The convention," Betty said.

Arthur looked blankly at her. "What convention?"

"Oh my God," Betty said. "You don't know anything about the Democratic convention? The police riot?"

"I guess not," Arthur said. "I've been pretty busy, haven't seen a newspaper in months. And not much TV."

"I can vouch for that," Stu said. "The army's very insulated, sweetheart. You don't hear a lot of civilian news when you're in training."

"Well, Humphrey got the nomination," Betty said. "Bobby would have gotten it if—"

"I did hear about the Kennedy shooting," Arthur said. "Terrible. A couple months ago? In California?"

"Yes. June."

"It happened toward the end of basic," Arthur said. "A couple guys in the platoon were going to get weekend passes, but the base canceled them all. The whole base, everybody. Worried about riots or something. I heard the same thing happened in April when King got shot."

"Yes, I bet," Betty said. "So sad. Bobby was pretty much guaranteed to get the nomination. And probably would have been elected. But now with Humphrey getting it, I don't know. I think they should have gone with McCarthy, myself."

"Betty, Nixon would have destroyed McCarthy in the election. The Republicans would have eaten him for lunch!"

"Fuck Nixon," Betty said. "Mark my words, he's going to be trouble one day. I sure hope Humphrey wins."

"I hope so too," Stuart said. "Not saying he's a shoo-in, but he's got a better shot at winning than Clean Gene would have."

They continued to discuss politics, although Arthur said little. He had only the vaguest idea what they were talking about.

During dinner, no one mentioned Sharon.

iv

After dessert and coffee, Betty said, "I'm going to go for a walk around the block, get rid of some of these calories. Great dinner, Mom."

"Thank you, dear," Mrs. Tibbets said, starting to clear the dishes.

"Arthur, you want to come along on my walk?"

"I'd love to," he said. "You mind, Stu?"

"By all means, go," Stuart said, chuckling. "Keep your eye on him, Betty. If he tries to cop a feel, deck him!"

"You two!" Mrs. Tibbets laughed.

"I will," Betty laughed. "Come on, Art."

They walked outside and started down the street. Betty pulled out a pack of cigarettes and offered one to Arthur. "No thanks," he said. "Tried it, didn't like it."

"I should probably quit," Betty said. "Look, thanks for not bringing up Sharon. She's kind of on the outs with Mom and Dad. Dad, especially."

"What happened?"

"She went crazy. Fucking. Over. *Night.* Picked up by the cops a couple times, drinking. It started right after you left. She even got busted with pot once. Dad got that

311

taken care of, though. Anyway, in July, after she graduated from high school, she moved out of the house. A big scene, let me tell you. Mom didn't leave her room for two days. Shar's hanging out now with really weird people, living in an old house near Union with four or five druggies. Acid and grass, not so bad. But I'm thinking more than that."

"Wow," Arthur said.

"Yeah," Betty said. "Dad is beyond furious. If you'd brought her up at dinner he'd have left the room."

"How's your mother handling it?"

"Better now. She goes to see Sharon every week or so. Brings her food, does her laundry." Betty smiled. "A mother's love. But at least she has a job. So that's something."

"She stopped writing to me in July," Arthur said.

"Yeah, she told me she was just tired of worrying about you. She thought it best to break it off."

"I thought something like that. Do you think I should go see her?"

"I don't know, Art," Betty said. "She's not the same person. I mean, you wouldn't believe it." She stubbed out her cigarette. "Let's get back. I'm glad we could talk." She kissed him on the cheek. "You're a great guy, Preach. Sharon's lucky, but of course has no idea. Please, be fucking careful over there, Vietnam. You promise?"

"Of course. And don't worry."

"Right, don't worry," she scoffed.

V

The next morning, Arthur drove to Searsport. He walked into the FoodMart and saw Higgins at the deli counter, talking to the counter man. Higgins looked up and saw him, smiled, and hurried over. "Arthur!" Higgins said. "It's great to see you. Home on leave?"

Arthur nodded. "I am, Mr. Higgins. I just wanted to stop by and say hello. See how the store was doing, you know?"

"I understand. It's doing fine, Arthur, just fine. You really got this place going during the time you were here. What, less than a year, and it was one of the most profitable small FoodMarts in the state when you left. You, sir, are a tough act to follow." He laughed. "You want a job? I could use some help."

Arthur smiled. This possibility had not occurred to him, but he was growing tired of sitting around, thinking about Vietnam. "Actually, if you need me for a week or so, I could use the money. PFCs don't exactly make a fortune, you know."

"Seriously? Well, I could swing thirty bucks a day for a week, if that works for you. Cash. It's not much, but..."

Arthur laughed. "Mr. Higgins, you just offered me more than my monthly salary for a week's work. Of course I'll take it. I'll start tomorrow morning. What do you want me to do? I see you've got a deli counter man."

"Oh yeah." He gestured to the man behind the deli counter. "Jorge here is doing just fine. Renato, bless him, recommended him. He's Renato's brother-in-law. Well, was."

"Was?" Arthur asked.

Higgins looked at him, and then grew serious. "Oh God, you haven't heard. Arthur, Renato was killed in Vietnam a month ago. He left a wife and two little kids. Just terrible."

Arthur flinched involuntarily, as if he had been slapped. "Oh no," he said.

Arthur thought of little else the rest of the day. "How awful," Aunt Esther said when he told her that evening. "I'm so glad you're not there." Arthur, not knowing how to respond to that, thought it best to say nothing.

The phone rang that evening. Arthur had taken to watching the evening news of late, paying particular attention to the upcoming presidential election and of course news from the war. "Arthur, it's for you," Esther said.

"Hi, you." It was Sharon.

"Well hi there, babe," Arthur said. He tried to keep the sarcasm out of his voice, not very successfully. "Nice to hear from you. Finally."

"I'm sorry. It's been difficult. I didn't know you were back until Betty told me this morning. I would have called sooner."

"I did send you a letter."

"Did you? It must have gone to my folks' house. I don't live there anymore."

"I know, Betty told me. You know, she's worried about you."

Sharon said, "She doesn't need to. Or you, either."

"Okay," Arthur said. "Not trying to pick a fight here."

She was silent a moment. "I'm sorry. Look, I'd really like to see you. Maybe I can come over. It's a nice night, we could sit in the back yard or something."

"Sure," Arthur said. "My aunt goes to bed at like eight o'clock now. Sleeps like the dead til about dawn. If we're quiet she won't even know you're here."

Okay, I'll be over at 8:30." She hung up.

"Hi," Sharon said, when he opened the door. Then she fell into his arms and began kissing him. "Oh, Artie, I've missed you so."

They more or less stumbled into the living room and collapsed on the couch, frantically struggling out of enough of their clothes to be able to make love quickly and frantically, both coming in a sudden outburst which they

314

were hard-pressed to keep quiet, Arthur having to whisper *"Shhh—shhh"* while clapping his hand over her mouth.

They sat quietly after, holding each other til their hearts quit pounding. "Oh my God," Sharon said. "That's the first time since…the last time."

"Really?"

Sharon looked at him. "Well of course, silly, why would you think otherwise?" She winked at him. "Didn't you like my pictures?"

He laughed. "I did," he said. "But then you stopped writing all of a sudden. I didn't know what was going on. And after what Betty said about you living with a bunch of folks out toward Union…I guess I thought you'd moved on."

She leaned against his shoulder. "No," she said. "I haven't moved on. I thought maybe I had, for a while there, but…no. I haven't. I have to tell you, I still don't want to marry you until—until you get back. But when you do, yes. If you'll still have me."

"Of course," Arthur said. "But you have to promise to write to me. And keep writing to me. And if you stop, please tell me why before you do. Will you?"

"I promise. I do. Honest." She then said, "Now, look what I've got." She reached in her purse and pulled out a joint. "This is great stuff. You want to toke up? You will be blown away."

Arthur laughed. "Sure," he said. "I haven't done any of that since junior prom. Lord, that was a while ago, wasn't it? But outside. There's a glider in the back yard. Come on."

He showed her outside to the glider. "You get that ready and I'll make us a couple of drinks."

"Do you have any wine?"

"I don't think so, but maybe there's else something around. I'll look. I'll be right back."

He found a bottle of bourbon in the back of one of the cupboards. He had no idea how old it was, but he poured a couple of fingers into Sharon's coke, and then went outside and crossed to the glider.

Sharon, naked, reclined in the swing seat, her clothes in a pile on the floor. "What took you so long?" she said.

She wouldn't let him touch her, but teased him as she touched herself, until they had finished the joint and their drinks. It was worth the wait.

.　.　.

CHAPTER 33
i

Searsport, Maine
September 1968

During his fifth day at the store, a middle-aged, portly man came in wearing a suit, tie, and a battered fedora. He spoke to Higgins for a moment. Higgins led the man over. "Arthur, this is Mr. Baker, a private investigator from Augusta. He wants to talk to you for a few minutes."

"Sure, no problem." Arthur shook hands with Baker. "Can we use the office, Mr. H?"

"Of course," Higgins said.

"What can I do for you, Mr. Baker?" Arthur said, when they were seated.

Baker opened a small notebook and took out a ballpoint pen. "Thanks for agreeing to talk to me, Mr. West," Baker said. "I'm looking into the murder of Officer Oscar Loudermilk from the Searsport PD. Last November. His parents hired me. They didn't think his death was being investigated vigorously enough."

Arthur nodded and smiled. *Best be careful here,* he thought. "Well, I didn't do it, if that's what you think."

Baker smiled and said, "No, I don't think that. But you did know the officer?"

"I did."

"When did you meet him?"

"I've known him since grade school."

"Was he a friend of yours?"

Arthur scoffed. "Hardly."

"Oh? How so?"

"It's a long story. He was a bully when we were kids. Everybody hated him, except for three or four of his toadies. Heck, they probably hated him too, really."

"What about Clement Paul? Did he hate him?"

Why had he brought up Clement? Arthur thought. He nodded carefully. "Probably more than anyone." Arthur recounted how Oscar had shot Clement's dog. He did not tell him the quarry story. "If you want more than that, you should probably talk to Clement."

"I intend to," Baker said. "But let me ask you, Mr. West. Do you think Loudermilk shooting Clement's dog would have been enough provocation to cause Clement to murder him? Years later?"

"I don't think so," Arthur replied. "Like you say, that was a long time ago. Clement got his revenge at the time. Kid stuff, nothing fatal." He moved on quickly before Baker could ask questions about this. "No, Clement has a temper. But a killing temper? I don't think so."

"I see," Baker said. "I gather the Officer had a bit of a turnaround in his personal life a year or two back, is that true?"

"Supposedly. Made a big show of getting religion. I didn't much believe it, myself. He'd taken up with the widow of another man, the fella who used to run this store, in fact. He ended up killing himself." Arthur did not mention any further details, although he was keenly aware

317

of them being in the very room where it had happened. "His widow is very religious, so I think Loudermilk was just humoring her."

"I see." Baker jotted a few sentences down in his notebook. "Now, did you know a friend of Clement's, a teaching assistant at the university up Orono?"

Arthur knew he had to be *very* careful here. "Some guy named—what, Crockett?"

"Yes, exactly." Baker checked his notebook. "Ted Crockett. What do you know about them?"

"About *them?*"

"Yes. Clement and Mr. Crockett. Would you say they were close?"

"I don't know," Arthur said. "Clement hung out with him for a while. He told me Crockett left, though. He moved back to Portland about a year ago. I guess about the time—" Arthur stopped. "About the time Loudermilk was murdered." He shrugged. "Do you think there's a connection?"

"I don't know. Do you?"

Arthur shrugged again. "Probably coincidence."

"Maybe," Baker said. "Was there anything…how should I put this—unusually close in their relationship, that you knew of?"

"What do you mean?" Arthur asked, buying time.

"Mr. West, to put it bluntly, do you know if they were in some kind of…some kind of unnatural relationship?"

Arthur laughed. "You mean like queers?"

Baker nodded, clearly embarrassed. "Yes. Homosexuals."

"Mr. Baker, I've known Clement all my life, and never once did he ever make any kind of move like that on me. Or on anyone that I ever heard of. If he's queer, he's kept it pretty hidden. And let me just assure you, I like

women, myself. I'm engaged to one right now, in fact."
Arthur didn't know why he felt compelled to say that.

Baker laughed. "Okay, I got you." He put away his
notebook. "Well, thank you, Mr. West, you've been very
helpful." He stood and shook Arthur's hand. "You take
care of yourself."

"What was that all about?" Higgins asked after
Baker left.

"Some kind of investigation," Arthur said. "So
when's that produce due to arrive, Mr. H?"

ii

"Shit, a private investigator?" Clement said. He and
Arthur were having lunch at Jordan's.

Arthur recounted the interview. "Then he asked
about Ted."

"Oh fuck," Clement said. "What did he want to
know?"

Arthur sighed. He decided to be blunt. "He wanted
to know if you and Ted were queers. I told him if you were,
you've sure kept it hidden from me."

"Shit," Clement said. He shook his head. "Goddamn
it." Clement rubbed his chin and drummed his fingers on
the table top, apparently lost in thought for a few moments.

"Clement, what's going on?" Arthur asked.

Clement stood, his burger only half-eaten. "You
don't want to know, buddy. Believe me. Look, I gotta go."
Clement started out, then stopped and put a fiver on the
table. "For the burger." He looked at Arthur. "Listen,
dumbass—you take care of yourself over there. You get
yourself killed, I'll never forgive you."

Then, a lifetime of memories overcame Arthur. He
was almost unable to speak. But he stood, and said, "Come
here." He gave Clement a huge bear hug, even lifting him
off the ground an inch or two for a second. "You take care
of your own self, my old friend." The last word was almost
a whisper.

Arthur knew this was the last time he would see Clement Paul.

Clement chuckled a little, patted him on the shoulders. "Yeah yeah, now don't start bawling on me like a damn sissy." Arthur choked out a laugh. Clement left the embrace, wiped his right eye, and looked at Arthur. He grinned and shrugged. "I'll be fine, man, what could happen? And drop me a note once in a while. I'll…I'll try to write back…Fuck, Preach, I'll miss you." He hurried out.

iii

"Hey Preach." It was Hag calling.

"Hag, how the heck are you?" Arthur said. "Nice to hear from you. Are you home?"

"Nope. Still in Rumford. Mom told me you were home on leave. Sorry I can't come home. Big test tomorrow."

"No problem, buddy." They chatted idly for a bit. Hag told him about school, and his plans to get ordained. He wasn't sure what denomination.

Arthur wondered if Baker had visited Hag yet. Not wanting to ask directly, he said, "So, you heard anything about Clement lately?"

"Oh man," Hag said. "That's a question. How much time you got?"

Arthur chuckled. "Not that much. I leave in a few days."

"Preach, I don't know for sure, but…you might want to be real careful around him. He's very bad news. Everyone…" he fell silent a moment, then continued, "I told you once the word was going around that Clement was a…a queer."

"I remember. Is that all?" *This was getting more than a little tiresome.*

"No, there's something worse." Hag lowered his voice. "Preach—there's another rumor going around. That—that it was Clement that killed Loudermilk."

"What?" Arthur said. "Are you kidding?"

"I wish I was."

"Why would he do that?"

"I don't know. But I have my suspicions." Hag continued, "You know he was friends with that guy up Orono, right?"

"Ayuh."

"Well—maybe Loudermilk found out something about the two of them. Maybe caught them...at it. You know."

Arthur hadn't considered this. "Wow, Hag. Why would you think that?"

"I dunno, Preach. No hard evidence. Just a feeling. Listen, I've got to go now. It was good to talk to you. I wish I could come see you. But I'll pray for you while you're gone. Every day."

"I'm sure that will help, Hag, but I'll be careful just the same. You take care, buddy, see you in a year."

And Hag was gone.

iv

On his last night at home, he and Sharon made love frantically, desperately, trying to stop time itself but knowing it was futile. It was good that Aunt Esther slept soundly.

Arthur awoke at 4:00 a.m. He dressed, woke up Sharon, and after she dressed, they quietly went downstairs. He made some coffee, and they sat at the kitchen table sipping quietly. "How are you doing?" Arthur asked.

"Arthur, please don't go." She looked away from him. "I'm worried. Scared to death, in fact."

"I'll be fine, I promise." He reached out to hold her hand.

321

"I know. I think you're going to be fine. I really do. I'm worried about *me*." She paused. "I don't know what's going to happen to me." She began to weep. "You keep me sane. With you not here…"

"Now now, come on, your parents and your sister love you. You could probably move in with Betty if you wanted to."

"No. Seeing Stuart all the time would just make me worry more that the same thing—or worse—could happen to you. I couldn't bear it if it did. I'm sure you'll be fine, but you know. There's always that chance."

He nodded. "I know, but it's too late now. I've got to go."

"It's not too late. We could go to Canada. We could be there in a few hours."

"No." He shook his head. "No. I'm not a deserter. Shar'."

Sharon grew angry. "Oh sure, the great American patriot, afraid to be seen as a coward. And never a thought for *me*. Or your friends and family."

He sighed. "You know that's not true. I think of you and my friends and my aunt every single day."

There was no point in going on with this.

Arthur looked at his watch. "Look, we've got to go. You need to drive me to the bus station. I've got to be at Fort Dix by tomorrow night and I've got a train to catch this afternoon in Portland."

Sharon wiped her eyes. "I love you, Arthur. And I need you. I need you so much."

"I'll be back, I promise," he said. He kissed her and went upstairs to say goodbye to Aunt Esther.

She woke up and stared at him sleepily. "Okay Arthur, I'll see you next week. Be careful and do a good job, and you'll be hired again, certainly. FoodMart needs young men like you. Please call me when you get there safely."

Arthur nodded. "I will, Aunt Esther. Maybe I'll write a letter to you instead once in a while, would that be all right?"

"Oh of course," she said. "For land's sake." She hugged him. "You'd better get going now, the wagon's waiting." She rolled back over and was soon asleep again. Arthur leaned down and kissed her gently on the cheek. She smiled but didn't awaken. He left quietly.

Sharon got him to the bus station just in time. He saw her standing by the Chevrolet as the bus pulled away. And he wondered—not for the first time over the past six months, he had to admit—if he would ever see her, or Maine, or anyone or anything he knew, ever again, in spite of his ritualistic assurances to everyone that he would be fine.

But then, as young men since the Bronze Age had done when going off to war, he put his doubts and sudden loneliness behind him, and turned to face his destiny.

. . .

NIGHTMARE

In the darkness and rain halfway through Arthur's second watch—it was a little after two—his radio emitted a short burst of static, causing him to jerk erect. He had started to nod off. Gotta keep awake.

He picked up the handset and pressed the push-to-talk button twice, sending back two bursts of static, indicating everything was quiet. He sat up as straight as he could, deliberately making himself uncomfortable to help him stay awake. He looked around, trying to think of something, anything, to keep his mind busy.

The rain abruptly stopped, and the near silence around him was suddenly overwhelming, the dripping of

323

*water from the trees above him the only noise he noticed at
first. But gradually he became aware of other noises. The
faint whistle from Pappy's nostrils as he slept. A sudden
murmur from Turnip as he rolled over, wrestling with the
demons that only came with sleep. Faint artillery fire
echoing far away.*

*The fire sounded a little like thunder, and it
reminded him of summers at home. He found himself
wondering about his friends back in The World. He had
received no mail in weeks. He began thinking of Sharon.*

He grinned.

*In spite of his exhaustion from the past two days,
and the remembered emotional pain of their parting, the
memory of them being together during the two years before
he got drafted made him stir a little. I'm not dead yet, he
thought.*

*Then the doorway to hell opened, and the devil
came to call.*

*He came in blinding flashes and explosions and
flying metal and the crackcrackcrack of AK-47 fire. He
came from the thick underbrush lining the opposite bank of
the river.*

*Turnip's scream was cut wetly short as Arthur dived
into the shallow watery foxhole behind the now pathetic
berm that should have been higher, should have been
reinforced with logs, should have been sturdier.*

*Keeping below the berm, Arthur pointed his M-16
across the river into the brush on the other bank and began
to fire against the wave of steel pouring over them.*

*Pappy dove in on top of him, bellowing. "YA
SONSABITCHES! GODDAMN YA TO HELL! HERE'S
SOME BACK AT YA!" Pappy popped the first claymore
and was reaching for the second when Arthur grabbed his
arm.*

*"WAIT, PAPPY! DON'T POP EM!" Arthur yelled.
The claymores were not pointed into the brush across the*

stream, where they could have done some good, but instead into the river where he had expected their targets to be.

The roars and flashes and flying steel continued to cascade over them in unending waves.

"BEAR!" Arthur yelled to the adjacent hole. "LURCH! NOSE!" No answer.

Arthur crawled through the explosions to the hole. He felt a slight sting on the back of his left arm but ignored it.

Lurch and Bear lay twisted and broken and unmoving in bloody poncho liners behind the hole. Nose cowered in the red water in the bottom of his hole, clutching his guts, curled up and gasping. "Oh fuck it hurts. Preach, it hurrrrts! I want my mamma, Preach!"

Then he knew what had to be done.

Re-aim the claymores.

Before he could talk himself out of it, Arthur crawled to the river bank and, keeping as low as possible— bullets were passing within inches of his head—he adjusted the three claymores in front of Lurch's hole so they were again facing across the river into the thick brush on the opposite bank. Then he crawled to the two remaining mines in front of his position and readjusted them.

"DON'T SHOOT ME GODDAMMIT!" Arthur yelled to Pappy as he crawled back to his hole. Once back, he yelled at Pappy, "NOW POP THOSE BASTARDS!" and then crawled to Nose's hole—Nose now silent and unmoving—and popped the three there. He thought he detected a slight diminution of incoming fire after he had done this.

Arthur became aware of LT yelling into a radio, trying to make himself heard above the din. "DRAC SIX, WE NEED FIRE SUPPORT. ANYTHING. WE—ARE— UNDER—ATTACK. DO YOU COPY? OVER."

The incoming ceased.

Arthur cautiously raised his head and listened. All he heard at first were the sobs and ravings of the wounded.

And then, Arthur heard something that he would remember for the rest of his life.

From across the river, he heard exultant, departing laughter.

PART IX: THE ROAD
CHAPTER 34
i

River City, Iowa
October 17, 1969

It was late afternoon in River City, Iowa, the yellow light casting long shadows behind the trees, just starting to turn. Arthur had called a cab from the gas station at the I-80 exit where his ride had dropped him off. He paid the cabby and went inside. It was the local Y, which the cabby had recommended as clean and cheap.

"You're lucky, not many people here tonight, got a room to yourself," the clerk said as Arthur checked in. He went upstairs, unlocked the door, put his bindle on the lower bunk bed and sat down beside it. He opened it, fished around for a minute, then withdrew the handkerchief Marie had given him. He put it in his jacket pocket. He went back downstairs and asked to use the phone.

The clerk gestured. "Pay phone at the end of the hall, by the exit."

He half-expected her not to be listed, but sure enough, there she was in the phone book: "Hoye, M/439 S Johnson St/RvrCty" followed by the number.

Gathering his courage, he called.

"Hello?" It was she.

"Marie Hoye? It's Art West."

"Who?"

"Art West. From Reno." There was silence. "I wanted to return your handkerchief."

"Oh!" she said. "Uh, well, yes. I remember you." Her question, although unasked, hung in the air.

"I was passing through," Arthur said, plunging ahead, "and remembered what you said about River City and stopping by if I was ever, uh, you know—here. So. I'm at the Y downtown, and was wondering if...you wanted to have dinner with me or something." He was starting to feel ridiculous. *What the heck am I doing?*

Marie was silent for a long moment. "You're at the Y?"

"It seems okay. It's clean."

"Yes. Well...thank you for thinking of me, Art. My girlfriend and I had a lovely time in Reno. But, it was Reno, yes? Not River City, Iowa. You know? When I said...what I said, about you dropping in, I'm sorry if I gave the wrong impression. I was just trying to be...well...I don't know. But—"

Arthur said, "No, it's all right. I completely understand. I'm just some random guy you had a conversation with at a casino in Reno. I'm sorry to have bothered you. You take care." He started to hang up. *What was I thinking?*

"Oh no, it's okay," she said. "In fact, I'm kind of flattered." She chuckled. "Now, I can say that men come half-way across the country to see me!" She grew serious again. "But...in any case, I wish you safe travels."

"Thanks," Arthur said. "Look, I've still got your handkerchief. I'll leave it with the desk clerk. It's really nice, I don't feel right about keeping it. Thanks for talking, and I wish you the best. Good bye."

"Good bye, Art. Take care of yourself." She hung up.

So much for that, he thought.

Arthur went to the bathroom down the hall and took a hot shower, which felt good, it being his first one since leaving Reno. He noticed in the mirror that his black eye was better, the green tint around it almost gone. He returned to his room and changed clothes, then realized he was hungry.

Someone knocked at the door. It was the desk clerk.

"There's someone downstairs to see you." He seemed mildly annoyed at having to come upstairs to deliver the message.

Arthur, mystified, said, "Who is it?"

"I don't know, some woman. Come see for yourself."

Arthur went downstairs. Sure enough, Marie sat in a chair in the lobby. She stood and smiled when she saw him. "Hello," she said, extending her hand.

He smiled. "Wow." He shook it. "This is a surprise."

She nodded. "I know. For me, too." She looked at her watch. "Is that dinner invitation still open?"

He nodded. "You bet. I was just thinking about dinner. What do you recommend?"

"There's a steak and pasta place just around the corner."

"Sounds perfect."

ii

After they were seated, the waitress gave them menus and took their drink orders. Marie ordered a bottle of red wine. "I hope you'll join me," she said.

He laughed. "Ordinarily, no, but I will tonight."

"Good, if I drank a whole bottle of wine you'd have to carry me home!"

The wine came a minute or so later, and the waitress unscrewed the cap and poured a glass for each of them. They ordered salads and entrees—a steak for Arthur, shells alfredo with ham and peas for Marie. "Well, cheers!" Marie said, taking a large swallow of wine.

"And to you," Arthur said. He sipped his wine. "So, you're from here?"

"Yes," she said. "After I finished high school, I worked in a bank. I married a farmer ten years ago. But I was just twenty-two then. We got divorced a year ago. I couldn't face a life of worrying about corn prices. Besides…it was boring."

"Any kids?"

"Oh my goodness, no." She smiled. "I dodged a bullet there, I can tell you, mister. Anyway, the trip to Reno was kind of a new beginning for me. I'd been moping around and then I decided to do something different and exciting, so I talked my friend Iris into coming along. We had fun." Marie took another large sip of her wine, then topped off the glass.

Arthur smiled. "What kind of fun? Or was it an 'I'll never tell'" kinda trip?"

She laughed. "Something like that." She winked at him. "What about you? What were you doing in Reno?"

"Passing through," Arthur said. "I just got out of the army. I'm heading back to Maine."

"Why didn't you just fly?" Marie sipped her wine again.

He shrugged. "I figured I'd make an adventure out of it and see the country. I guess I'll be back in a week or two. I'm not in any particular hurry."

Their salads and rolls came and they ate in silence for a few minutes. He wondered if her blouse was unbuttoned that extra button just for him. "You're looking good."

Marie smiled. "Well, thank you. That's nice to hear." She grew serious. "I haven't heard that much."

"I'm sorry."

"My ex wasn't one for saying such things." She seemed to want to elaborate, but then the waitress showed up with their entrees. Marie finished her wine and the waitress refilled her glass and topped off Arthur's.

They finished dinner, chatting idly. Arthur wished he had ordered the pasta. The steak was tough, and barely pink inside; he had ordered medium rare. He took a few bites and left the rest, concentrating on the potato. He loaded it up with sour cream.

Arthur suggested dessert when the waitress returned to clear the dishes. Marie declined. "No, I've got to keep my girlish figure." She winked again. They had finished the bottle of wine, Marie drinking most of it. "I'm a little tipsy, I guess, but the walk home will clear my head. Thank you for the lovely dinner."

"Maybe coffee?" Arthur asked.

She appraised him a moment or two. "Art, how old are you?"

Arthur smiled. "Don't you know you never ask a gentleman that question?" Then, seeing that she still seemed to want an answer, he decided he was not going to lie. "I'm twenty. I'll be twenty-one in June."

"I see." She nodded slightly, almost to herself. Then she decided. "I can make coffee back at the house. If you really want some."

"I'd love some," Arthur said.

iii

The house was only a few blocks away. It was a yellow Victorian with a large front porch and two gables above the porch roof. The top half of the front door featured a large, ruby-colored diamond of cut glass.

As they turned into the walkway, a voice came from a car parked across the street. "Marie?"

She looked at the car. "Oh Lord," she breathed. "Wait here." She walked to the edge of the street. "Yes, Robert?"

"Are you all right?"

"Of course I am. But what are you doing here?"

"Nothing. It's just that I wanted to say I was sorry for...you know."

Marie shook her head. "Robert, you should have thought of that before you started yelling at me."

Robert nodded. "I know. But—" He looked at Arthur, started to say something, then shrugged and sighed. "Oh never mind. Good night." He started the car and drove away rapidly.

Arthur looked at Marie. "Who was that?"

"No one," she sighed. She gestured toward the house. "Come on in, it's getting cold out here." They walked up the steps to the front door. Marie opened it. "I never bother to lock up," she said, entering the house.

From the foyer, a set of stairs ascended on the left. To the right was a living room, demarcated from the foyer and hall by sliding, darkly stained wooden doors that were partly open. A Siamese cat was licking itself on the sofa. At the end of the hall leading to the rear of the house, Arthur could see what appeared to be a kitchen beyond an open door. "Beautiful house," he said. "Yours?"

"Yes, I inherited it from my mother. It's been in the family since 1881. I have three bedrooms upstairs I don't use, so I rent them to students. We're a university town. Eastern Iowa State."

"I've heard of it," he said. He actually hadn't.

She laughed. "I'm surprised."

"Where do you stay?" he asked.

"I have the whole first floor," she said. "I can lock the kitchen door at the end of the hall, and I pull the sliding doors to close off the living room entrance." She smiled. "Once I go to bed, I lock up. I like my privacy."

"Are the students that much of a worry?"

She laughed. "Oh my goodness, no, of course not. I'm pretty careful about who I rent to. Of course, once in a while I can smell marijuana—at least I think it's marijuana—but I don't make a fuss about it. As long as they're quiet and don't cause trouble, I live and let live. So no," she finished. "I just want to relax in the evenings. Sit in the living room and watch television in my bathrobe with a glass of wine, you know. That sort of thing."

"Other than the students, you live here alone?"

Marie nodded. "Yes. For now."

"For now?" he asked. She didn't answer.

iv

Marie made coffee, and they sat on the sofa in the living room. She pulled shut and locked the sliding doors, then turned on the TV and they watched idly for a few minutes. "Would you like something a little stronger?" Marie asked when she'd finished her coffee.

"Like what?"

"I have some brandy. Maybe a nightcap?"

"Well—okay," Arthur said. "A small one. Then I'll have to go."

Marie went into the kitchen. Arthur petted the Siamese lightly. It didn't wake up but purred softly.

Marie returned with two glasses. She gave the one with the smaller amount to Arthur. "It's just Korbel," she said. "Everybody here drinks it." She laughed. "The pride of the Midwest."

Arthur raised a toast. "Cheers." They sipped. Then he remembered. "Oh—almost forgot." He reached into his jacket pocket and pulled out the handkerchief she had given him in Reno. "Here. See? I told you I'd return it." He held it to his nose, inhaled delicately. "It smells like violets. I'm glad I kept it."

"I am, too." Marie took the handkerchief and inhaled its scent. She then knocked back the brandy in one swallow, then looked at him and said, "All right, then."

Everything happened at once.

She pushed the cat off the sofa and slid over to him and threw her arms around him and started kissing him, her tongue flicking over his lips. "Baby," she whispered. She took the drink out of his hands and put it on the coffee table and then quickly straddled him, kissing him hungrily, holding his face steady so she could probe his open mouth. "Please," she whispered. "Baby, please. I need you. *Ball* me." She said the words as if overcoming something: inhibition, guilt, fear. Arthur couldn't tell.

"Are you sure you—" he said, but she was already on her feet, pulling him to the back of the house and her bedroom.

v

"Wow," Arthur said the next morning when he woke up and found her on her side, looking at him, smiling gently. "You are one great lay. Holy moley."

Marie chuckled and stretched beside him, then curled up and laid her head on his shoulder, her right arm across his stomach, content. "My, that was fun," she whispered. "I'm going to be sore for a week."

"I don't know if I can walk," Arthur said, and they both chuckled.

She grew serious. "Baby, can I ask you something?"

"Sure."

"Do you know you moan—even tremble in your sleep a little?"

Arthur looked at her. "I do?"

"Yes. You were so loud you woke me up once. I had to kiss you to get you to stop."

Arthur chuckled. "Thanks," he said. "I think I remember." He didn't.

Marie waited a beat or two for further explanation, but when none was forthcoming, she shrugged. "Oh well." After a moment, Marie pressed closer against him, then her hand slid lower. "In for a penny, in for a pound," she whispered.

Arthur smiled, but gently held her hand from further advances. "Let's get something to eat first," he said, kissing the top of her head. "But hold that thought."

Marie pretended to pout. "Oh poo, you're no fun." But she sat up and looked at him fondly. "What would you like?"

"Coffee, to start."

"Sure. Let's make some." They went to the kitchen.

After scrambled eggs and hash browns and toast, Marie poured them each another cup of coffee. "Care for a shot of Korbel in your coffee?" she asked.

"No thanks," Arthur said. "A little milk, maybe? But you go ahead."

She did so, then pouring some milk into his mug. The telephone rang.

"Hello," she said. Then her voice went oddly flat. "Yes. No, not today. I don't know. All right. I'll call you soon. A day or two maybe. Goodbye."

She hung up. "Iris," she said. "Wanted to get together. I told her not today."

"Ahhh," Arthur said. Somehow, it did not sound like she was talking to her girlfriend. He began to clear the dishes.

"No, sit still," Marie said. "I'll take care of them later. I'm going to go freshen up. Take a shower."

"Okay," Arthur said.

She looked at him, inviting. "Ummm, we could—"

"What?"

She smiled, nodded slightly toward the bathroom. "Take one together? I have an extra toothbrush."

Arthur grinned. "We could do that," he said.

By eleven, they were both asleep again.

vi

Dusk was just falling when Arthur awoke. Marie was not there. He lay still, staring at the ceiling, thinking about what to do the next few days. *Stay here for a while? Certainly.* How long? He did not know. There was much to consider. Then he heard the telephone ring. Marie answered it.

"Yes, Robert. Yes. I don't know. I'm sorry, you should have thought of that. It's not my fault. I'm just not ready, so… Okay. Good bye, then."

It was definitely not Iris, this time.

Arthur got up, dressed, and walked through the kitchen into the dining room and then through to the living room. Marie sat in a chair next to the telephone. She smiled. "Hi."

"Hi, yourself." He sat on the sofa. "How are you doing?"

"Fine!" she said, a little too brightly.

"I heard you on the telephone. Bad news?"

"No." She sighed and then crossed to the sofa and sat next to him, leaning her head on his shoulder. He put his arm around her. "It wasn't bad news. It was Robert."

"The man from last night?"

"Yes."

"Who is he?"

Marie sighed. "He wants to marry me."

"What?" Arthur said, turning to face her. "He wants to *marry* you?"

"Yes."

"But—but—then what about—?" He gestured. *This.*

"Having fun, I hope," she said. "I sure am."

"I guess you don't want to marry him, then?"

Marie was silent.

"Wait—you *do* want to marry him?"

She sighed. "I don't know." She looked at him. "I'm so ashamed. I shouldn't have gotten you involved in this."

"Involved in what?"

"My—troubles."

"What troubles?"

"I don't know. It's just..." She sighed again. "Art, I'm thirty-three and divorced in a small town, with very few eligible single men around. I had nothing before me but a life of being alone. In a small town in the middle of cornfields and hog farms. Then Robert appeared."

"Who is he?"

"A new manager at my bank. My age. Also divorced. Kinda square. More so than me, anyway," she laughed.

Arthur grinned. "You're not square. Hardly."

Before she could answer, the doorbell rang.

"Oh my," Marie said. She went to the front door, then turned and looked at Arthur. She opened it. "Hello, Robert," she said.

"Hello, Marie," Robert said, coming into the foyer. "I think we need to—" He saw Arthur in the living room.

Marie led him into the living room. "Robert, this is Arthur West. He's a student. I've rented him a room."

"Arthur, nice to meet you," Robert said, offering his hand. His tone was cordial, but he was definitely not smiling.

Arthur stood and shook it. "Nice to meet you." Then, thinking on his feet for once, he said, "thanks for renting me the room, Miss Hoye. I'll have the check for you whenever you're ready." He nodded at Robert again and went into the foyer. Marie pulled the sliding doors closed behind him.

Arthur went upstairs and opened the door to the room in the front of the house, apparently vacant. Leaving the light off, he sat quietly by the window overlooking the

336

street out front, hearing only vague murmurings from downstairs. Finally, after a half hour, Robert left, and Arthur watched him get into his car, slam the door and drive away quickly, as if angry.

When the car turned the corner at the end of the block, Arthur went downstairs. Marie was opening the sliding doors. She smiled. "I was just coming up," she said. "You want some coffee?"

"Sure." He followed her to the kitchen. Marie put the kettle on to boil.

"He asked me to marry him," she said, sitting down. "Officially this time."

"Wow," Arthur said.

"And, I told him...I'd think it over."

"Umm, you didn't, uh..."

She laughed. "Oh my goodness, no. You are one thing he does not need to know about, mister. He was already upset I ran off to Reno with Iris," she said. "I'd never see him again if he knew about us." She took his hand, squeezed it. "Baby." She touched his cheek tenderly. "Thank you for thinking so quickly. He thought you were one of my student renters. Well, maybe not really, but it gave him something to believe."

The kettle started whistling. Marie got up and made the coffee. Arthur waited. They sipped. "I don't know what to do."

"Do you want to marry him?" Arthur asked.

"I think so, but I'm not sure." She smiled. "I probably would have said yes, if you hadn't come along. When you called me, I was surprised and flattered, but I wasn't planning on seeing you at all. But...a little while after you called, Robert called, and we had a fight over the phone. So I decided, what the heck. It was only dinner with you, after all, right?" She smiled. "Well, it started out that way. But, after Reno...you know. Lost opportunities. Who would have known?"

337

"I know," Arthur said.

"Darn you," she said, smiling. "It would have been fun, there."

Arthur sipped his coffee. "Ayuh. But we're having fun now. Right?"

"Oh yes," Marie said. "I mean...*whoa,* mister." She laughed. "This has been wonderful. I've never, uh—had a...a fling before. Not like this. I mean, that's what this is, isn't it? A fling? Nothing wrong with that, people have them all the time. Except me. So I guess I was due. But we're not really a serious thing. Are we?" she asked. "I'm thirteen years older than you, you're on your way back east...It would never work, I don't think? Not long term?"

"I don't know." After a moment, he added, "Probably not." *He couldn't lie to her.*

"It's been fun, though."

"It has." He smiled. "You're terrific, Marie."

"You are, too." She put down her coffee mug. "Oh who am I kidding? Come on, you." She led him back to her bedroom and she made love to him desperately.

vii

After, they lay quietly, Marie on her side, back to him. Arthur could tell she was awake.

"Art?" she said. "I'm sorry."

"About what?"

"Nothing bad, believe me. Hardly. I just—just need space. Time."

Arthur nodded. As much as he wanted to stay longer, he knew Marie was right. He sighed. "Okay. My stuff is still at the Y. I can stay there."

"That would probably be best. I'm sorry."

They both dressed.

When he finished lacing up his jungle boots, Marie walked him to the front door. "Good bye," he said. "I'll never forget you. Ever." He leaned in to kiss her on the cheek.

Suddenly, Marie hugged him fiercely, squeezing him to her. "You deserve the best. Not someone like me." She opened the door and he stepped onto the porch. "Good bye, Art."

"Marie..."The door closed.

As he started down the porch stairs, he may have heard a single sob, choked off immediately.

.   .   .

CHAPTER 35
i

River City, Iowa
October 21, 1969

Arthur was eating breakfast at the counter in the Howard Johnson's at the I-80 entrance ramp. He had been planning to walk down to the interstate and stick his thumb out, but decided a hot breakfast should definitely be part of the plan. Then, everything changed when *The Coolest Guy Ever* walked into the restaurant.

Everything about him was perfect. He was wearing pressed bell-bottom jeans, a black turtleneck sweater, a mahogany leather jacket, and matching, well-polished cowboy boots. The clothes fit him perfectly, and he wore them with an easy grace that Arthur could never hope to match. He was older than Arthur, maybe mid-twenties, with a dark beard and moderately long hair, clean and well-cared for, tied back in a ponytail.

The Coolest Guy Ever nodded to Arthur and sat a few seats away, exhaling heavily as he sat. They were the only customers at the counter.

"You look tired," Arthur ventured.

"Oh yeah, man," he said, grinning. "Fifteen hours on the road yesterday. From Denver to here. Eight hundred miles. It was good to catch some Zs. But I still got another thousand to go."

"Long drive," Arthur allowed. He couldn't explain it, but he was flattered; *The Coolest Guy Ever* was actually talking to him.

"Name's Ben Stetler."

"Nice to meet you. Art West. People call me Preach."

Ben laughed. "Why?"

Arthur smiled. "Long story."

"I hear you, Preach. Nicknames always have a story. I wish I had a cool nickname like yours, but people just call me Ben." Arthur chuckled, embarrassed but pleased. *He thinks my nickname is cool.* He took a bite of his pancakes. Ben said, "That actually looks good."

Arthur nodded. "Yeah, they're all right."

"That's good enough for me." The waitress appeared and poured Ben some coffee. "I'll what he's having," Ben said. She took the order and went back into the kitchen. Ben looked at Arthur's jungle boots. "When did you get back?"

Maybe I should lose the jungle boots, Arthur thought. "A couple weeks ago. Damn boots are comfortable. Couldn't throw 'em away although I kinda wanted to."

"I hear you. I was there, too. Army. You?"

"Army. Big Red One. I was a grunt."

"Holy shit, Big Red One? Me too! Engineers, 66-67. Heavy equipment operator. My outfit built the Quan Loi air strip."

"Seriously? Quan Loi? I spent half my tour there."

"No shit? Damn, small world. An Loc still a pit?"

Arthur laughed. "Oh yeah. The garden spot of the world."

"I hear you. At least in Lai Khe there was the village you could go to. Beer, music, girls to flirt with if you bought 'em tea."

"I remember."

Ben laughed. "Where you headed?"

"Maine."

"Heading to New York, myself. But I grew up in southern California. Riverside."

Ben's food came and they ate in silence. When they were finished, Ben lit a cigarette. "Smoke?" he offered. Arthur declined. Ben then said, "Listen, Preach, let me ask you something." Arthur nodded.

Ben leaned forward and lowered his voice just a touch. "I got a proposition for you," *The Coolest Guy Ever* said. "I could use some help driving. I don't want to spend any more 15-hour days behind the wheel without a break. Can you drive a truck?"

"Not an 18-wheeler."

Ben laughed. "Nah, it's a 12-foot cargo van. Drives like a car. It's even an automatic. We can trade off driving. Three or four-hour shifts."

Before Arthur could say yes, which he fully intended to do— he sure needed the ride and Ben was *The Coolest Guy Ever*—it got better. "I'll even pay you," Ben said.

Arthur couldn't believe his luck. "Sounds good to me, man."

"Great," Ben said. "Let's pay, and we can talk outside."

ii

Outside, Ben said, "So I've got something to smoke that's better than Marlboros." He pulled a joint out of his pocket.

Arthur grinned. "Now you're talking."

They walked across the parking lot to get away from the building, and Ben lit the joint. They walked

341

around the parking lot until they finished it, Ben shredding the roach, scattering the remains.

"Good stuff," Arthur said, impressed. It was, in fact, the best marijuana he had ever had. "Really good."

"Yeah, I thought so, too," Ben said. "Very good shit. Hey, come over to my truck for a minute." They walked to his van, a nondescript, white Chevy Sport with California tags. "Here, let me show you something." Ben glanced around the parking lot, then opened the back of the van, lifting a tarp covering the cargo. "Take a look at this."

The cargo bay was filled almost to the ceiling with green bricks of marijuana in sealed plastic bags.

"Wow," Arthur said. "How much is there?"

"Two hundred keys," Ben said. "Four hundred and forty pounds. Primo grade Colombian. What we were just smoking. In New York, on the street, grass this good would go for three hundred a pound, easy. Maybe even more."

"And you want me to help you drive this to New York?"

"Yup. Now don't worry, it's going to go very smoothly. This is my fourth trip with weight, and I've never had a problem. I've got my contact all lined up. I'm meeting him in two days. A guy I knew in the army, we kept in touch."

"What if we get stopped on the way?"

"It's never happened. I drive very carefully, obey all the traffic signs, speed limits, all that shit. I am completely clean, too. I've never been busted for so much as a joint, and I have a spotless driving record." Ben then asked, "You do have a license, right?"

Arthur nodded. "And not even a parking ticket."

"Good," Ben said. "Anyway, the van is registered and inspected, and in great shape, so we're not gonna get pulled over for a busted tail light or something. All I need is for you to help me get it to New York. You just drive safely and don't speed, and we'll be fine. I'll cover food, and hotel for tonight. And I'll pay you five hundred when we close the deal."

Arthur, astounded, said, "Five hundred bucks?"

"Yeah. In fact, here, I'll give you half up front." *The Coolest Guy Ever* pulled a wad of bills out of his pocket and peeled off 5 fifties. "The rest when we finish the deal. I can't give it to you now, but once I get paid for this cargo, you got it."

Arthur nodded. "Works for me."

"I was thinking about not telling you what I was carrying, but I decided I probably better," Ben said. "I didn't want you finding out during the trip and freaking out or some shit."

"I appreciate that," Arthur said dryly. "But it's cool, man, I'm up for it. Sure, I'll help you." For the first time, Arthur was actually looking forward to the rest of the trip. *What could go wrong?*

Ben handed Arthur his money. "Far out. Let's get rolling."

iii

That night they stopped at a motel outside Cleveland and got going again early the next morning. Ben took over when they got close to New York; they left I-80 and spent the next two hours, in New York rush hour traffic, covering the last fifteen miles. Finally, around dusk, they found their destination, a townhouse in the East Midwood neighborhood, a few blocks from Brooklyn College.

"Everybody in New York must have decided to go for a drive about the time we got here," Arthur said.

"I hear you, Preach," Ben said.

Ben drove around the block and turned into an alley, then parked behind the townhouse. He shut off the engine, exhaling heavily. "Far out," he said. "We are finally here. Let's go. Panther's expecting us."

"Panther? That's his name?"

Ben laughed. "Oh yeah. You'll understand when you see him."

They got out, Ben locked the van, and Arthur grabbed his bindle. Ben knocked on the back door of the townhouse.

A muffled voice from inside said, "Yo?"

"Ben, man. We have arrived."

The door opened. "About damn time you got here, Home."

Standing before Arthur was the blackest man he had ever seen, his hair teased in a disheveled afro. He wore a pair of jungle fatigue pants and a wife-beater t-shirt. "Hey, bro'," Ben said. He gestured to Arthur. "This here's my buddy Preach. Preach," he said, "this here's Panther."

Arthur nodded. Panther seemed unimpressed. He looked at Ben. "He cool?" he asked, gesturing toward Arthur.

"Absolutely," Ben said. "He's been helping me drive."

Panther appraised Arthur a moment. "All right," Panther said. "Come on in."

"Nice to meet you, Panther," Arthur said. Panther grunted.

Two women sat in the living room—both young, one black, the other blonde and very pale. The blonde smiled vaguely at him. The black woman looked him up and down briefly, almost studying him, then turned away, ignoring him further.

"Who are they?" Ben said.

"They're cool, don't worry," Panther said. "Let's talk." They moved to the dining room table. Arthur started to sit down with Ben, but Panther stopped him. "Naw, Home," he said to Arthur. "You need to go sit with them." He pointed to the girls. "Ben and me got business."

Arthur glanced at Ben. "It's okay, Preach," Ben said. "We'll be done here soon."

Arthur nodded. He couldn't exactly say why, but he was starting to get nervous; *something's not right.* But then he figured *The Coolest Guy Ever* must have known what he was doing, so he returned to the living room and sat down across from the women on the sofa, dropping his bindle beside his chair. He smiled at them. "Name's Preach," he said.

The blonde said, "I'm Liria. This is Roxanne." Roxanne, ignoring him, glanced at her watch.

After a brief conversation, Panther stood and walked to the back of the house. He returned a moment later with a zippered athletic bag. He placed it on the table and pulled the zipper open, tilting the bag to show Ben the money.

"Sixty?" Ben asked.

"To the dollar," Panther replied.

"Then we are good," Ben said, standing, taking the bag. "A pleasure doing business with you, Panther, as always." Ben zipped the bag shut. "Preach," he said, "let's help Panther unload—"

Bump—BumpBump—Bump.

A knock at the door.

"What the fuck?" Panther said, annoyed. "Ain't nobody—"

"Don't anybody move!"

Holding an automatic pointed straight at Panther, Roxanne jumped to her feet and swiftly crossed to the door.

Arthur raised his hands. *Holy fuck.*

Roxanne opened the door and six cops swarmed into the room, each brandishing a pistol and wearing dark clothes, body armor and ski masks. *"ON THE FLOOR! NOW!"* one of them yelled.

Liria began to scream as she fled to the back room. A cop chased after her. A cop apiece moved on Arthur, Ben and Panther.

Then, appallingly, Ben fell to his knees and began to scream. *"Oh God please don't kill me please please!"* He threw his hands in the air, sobbing.

Arthur's view of Ben as *The Coolest Guy Ever* immediately evaporated.

"SHUT THE FUCK UP!" Roxanne yelled. Ben, now sobbing uncontrollably, collapsed as one of the cops shoved him to the floor. Another shoved Panther down. Arthur dropped to the floor before the cop headed toward him could shove him.

In the back room, Liria was screaming. *"No, please!"*

One of the cops said to another one, "Get back there and get Maurice. We don't have time for this shit."

The cop on Arthur grabbed his hands and pulled them roughly behind his back and began tying them with twine as the other cops did the same to Panther and Ben. The cops then pulled paper sacks over their heads and pushed them to the ground.

From the bedroom, bed springs began creaking. *"Please no, please, stop!"* Liria cried.

"KEYS TO THE VAN? WHERE?" one of the cops yelled.

"In my coat pocket just don't kill us please!" Ben sobbed. Arthur heard the cop rooting around for the keys.

The cop then said, *"WHERE'S THE FUCKING MONEY?"*

"In the bag there on the table! Please! Take it!" Ben wailed. Arthur heard the zipper opening.

Arthur put his fear aside and began to think. *The cops had bound their wrists with twine not handcuffs and Arthur had never heard of cops putting paper bags over suspects' heads and he didn't know cops wore ski masks and no one had actually said 'You're under arrest' yet and he certainly didn't think raping female suspects during a raid was standard procedure and what in the hell have you gotten yourself into, dumbass?*

As Arthur mulled over various possibilities, he did not at all like his answers.

After Nam, dying like this?

He grew very still, trying to make himself invisible.

Arthur could hear Liria sobbing softly in the back room as the man who had raped her returned with the other one.

"Fuck, Maurice, zip your damn pants up," the leader said.

Maurice laughed. "Sorry *jefe,* but she had a *fine* ass."

"She did," chuckled the guy who had gone in after Maurice. "I almost cut a slice myself." Then Arthur heard the back door open, and the sound of people...*leaving? What was going on?*

"All right, dickheads, here's how it is," the leader announced. "We're confiscating the van and the money, and y'all are gonna be hauled downtown very shortly. Now shut the fuck up and don't move a goddamn *inch* until the paddy wagon gets here."

Arthur heard the back door shutting, the van doors opening, the engine turning over, and then the van pulling away. Then it was quiet, except for Liria, keening in the back room, and Ben, who continued to sob softly. *"Oh fuck, ohhh mother fuck..."*

In fact, after a minute, Arthur realized that he hadn't heard another sound since the van left. Then he knew. "Panther, I think they *all* 1—"

"SON OF A BITCH!" Panther yelled, arriving at the same conclusion almost simultaneously. *"WE BEEN RIPPED OFF!"*

"Quiet!" Ben cried, *"they'll kill us!"*

"Get a fucking grip, Ben, Jesus!" Arthur yelled. *"Panther!"*

"I'm here, Home!"

"Can you move over toward me? I'll come your way. If we can get our backs to each other with our hands lined up, maybe I can untie you."

After a moment, Panther said, "Cool, Home, let's do it."

It took a few minutes, but Arthur managed to untie Panther, who then quickly reciprocated. Arthur ripped the paper bag from his head and ran to the back room as Panther began untying Ben.

Liria lay face down on the bed, skirt hiked up and panties around her ankles, hands tied behind her. Liria screamed when Arthur touched her. *"No no! Please, no more!"*

"Shhh, shhh, I'm not gonna hurt you, I'm tryin to untie you." Liria opened her eyes and looked at him, then nodded, panting. When Liria was untied, they returned to the living room, Liria shaking but trying to get control of herself.

Ben and Panther were sitting quietly, rubbing their wrists, Ben, shivering, eyes wide, no longer weeping but clearly still shaken.

Panther looked at Liria, started toward her. "Baby, you okay?"

Liria looked at Panther, and started to nod, but then, suddenly enraged, charged him and began slapping desperately at this face, spitting invective. *"YOU BASTARD! YOU COULD HAVE GOTTEN ME KILLED! WHAT IS FUCKING WRONG WITH YOU! BRINGING ME INTO A DRUG DEAL!"*

"Baby, come on now," Panther said, trying to soothe her as he dodged and blocked her slaps. "Now just calm down. *Calm down!* Want me to take you to the emergency r-"

"I—want—nothing—from—you!" Liria screamed, having none of it as she punctuated each word with a slap.

When she had slapped herself out, she hissed, still shaking with fury, shame, pain, fear, "I'm *outa here*. Jesus *Christ.* And don't you even *think* about calling me, ever *again!*" She grabbed her purse and ran out the door, sobbing, slamming the door behind her.

"Holy fuck," Ben said, sniffling. Although still terrified, he was finally calmer. "I've never been so...fuck. Those bastards...shit, they might have killed us." *The Coolest Guy Ever* wiped his nose on his coat sleeve. Arthur then noticed the wet spot in the crotch of Ben's jeans. He was appalled.

How could I have been so fucking stupid?

Panther went to the kitchen and returned with a bottle of Southern Comfort and three glasses. He poured each of them a generous shot. Arthur knocked his back in one gulp.

Panther looked at him. "Thanks, Home. Untying me. That bitch Roxanne. "

Arthur scoffed. "Ya think?"

Panther didn't reply.

Ben looked at Arthur, who, silent, stared back evenly. "I'm—I'm sorry, Preach," he said. "It was just that—"

"I know, Ben." *Please shut up now,* Arthur did not say.

While Ben and Panther began to talk things over, Arthur took stock. He decided he was probably all right. He had his bindle, his wallet and ID, plus his cash. More importantly, Panther didn't know where he was from, and all Ben knew was he was from someplace in Maine.

All he had to do now was ditch these guys, especially *The Coolest Guy Ever*. Which he did a short time later, slipping out the front door when Ben went with Panther into the alley to see if there was any sign of where the van had gone.

iv

The cabby stopped in front of the Livingston Street Greyhound terminal. Arthur bought a bus ticket to Bangor, transferring in Boston, leaving in an hour. He sat in an inconspicuous corner of the station where he could see all the doors but not be readily noticed himself.

When the bus pulled out at 9:30 that night, Arthur finally began to relax, very relieved to be alive, and out of the drug running business—*forever,* he vowed. He realized he had been very lucky. And, he also realized, for the first time in his life he felt ashamed.

.   .   .

PART X: MAINE
CHAPTER 36
i

Belfast, Maine
October 24, 1969

Mrs. Hall pulled up in front of the house on Congress Street. It looked the same as it had thirteen months before: well-maintained, the lawn newly mowed, the Bel Air parked in the driveway, tailfins as impressive as Arthur remembered them. The car had been freshly washed and waxed.

It was good to be back. Finally.

"Arthur, it's all yours now." Mrs. Hall reached in her purse and pulled out a key ring. "Here are the keys to the house. I think you'll find the car keys hanging inside the front door. And, a few months before Esther passed, she and I arranged for a lawyer here in town to handle the estate. You'll want to go see him soon. His card is on the dresser in the foyer."

"Thank you, I will."

"Also, I bought some groceries for you. Eggs, bacon. A few cold cuts. And coffee, of course. I remember how you like coffee."

"You're very kind, Mrs. Hall. How much do I owe you?" He reached for his wallet.

"Oh for heaven's sake, Arthur, not a penny," she said. "We're all just glad you're back."

He smiled. "I'm glad I'm back, too."

"It must have been awful over there. Esther was so proud of you."

"Where..." Arthur couldn't bring himself to say it, but Mrs. Hall knew what he was asking.

"Grove Cemetery. It was a lovely funeral. Half the town turned out. Your aunt was respected and loved, Arthur. You should be proud."

"I am, Mrs. Hall."

"Would you like to have supper with us? We have plenty. Henry Senior's not doing very well, but he said he wanted to see you when you could come by."

"Mrs. Hall, thank you for the invitation and the ride, but I'm really tired; it's a long bus ride here from New York, almost 24 hours, what with all the stops and transfers. I need a shower and some sleep before I do anything."

"Of course. Well, I'll tell Henry Junior you're home. I know he'll want to see you when he's home next."

"Thanks. Please do. Has Hag talked to Clement? I'd like to see him, too, if he's still around."

Mrs. Hall said, "I guess you haven't heard." She sighed. "Clement was arrested for the murder of Oscar Loudermilk. This past spring."

Arthur stared, speechless. *Holy fuck.*

Mrs. Hall nodded. "I know, it's a shock. He pled guilty too, at his trial. Didn't even mount a defense. He said he did it, and would do it again. Well, you can imagine how that went over with the judge. Life without parole. He's in Thomaston now; been there three months. Just terrible."

Arthur nodded. "Oh man, I'm so sorry to hear that, Mrs. Hall. I can't say as I'm surprised, though. He hated Oscar, always did. Of course, he wasn't alone."

"I know," Mrs. Hall said. "Henry Junior finally told me about the incident at the quarry all those years ago when Oscar threw Clement off the Cliff. It's so sad. You never know how ugliness you committed so long ago will reach out for you, but it usually does, eventually." She sighed. "Well, I must be going. Get some sleep and call us when you're rested and ready."

"Thank you, I will. Good night, and please give my best to Mr. Hall. I'll be over to see you both soon." As he watched Mrs. Hall depart, he thought of Clement.

Of course he'd tell the judge he'd do it again, the moron.

He would write to Clement as soon as he could.

ii

Arthur let himself in and stood in the foyer, looking around. He breathed in deeply the familiar and evocative scents of the house. *His house, now.* The smells were so indelibly imprinted that they brought his aunt to mind: a little mustiness, ash from the fireplace, sun-bleached curtains, the faint odor of baking soda and vinegar, two of the few cleaners she was willing to use, along with the tiniest lingering scent of cooking from the kitchen. He half-expected her to walk in and tell him to wash up for supper. He smiled, and exhaled deeply. It had been a long three weeks.

He went upstairs and entered the main bedroom. He still thought of this as his aunt's room, although he supposed it was his now, if he wanted it. But he could not bring himself to sleep tonight in the large feather bed there. Instead, he went to his old room, further down the hall. The bed was made, probably with the same sheets the cleaning lady had put on it the day he left, thirteen months ago. The rest of the room was equally unchanged, as if he had just been gone overnight and had now returned.

The photograph of Stu next to his track from Nam was even there, on the dresser precisely where he had left it more than two years ago. But it had faded a little after two years in the sun, he noticed, so he put it in the top drawer of his dresser. He put his film can in with it.

He decided he would sleep here for now, and maybe move into the main bedroom later. Sleeping in Aunt Esther's old bedroom just felt...*wrong.*

He put his bindle on the bed and then walked down to the bathroom at the end of the hall. After he showered, he opened his closet and dressed in some of his old clothes. It seemed strange, putting them on, as if he were donning a costume. He went downstairs to the living room and turned on the news.

Two big hurricanes were bearing down on Vietnam, with major flooding and loss of life feared.

A large operation in Quang Tri Province was underway with heavy fighting involving the 101st Airborne.

Paul McCartney announced he wasn't dead.

He turned the TV off and went to the kitchen and made a sandwich. Then he called the Tibbets'. Mr. Tibbets answered. "Damn, Arthur, welcome home," he said. "I'm very happy to hear your voice, son."

"Thank you, sir, it's good to be back."

"I'm so sorry to hear about your aunt. My deepest sympathies."

"Thanks. She was really something. I wish I'd been here. Mr. Tibbets, I was wondering if you could give me Betty and Stu's number? Are they still living in Boston?"

After a brief pause, Tibbets said, "No, Arthur, Betty is here now. Let me get her, I'll see if she'll speak with you. She's not doing well."

A few moments later, Betty picked up. "Hello, Preach." She sounded flat, weary. "I'm glad you made it. Are you all right?"

"Ayuh. I'm all right. I was lucky. How are you?"

Betty sighed. "Not too well, I'm afraid."

"I'm sorry to hear. What's up?"

She was silent.

"It's Stu, isn't it?" he said.

She sniffled a little. "Yes. Preach, he—he—isn't with us anymore."

Fuck. "Oh no."

"Yes. A month ago. He overdosed on sleeping pills. A whole bottle. He died during the night. I found him the next morning when I went in to help him get dressed. He'd been complaining about the pain lately; he never used to. Plus he was getting more and more depressed. I tried to get him to see a therapist or something, but he wouldn't. In the end he was just mean, ugly, taking pain killers that weren't working. Nothing I did helped. I couldn't stand to be with him and—and so I moved into the guest room in our apartment. Oh Preach, I feel so guilty. I should have been—"

"Stop it," Arthur said. "No one could have done more for Stu than you did. You married him, did your best by him. Come on."

"I know, but it won't go away. The guilt."

"Well...I'm sorry. Stu was a good man."

"He was."

"Where is he buried?"

"The family plot in Connecticut."

"Well, if there's anything I can do, let me know," Arthur said.

"I will. Thank you. This fucking war. I hate it."

"Me, too. And we're going to lose it, too, now, I'm pretty sure. It's only a matter of time."

Betty didn't respond.

He continued, "So. If I could ask, how's Sharon?" Despite her promises, she had stopped writing to him a few months after he left—again, with no explanation.

Betty sighed. "Oh we are just full of good news on that front, too," she said. "I hardly speak with her anymore. She's living in a trailer near Searsport with some guy who works at a lumber yard. She's also pregnant. My parents are sick over it. Dad can't even bear to say her name. I'm so sorry, Preach. I wish I had better news."

Arthur had suspected something like this, but was still more shocked than he had expected to be. But he merely said, with a dry chuckle, "Well—it sounds like we both have relationship problems."

Betty chuckled. "I'll say." She said, "I was sorry to hear about your aunt."

"Thanks. She was something. A huge part of my life. I didn't tell her that when I had the chance. I wish I had."

"Yes. We all have regrets, don't we?" Arthur didn't answer. "Well, I'll let you go," she continued. "Do you want Sharon's phone number?"

"I guess so," Arthur said. "I probably ought to talk to her."

Sharon gave him the number. "That's the trailer number. She's waitressing at Ivy's downtown now."

"Ivy's?"

"Yeah, it used to be Johnson's. The family sold it after you left. Anyway, call me again, we can commiserate."

"I will. Take care." He rang off.

Arthur went to the living room and watched television for a few minutes, then found himself growing morose over…his aunt. *Stu. Clement.* And of course his war buddies, dying miserably in a losing cause along some nameless sewer in Vietnam, with no say in the matter.

Exhausted, but at last safe, he let the grief wash over him. *He was back. But to what?*

Finally, he went to bed. He slept for fourteen hours. Only once did he wake up in the night—panting and frightened, but unable to remember why.

iii

Arthur got up late Saturday morning, hungry and thirsty. He went downstairs and drank half the carton of orange juice Mrs. Hall had bought, right out of the carton, and then made a pot of coffee. While that perked, he made bacon and eggs.

After breakfast, feeling considerably better, he walked downtown and bought a *Bangor Daily News* at the drug store, then returned home, resolving to get a subscription first thing Monday morning. He called John Tripp, the lawyer Mrs. Hall had mentioned, but the office was closed. He left a message.

Arthur read the paper while finishing the rest of his coffee, then decided to do what he knew he had been putting off since he got up.

iv

ESTHER L. MCLACHLAN
JUNE 15 1885 –
SEPTEMBER 26 1969
A LIFE WELL LIVED

It was that, Arthur thought as he stared at the grave.

He stood quietly, everything around him still. After a time and without thinking about it, he stepped forward and touched the gravestone, hand lingering a long few seconds. He walked back to the Bel Air, and drove home.

v

He called Clement's family. Mr. Paul answered. Arthur asked for Clement's address.

"What do you want to write to him for?" Paul asked.

"He's my best friend, Mr. Paul," Arthur said. "He could probably use some mail."

"You want to waste your time, go ahead," Paul said. "He won't answer." He read him the address for the prison in Thomaston.

"Thanks. Do you ever go see him?"

"Hell, no." Paul hung up.

vi

Dear Clement,

Hey, buddy. I just got back from Nam a couple weeks ago. I hope you are doing okay, or at least as well as can be expected.

I'm doing okay myself, I didn't get shot or anything, and wanted to write. I guess getting mail is a good thing for you? Getting mail in the army was always nice. I'll write often if you want.

Can you get packages? Is it okay to send you stuff? Is there anything you need? Smokes or candy or something like that? Is that allowed?

Let me know also if you'd be up for a visit. I could come see you. If you are allowed to make phone calls, give me a ring. Same old number at the Congress Street house.

Of course, if you'd rather not hear from me, just don't write back or call and I'll understand.

Take it easy, buddy. Try to be optimistic, although I guess that's probably hard.

Sorry if I sound like an idiot.

Best,
Preach

vii

Arthur showed up at Ivy's mid-morning on Monday. He walked in and sat down at a booth; the breakfast rush was over and there were only a few customers. Sharon came out of the kitchen with a menu and her coffee pot. She saw him and stopped. Arthur waved.

357

Sharon looked startled, but then, with a slight smile, she walked over. "Hello, stranger." *She was definitely pregnant.*

"Hi."

"You want breakfast?" she asked.

"No. Just coffee. Betty told me you worked here. I was hoping you'd have a few minutes. Do you get a morning break?"

"Yes." She looked at her watch. "I have fifteen minutes. I'll let the boss know." She went back into the kitchen and emerged a few moments later. She sat down and lit a cigarette. "So…you're home. Glad you made it."

"Me, too. What have you been up to?" He gestured to her abdomen and smiled. "Besides the obvious, I mean."

She smiled slightly. "Yes, the baby's due in March. Did you ever meet Adam Garcia from high school? He was a couple years ahead of us."

"I remember him."

"Well, Adam and I have a nice little place just the other side of Searsport. He works at Cabot's lumber yard in Ellsworth. We're gonna get married after the baby's born."

"Good," Arthur said. "What's Adam like?"

"He's all right," she said. "Has his moods."

"Is he good to you?"

"Mostly. I try to keep him from drinking too much."

"I hope you're successful at that."

"Sometimes yes, sometimes no. I'm not drinking at all now, of course. The baby and all. How are you doing?"

"I'm good. Seeing the lawyer this afternoon to take care of the paperwork on the house and all. I own it now. My aunt willed it to me."

Sharon smiled thinly. "I'm happy for you."

"Too bad you're taken," Arthur said. "We'd have been happy there."

Sharon scoffed. "Maybe. I don't know. But things happen, don't they? Ah well." She shook her head dismissively and stubbed out her cigarette. "Look, I've got to get back to work. Was there anything in particular you wanted to talk about?"

"I guess not," Arthur said. "I just wanted to see you. I want you to be happy."

Sharon shook her head. "No, you don't. You came in here to lord it over me, Arthur West. You and your house. And your car. And all your aunt's money."

Where was this coming from?

"What are you talking about?" he said. "I didn't think any such thing."

"Yes, you did," she said. "You and Betty and my parents and everyone else. You all hate me. At least Adam loves me. So now that you've had your fun, please leave. And I work here full time now, so you might find another place to eat."

Arthur looked at her, stunned. He started to say something, but changed his mind. He finished his cup of coffee and stood. "Okay. Fine." He tossed a five dollar bill on the table. "Keep the change." He immediately felt small.

"There, see? Keep your money!" Sharon shot back. "It's on the house. Good *bye.*" She walked back to the kitchen and disappeared.

Arthur left the fiver, walked back to the house and, still annoyed, entered to a ringing telephone. It was a reporter from the *Republican Journal*. "Sergeant West, the paper would like to interview you," the reporter said. "You're a hero, a Silver Star winner. What time could I come over for an interview and a photo?"

"I don't want to be interviewed. And please don't call me again." He hung up.

The paper ran a 100-word story the following week, and included his high school yearbook photo.

viii

The meeting that afternoon with Tripp went quickly. "Your aunt did indeed leave you everything, Mr.

West," he confirmed. "House, car, plus the rest of her estate, a considerable sum. However, she asked me to manage it for you until your 21st birthday. That will be next June, I think?"

"Yes sir," Arthur said.

"Very well. I'll send you a thousand dollars a month until June, which should be more than enough to take care of your bills and so forth. Maybe you could open a bank account someplace?"

Arthur nodded, stunned at the size of the allowance. "Of course."

Tripp continued, "On your birthday, the entire estate will come under your control. Should you wish to retain professional financial management, I can recommend an advisor. Please let me know when the time comes. Here is your first check." Tripp handed him an envelope with the check, as well as a copy of Esther's will, the deed to the house, and the title to the car.

Clement called him on Friday.

ix

"They let us have one phone call a week," Clement said. "They take it away if we piss 'em off. I don't get to make many calls."

Arthur laughed. "Why am I not surprised. You never could keep your mouth shut."

"Yeah. But I fight, thank fuck. I don't win much but that's not really the point. If you don't fight here you're as good as dead. Maybe worse off."

"Any chance of you getting out of there?"

He scoffed. "Yeah. In maybe twenty years. But probably not. I try to behave myself, but that ain't happenin."

"Twenty?"

"Probably longer."

"You can't appeal or anything?"

"It wouldn't do any good. I killed a cop, Preach. The law ain't gonna let me out. I'm lucky they didn't give me the chair."

This was the first time Clement had ever admitted to killing Loudermilk. "So…you actually did kill him?"

Clement was silent a moment. "Everybody thinks I did. Same thing. But killing a cop makes you golden in the joint. Most of the other guys respect you, leave you alone. And I've made some friends here. Anyway. I just wanted to say hello, welcome you back from fuckin' Vietnam. I'm glad you didn't get shot over there. Now be careful, understand? It'd suck to get home alive from that fucking place and then get killed in a car wreck or hit by a bus or something. And keep out of trouble with the law. You wouldn't like it here, trust me."

"Don't worry. My one brush with the law was enough for me."

"You had a brush with the law?"

"Something like that. Look, man, is there anything I can do? Do you need anything?"

"Yeah, smokes and candy, like in your letter. The guards search all the packages of course, usually take some of the stuff like that, but I'll get most of it. Useful to buy shit inside. Favors, you know. Thanks for writing, by the way."

"I'll get a care package together for you next week."

"Cool, thanks. Preach, you've always been my best friend. Don't worry too much about me. I've been better, but I'm all right. I gotta go now, time's up. I'll look for that package. Good bye." Clement hung up.

x

Arthur sent Clement the package as promised, but a week later, Mr. Paul called him. "Clement's dead," he told Arthur. "Guards found him yesterday, shanked in the shower. Little bastard finally mouthed off to the wrong man. The warden's looking into it, but none of the prisoners are gonna talk. They never do."

"I'm sorry to hear," Arthur said, when he was able to speak. He found himself shaking. Paul's words sounded far away, hollow. "Clement was a good friend. We'd— we'd been through a lot together."

"Good riddance, you ask me. I'd just as soon throw him in the Penobscot, but we're having a funeral. His mother insists. It'll be two weeks from today. Grove cemetery. One o'clock. Come or not." Paul hung up.

That evening, Hag called, and Arthur told him the news. Hag started to weep, and said he'd be at the funeral.

xi

Arthur woke up Saturday morning exhausted. He had not had a quiet night. He remembered vague dreams, the details of which were not clear but at an unconscious level still had the capacity to disturb. A cup of coffee would make him feel better.

He went to the kitchen and soon was sipping his first cup. It was a bright but nippy day outside, a touch of frost on the Chevy.

On impulse, he called Betty. "Hey. It's Preach."

"Preach," she said, sounding pleased. "Thanks for calling. I was wondering if you'd forgotten."

"Nope," he said. "I said I'd call you, so here I am. Listen, I was going to go for a ride later this morning. Want to come?"

"Where to?"

"Out to the old quarry. Used to swim there when I was a kid."

"It's all closed off now. Has been for years. After that little kid drowned."

"I remember. I wasn't gonna go swimmin'," he said. "Trying to bury some ghosts, really."

"Sure, I'll go with you," Betty said after a moment. "Maybe we can get some lunch after?"

362

"That'd be great. I'll see you about eleven."

xii

They parked near the quarry and walked the last hundred yards. They passed the spot where Loudermilk's car had been parked those many years before. He smiled, but decided he probably should not tell her the circle jerk story.

When they got closer they saw several kids' bikes beside the trail. "Uh oh," Arthur said. "Looks like we're not alone."

"Whatever they're doing, I bet they're not swimming," Betty said. "Brrrr, I couldn't imagine." They reached the fence.

The fence was in considerable disrepair. Several gaping holes were in the chain link, easily big enough to allow a person to go through. "I guess the cops don't come out here anymore," Arthur said. Then they heard yelling and laughter across the quarry. Arthur looked over at The Cliff, still impressive, even now through the eyes of an adult and not a nine-year-old.

A small group of boys stood at the top, gingerly approaching the edge and peering over. One of them suddenly grabbed another and yelled *"Don't jump!"* but at the same time pulled him back. The other kid yelled in surprised fright, and after a little more yelling back and forth they both started laughing. They noticed Arthur and Betty across the quarry and waved. Arthur waved back. The boys started back toward them.

"The owners of the bikes, I'll wager," Betty said.

"Ayuh." Arthur had to look away.

Betty, sensing his mood, moved closer to him, put her arm around his waist and leaned her head on his shoulder.

"Vietnam," Arthur said. "Everything is different."

Betty nodded. "I know exactly how you feel." She sniffed, dabbed at her eye. "Look, if you're ready, I could go for a grilled cheese and some tomato soup. There's a place in Winterport that makes it. Their own recipe."

"Sure."

The boys arrived about this time. "Hey Mister," one of them said as he climbed through the large hole in the gate fence.

"Hi," Arthur said, brightening a little. "Any of you guys jumped off it yet?"

"Ayuh," two of them said eagerly. "Will here hasn't, though. Maybe next summer. If he doesn't chicken out like he did *this* summer!"

But Will was game, and just shook his head, rolling his eyes. "Call me chicken if you want. You guys are crazy, doing that. You could get yourselves killed."

"You'll do it when you're ready, Will," Arthur said. "I bet next summer. It was scary the first time I did it, too."

"You did it, Mister?" Will said.

"Ayuh. When I was ten."

"Wicked," one of the others said. "Well, good bye, we gotta get home." As they started down the path toward their bikes, Will turned and said, "You sure got a pretty girlfriend, Mister." They ran off giggling.

Betty laughed. "Well, wasn't that nice," she said.

Arthur smiled. "He was right, too," he said.

She looked at him and kissed him. "Thank you."

Arthur said, "Let's get that grilled cheese sandwich."

xii

"Artie!"

Arthur heard his name called and he was trying to run and trying to escape from the rats and Puppa was screaming and on fire but his legs weren't working fast enough like running in mud and blood and rats were coming and—

"Artie! Wake up!"

He opened his eyes with a start and propped himself up on his elbows. He looked around, it abruptly dawning on him that he was in the main bedroom at his house. Betty was beside him, sitting up, staring at him in the pale moonlight.

"Hi," he said, panting. "Wow."

"You were having a nightmare," she said. "You started moaning in your sleep, then thrashing around."

"Thanks," he said. He lay back down, taking deep breaths to slow his heart.

Betty lay back down next to him and snuggled closer. "Stu used to have nightmares. Fucking Vietnam. What did they do to you guys over there?"

"I didn't used to have nightmares. Ever. Until six months ago."

"Have you thought about...seeing someone?"

"Like a shrink or something?"

"Yeah. Someone to talk to. There must be programs. Isn't the VA supposed to help with things like this?"

"I guess. I don't know, Bett'. I'll call the VA hospital in Togus. Just come here. That's what I need now."

"Good." She snuggled closer to him and chuckled. "My folks would be scandalized about me being here."

"I'm not," Arthur said. "I'm glad you're here."

"I'm glad we found each other," Betty agreed.

Arthur kissed her on the forehead. They were soon asleep.

.   .   .

CHAPTER 37

i

Belfast, Maine
November 1969

Clement's funeral was on a blustery and gray day, with a strong hint of snow in the air. It was the last weekend Grove cemetery was allowing burials this year. Interments after mid-November had to be postponed until spring because of the frozen ground.

Betty was unable to come, having already planned to go to Washington DC that weekend for a large antiwar rally.

"Are you sure it's okay?" she had asked. "I know Clement was a friend of yours. I'd come except for the march. I helped organize it, so…"

"It's all right," Arthur had said. "I'd go with you if not for the funeral. But I have to be there."

There were almost no other people present except for Clement's immediate family: Mrs. Paul, now wheelchair-bound; May; and, surprisingly, Mr. Paul, the last person Arthur had expected to show up. Mr. Paul did not look well.

Then Arthur noticed another man, standing by himself a bit away from the gravesite but close enough to hear. He looked vaguely familiar, but Arthur could not quite place him.

The service started. The pastor opened with a welcome and a prayer, and then began his graveside homily. He spoke of compassion and redemption and God's unceasing love, and of his willingness to answer prayers that were "sincerely offered for the souls of even the worst of us." Arthur had little doubt as to whom he was referring.

Mrs. Paul cried softly into a handkerchief and May leaned against her, an arm around her shoulders. Arthur was surprised to see Mr. Paul openly weeping, wiping his eyes repeatedly as the pastor continued. Finally the pastor asked if anyone wanted to say a few words, and Mr. Paul stepped forward.

"Clement and me weren't close," he said. "He was a trial to me from when he was little. But he was my son and as bad as he was, and as many mistakes as he made, I will miss him and hope the Lord will forgive him."

He was silent a few moments.

"Guess that's it," he finished. He stepped back with his family.

Arthur could imagine Clement's sarcastic reaction to his father's remarks. Hag was praying fervently to himself.

The man standing alone was staring silently at the ground. Then Arthur recognized him. He had grown a beard since he had last seen him.

Ted.

After a moment, Mrs. Paul said quietly, "I say, thank you, Clemmie's friends"—she gestured to Arthur and Hag but had not noticed Ted—"for coming. Clemmie was good boy in his heart, just turn down the wrong street. I hope God forgive him, keep him safe." She began to weep.

Then Hag raised his hands up high, eyes closed. "Oh Lord our God," he intoned, "who made and sees and knows all things, look down on my friend, this lost soul Clement Paul, and raise him up to be part of your fellowship from now until the end of days. Let him be reborn in your glory and live forever to do honor to your name. Bring comfort and peace to his family. Bring the knowledge to his friends that if they only repent of their sins, and welcome you into their lives, that they too can be saved and be a part of your kingdom and know your peace and love. Hallelujah!"

Hag paused to take a breath. "Thank you, young man," the pastor quickly said before Hag could continue.

After a verse of *The Old Rugged Cross* and a benediction, the service ended. As Ted left, Arthur nodded. "Hey. Ted, isn't it?"

Ted stopped and nodded. "Yes, hello. You were a friend of Clement's I think?"

"Ayuh. We met years ago. Art West."

"Ted Crockett."

"I thought so, just didn't recognize you at first with the beard." Arthur introduced him to Hag, then said, "I won't be a minute, Hag." Hag nodded and walked to the car. "Sorry to meet again under such circumstances," Arthur said. "A sad day."

"Clement was a good person under all that shit he had to deal with in his life," Ted said. "His father. And all the rest. You know, a small town with its prejudices. He was lucky to have you as a friend."

"A lot of good it did him."

Ted said, "That vile piece of shit, Loudermilk."

"Clement told me," Arthur said. Ted looked at him, alarmed. "Of course, he never told me exactly how it…what happened."

Ted nodded, relaxing a little. "He told me he wouldn't."

Arthur said after a moment, "There were rumors."

Ted laughed shortly. "I bet." He looked hard at Arthur. "About how he didn't actually kill Loudermilk, but said he did to cover for a friend?"

What? Arthur returned Ted's gaze, but said nothing.

"About how he gave up his freedom, and even his life, for his friend? Because his friend had so much more to lose than he did? And about how his friend thinks about him every day, and what a gift he gave him? And how he wishes he was half the man Clement Paul was? And how he's got to live with it now, knowing he's too much of a coward to tell the truth? Those kinds of rumors?"

Arthur nodded, stunned. "Something like that, I guess."

Ted smiled bitterly. Then he shrugged. "Yeah, well, don't believe every rumor you hear. Look, it's nice to see you again, Art. I've got to get back to Portland." He paused, then added, "I don't expect we'll meet again."

Arthur said, "Ted, I appreciate you coming, even if the Pauls don't. Clement was a good friend."

"More than a friend. To me. Good bye."

Arthur watched him depart, then returned to the car. As they drove away, Hag asked, "What was that about?"

"Nothing," Arthur said, turning left toward town.

ii

A few days after the funeral, a brief story in the *Bangor Daily News* noted that a former instructor at the University in Orono, Theodore Crockett, had been found dead in his Portland apartment, apparently a suicide.

The peace of the dead, their secrets safe, returned to Grove Cemetery.

iii

Arthur had Thanksgiving dinner with Hag and his family. When he returned home, he found Betty at the house, working.

With Arthur's permission, she had set up a small office in the parlor. He had arranged for a second telephone line to be installed. Betty brought in a filing cabinet, and put up a couple of bulletin boards. She bought a radio and usually kept it tuned to a Boston all-news station.

The house soon became the center for antiwar activism in the area. In return for Arthur's generosity, Betty insisted that her friends keep the downstairs clean and neat, and also chip in money to pay for the phone line, some of the utilities, and part of the cleaning lady's pay.

Arthur was fine with all this, but he laid down the law on the issue of drugs. "Bett', we can share a joint when we're here by ourselves. But I don't want a bunch of

369

strangers smoking dope in here. We might well be a target for the cops once word gets out what's going on here, and I don't want to give them any excuses to come calling." Remembering Brooklyn, he added, "Or anyone else."

"Agreed," Betty said.

Arthur was prescient on this. A week later, he caught a guy selling an ounce of grass to another of Betty's friends. Arthur unceremoniously kicked both of them out of the house. The fact that Arthur was a Vietnam veteran, a group already rumored in the popular imagination to be crazy and prone to violence, helped him in his efforts.

Arthur was surprised to find strong support for this action from most of Betty's activist friends. They did not want their efforts to end the war compromised by "a bunch of dope-smoking hippies," as one of them put it.

Over the next month he became used to Betty's friends being there at all hours, even on occasion finding one of them asleep on the sofa when he got up in the morning. He didn't mind; he cheerfully made coffee and pancakes for them. In truth, the house was huge and empty when he was there by himself, and so he mostly enjoyed the company.

Still, becoming active in the antiwar movement wasn't for him. He certainly supported an end to the war. The problem was the ugly language that he frequently overheard directed at the country, and even the concepts of democracy and the Constitution. In particular, some of the rhetoric he overheard directed at the ordinary soldiers who fought in the war bothered him, the term "baby-killer" being the best example, although everyone mostly avoided using it in Arthur's presence.

Arthur also found that Betty's increasing activism was beginning to affect their relationship. She rarely seemed interested in spending personal time with him. She would often come to bed only after he had already done so, and mostly seemed uninterested in any sort of physical intimacy. Arthur soon realized, to his disappointment, that Sharon had been far more interested in sex than Betty was. To make things more difficult, his troubled dreams continued.

iv

January 1970

Arthur walked into his bank downtown on a Saturday shortly after the New Year to deposit his January allowance check. As he stood in line, he heard a familiar voice behind him shrieking, "Preachee! Preachee! My goodness, it's you!" He turned just in time to have Wilma Osgood grab him and plant a big smooch on his cheek. Next to her was a toddler, staring wide-eyed. "Oh my heavens, Preachee, it's so good to see you! I'd heard you were back but—"

"Ayuh," Arthur said, smiling. "I am. Got out in early October. How are you doing, Wilma?"

Wilma looked and sounded far better than the last time he seen her, shortly after Dick had run off more than three years before. The boy was small and his features were oddly malformed, but he smiled and seemed pleasant enough. "This must be Justin?" Arthur said. The boy looked at him at the mention of his name, then pressed close to his mother, face buried against her hip.

"Oh yes, this is little Justin, my gift from the Lord. We're going to be starting pre-school soon, aren't we, Justin? At a special school, for kids who are just as special as you." Justin nodded into her hip.

"I'm glad to see you," Arthur said. "You seem to be doing well."

Wilma smiled. "Yes, I am. I am blessed, I truly am. Oh—and I have some great news. I heard from Dick. Preachee, he's coming home!"

"What?"

"Yes. He called a couple of weeks ago. Well, you can imagine how upset I was. In fact, I hung up on him the first time. And the second. But he kept calling back, so after a while I started talking to him. We've been talking every night for the last two weeks. And yesterday, he asked if I'd take him back."

"Will you?"

Wilma smiled. "Yes. Justin needs a father. But, there will be certain conditions."

Arthur nodded. "I bet," he said, voice flat. *The bastard.* "Well, tell him I can't wait to see him, if he wants to look me up."

Wilma invited him to supper when Dick got back. Arthur said he would get back to her on that.

v

A few days later, during one of his usual visits to the library—he had been pleased to discover that the library subscribed to several big city papers—an AP article on page 2 of the *Boston Globe* caught his eye: *"Utah Cult Leader Arrested on Murder, Drug Charges."*

The cult leader, Carl Mumford—known as "Blue Hawk" to his followers, the story noted—had been arrested after a pre-dawn raid on a ranch in the desert about 75 miles south of Provo. Fifteen of his followers, all but two of whom were young women, were also taken into custody. An infant, the son of one of the women, was placed with Salt Lake City Child Protective Services. A third male associate wanted by authorities, Frederick D'Angelo, of Los Angeles, was still at large. Authorities feared he may have been the victim of foul play, and teams were searching the ranch for possible remains.

Mumford and his followers were charged with murdering three people in the Salt Lake City and Provo areas. No motive had been revealed by the authorities so far, but a source who spoke off the record in order to share information with the public reported that a number of "really crazy theories" were being pursued: "End of Days stuff, a race war, you name it."

The story moved on to background information, most of which Arthur already knew. Arthur asked the reference librarian to make a Xerox copy of the article. He brought it home and showed it to Betty.

"I met these people," he said, handing her the article.

Betty read it. She looked at him, bemused. "Come on. Seriously?"

"Ayuh," Arthur said. He told her the story. "I'm pretty sure this Frederick D'Angelo they're looking for was the guy who picked me up hitching in Nevada, back in October."

"My, you do know some of the most interesting folks, Artie." After a moment she asked, "Umm…you don't think…?"

"Oh no," Arthur said. "I'm not worried. I got out of there two days after we arrived. No one knew who I was or where I was from."

"You might want to call the cops out there, tell 'em you have information."

"I already did," Arthur said.

vi

Arthur opened the door at a knock a week later. He was not surprised at who stood before him.

"Hey, Preach."

Dick sounded tentative, clearly not sure how Arthur would react.

Arthur nodded, keeping his expression neutral. "Wilma told me you were back."

"Ayuh." After a moment, Dick said, "Umm…can I come in?"

Arthur grudgingly stepped aside. Dick walked into the foyer and stood there.

"You want some coffee?" Arthur finally said.

Dick nodded.

"Well...come on, then." Arthur led him to the kitchen.

After he had poured them both a cup, they headed to the living room. They passed the parlor. Betty was on the telephone and waved him away. "Betty Tibbets," he said. "Sharon's sister."

Dick smiled. "Yeah, I remember." They sat and sipped coffee quietly for a moment. Then Dick said, "I half-expected you to deck me when you opened the door."

"It's early yet," Arthur said.

Dick chuckled. "Okay. I wouldn't blame you if you did. I deserve it. But Preach, I'm back. For good this time. I'm staying with my folks at the moment. They were good enough to let me move back in, bless 'em. And I've been talking to Wilma, and she's going to let me move back in. With her and Justin. I put off seeing you til now. I wanted to concentrate on Wilma."

Arthur nodded. "Good idea."

After a moment, Dick sighed. "Preach, I want to apologize for what happened in San Francisco."

Arthur said nothing.

Dick sighed again, but pressed on. "I've been just awful for a long time, Preach. For years, even in high school. I have a lot to make up for. But I'm going to try. I've got to go see Jeanette's mom too, apologize and see if there's anything I can do. Give her a chance to unload on me, if nothing else. Not looking forward to that conversation, I can tell you. Anyway, I hope Wilma will eventually forgive me. I wouldn't blame her if she didn't. It'll take a while, I know."

"Why the change of heart?"

Dick sighed again. "I don't know, just happened. After you left, I lasted about 48 hours with that Amanda chick, but she ended up booting me out just like she did you. A few days later I caught her hitting up some meth in the living room. Pilgrim was tying her off. I didn't want to have any part of that shit, so I went back to the apartment in the Castro where I'd been staying, packed up, and hitch-hiked to LA."

Dick drained his coffee. "I thought leaving San Francisco might help, but I found out when you move, you don't leave your problems behind. The problem, of course, was me. Also of course, I got worse. Drinking way too much, starting to do uppers to boost me, then reds to mellow out. Then uppers to pick me up again. Pretty much rock bottom. When I started thinking about using needles, I knew I had to do something. Hell, I even went to a Billy Graham crusade at the Coliseum one night, hoping. Crazy, huh? Didn't do anything for me, though. Don't know why I thought it would."

"Ayuh," Arthur said dryly.

"Anyways, the next day I passed a storefront free clinic downtown. A sign in the window said they offered drug and alcohol counseling. I figured let's give that a shot, so I went in. They referred me to a shrink who did volunteer work with them. And damn if it didn't help me. I saw the guy an hour a week for like two months. Well, that was one of the smartest things I ever did. It turned my life around. It really did. You, my friend, are looking at a new man. I'm clean, first off. No booze, no drugs, not even cigarettes. Two months, eight days as of today. So—one day at a time and all, but so far, I have renounced my rowdy ways," he laughed. "Maybe someday I'll be able to have a beer or a smoke, but not today. Gonna try to make a go of it now, as a good husband and father."

In spite of himself, Arthur thought, *Maybe he's okay. Guess we'll see.* "So what's next?" he asked.

"Last week, I talked my way into a job selling cars at a Ford dealership in Augusta." He quoted his pitch. "'If you want a great ride, I can put you behind the wheel of a brand new Ford today!'" He chuckled. "Seriously—I already sold my first car. A Bronco. Second day on the job. The boss tells me I'm good at it."

"That's great news, Dick," Arthur said.

"So what have you been doing?" Dick asked.

Arthur gave Dick a brief summary of his trip across the country, leaving out Megiddo Ranch. Dick had heard about Clement. Arthur finished with his new relationship with Betty. "So that's about it. I'm sitting here most days, trying to think of stuff to do. I help Betty with her antiwar stuff, but my heart's not really in it, you know? Things seem to be starting to wind down in Nam and…" He sat back. "So I'm considering my future, I guess. I'm not even twenty-one yet. I have lots of ways I can go."

They visited another half hour, then Dick stood. "Preach, it's been great to see you. I've got to get on over to Wilma's. I told her I'd help her out with Justin this morning; I'm not due at work til noon. I just wanted to stop by."

"Sure, thanks, man, I'm glad you did."

"So…are we square? It's more than I deserve, but…"

After a moment, Arthur said, "We are." He offered his hand. "I'm glad you're doing better, my friend. I really am."

They shook. "You too, man. I'll be in touch. And thanks." Dick left and Arthur shut the door behind him.

Betty emerged from the parlor when her telephone call was over. "Sorry, Artie, a conference call. I couldn't miss it. Big demonstration in the works for Boston next month, as soon as it gets warm. I'm going to try to organize a busload of folks from up here. Who was that?"

"You must remember Dick Osgood. An old friend of mine."

"Really? The guy who ran off with that girl years ago?"

"Yep. He's back and wants to make amends, start over."

Betty sighed. "Well, good for him," she said, not sounding very convinced. "Anyway, I hope you'll come with us to Boston. You've never been to a demonstration, have you?"

"Actually, I have," he said. "Maybe I'll come to this one. I'll let you know." But he knew he wouldn't.

.   .   .

CHAPTER 38
i

Belfast, Maine
April 1970

The one time Betty and Arthur did acid together, it did not go well. Betty had done it several times before and knew how to act as a guide, so she convinced Arthur to give it a try. He reluctantly agreed to do so the following night.

That evening, Betty locked the doors of the house, turned off most of the lights, put on soft, relaxing music, lit a scented candle, and then they dropped. They began to get off about a half hour after. Ninety minutes in, Arthur was laughing hysterically at pretty much everything that Betty said or did. He found her unaccountably hilarious.

At two hours in, the terror hit. And Arthur remembered little after that.

ii

He woke up in their bed. His mouth was dry like sandpaper in a desert. He felt limp, worn, *off,* as if somehow out of phase, but most of the effects had faded. He looked at the bedside clock. It was almost four in the afternoon. They had dropped at about eight the night before. Twenty hours ago. Most of that time was a complete blank; he had only the vaguest recollections.

Betty holding him as he sobbed—

He apologizing for being awful and boring—

His father screaming and on fire and his mother freezing and singing Rose of Culloden—

The killing of Lima—

And the rats—

Enough.

Arthur stood, and then had to put his hand on the mattress to steady himself. Regaining his balance, he walked into the bathroom and pissed a gallon. He drew a large glass of water and gulped it down. His mouth tasted terrible. He brushed his teeth, feeling every single one of the bristles individually massaging his gums. A rainbow played around the edge of his field of vision, more sensed than seen.

Must still be tripping a little.

Someone knocked on the bedroom door. "Hello? Artie?" It was Betty.

"Come in," Arthur croaked. He cleared his throat, tried again. *"Come in,"* he said. She did so. With coffee. "Ohhh, thank you," he said. "You are the woman of the hour."

She smiled. "I heard you get up. I thought you could use a cup. There's more. And I've made pancakes."

He sipped the coffee. It was hot, burning, but *oh so good.*

"I think I'm still tripping a little," he said.

"Probably. I am. It takes a day or two to get back to normal."

"Well, it's not so bad. Now. Just kinda weird."

She smiled. "It was sure bad for you early on. Why don't you get cleaned up and come down, and we can talk."

"Was I awful?"

"You were terrified, and then unbelievably sad. But you were not awful. You're not an awful person, Artie. Plus, it was good acid. Really good. If I'd known how good, I'd have had you take a half a tab. Anyway, we can talk about it over breakfast. You need some food. I'll see you in a few minutes."

iii

"So there's a lot going on here with you, I think," Betty said. "Most of which I don't know. Of course we've only been together a few months."

Arthur played with his breakfast, eating some of the bacon and picking at his pancakes. The act of chewing, feeling the masticated food in his mouth, was vaguely off-putting. "Ayuh," was all he could manage.

"So, I could tell you what I think based on what you were saying last night, but it will just be my speculation. I mean, I don't know anything about the background here."

"I'd be interested," he said. "Mostly in what I said, first off. I don't remember very much."

"Well, something terrible clearly happened to you in Vietnam. I mean more than usual. It involved night, and rats, and lots of people getting killed. I'm guessing some kind of battle or something."

He nodded. "True."

"Rats?"

"Crawling over me in the night. That happened."

Betty sipped her coffee. "Jesus fucking Christ," she muttered. "That's awful."

"The killing was worse."

"Go on."

"A bunch of my buddies killed, more wounded. We were ambushed. Only six of us were unhurt. My squad was wiped out, except for me and another guy. Pappy. Twice my age. Just luck, fate, whatever. It happens. Pappy and I got medals." He scoffed. "Basically for surviving. I even got a purple heart. Which I did not deserve; they gave it to

379

me anyway." Then he remembered. "Wait one, I'll be right back." He ran upstairs.

He returned a minute later with his film can. He took out the tiny piece of shrapnel. "This is the piece that hit me. That night."

"Really?" Betty asked. She examined it closely.

Arthur nodded. "I wanted to save it for some reason. To remember I guess. I dunno. The medics gave it to me." He felt kind of foolish now.

"Well, it makes sense you'd be angry," Betty went on, handing it back to him. "And you relived it a bit last night, clearly. That also makes sense."

"I guess." He smiled and returned the piece of metal to the film can. "But what I don't understand is, how when I started to get off, everything was so funny. Then the next thing I know I'm scared shitless, I mean like I was going to die. I haven't been that frightened since Nam. Worse, in fact."

She smiled. "You know Timothy Leary?"

"I've heard of him. The acid guy."

"Yes. He once said that people who trip for the first time, and start out laughing, always feel the terror. He said, 'They realize the joke's on them.' I always remembered that."

Arthur smiled. "So that's common, I guess. The laughing."

"Yes, very, apparently."

Arthur thought a moment. "I guess I haven't gotten over Nam. I think that was part of it."

Betty nodded. "How could you have gotten over it?" she said. "You were there like six months ago. Fuck, I haven't gotten over it, and I didn't even go. I don't know if I'll ever get over it. Stu's death. All the others. And the tens of thousands of Vietnamese. *Hundreds* of thousands. With no end in sight. And of course, what the war's done to us,

as a country. And most of all, now…what it's done to you."
She reached out, took his hand.

Arthur nodded. "If I could just get over the dreams,
you know? They're—" He stopped, collected himself. "If
they could just be gone. I'm not asking much, for fuck's
sake."

"Oh, Artie."

"Every day. Every *day* I think about that
goddamned place. I can even smell it sometimes. If I could
just stop thinking about it. Just a day off once in a while.
That's not too much to ask, is it?"

She smiled. "Yeah, you probably shouldn't do acid
again." Arthur laughed shortly. "At least 'til you've put all
this to bed. Which isn't going to be any time soon, I don't
think. If ever." She said, "Tell me, have you thought any
more about talking to someone at the VA? Might that help,
you think?"

"Yeah, maybe," he said. "I keep it bottled up. I
don't talk about it to anyone. You don't know how folks
will react these days. A lot of people blame the grunts. Like
they make the policies."

"I know. It's awful. I'm bothered by some of what I
hear said here. In front of you, for God's sake. In your own
house." She took a sip of coffee. "But," she said, "there's
something else too, inside you. Deeper."

Wonderful, Arthur thought. After a moment, he
said, "What else did I talk about?"

"Artie, what about your folks? I mean, you've been
living with your aunt since you were little. What happened
to your mom and dad, Artie?"

"They both died," he said. "A few years apart."

"How?"

"I don't remember real clearly about my father," he
said. "It was some kind of accident, involving a tractor."

"I'm sorry. How old were you?"

381

"Pretty young. Six or so. Like I said, I don't remember really clearly." *He wished she would talk about something else.*

"And your mother?"

"She died in a mental hospital when I was nine. My father's death was very hard on her. She went crazy. Almost froze to death one night. I found her outside." He sighed. "I went to live with my aunt after that."

"Oh Jesus," Betty said. "How do you feel about all this?"

"How do you *think* I feel?" he snapped at her, suddenly irritated. "You think I'm happy about it or something?"

"Hey, just trying to figure this out. Sorry."

Arthur immediately regretted his outburst. *What was that about?* "No, I'm sorry," he said. He thought for a minute. "I think…I think I maybe was kind of responsible. For both of them dying like they did."

"Artie, you were a kid. How could you be responsible?"

Arthur thought a minute. "I remember I got sick or something. Pneumonia, maybe? I dunno. But I had to go to the hospital. I remember a trip in the dark with my mother, bright lights, shots. Anyway, I got better. But we didn't have a lot of money. I'll take you by the old farmhouse sometime, if I can remember where it is."

"It's okay, we don't have to do that if it's too painful to—"

"I didn't say it was *painful!*" Arthur snapped again. "Stop putting words in my mouth! You don't know anything about—"

He stopped when he saw her expression. "Sorry. Again." He shook his head. "You must have struck a nerve. Fuck, what is going on inside my head?"

"Do you want to stop talking about it?"

Arthur thought a moment. "No. Let's keep going. I'll try." He collected his thoughts. "Puppa..." He stopped and smiled, chuckled slightly. "I used to call him Puppa. Damn, I hadn't thought about that in years. Anyway, he had to work more to pay the hospital bill. He already worked hard, now that I think about it. Harder than any man I ever knew. He almost never stopped. But when I got sick, he had to work even more, you see? He couldn't have had any health insurance, and I remember Momma telling me he wouldn't accept charity. Hell, he wouldn't even let Momma work. He was always tired there, toward the end. He must have been."

Then the guilt came to him in a wave. "Oh God," he said, stomach churning. "Don't you see? He might not have had the accident if he hadn't been tired from working so much. I don't remember the details, but that's the connection. Hag and me were playing in puddles, I got sick, and—and he had to work more to pay off the medical bills. You see? I killed him. My fault. Or just as well could have been."

Then it came pouring out. "And not just him. My mother too, you see? She had some kind of breakdown after he died. She wouldn't have if—if I'd not gotten sick. And so many others I knew. All dead. Clement. Loudermilk. Laverdiere at the FoodMart. My aunt. *Stu,* for fuck's sake. And the guys in my squad. Four of them. What is it about me? Everyone I know ends up fucking *dead*. I'm a walking, talking grim reaper. *Shit."*

"Do you really blame yourself for Stu? Or fucking Loudermilk? Or the guys who were killed in your squad in Nam?"

"Loudermilk? I dunno. Maybe. Stu? No. But the guys in my squad? I think so," he admitted. "At least some." He told her about the misplaced claymores and he having to move them under fire. Then Arthur said, "But *I* didn't get killed, see? *They* all did. I don't know why. How did I luck out? I should have died out there that night, but hardly got a scratch. Anyway, so I'm living with that. It's like I'm guilty of something, I dunno."

"Artie, I—" Betty started but Arthur waved her off.

He stood. "Look, Bett', I don't want to talk about this anymore. I need to—to go take a shower or something. I stink." He left the kitchen and hurried back upstairs and turned on the shower. He needed to get clean.

After, he went back to bed. He slept another six hours.

The dreams had not gone away.

iv

May 1970

Arting hur came downstairs one Friday morning to much urgent activity and general commotion. Normally, most of Betty's friends didn't show up until late morning. But today, it was barely nine and they were all in the office, Betty pounding away on a typewriter while simultaneously talking on the telephone.

"Yes! Fucking Nixon! I just heard it. No, I'm not making it up. Yes, unbelievable. Sure, come on over. We need to call everyone." She hung up. Another of her friends was on the house line, furiously taking notes. A third was watching a press conference on TV, also taking notes, handing each page to yet another of Betty's friends, clacking away on the office's second typewriter.

Arthur glanced at the TV screen. A Nixon administration spokesman was gesturing to a map of northern III Corps—he saw the town of An Loc—and two areas of the Cambodian border labeled "Parrots Beak" and "Fish Hook." Arthur knew these areas well. His unit had spent many a week conducting combat operations there.

"What's going on?" Arthur asked, coming up behind her and kissing her on top of her head. He tried to hug her.

Betty impatiently shrugged off his embrace. "Stop it, Artie. We've gone into Cambodia. *Cambodia!* It's not bad enough that we're destroying Vietnam. Now we're destroying fucking Cambodia!"

"What are you talking about? Cambodia's neutral."

"It is! But Nixon's gone in to try to take out the North Vietnamese command center there."

"Oh," Arthur said. He started to the kitchen. "I need coffee."

"Wait, what?" Betty said. "What do you mean, *'oh'*? You don't see this as a big deal?"

"Sure. And long overdue."

"What?"

"Bett'," he said, patiently explaining "the gooks use the border as a safe zone, see? I spent a lot of time up there where this is going on." He gestured at the TV. "The gooks'd carry out an operation, then retreat back across the Cambodian border to avoid getting attacked. They knew Cambodia was safe. We couldn't bomb there, and we couldn't send troops in after them. But now, we're finally leaning on them."

"Wait, what, you *support* this?"

Arthur shook his head. "Don't misunderstand me, I want us out of Vietnam, of course," he said. "But as long as we're gonna be there, the guys in Three Corps need for there not to be a place the gooks can run to when they get in trouble."

Betty looked at him, and then shook her head in disbelief. "Go get your coffee." She went back to typing. "And stop calling them gooks. Jesus. You sound like a racist."

v

Activity in the office increased during the weekend. They were working to organize a massive turnout next Saturday in Portland of opposition to the Cambodian incursion.

Then on Monday afternoon, another one of Betty's friends burst in the front door without knocking, and ran to the parlor. "Fucking shit!" he yelled. "The army just murdered four students in Ohio!" The house erupted.

"Fuck," Arthur breathed. *He had to get out of here.* Amidst the uproar, he quietly slipped off to the library.

When he returned late that afternoon, Chevy was waiting for him, sitting in a lawn chair by the front door.

vi

"Chevy!" Arthur said, grinning and crossing to him. "Damn, it's good to see you!"

Chevrolet got up and grabbed Arthur's hand and pumped it, slapping him with a massive hand on the back, so hard it stung. "How the hell are you, Preach? You made it back home, I see. How long did it take you?"

"About three weeks," Arthur said. "How the hell are *you,* buddy? Still hoboing?"

Chevrolet laughed. "I guess so, my friend. My travels took me to Augusta, and I knew that wasn't that far from Belfast, so I stuck my thumb out, and two rides and a few hours later, here I am. I remembered you told me Congress Street, but you didn't tell me an address. So I asked around downtown. Lots of people know where you live, Preach. You're kind of a home town hero. A Silver Star? I am impressed. Damn, son."

Arthur laughed. "Small town," he said. "Everybody knows everybody else. So come on in. Had anything to eat lately?" He looked at his friend's substantial girth. "Never mind, you probably have."

Chevrolet roared with laughter. "Now don't you be making fun of my movie star figure," he said. "But yeah, I could eat, since you asked."

"Come on in, I'll make some lunch." He led Chevrolet inside and they walked through the crowded living room into the kitchen. Chevrolet's size, long white

386

beard and bindle over his shoulder attracted more than a little attention. He looked like a raffish Santa Claus.

He sat at the kitchen table while Arthur made coffee and got bacon frying. "So where'd you go after Reno?" Arthur asked.

"Denver," Chevrolet said. "I needed to visit my bank to pick up some money. I lost all I had shootin' craps that night, as you may recall."

"I recall."

"I've also got family there now. My daughter and her new husband. They just moved there. I hadn't seen her in years, thought I might as well stop by. They put me up for a few weeks. But I got the urge to start wandering again, like I always do. Plus Colorado is so damned cold in the winter. So I left, hopped a freight south, picked fruit down in Texas, then gradually worked my way back north as the weather got warmer. And here I am."

Arthur made BLTs, and served them with some mac salad he'd made. "Damn, you've learned to cook since I saw you last," Chevrolet said, polishing off the sandwich in short order. "Thanks, that hit the spot."

"So, where are you staying? Is there a jungle someplace around I don't know about?"

"Nope, nearest one's near Ellsworth. I was hoping I could get a flop here for a day or two. Would that be all right?"

"Heck, of course it would," Arthur said. "Come on, I'll show you to your room." He led Chevrolet upstairs to the third bedroom. "Here you go," he said.

"Well, I sure appreciate it," he said. "I could use a shower. You mind?"

"Of course not. Down the hall, last door on the left." He gestured. "I'll leave you to it. See you downstairs in a bit."

Arthur went downstairs. Betty was in the living room, apparently waiting for him. "Artie, I need to speak with you," she said. They walked into the kitchen and she shut the door. "Who is that man?"

"Chevy. A road friend of mine I met last fall, just after I started hitching back here from San Francisco."

"Chevy? What's his real name?"

Arthur smiled. "That is his real name." Arthur explained.

"I don't believe that for one minute," Betty said. "Chevrolet *Ford?*"

"Believe it or not, but it's true."

"I had no idea who he was when he knocked on the door but he said he knew you, so I told him he could wait outside. But now, you let some bum into the house and you don't even know his real *name?*"

"Look, I spent time with him on the road," Arthur said. "Believe me, you get to know people doing that. He's smart, honest, taught me a lot. And he's not a bum. He's a hobo. There's a difference. He's not some derelict. He's even got a bank account."

"But you didn't even ask me!"

"I didn't think I had to. Don't you trust me?"

"Well of course, just not him!"

"I just told you, you can trust him. I guarantee. Besides—" he stopped. "Never mind."

"No, what?" Betty said. "What were you going to say?"

Arthur sighed. "I mean…whose house is it, anyway? Not to put too fine a point on it? Huh?" He felt the anger growing. "Answer me that. I can invite anybody in here I want. Right?"

"But he's a stranger!"

"Well look around, Bett'," Arthur said. "I don't know anyone in here right now except you and Chevy. There's like, what, ten strangers in here? Right this very minute. Who the heck knows who these people are? They might even be FBI for all you know!"

"You're—you're impossible!" Betty shouted, and stormed out of the kitchen.

vii

At the end of the day, after Betty's friends left, she joined Arthur in the back yard and they sipped drinks, Arthur with his DP and Betty with a glass of wine.

"Whew," Betty said. "Long day." She had calmed down.

"I guess you got a lot done," he said.

"Yes. We dropped the Portland idea. We're organizing a demonstration on the Orono campus now. I've talked to friends at other universities around New England. A bunch of demonstrations are set for Saturday. And all around the country, too. A huge one in Boston. So." She sipped her wine. "Are you going to come to this one? You haven't been to one since you got back."

Arthur sipped his DP. "No, I don't think so."

"Oh for god's sake," she said. "Artie, you need to start coming to these. We're trying to end the fucking war. I thought you wanted to help."

"I have helped," he said. "Giving you the space here, rent-free, I might add. I never complain about your friends here all hours of the night."

"So come, then. Take it up a step." Arthur was silent. "What's the problem, Artie?"

"The movement just isn't my passion, I guess," he said. "I know it's important and all, but…"

"But what?"

"Bett'…I was proud of my service in the army. I know I was drafted and only served 18 months and it's a very bad war and we shouldn't be there. But the guys I met were the best. They—*we*—were serving under very tough circumstances. Doing what our country had asked us to do, for better or worse. And a lot of them didn't make it home. So, for me and the other survivors to come home and—and be blamed for the war is a bit much. And now, to hear us

389

called 'baby killers'…" He stopped, and took a couple of deep breaths.

"Sorry, I'm getting worked up here. It just bothers me, is all. It wasn't the grunts I served with who started this war. It was the politicians. Sure, yell at them, blame them all you want. But I just wish your friends would leave the grunts alone. I never killed any babies. Nor did one single soldier I knew. To hear you all using that kind of language—don't you know how insulting it is? And some of you throw it around like I'm not even here."

"Artie, I've never called you that, and I never would. I know others have said that, and I tell them not to." She shook her head. "I'm sorry, I didn't realize you were taking it so personally. Of course they're not talking about you."

"Well it sure comes across that way," he said. "And Betty, some of them do mean it about me. I notice the nasty looks I get, you know."

"No one gives you—"

"And another thing," Arthur said. "The Cambodian operation is a good idea, so I'm not sure I even support the idea of having demonstrations about it anyway."

Betty looked at him. "And what about Kent State? Do you support demonstrations about that?"

"Of course, Bett'," Arthur said. He sighed. "But Kent State was a bunch of weekend warriors. National Guardsmen. Most of them joined the Guard to keep out of going to Nam. Poor attitudes, poorly trained, poorly led— hell, some of them show up for their monthly training weekends and don't even have uniforms. And these clowns get sent off to some college campus in Ohio, with *live ammunition.* That right there is the reason those students were killed." He shook his head. "So yeah, demonstrate away about it. But I guarantee you, if regulars had been there, none of that would have happened."

"Well someone should have stopped them. Some of them need to go to jail, too. Even the governor. He ordered them to the campus." Betty snorted. "Fat chance of that happening, though." She sighed, finished her wine. "God. All right, so, look. You don't support what we're doing, really. Do you want us out of the house? Move the office someplace else?"

He said, "No. That's up to you. I don't care."

"You don't care?"

"No."

"What about me? Do you care about me?"

Arthur said, "Sure, of course I do. But where are we going, Bett'? We never do anything. We haven't been to a movie or out to dinner in months. Your whole life is devoted to this war and your political friends. I'm tired. If you can't manage to spend some time with me and not worry about the war, I don't know why we're even bothering. Do you realize we haven't screwed in a month?"

"Well I'm sorry," Betty said, jumping up. "I didn't realize you were keeping track! Excuse me, but there are more important things than screwing. Jesus, if it's that tough for you, go jerk off or something."

Then Arthur got mad. "Well that'd be better than sex with you lately. Boy, do I miss your sister. At least she *liked it.*" Arthur immediately regretted saying this. But he did not take it back.

Betty glared at him, enraged, started to speak, then stopped, stunned. After a moment, she said flatly, "Okay, I'm out of here. I'll be at my folks tonight. Don't bother to call. I'll come around with a truck in the morning to get my stuff and clean out the office. Good bye, Arthur." She stalked back into the house, stopping at the back door and turning back to him. "And—and have fun with your friend Chevy!"

She disappeared into the kitchen, and a few moments later he heard the front door slam. Arthur finished his DP, feeling upset, but oddly elated, at the same time.

Arthur heard the kitchen door open and turned to look. Chevrolet was crossing the lawn, holding two beers. He sat down in the lawn chair Betty had been occupying. He handed Arthur one of the beers. "I took em out of the fridge. Hope you don't mind."

"No problem." Arthur took a sip.

Chevrolet sipped his beer, looked at Arthur and smiled. "Preach, I gotta hand it to you. You sure got a way with women."

Arthur laughed. "Yeah, I do, don't I?"

Chevrolet sipped again. "So. I was in the bathroom taking a crap and opened the window for some ventilation. You can thank me later," he laughed. "Anyway, I heard y'all arguing. And my name coming up. Sorry, couldn't help it. She was sure pretty, anyway, I'll give her that."

"She was," Arthur said. "Smart, too. But not much fun."

"I guess I contributed here, and I'm sorry about that."

"No you didn't," Arthur said. "It would've been something else if you hadn't been here. We really weren't going anywhere anyway."

"What are you gonna do now?"

"I dunno," Arthur said. "I'm bored here. I feel like I gotta get out, get away. Do something different." He smiled. "To be honest, I kinda liked it on the road. You never knew what was coming next."

"Yeah. It has its appeal. I'm not gonna stay here long myself, in fact. Maybe a day or two, if that's all right?" Arthur nodded. "Settling down isn't for me. Never has been. So I'll be shoving off here soon. You might want to consider doing some hoboing. Hell, come with me, if you like. It's a big old country, lots to see."

"I was thinking that," Arthur said. "Only…"

"Only what?"

"It's not just a big old country. It's a big old world."

"That's true," Chevrolet said. "There's lots of places to see. Places where the beer is cold and the women are warm. And where the locals aren't trying to kill you."

"I hear Amsterdam's nice," Arthur said.

"It is," Chevrolet said. "I've been there. What are you going to do with the house?"

"I don't know." Then he thought of Dick and Wilma. "I guess I could rent it."

viii

The next day Arthur applied for a passport.

. . .

PART XI: HOME
CHAPTER 39
i

Amsterdam, the Netherlands
May 1, 1975

The dreams had redoubled the past several weeks.

Arthur sat on the sofa in their Amsterdam apartment, watching the TV, numb. Images of defeat filled the screen. He watched a slick land on the roof of the American embassy in Saigon, a line of people on stairs going up to the landing pad, the desperation radiating from them, captured even in grainy tape a day or two old. There were easily fifty people in line that he could see, far more than could board the little slick, and with more people undoubtedly in line inside, waiting for their increasingly unlikely turn to board, and escape.

He had the *BBC World News* on, as his Dutch, while improving, was a little shaky; while good enough for casual conversation, he still had trouble with television. "Saigon has fallen," the reporter intoned, "and the last Americans, and some desperate Vietnamese who had helped them, are catching what are no doubt the final flights out of Saigon. Tan Son Nhut Airport is no longer operational."

The images shifted to the deck of an American aircraft carrier in the South China Sea. A slick had landed on the deck, flown from the mainland by a terrified South Vietnamese pilot, desperate to escape from the communists. With the pilot and his family safely disembarked, it was pushed overboard by a large group of crewmen. More terrifyingly, still another slick, easily two hundred feet above the sea, began to bank on its final, clearly fatal descent, and a man jumped from it as it fell, plummeting to his likely death along with the slick. All caught on camera as it happened. Arthur was appalled.

Fuck.

The apartment door opened, and Mila came in from her trip to the market, basket filled with some kind of leafy produce, a few lemons, other things. *"Hallo,"* Arthur said.

"Hallo, mijn liefste," she replied.

Mila was young, blonde, pretty. She was a student at the University—accountancy and finance. He loved her for many reasons, including her brain, wired very differently than his own. He found her interest in numbers fascinating, if incomprehensible. "Numbers make the world turn," she once told him. "And if you understand them, they never lie."

"A successful trip to the market?" he asked.

"Yes," she said. "Fresh herring. See?" She held up a package wrapped in pink paper. "Fresh lemon to squeeze on them. We'll sauté them tonight with a salad."

He smiled. "I should try to find some Maine lobsters for you sometime," he said. "Best seafood in the world."

She laughed happily. *"Mijn liefste,* I would love that. I hope we go to Maine sometime."

Arthur smiled. "Maybe we will. Now that that's over," he said, indicating the television. More images flashed across the screen, of boats, barges, anything that would float, adrift in the South China Sea, filled with people waving frantically at the cameraman, imploring to be rescued. Arthur saw fear, shame, chaos...defeat.

"Ahh, terrible," Mila said. "Those poor people."

"It's finally over," Arthur said. "I thought I'd be happy. And I am, but it's just...so sad. Shit. I don't know."

"How so?" Mila asked, starting to wash the salad greens. She had adopted the practice—for which Arthur was grateful—of merely offering a prompt or two, listening, not talking, when he spoke of Vietnam. It had always been hard to find people who would listen, especially lately, when no one seemed to care any longer.

"I'm glad it's over, of course," he said. "But I'm sad about the waste." Another shot of a chopper being pushed overboard. "I rode in those. I just..." He stood. "Fuck it," he said. "I'm going for a walk."

"Please stay, *liefste.*"

"I'll be back soon. I'm just going to the square for a bit." Their apartment on the Herengracht was a few blocks from Dam Square. "Do you need anything else for dinner?"

"No," she said. "Are you all right?"

"Yes, I just need some fresh air."

"Are you sure? You don't look—"

"I'm fine, I said!"

Mila said nothing; she returned to preparing dinner.

He immediately regretted his shortness with her. "I'm sorry, Mila, I—"

"Go for your walk. It's all right."

Arthur sighed, went downstairs, and headed for the square.

Dam Square was crowded as usual with lots of Dutch young people, many openly smoking pot as a small bluegrass combo played near a monument. Arthur had seen them in the square before. He had come to enjoy them; they specialized in bluegrass arrangements of American rock songs. Some of the young people in the small crowd near them were dancing—exuberantly, if not particularly skillfully—as they imagined American hillbillies danced, knees and elbows flying as they attempted clumsy do-si-dos and allemandes.

Arthur smiled at the spectacle. He had come to love Amsterdam and its relaxed tolerance, so different from America, especially during the past decade.

Mila wanted him to take her there for a visit. He had told her of Maine many times, and now that they were getting serious, she wanted to see where he came from and learn more of his life. Mila was Dutch to the core, of course, and Arthur knew it was unlikely they would ever move to the States permanently. Nevertheless, a visit might be doable.

Someday.

Arthur sat on a bench and listened to the music for a bit. The hippy next to him offered him a toke on his joint. Arthur accepted. *"Dank je."*

"Geen probleem."

Arthur asked if he had one to spare, and the hippy nodded. Arthur offered him a guilder but the hippy shook his head. Arthur thanked him again, then lit it and took several tokes. The band finished its take on a Steve Miller tune, then switched to an upbeat *If You're Going to San Francisco*.

Perhaps it was the excellent grass, perhaps it was something more fundamental, but within moments, Arthur found himself remembering again that first—and only—time he had ever been there.

For once, he let the memories come without fighting them.

ii

Arthur returned to the apartment an hour later. Mila had tossed the salad and set the table. The fish was prepared and ready for sautéing, and a fresh lemon was sliced, in a serving dish, next to a small dark loaf with butter.

"Ahhh, back at last," Mila said. She crossed to him and kissed him as he entered.

"I'm sorry I was short with you," Arthur said. "The news was difficult."

"I know, *liefste,*" she said. "Here, have a glass of wine." She poured him a glass of chilled Kabinett, and smiled. "The Germans may be horrible people, but they make good wine."

Arthur chuckled. "They do."

Mila lit the burner on the stove, and soon had the herring sautéing in wine, herbs, and a little olive oil.

After they ate, Mila poured the last of the wine, and they sipped it quietly. Arthur said, "So I'm thinking of starting University in the fall. Here. History, maybe. Literature. Do you think that would be possible?"

Mila was delighted. "Oh yes, very much so. You should. Your Dutch is good enough, and getting better. Everyone at University speaks English anyway, so you will do fine."

"Okay, then, I will." He finished his glass, and they began to clear the table. "I love you, Mila."

"And I love you, Arthur."

Then, at last, he asked. "So, do you think you might want to get married?"

"Oh Arthur, yes, yes, of course I do!" She put down the dirty dish she was holding and hugged him fiercely. "I have been hoping you would ask. It may be a few years, if

397

you can wait; I want to finish my doctorate, but yes. Yes, Arthur, I will marry you."

iii

Belfast, Maine
May 17, 1980

He married her five years later, in the back yard of the Congress Street house on a lovely spring day. Mila's parents had flown over for the wedding and were staying at the house; Arthur had kept it vacant after Dick and Wilma had bought their own house a year earlier. He had had his property manager get it cleaned up and stock the fridge a day or two before they arrived.

Arthur shared a beer with Dick and Hag before the service. "What a trip it's been, buddy," Dick said. "Thanks for asking me to be best man."

"Who else would I ask, man?" Arthur said, smiling. "It's good to see you again." Dick, in the space of ten years, had parlayed his job as a car salesman into running a Ford dealership in Augusta. "And I'm glad you're doing well. You and Wilma will have to visit us in Amsterdam sometime."

"We will, buddy."

Hag sipped his beer. "You're my first wedding this year, Preach," he said. Hag was, at last, pastor at a small Pentecostal church near Waterville.

Arthur smiled. "Just don't go getting all fire and brimstone on us or I'll start telling everyone about your antics when we were kids."

Hag guffawed. "You had some antics in there too, don't forget! Be careful, or I'll use you as a bad example!"

Arthur looked around. Wilma and Justin were there, of course; Justin was chasing Arthur's son Finn around the garden, both giggling. Finn had been born in 1977. "You and Mila sure made a good-lookin' boy, there, Preach," Dick said, watching them. He grinned. "Good thing for Finn that he takes after his mom."

Arthur laughed. "Tell me about it."

Higgins, now FoodMart's state manager, and his wife had driven over from Augusta. Hag had brought his mother, but Henry Senior had finally succumbed to the cancer several years before. The Tibbets were also there. To Arthur's astonishment, Betty had come, too.

"I didn't think you'd be here," Arthur said as he and Betty embraced. "But I'm glad you came, Bett'. Thank you."

"Thank you for inviting me," she said. "I was surprised. But very happy to get the invitation. Artie, I've thought for a long time that I acted terribly—no, don't interrupt, let me finish—that I acted terribly when we went our different ways. I was so stupid. Jesus, you'd been back from Vietnam for what, eight months? And I was expecting you to just forget all that and take up with me in the antiwar movement. When what you really needed was peace and quiet. And time to process, and forget. I'm surprised you put up with me as long as you did."

Arthur smiled and leaned in and hugged her. "It's okay," he said. "I was an asshole. I should have realized you had your issues, too. I mean, you had just been widowed, and here I was, upset that you were focused on ending the war that killed your husband. While I was worried about not getting laid more."

She looked at him, then they both chuckled. "So, what do you say we both move on?" Betty said. "I'm ready."

"I am too," Arthur said, grateful. "Thank you. But I have a present for you." Arthur took from his pocket the old Polaroid Stuart had sent him: Stu, proud and strong, pointing to the RPG damage on his track. "Here. Stu sent me this thirteen years ago, just before…You should have it."

Betty looked at it, tearing up. "Thank you." She kissed him on the cheek. She smiled. "Look at me, ruining your wedding like this. I'm sorry."

Arthur smiled. "Don't be. Who might have ruined it would have been your sister. I thought about inviting her, but it would have just made her mad."

Betty nodded. "If it's any consolation, she hasn't spoken to me or Mom and Dad in years."

Mila came over. "Arthur, who is this lovely lady?" she asked. "You are making me jealous." Arthur introduced them. They walked off together, and in a few minutes were whispering to each other, glancing at Arthur and giggling.

Chevrolet's appearance was another surprise. He had called Arthur in Amsterdam several weeks earlier to rsvp to the invitation Arthur had sent to his Denver PO Box.

"Yeah, Preach," he said upon arriving, "After I visited you here—what, ten years ago? Damn, a long time—I got back on the road again, but then, when I got to thinking about what a nice place you had here and all, I decided what the hell, do I really want to spend my dotage hanging out in jungles? So, I moved in with my daughter in Denver, who'd been after me for a year to do just that, bless her." He leaned toward Arthur and whispered, "And let me say, you sure know how to pick 'em. Mila is one gorgeous lady!"

Arthur laughed. "She is that. And an accountant, God help me. Let me introduce you around." Chevrolet was soon holding court near the punch bowl, his tales of the road provoking gales of laughter from Wilma, Mr. and Mrs. Tibbets, Mrs. Hall, and Mila's parents. Arthur was very grateful to see him shake hands with Betty, who then hugged him.

"Chevy's quite a character," Hag said.

"I'll say," Dick chortled. "Where'd you meet him?"

"On the road, heading home from Nam," Arthur said. "He's the best." He sipped his beer. "Gotta say, it's nice to see you guys again. But, I wish...you know. Clement."

"Yes," Hag said, growing somber. "I know. I miss him."

Arthur nodded. "Me, too."

Dick raised his beer. "Peace to him, wherever he is, the little bastard."

"Amen," Hag said. "I pray for him every day. Still."

They sipped their beers.

Then Hag brightened. "Man, we sure had us some times together, though, didn't we?" They all nodded, chuckling, grateful for the mood change.

Hag put his beer down. "Well, the Lord probably wants me to be sober during the service, so I ought to stop at a half a beer for now. I'll finish this after I get you and Mila hitched. Get ready, Preach. You've got ten minutes!" Hag went off to let Mila know to start rounding everyone up.

"You have the ring?" Arthur asked.

"For about the fifth time, right here," Dick laughed. "Don't worry, buddy. Everything is going to be fine."

iv

After the wedding, they spent the next ten days in small inns along the Maine coast, making love and eating lots of lobster. Arthur got Mila to take a dip in Penobscot Bay, which she said reminded her of the North Sea, only colder. Mila's parents stayed at the Congress Street house and watched Finn.

After the honeymoon, they flew back to Amsterdam. Arthur got work as a freelance journalist, writing about American affairs for several English language papers on the continent. Mila became an accountant at a large international consulting firm, soon rising to management.

A year later, Arthur sold the Congress Street house, and they used the money to buy outright a small house in Amsterdam's Jordaan district. Finn was joined by Esther in 1982. The children and Mila were now the center of Arthur's world.

v

Home
June 3, 1984

One night, two years after Esther was born, Arthur couldn't sleep, and, restless, he quietly dressed, then looked at a certain film can on his dresser. He put it in his pocket, and went outside. After walking a bit, enjoying the cool of the evening and the stars above, he came to a bridge over the Herengracht. He paused there, leaned over and, smiling, watched the placid water below him.

He realized he was happy.

He opened the film can and shook the tiny fragment of metal into his palm.

It was time.

With a last look, he tossed the shell fragment, followed by the film can, into the canal.

West headed home.

THE END

Made in the USA
Columbia, SC
13 October 2023

24005444R00220